LEAVING
DIXON'S
CROSSING

Books by Janet Brantley

Murder by Any Other Name

LEAVING DIXON'S CROSSING

JANET BRANTLEY

Gulf Park Press
Ocean Springs, Mississippi

LEAVING DIXON'S CROSSING
Janet Brantley
ISBN – 13: 978-0-9908795-1-0

Published by Gulf Park Press 2021
©2021 by Janet Brantley

This is a work of fiction. Certain historical events may appear within this book, but names, characters, and incidents are all products of the author's imagination *or* are used for fictional purposes.

Book design by Laura Lis Scott, Book Love Space.

Cover Image of Texarkana, Arkansas/Texas, c. 1940, from the **Texarkana Museums System, Wilbur Smith Research Archives.**

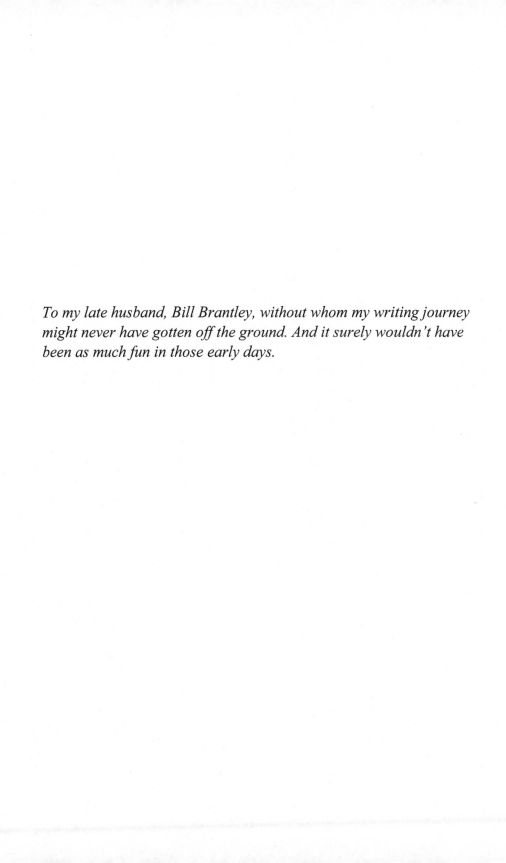

To my late husband, Bill Brantley, without whom my writing journey might never have gotten off the ground. And it surely wouldn't have been as much fun in those early days.

LEAVING
DIXON'S
CROSSING

PROLOGUE

Dec. 29, 1940 President Franklin D. Roosevelt's weekly "Fireside Chat"

Excerpt:

". . . As planes and ships and guns and shells are produced, your government, with its defense experts, can then determine how best to use them to defend this hemisphere. The decision as to how much shall be sent abroad and how much shall remain at home must be made on the basis of our overall military necessities.

We must be the great arsenal of democracy. For us this is an emergency as serious as war itself. We must apply ourselves to our task with the same resolution, the same sense of urgency, the same spirit of patriotism and sacrifice as we would show were we at war.

We have furnished the British great material support and we will furnish far more in the future. There will be no 'bottlenecks' in our determination to aid Great Britain."

ONE

GRADUATION

MAE JOHNSON FIDGETED ON the hard wooden chair, trying to keep her butt from going to sleep. Superintendent Browning droned on, his words about as distinct as the fluttering of the moths attacking the light fixture over his head. *How much longer before I can get that diploma? How much longer before I can get out of Dixon's Crossing for good?*

She stuck out her bottom lip and aimed a puff of air at her drooping bangs, damp with perspiration. *My Lord, it's hot in here!*

Her eyes roamed across the audience, lighting with distaste on Mr. J.T. Wheeler's back, right at the front of the stage. *Well, where else would he be? After all, he's the richest man in Dixon's Crossing, president of the School Board, and an elder in the First Baptist Church—my church.* The thought made her ill.

Ten years of Depression had left Dixon's Crossing a poor community—well, poorer. *Is that a word?* Miss Jenkins would have her hide if she used a simple word like poor in the wrong way.

Mae eased her head around so she could see her English teacher on the other side of the stage. *Golly, Miss Jenkins is pretty. Wonder why she's not married.* The teacher was about twenty-five, still plenty young to start having kids. She was nice and sweet, pretty and smart. *Hmm—maybe that's it. Maybe she's too smart to get married.*

At the thought, she looked at Miss Jenkins with a new respect. Mae didn't plan to marry for ages. She'd already promised herself not to get hitched anytime soon. She was going to make it on her own. She couldn't imagine ever getting desperate for a man to take care of her. A snicker escaped her, and she shrank back into her chair as Miss J. gave her a sharp look, pretty lips drawn down into a frown, one perfectly drawn eyebrow raised.

She turned her attention to the audience. There was Mama and Daddy in the second row, with her brother Thomas, his wife Annette, and their three brats filling up the rest of the row. The kids weren't really brats, but the idea of being saddled with three kids by the time she was twenty-four, like Annette, just gave Mae the heebie-jeebies.

Her gaze fell next on Oliver, her best friend in the world, except for Graydell, of course. Oliver was three years older than Mae; he'd always been like a big brother—much more so than Thomas. Oliver worked with his daddy on Mr. J.T.'s farm, just like her daddy, plus he worked in the store sometimes.

There wasn't much to do around Dixon's Crossing except for cotton farming, and Mr. J.T. had a handle on that. His 300 acres of river bottom land was the best in the county. It was way too much for one man to farm, though, so he let several other families have small houses to live in while they farmed forty acres each on shares with him. Having those houses close by was about all Mae could think of that was good about her life. She had grown up with plenty of kids around to play with. They'd all meet up in the middle of the fields and play for hours, until their mothers started calling them home for supper.

Mr. Browning's voice changed suddenly, and Mae straightened. "And so, good folks of Dixon's Crossing, Arkansas, I present to you the Graduating Class of 1941." Wild cheering greeted these words. He motioned for quiet. "Let us bow our heads as Brother Williams leads us in prayer."

2

"Heavenly Father," Brother Williams began in his lovely baritone.

Now this is something I can listen to with pleasure.

"We come before you this evening to ask your blessings on these young people as they set forth on the next stage of their lives. We pray that You will guide them in the direction that You would have them to go."

Yes, Lord, straight up the road to Texarkana!

He prayed at length for the countries at war in Europe, and he prayed for America not to become embroiled in the fighting there.

Yes, leave our boys out of it, please.

"Help our young men to find employment that will allow them to provide for the families they will very soon begin to establish. Help our young women to prepare themselves for their intended purpose as well. We know, Lord, that the heart and soul of the family lies with that wife, that mother, who nurtures and cares for her loved ones."

Not me—not yet! Please, God!

He closed his prayer by asking God to keep them all strong in their faith and strong for Dixon's Crossing.

What a sweet man!

"In Jesus' holy name, Amen."

"Amen!" someone behind Mae muttered, and two or three snickered.

"Hush!" she hissed through clenched teeth, without turning.

A rustle of excitement moved through the crowd. Men rose from where they had been kneeling at their seats, and women shushed restless children.

"Miss Jenkins, if you would help Mr. Wheeler, the president of our Board of Education, with the diplomas, we'll see about getting these young people out of our hair. Forever!" There was a bit of laughter at this, and even Mae was impressed that sour Mr. Browning would try to make a joke.

Her place was halfway through the ten students who were graduating, and she hoped to High Heaven she didn't mess up when her time came. She rose with the others, as they had practiced, and took a deep, steadying breath as Mr. Browning called, "James Bradford Adcock."

"Right hand over, left hand under." She repeated the phrase in her head as James walked forward. *I can see James in five years. He'll be married to Jo Beth and they'll have at least two kids. They'll probably be on Mr. J.T.'s farm. Hardscrabble life. Not for me, thank you very much.*

Mae had a prediction for each of her classmates. Rebecca was marrying her longtime sweetheart Ronnie in three weeks. No prediction needed.

"Morris Olen Harkness," Mr. Browning boomed. Mae expected Morris to be valedictorian.

As Morris reached for his diploma, she thought back to the conversation they'd had a few days ago. Sitting on the verdant carpet of clover at lunch, they had discussed their futures. Reaching down to pluck a four-leaf clover, he laughed at his luck. "That settles it," he crowed. "I'm getting out of here as soon as that diploma is in my hand. I'm headed to Missouri to law school." *I hope he makes it.*

"Eula Mae Johnson." *Lord, I hate my name.* She walked forward, too afraid of losing her concentration to look Mr. J.T. in the eye. She hated taking her diploma from him—but she was resigned. She would have taken that diploma from the devil himself.

Right hand over, left hand under. And like that, it was done. She was a graduate. Her diploma said she was a grownup now. She *was* ready to make her place in the world, corny as that might sound.

She returned to her spot and looked toward her folks. Mama was wiping tears, and Daddy had a smile as wide as the Red River. Even her irritating brother and sister-in-law were clapping. She looked at Oliver and their eyes met. He nodded in approval.

"Priscilla JasmineThibodeaux." Prissy sashayed up to get her diploma and it was all Mae could do to keep from busting out laughing. Then Graydell (no middlename) Upton. Finally, Buzz Wilson stepped up, the last to get his diploma. The audience again erupted in applause. Whistling. Stomping. She felt herself grinning like a possum. *Oh, boy, I'm out of school! On my own. Let's get this show on the road.*

* * *

Mr. Browning deferred to Mr. J.T. to announce the honor graduates. Like a man on a mission, he strode to the podium and cleared his throat. He looked at the two envelopes handed to him.

As anxious as if it were Christmas morning, Mae waited. "This year's salutatorian, the person with the second highest average over the last four years is . . . Morris Adcock."

She jerked her head toward Morris in surprise. She'd been sure he would be valedictorian. He was the hardest working, most ambitious person in her class. Morris moved to shake hands with Mr. J.T., who urged him toward the podium. Mae was glad it was him instead of her. She hated the idea of talking in public.

The young man stood quietly for a moment, red creeping from his collar toward his hairline. He moved as if to put a hand in his back pocket, but his long, too large suit jacket made that too much work, and he soon gave up, clenching his hands behind his back instead. Mae could feel his nervousness like a curtain descending over them. But when he started to speak, she was caught up in the flow of words. *My, how that Morris can talk. If I ever need a lawyer, I sure hope he's available.* The applause was warm when he finished, and Morris bobbed his head in thanks before returning to his seat.

"Now the moment you've all been waiting for," Mr. J.T. said. "It is my distinct honor to present to you the Valedictorian of the 1941 graduating class." He unsealed the last envelope, taking his time, letting the tension build to a crescendo in the audience as he slid the certificate out. The paper in his hand began to shake.

What the heck?

It was so long before he spoke that a murmuring began in the audience.

"Your 1941 Valedictorian . . . Eula Mae Johnson."

What? No, that has *to be wrong. Surely my grades weren't the best!* The stony expression on Mr. J.T.'s face was what finally convinced her she had heard correctly. Still, she sat, not moving, as friends clapped her on the back.

A faint smattering of applause began, then grew in intensity. When she looked down from the stage and saw her daddy standing and clapping for her—only her—she knew it was true. Her knees started shaking, and there were about a thousand butterflies in her stomach, though, in truth, it felt more like a thousand caterpillars twisting and grinding away in there.

Then her classmates were gathering around her, and she was being pushed and pulled toward the center of the stage, where Mr. J.T. was waiting for her. No way could she walk over to him . . . not after the run-in she'd had with him the other day in the store.

Then Graydell was in front of her, grasping both her arms and shaking her. Graydell, who knew everything, almost. "Now, you listen to me. I know what you're thinking—but you will *not* let him take the glory of this moment away from you, do you hear me? You march right on over there and take that certificate, say thank you, and let's get the hell out of here. I mean it, now. Oh, gosh, Mae, I'm so happy for you!" She threw her arms around her friend for a quick hug that almost toppled them, then propelled her forward. Just a bit at first, but with each step a little more, Mae began to believe. And to smile. Until she looked up into Mr. J.T.'s face.

She stumbled toward him, trying to wrap her mind around this most unexpected event. She was supposed to say something, wasn't she? But what? *Morris talked so good. What do I say? Well, if Morris can do it, so can I. I'm not going to let anyone show me up. Not tonight.*

Mr. J.T. held out the certificate the way he had handed out the diplomas, the way they had practiced. Right hand over, left hand under. Shake with the right, accept the certificate with the left.

A simple thing, really. So why couldn't she do it a second time?

Because when she looked at him, she heard those hateful words he had said to her last week: "You're too young to understand how the world operates, Mae Johnson. I advise you to go home and talk to your mama about these things. It's about time you come to see how things are done

6

around here." Worse than that, she remembered the day he'd sneaked up behind her while she ironed his sheets. She felt her skin crawl as she reached him.

She lifted her chin and reached, with her right hand, for her certificate. She did not say thank you. She did not shake the extended hand. She walked to the podium and looked down at her family. Mama's face was a mixture of pride and anger. *There'll be hell to pay tonight. But right now, I guess I have to say something.*

Miss Jenkins had always stressed to them that if they had to make a speech, they should pick somebody out in the crowd and pretend they were talking just to them. Her green eyes roved over the faces. Not her family. She'd be more nervous than ever. Then her eyes met blue ones so still and deep she felt herself relax. *Oliver. Yes, who else? My best friend in the world—except for Graydell, of course.* He nodded encouragement, his broad smile punctuated by a wink. She smiled back, then spoke, feeling calmer than she would have believed possible.

She managed about four sentences, at first congratulating Morris. A few more words and she was done. Later on, she would be pretty sure she had thanked her parents and her teachers, especially Miss Jenkins. But she was absolutely certain she had *not* thanked Mr. J.T. Wheeler.

The class song, a brief prayer, and it was done. Prissy's mother started the piano march for them to file down the aisle and outdoors, where lightning illuminated bumpy clouds and a heaviness in the air made it hard for her to breathe, even outside. The rain was sure to come soon. There was the prickling of her skin, too, which Daddy told her she got from her Grandpa Johnson. She so wished she'd known her grandparents.

"Hey, girl! I'm so happy for you, you rascal!" Graydell hugged her from behind, swinging her around.

Morris smiled and held out his hand. "I'm proud to be in the same class with you, Mae. You've worked really hard, harder than most of us. You sure deserve this."

She shook his hand and nodded, too tongue-tied to speak. He moved aside and there stood Oliver, for once not so serious. In fact, he was still grinning from ear to ear. "I'm so happy for you, Maisie. Now, I expect you to go out and change the world!"

"Oh, Mae, look at us. We're all grown up now." Prissy was waving her rolled-up diploma around like a wand. She touched it to Mae's forehead. "You, Mae Johnson, may now go out to seek your fortune."

Between Oliver and Prissy, Mae was brought back down to earth in an instant. It was 1941. For generations things had been the same. Did she really expect this award to make any difference? Would her plan be any easier to carry out with this award? Then again, maybe it *would*. Who could tell? She wanted to talk to Oliver about it. Graydell already knew, of course, since she was in on it. Mae realized Oliver's approval was also important to her. She leaned toward him and whispered, "I need to talk to you about something. Need your advice. Give me a ride back home?"

"Sure. I'll just be out by the car. Take your time."

TWO

OLIVER CRANFIELD

"THINK WE'LL make it back to your house before the rain hits?" Oliver scowled at the lightning flashes streaking across the sky. "Don't want you to get those pretty clothes wet."

"If I do, I'm sure it won't be the last time. I won't melt, you know." She leaned back against the slick leather car seat.

"Oh, I know that. You can be sweet when you want to be, but we both know 'sweet as sugar' wasn't meant to describe you."

"Thanks a lot! So, what *would* you say about me?" She shoved her head out the car window, reveling in the cooling breeze. "My Lord, it was hot in there!"

"Yeah, we were all feeling the heat. I'm going to have to think about that for a bit. You're not too easy to pin a label onto." She grinned to herself. She liked being different.

Oliver pulled into the old Wharton place, left deserted since the family had packed up and departed for greener pastures a few years before. He put on the parking brake, turned off the key, and turned to Mae, his eyes examining her face in the now frequent lightning flashes—sheet lightning so far—streaks racing through the clouds, illuminating everything like a golden, hazy afternoon. Just flashes, the darkness feeling even deeper when the streaks faded away.

"So, what's up, Maisie?"

Now that the time had come, Mae didn't seem to know how to start. Any other time she would have jumped in with both feet. After all, this was only Oliver, one of her best friends.

"Maisie? What's wrong?"

"Nothing's wrong. I just don't know how to start, *where* to start."

"Daddy always says to start at the beginning—but knowing you, that may not be a good idea. Ow!" This, as she punched him in the shoulder. "No, really, we only have a few minutes, and then they'll be looking for you at home to celebrate."

"Okay." She sat up straight. "You know how I've been saying I was going to leave Dixon's Crossing when I turned eighteen?" He nodded. "Well, you know my birthday was at Christmas, and now that I've graduated . . ."

"I know," he said, and she could hear the question in his voice.

"Well, Graydell and I have been talking. We're going to Texarkana the first chance we get, and we're not coming back till we both have jobs." There. She'd said it. She tried to see his reaction, but the lightning didn't cooperate. The darkness held, as if it, too, were waiting. The night was dark as Lazarus's tomb.

"Why, that's great. Really great, Mae. I'm really excited for you."

Uh-oh. He called me Mae. Could he be upset? He doesn't sound one bit excited. "Now, even though I'll be moving to Texarkana, I'll still be back often. That bus runs through here every day, down to Shreveport every morning and back to Texarkana in the evening. I can come spend the whole day on my day off."

"That'll be fine, I expect. Do you have any idea where you might be able to find a job? There aren't many out there these days."

"Yeah, I know it's just next to impossible for you men to find jobs, what with the country in the shape it's in."

10

"You're right about that. If you aren't married with a houseful of little ones, they won't even talk to you."

"Well, there you go!" she teased. "Just find you a woman and start raising babies."

"And how am I supposed to raise them, working for my daddy on a sharecropper's farm?" The anger in his voice surprised her. She felt all at once almost sorry she was leaving, sorry that she could, maybe, when he didn't have a chance.

"Oh, Ollie. I'm sorry. Just running my mouth as usual, not thinking about anybody but me."

He seized her wrist and tugged, but without pressure, as if she were a China doll. "No, Mae. I'm the one who's sorry. I should be glad you're doing what will make you happy. Well, I am glad, really. It's just that—I'll miss you, you know? This place just won't be the same."

"What, without my motor mouth and my way of always getting in trouble?"

"You know that's not true. Everybody loves you. You're a heck of a girl."

"Aw, thanks. I promise I'll come back to visit. You'll always be my best friend in the world, except for—"

"Graydell, of course," he finished for her, and they both laughed, easy with each other again. "We better get you home, girl. You've got a celebration to get to." He started the car. "And Maisie?"

"Yeah?"

"I'm really and truly proud for you that you made valedictorian. It's nice to have a smart friend. Maybe it'll come in handy one of these days."

She slapped at his shoulder again, and he drew back as if hurt. Then on an impulse he put his arm around her shoulder, drawing her into a warm hug. "I'll miss you, Maisie."

"I'll miss you, too, Ollie," she said against his shirt sleeve, and realized how much she meant it.

He put the car in gear and pulled back onto the road. They were silent during the rest of the ride, which took all of two minutes.

11

"Come in with me?" she asked, putting her hand over his on the wheel.

"Oh, I think this should be a family night. I'll see you soon." He leaned across and opened the car door for her.

"Thanks for the ride, and for the talk." She stepped out, stood up straight, and turned toward the house.

"Good luck, Maisie!" He backed from the yard.

A thunderclap, loud and echoing, made her jump. She took a step—and the clouds, having threatened all afternoon, opened with a vengeance. She was drenched before she reached the screen door.

* * *

Later, with the cake eaten and Thomas and family long gone, Mae retreated to her room and pulled out her diary.

Friday, May 16, 1941

I can't believe this night finally got here! I've been counting the weeks, then the days, finally the hours. And now it's over. I am a high school graduate.

The most amazing thing happened tonight! I won the Valedictorian spot! Me—"Eula" Mae Johnson. I couldn't believe it at first, but I finally made it up to the podium. I had to get my certificate from Mr. J.T., which I couldn't hardly stand. But then Miss Jenkins put a medal around my neck. I had to lean over a bit cause she's so short, and when we were face to face I could see her eyes were all wet, but she was smiling. She said, "I am so proud of you!" And that meant as much to me as anything.

Thomas and his family came by the house—they were waiting when I got there. Oliver drove me home, and the lightning and the heaviness had my skin prickling, but the rain held off. Then it hit, and before I made it in the house the bottom fell out! I got my new navy skirt and weskit soaked, but I don't care. I'm just too happy to care about something like clothes.

I talked to Oliver about moving to Texarkana, and he wasn't happy, but he did wish me luck. Now I just have to get up enough nerve to face Mama and Daddy. But not tonight—they were just too happy, and I was, too. I'll have to wait to find the right time. Surely I'll be able to make them understand.

Lord, thank you for this blessed night. I didn't think anything could be better than graduating. But to be Valedictorian! That's just almost too much for me to stand.

THREE

PRISSY THIBODEAUX

MAE BIT INTO HER chicken leg and stole a peek at Prissy. The younger girl had stopped eating and was staring at her. Finally she spoke.

"You're going to do what? You're joshing me, aren't you?"

The two were lounging on a quilt under one of the giant oaks surrounding the churchyard. A gentle breeze teased the curls at Prissy's neck. She had pinned her mass of glossy black hair atop her head, a few tendrils escaping right away, more slipping loose recently.

"No, I'm not teasing, I'm serious. Prissy, you know I've talked about this for a long time now."

"Yes, but I thought that was just you being you—that you were just mouthing off."

"Oh, I see. I lay out my hopes and plans, confessing my most secret thoughts, expecting my friends to support me, and all that time you've not been taking me seriously." She stopped, hurt. Not knowing what else to say.

"Mae, don't be like that. You know I'm your friend. We've known each other forever."

Mae didn't respond, and the silence grew strained between them. She gazed across the field of cows next to the churchyard. The herd had three new baby calves—two red with white faces, one solid black. The black one was a little boy, and today he was being rambunctious, running in circles, kicking up his heels, head butting the little girls, who ignored him while concentrating on the tender green shoots of grass, ripping hungrily at the blades. Somewhere a bull bellowed, letting his womenfolk know he was still around.

"It's not like I'm leaving and never coming back. I'll be back as many weekends as I can. We'll see each other at church, and at dinners on the ground like this one, and I promise I'll come see you from time to time."

"I just don't understand why you even want to leave here. You have a nice family, a good church family, real friends."

"I know I do. It doesn't have anything to do with any of that. I just need to spread my wings, live a little. I'll only be a couple of hours away. It's not like I'm going to Dallas or New Orleans."

"Well, at least I could understand it a bit more if you were moving to New Orleans. It's a beautiful, exciting city," Prissy said. Her daddy's parents were from New Orleans, and Prissy visited every summer. She was enamored of the place. "But I just don't see anything special about Texarkana."

"What's special is that it's *not here*. And it's a place where I can get out on my own. I want a husband—someday—but not now. And if I stay here, I'll be pushed to find a man, to get married soon."

Prissy wrinkled her forehead and shook her head from side to side. "Now, Mae, I just don't think that's true. I can't see your mama and daddy pushing you into getting married if you don't want to. Do you honestly think they would?"

Mae shrugged her shoulders and stretched her long legs out in front of her, rearranging her skirt modestly. They were still at church, after all.

"Maybe not. But things aren't easy at home these days, Prissy. My family's not like yours. We don't have any money to speak of. The only way I've had spending money for the past few years is by working for Mrs. Wheeler. You know that. And I really don't know which is worse, the

15

thought of cooking, cleaning, and taking care of her little girl, or having a family of my own to do for."

At this, finally, Prissy barked out a not very feminine laugh. "Oh, Mae, you're right. I just can't see you remaining an old maid and still working for Mrs. Wheeler, and then someday moving on to care for Hope's household and her children, *ad infinitum*, until your dying day!"

"Bite your tongue, woman! Do you want to put a hex on me?" But Mae was laughing, too.

"Who is this talking about hexes, right here on the church grounds?"

Mae jumped at the sound of the baritone voice she knew so well. Oliver. She leaned back on her elbows and looked up to see him laughing down at her. He looked about seven feet tall from her vantage point.

"Never you mind. It was a bunch of silly girl talk, that's all. Right, Prissy?"

Prissy murmured her assent. "Why don't you join us, Oliver? Maybe you can talk Mae out of this silly idea about leaving Dixon's Crossing."

Oliver dropped onto a corner of the quilt and, plucking a blade of the slender grass, stuck it between his teeth and chewed for a moment, as if pondering what Prissy had said. Then he gave a little jerk of his head.

"I don't think so, Prissy. Mae's mind seems to be pretty well made up. We've already had this conversation, and she isn't going to listen to me any more than she is to you."

"That may be. But if she'll listen to anyone, it will be you or Graydell. And since Graydell seems to be ready to run off and leave us, too, I don't suppose it would do any good to try to get her to talk some sense into Mae. So I'm going to get myself another slice of Mrs. Williams' chocolate pie, and you two can talk it out one more time." She stood up and daintily smoothed her skirt. "And Mae . . . really listen to the man this time, alright?"

Mae sat up straight and gave Oliver a once over with a jaundiced eye. "Okay, Brother Oliver, give it your best shot!"

FOUR

THE WHOREHOUSE

MAE SAT FANNING HERSELF with a copy of the *Texarkana Gazette*, thinking how hot it was for it to still be May. Waiting for Graydell to get back to the car, she propped her arm on the window frame, leaned her head on her hand, hoped nobody she knew would come by and see her here—it was so embarrassing, sitting here in front of a whorehouse.

This morning Graydell had asked her daddy if she could have the car so she and Mae could come to Texarkana, and when he said they could they had rushed to get ready. Mae had spent the night with Graydell, so the two of them had already picked out clothes to wear. They wanted to look nice, but not dressed up to the point where Graydell's parents would get suspicious. In other words, jeans and nice blouses.

Just before they left, Mrs. Upton had thrown a monkey wrench into their plans. "Graydell, since y'all are going into town, I need you to take something to your sister."

"Aw Mama! I don't want to go to that place."

"Well, I'd just as soon you not go there, either. But Clara wrote last week and asked me to send the dress I made her next time someone came up that way. I have it packed, so it won't take you long to drop it off. I'll go get the sack."

As her mother left the room, Graydell had muttered under her breath, "I don't know why she needs another dress. It's not like she's gonna wear it."

Mae snickered, but she couldn't help blushing. Graydell's older sister Clara was living in one of the whorehouses down on the far end of Broad Street. Mae didn't like to stand in judgment. The last few years had been hard on everybody, and she knew Clara had looked for decent work before she'd done what she did. She had gotten in trouble when she was fifteen, and Graydell's mama was now raising her little girl, who was now seven years old.

Mae felt sorry for the pretty little girl. She would most likely have to go through some tough times at school when the kids got old enough to find out about her mother. Clara was a good mother, in her own way. She sent money back home to help out, and she also sent nice clothes for her daughter—but not so nice that the girl would stand out when she wore them. And Clara visited several times a year, as often as she could.

Still, Mae didn't like sitting here in broad daylight in front of a brothel. Never mind that nobody she knew had any business being here, either. She just wanted Graydell to hurry up. They had things to do.

She sneaked a look at the house. It was really pretty. All of these houses were. There were two more in this block Graydell had said were whorehouses, too. This one was the prettiest. It was a big, sprawling two story with a wide front porch that held a few rocking chairs, and there was a swing at each end of the porch. There were nine steps up to the porch from the street. A black wrought iron fence surrounded the front yard, which was filled with rose bushes, lilacs, and other blooms.

The house had fancy trim, with lots of little curlicues that must have been the devil to keep painted, but the paint on the house was fairly new—a pale, buttery yellow, with all the trim work painted a deep wine red, about the same shade as the rose on the vines trailing along the fence. The chairs and swings were painted a shiny black. At every window hung lacy white curtains that fluttered whenever a breeze passed by. She heard giggles drifting out of the house from time to time. *It must take lots of work to keep up a place this nice. Wonder how many times you'd have to . . .*

Graydell came out of the house and bounded down the steps as if chased by iniquity. "Boy, I'm glad that's over! Let's get out of here!" She started the car and pulled out into the empty street, swinging around in a wide U-turn so they were headed toward State Line, and safety.

"So, how's Clara doing?"

"Oh, she's doing," Graydell giggled. She drove, looking straight ahead. "I don't need to be laughing, I'm driving."

Mae snapped her head around and gave her friend's profile a disbelieving look. "You're *laughing about this*? My Lord, Graydell, we just left a *whorehouse*, for Pete's sake."

"I know! Believe me, I know." The giggles kept threatening to erupt again. "And you wouldn't believe what they were doing."

"I don't even want to think about it," Mae said, blushing.

"Not that. You think I'd have gone in there if there were men around?" She removed one hand from the steering wheel and tapped it against her chest over her heart. "Why, whatever do you take me for?" She reminded Mae of Miss Scarlet O'Hara in *Gone with the Wind*. They had both read the book last winter and been very impressed with the southern fireball.

Mae punched Graydell's shoulder. "Cut it out. You know what I meant." She tried to ask in an offhand way, "What's it really like in there?"

"Like you'd expect, I guess. It's like the outside—everything is fixed up just perfect. There's wallpaper with lots of roses, deep red velvet chairs and sofas. And a player piano, but it wasn't playing. You first go into a big entry hall that has a long rack with hooks on the wall—I suppose for all the 'gentlemen's' coats. But Mae, the floor is the most amazing thing! It's covered completely with silver dollars."

"What? The floor?" Mae couldn't imagine what that would even look like. "How many dollars do you think it took?"

"I wouldn't even know how to make a guess. But that hallway is as big as our living room almost. Anyway, the woman who runs the place is

Miss Nina. She's probably about thirty-five or forty. She's called a 'madam,' that's what Clara told me. Miss Nina was sitting at this big roll-top desk in the parlor—it looked like she was doing some figuring. Three of the girls were just sitting around in these satiny bathrobes."

"How old are they?" Mae couldn't keep the curiosity out of her voice.

"About our age, some probably as old as Clara. They have a colored maid—she opened the door for me. She had on this black dress with a white cap and white apron, and it was starched all stiff and proper."

"Sounds like the movies we see sometimes, you know, with those fancy people in New York City or somewhere."

"Um-hmm. About like that."

"A real maid," Mae murmured thoughtfully. Then, "Where was Clara?"

"She was upstairs in her room. I didn't go in. The maid went and got her. I've never been to her room. I'm not allowed."

"They won't let you?" Mae was huffy over this insult.

"Nah. I guess their rooms are fixed up all 'naughty' or something."

"Ooh, naughty." Mae rolled her eyes and waggled her eyebrows.

Graydell began to giggle.

"What?"

"I had to wait for Clara in the upstairs parlor, and there were four girls out there. One of them had this pair of red lacy underwear, and she threw them into another girl's face."

Mae laughed, but felt her face flush.

"Then *that* girl snatched them off her face and used them like a slingshot and . . ." Graydell couldn't continue, she was laughing so hard. After a moment she went on, "And she shot them into *my* face!"

Mae shrieked with laughter. "Were they new or used?"

"Oh, my Lord!" Graydell said, wiping tears from her eyes. "I have to stop somewhere. I can't see where I'm going."

They had been riding down Broad Street, and now turned north onto State Line Avenue. Texarkana was a city divided between two states, and now as they drove north, Texas lay to their left while Arkansas was on their right.

"Here's the Dixie Drive-in. Pull in here," Mae said.

Graydell stuck her arm out the window with her hand in the air, breezily letting anyone behind her know she was turning right. She stopped the car as soon as she was off the street. The girls sat for a couple of minutes, letting their hysterics run their course, their breathing slowly returning to normal.

"Oh, Graydell. How embarrassing. I would have just died if that had been me."

Graydell shrugged, turning serious. "I wouldn't have been there if Mama hadn't made me."

Mae heard a slight catch in her friend's voice. "Never mind that. Hey, let's get a soda while we're here."

Graydell hesitated, as if she wanted to say something more.

"What? Want to go someplace else?"

"No, this is fine. I just—well, I thought you might want to know who I saw while I was waiting for Clara. But I'm not sure—"

"You mean there's somebody else in there we know?" Mae's eyes were round with surprise. "Who was it?"

Graydell's nose wrinkled. "Evangeline."

Mae made a face as if she'd swallowed Castor oil.

"Mae, you okay?"

"I'm fine. I suppose that's a good place for her. I'm sure she's got the experience."

"Mae—"

"Well, every time Frank and I have broken up, he's gone running off to *her*, and you know how we'd see them all wrapped around each other. I always thought that's why he would stop seeing me, cause I wouldn't, you know—"

"Then it was his loss. And good enough for him, if his other girlfriend ends up in a whorehouse." Graydell slapped the steering wheel for emphasis.

"What was she doing? How did she look? Did she recognize you?"

"Oh, yeah, I'm pretty sure she recognized me. She wasn't doing anything when I got there, but when she saw me she got up and left the room."

Mae turned her head away and looked off across the parking lot, lost in thought.

"Hey, come on, let's get that soda." Graydell pulled the car into one of the parking spaces close to the building and tooted the horn. After a minute with no response, she honked again. "That's strange," she said. "There's always a girl out here right away. It's not even busy today."

Mae craned her neck to look toward the building's main entrance. "D'you think there's something wrong? They are open today, aren't they?"

Just then a squat little man of about fifty burst out the door and came bustling toward their car. "What can I get you ladies today?" He was carrying a small pad and pencil, as if he planned for them to place a complicated order.

"Just two Coca-Colas, please," Graydell said. "Say, where are your usual carhops?" The place was known for its roller-skating waitresses.

"Well, you see, there's the problem. The girls who were supposed to work today decided to up and move to Shreveport. No notice or anything. Just came by this morning with their car all packed up and asked for their last pay. I apologize for being so unorganized. Don't know what the missus and I are going to do. I know there's plenty of people out of work, but I need somebody soon."

Graydell turned to Mae and raised an eyebrow. Mae gave the man her warmest smile. "Well, now, isn't this your lucky day?"

* * *

Sooner than they had expected, then, Mae and Graydell found themselves with jobs. Mr. Robinson, owner of the Dixie Drive-in, seemed to be a nice enough old man, and his wife Dora was just a darling. As soon as he had said, "You're hired," she had begun bustling around, rounding up

22

uniforms for the two of them. They were told to wear their own jeans, but she found some pink polka dotted shirts for them.

Graydell almost backed out when their new boss told them they had to serve customers on roller skates.

"I've never had any luck with those things," she complained to Mae. "I'll probably fall and bust my butt."

"Probably so," Mae said cheerfully.

"Mae! You're supposed to be supportive, rah rah and all that!"

"I will be, once you put the skates on. Oh, c'mon, Graydell! This is going to be fun! An *adventure*!"

"Why do I let you drag me into these things?" Graydell was actually wringing her hands.

Mae snorted. "Maybe because you want to get out of Dixon's Crossing almost as much as I do?"

Her friend would not be mollified so easily. "*Nobody* in Dixon's Crossing wants out as bad as *you* do. It's all you have talked about for the past year and a half."

"And dreamed of for way longer than that," muttered Mae.

Mr. Robinson interrupted the girls. "I have one girl who can come in this afternoon, and she'll be able to help us out through next Thursday. Can y'all be here by Friday?"

"Well, I don't know—" Graydell began.

"Yes, sir, we'll be here. What time?"

FIVE

MRS. SWENSON'S BOARDING HOUSE

"NOW TO FIND A place to stay." Graydell's frown was deepening. "I've got to get the car back home before dark. It's the rule at our house, you know."

"Yeah—but I'm just so glad they let you have it today."

"Only because my sorry slut of a sister needed some stuff. Now, how do I convince them to let me use it again on Thursday, especially when I tell them it's to move all our things?"

"Don't worry about me," Mae said casually. "I'm not bringing much with me. After all, our room will almost surely be furnished, and we won't need anything to cook with if we get room and board. Just need my clothes, shoes, and makeup—and not all of that. Summer's creeping up on us, so I don't even need a coat. I can bring a bag of stuff back with me whenever I go home for a weekend."

"Good idea." Graydell navigated around the large post office and federal courthouse that straddled the state line between Texas and Arkansas. "I was thinking maybe we could look somewhere close to the new courthouse and police station, maybe in the Quality Hill Neighborhood. Want to try Laurel Street first?"

"Sounds good to me," Mae agreed. "You know I don't know my way around the town, but I've been by the courthouse several times with my folks, when they came to pay their poll taxes and such. I like the name, too—Quality Hill. It even sounds respectable. Maybe it would make out folks feel better if we could find a place they were familiar with."

"Well, aren't you sounding all grown-up all of a sudden? Guess that's what becoming part of the real work world does for you," Graydell laughed.

She slammed on her brakes, throwing Mae up against the dash. "Hey, take it easy! You don't have to be in such a tizzy over room hunting." Mae scooted back in the seat, adjusting her scarf.

"Mae, look! Didn't you see it?" Stopped in the middle of the residential street now, Graydell was pointing into the yard on their right. "I mean, he just ran right in front of the car! I almost hit him! And wouldn't that have put the kibosh on my getting to use the car again."

Mae looked where Graydell was pointing. There amid the shrubs and flowers in a beautifully kept front yard stood a magnificent white tail deer. He wasn't moving a muscle now, but stood with his back toward the girls in the car, his head turned so he could watch them from over his shoulder.

Mae reached to roll down her window, wanting a clearer view of the animal. "Well, would you look at that? He ran right in front of the car?" she asked softly.

"Yeah," her friend whispered back. "And then he went over there and stopped to look at us."

"It's a sign," Mae breathed. "He's sent to show us the way, just like the pillar of fire leading Moses and the Israelites in the Bible." A shiver went up and down her spine.

"Eek! He's on the move," Graydell squeaked. "Now where's he going?"

The stately, velvet-antlered animal was strolling his way across the lovingly manicured lawn. When he neared the flower bed next to the porch, he gave a fluid leap up and sideways and landed on the porch. Both girls

25

gasped. He trotted across the porch, ducked his head, and disappeared around the corner, following the wrap-around porch out of sight.

"Well, I never! Wonder where he's going."

"Maybe to see if the milkman left any fresh bottles this morning," Mae chuckled. Then her laughter broke off, and she grabbed at Graydell's arm. "Graydell, look! There, in the front window! I told you he was a sign."

Graydell squinted and read aloud: "Room for rent. Single Christian ladies only. Board provided. Inquire within." She had her hand on the door handle and was yanking it open when Mae muttered, "Wait."

The deer had circumnavigated the entire house, still traveling by porch it seemed, for he was now peering around the corner, surveying the place he had started from.

"Well, you little devil," Mae murmured approvingly. "Better safe than sorry, hmm?"

The deer's antlers seemed to be weighing him down. "That's a really nice rack," Graydell whispered. "My brother would love to have it mounted over our fireplace." Once again, the deer had stopped, and he seemed to be peering directly at the two of them again. "He kind of gives me the creeps, Mae."

"Aw, no. He's just a special gift, that's all. He led us right to this house, that has this sign, just what we're looking for. And look. There's the lady of the house."

A woman in her mid-fifties had opened the wooden front door of the house a few inches to stare out at the beast now just on the other side of a screen door from her. Suddenly she flung the door wide.

"Scat, you awful creature! Go on with you now. Shoo!" Her words were punctuated with sharp jabs from the business end of a hefty broom. "I mean it! Go back to the country where you belong!"

Far from intimidated, the deer simply leapt from the porch as if that was what he had planned all along, sauntered across the yard, and stepped into Laurel behind the girls' car. Looking back once, he gave his whole body a shake, his muscles rippling in the bright sunlight. Then he

26

broke into a canter, turned the corner at 6th Street, and disappeared from view.

"It's a sign, I tell you," Mae breathed again, reaching for her door handle.

The woman with the broom opened her screen door and started inside, but, spying the two girls headed up her sidewalk, stepped back outside, propping on the broom handle.

"Hello," Mae called out, waving. "Are you the mistress of the house?"

Seeing the woman nod, she continued. "I'm Mae Johnson, and this girl here is my friend, Graydell Upton."

"Pleased to meet you. I'm Laverne Swenson. Can I help you girls with something?"

"I hope so," Mae said, as they reached the porch. They all shook hands, and Mae said, "Graydell and I live down close to Dixon's Crossing, and we came into town today looking for work."

"I don't have anything I need help with," Mrs. Swenson said reaching for the door handle.

"Oh, no, ma'am, we're not here for that. We're here for *that*," and she pointed to the sign in the window. "I hope you haven't rented it out yet?"

"Well, no, I haven't, as a matter of fact."

The woman had a bit of an accent, but Mae didn't have enough experience with foreigners to recognize it.

"We'd sure like to talk with you about it."

"Are you girls old enough to be out on your own?" She sounded skeptical.

"Yes, ma'am," Graydell answered. "We're both eighteen, and we just graduated high school a couple of weeks ago."

"Is that right? Well, that's good to know. First, before I show you the room, I might as well go over the price and my rules. No need to even go inside if you aren't ready to agree to those things."

The girls nodded, and Mrs. Swenson began a litany of rules and regulations, everything from not having any men upstairs to the hours when they could use her washing machine to do their laundry.

"You'll be able to have all your meals here, except for Saturdays— I take that day off. And Sunday I fix one meal, at noontime, and I serve it after I get back from church. You girls churchgoers?"

"Yes, we both go to the Baptist church," Mae said.

"I'm a Methodist, myself, but we're all God's children under the skin."

Mae smiled. T*hink I'm going to like her.*

"The rent for both room and board is twenty-five dollars a month, and I need at least a ten-dollar deposit if you decide you want the room. I'll need the rest on the day you move in."

They looked at each other, both wondering just how much money the other had.

"That sounds okay," Graydell said. "You think we could see that room now? We have to be getting back home soon."

Mrs. Swenson looked at first one, then the other. "Come on in."

The downstairs of the old house was well-appointed. A parlor lay to their left, a dining room to their right.

"We'll eat in here each meal," Mrs. Swenson said, "I have two other women boarding here already, so there will be four of you at mealtimes."

"The room is lovely," Graydell said. "And I love your parlor."

"Why, thank you," the landlady said. "You may entertain gentlemen friends in the parlor if it is empty. The other tenants don't make use of it very often. They prefer to go out, I suppose. But remember, no men on the second floor."

They both nodded. Finally, she took to the stairs. "And I would appreciate very much if you used the stairs like ladies. No running up and down, making all sorts of noises. I run a quiet house, and I aim for it to stay that way."

Again, they simply nodded.

What, do we look like hooligans? Mae grinned behind Mrs. S., which is what she was already calling the woman. The room she showed them was a large, airy room with windows on two sides. There were three single beds: one under a window, one with its headboard up against a wall, and one snuggled into a far corner. *That's the one I want.* One wall had a short row of cabinets, and there was a sink and a tiny stove. A small table sat next to one of the windows, and French doors sparkled in the sunshine.

In the middle of the room there was a sofa and a low table. Graydell gave these only a passing glance. She opened the doors and peered outside. "Oh, Mae, come and look! We have a balcony! I mean, the room has a balcony."

"Yes," said Mrs. S., the tenants always seem to enjoy the balcony. It's nice and breezy when the weather's warm."

"Like now, you mean?" Mae grinned, stepping onto the balcony with Graydell. It appeared to run the length of the front of the house. "Nice view of the courthouse," she added.

"The bathroom is the next door down, in between this room and the next one. I'll leave it up to all you young women to figure out who uses the bathroom when. The other two girls have private rooms, but those run forty dollars a month. They have good jobs over at the courthouse," she went on. "I have one other room empty right now, but I'm showing you this one because I don't know what your budget is. I can show the other one if you'd like, but it costs more."

"No, ma'am," Graydell said. "I think this is about all we can afford, just starting a job and all."

Mrs. S. nodded, sizing them up. "What kind of job did you find?"

"We're going to be carhops at the Dixie Drive-In," Mae said proudly. "We went over there at just the right time. Two of the waitresses had just quit."

The landlady drew her brows together and frowned. "I'm not sure I like that idea. Carhops. How do I know if you're decent girls?"

"Mrs. S.!" Mae protested. "You should be able to tell by just looking at us. All we want is to live in Texarkana instead of out on a farm, and we're willing to work hard to make that happen. Now, do you want to rent to us or not?" Her hands were on her hips, and she could feel her face warming. But she couldn't help herself. She wanted this beautiful room.

"What did you call me?" Mrs. Swenson asked, scowling.

"She didn't mean anything by it, Mrs. Swenson," Graydell protested.

But Mae was ready to stand up for herself.

"No, I sure didn't. It's just that, well, you just seem like a Mrs. S. to me," she said, laughing self-consciously. "I tend to do that to people I like—just shorten their name down somehow. I felt comfortable with you, so it just came out." She shrugged.

Mrs. Swenson stared at her for a long moment, then she chuckled. "To answer your question, yes, I believe I do want to rent to you. The other two tenants are so serious all the time. They're in their mid-twenties, and they just go to work, come home and go to their rooms, eat dinner, and sometimes go out in the evening, but not very often. You girls will be like a breath of fresh air."

She went back through the room and out into the hall. "Well, are you coming to look at your bathroom or not?"

The girls hugged each other briefly and followed their new landlady, with Mae calculating in her head.

I sure hope we've got ten dollars between us.

SIX

CONFRONTATION

"WHAT IS IT?" MAMA asked, sinking into her chair at the end of the table, a small, tired groan escaping her lips. The sound sent a feeling of guilt washing over Mae. *Can I really do this?* She looked closer at her mother, at the shoulders rounded by tiredness, the face streaked with lines put there too soon by too many years in the sun, at the eyes with their resigned expression. Yes, she could. Otherwise, she would end up just like her mother.

Mae had started for the house when Graydell dropped her off, but Mama was in the side garden and called out to her. "Has the long-lost daughter finally decided to come home?"

Mae had hoped she could talk to Mama reasonably about her news, but that one sentence told her this wasn't to be. And when Mama followed her straight to the house, she prepared herself for battle.

Now she said, "You know I've said for the longest time now that after I turned eighteen and got out of school, I wanted to move to Texarkana and get a job up there?"

"Yes, Mae. We have all heard that from you plenty of times. But you know that's just not realistic."

"Why, Mama? Why is it not realistic? I'm a good worker. I work hard. I know how to do lots of stuff, not just here on the farm, but over at Mrs. Wheeler's house, too. I cook, clean, do washing and ironing—I'm even a good cook, thanks to you." She gave her mother a bright smile, wanting so much to hear agreement from her.

"All that's true, as far as it goes. But you still have a lot to learn. There's an awful lot that goes into really running a household all by yourself. It may look easy to you, but things were very different around here before you and your brother and sister came along. Y'all have made it much easier on me than it used to be."

"Well, I'm not ready to think about something like that just yet," Mae said, as she emphatically set down the saltshaker she'd been absently rolling back and forth between her palms. "I don't plan to get married for years and years. And I don't plan to stay here in Dixon's Crossing when I could move to Texarkana and have some fun."

"Fun," her mother spat out. "Fun! Is that all you think there is to life, Eula Mae?"

Mae cringed, only ever hearing her full name when Mama was upset with her. She had to try to make her understand. "I love you, Mama. I just don't want to *be* you." Too late, she saw the fresh pain in her mother's face. "I didn't mean it like that, Mama! I'm sorry. You know I can't say anything straight without putting my foot in my mouth."

"No, that's quite all right," Mama said, squaring her shoulders. "I don't suppose I would want to be me, either, if I were you."

Mae's guilt doubled with that statement, fraught as it was with a sadness and longing Mae had never heard, or at least never paid attention to, before.

"Mama, I'm sorry, but I do wish I could have your blessing on moving out."

Stomping on the back steps signaled Daddy's arrival. It was almost six. Mae's news had kept her mother from having supper ready. *Great. Another layer of guilt added to what I'm already feeling.*

32

Mama had risen at the sound of his boots, and by the time he was in his chair taking them off, she had all burners on the stove turned on, heating up leftovers from the noon meal.

"Did we have any of those greens left at dinner?" Daddy asked, heaving a sigh of relief as he set his boots against the wall and wriggled his toes.

Mama's voice was thick when she answered yes, and always one to pick up on cues, he looked sharply at her.

"Bessie, what's the matter?"

"Nothing, Will. I just got sidetracked out in the garden, and I don't have supper on the table like I usually do, that's all. I'm sorry."

Mae felt his eyes on her as he got up and went to stand beside his wife. "No, hurry, hon. I'm so tired I could use a few minutes to rest anyway. Mae, what have you been up to today? I saw Graydell drop you off a few minutes ago."

Mae hesitated, hating to worsen the mood before supper—but then she thought, "It will only get worse if you put it off."

She took an onion from the window ledge and rinsed it in the bowl of water sitting in the sink. Reaching for a match from the matchbox, she clamped the wooden end between her teeth and began to peel and slice the onion. Sucking hard, she drew a touch of sulfur into her mouth to keep her eyes from tearing up.

"Well, since you ask, we *have* had a pretty exciting day." She looked over her shoulder, trying to catch Mama's eye, but she was busy at the stove.

"Tell me all about it," Daddy said. "There hasn't been any excitement around here at all, huh Bessie?" He patted her on the back and returned to his chair.

"We went to the Dixie Drive-in to get a coke, and the owner had just lost two of his waitresses, so he hired us both on the spot. His wife helped us put together out uniforms—We have to work on roller skates!—and we start on Friday. Then we went looking for a place to live, and we found an apartment across from the Courthouse. The landlady seems real nice—and I know y'all will appreciate this—she is very strict about her boarders." Mae stopped to take a breath and reached into the cabinet for a bowl for the onion slices.

Mama kept stirring whatever was in the large pot on the back of the stove.

"My goodness, Mae, that's a lot of information in one breath," Daddy said. "Bessie, have you heard all this already?"

"Mostly. That's what we were talking about before you came in."

"I take it this news is responsible for the way you two are avoiding each other?" he said, continuing to look from one to the other."

"I'm not trying to avoid her," Mae said. "I just wish I could get a little bit of support from her, that's all." She rinsed her hands and wiped them on a dish towel, then came to sit on the bench by the window.

Her mother turned to face the two of them. "You might give a person time to get adjusted to news like that, young lady. In the first place—"

Her husband held up a hand, silencing her, then motioned for her to come sit in her chair at the table. Reluctantly, she did so.

"In the first place, I want to ask Mae a couple of questions. You may have heard enough, but I haven't."

Mama squared her shoulders. "That's fine. I suppose I can sit through listening to it again. Just so you pay attention to the fact that your daughter has pretty much gone out and done this on her own without discussing it with either one of us."

"Fair enough. Mae, why don't you start at the beginning and tell us—me—what you think you've done."

Mae bristled at the word 'think,' but she sat up straight and faced him.

"Yes, sir, I'd be happy to. First of all, you know I've been saying that after I turned eighteen and graduated, that I was going to get a job in Texarkana and move up there."

Despite his resolve, Daddy's eyes twinkled, and the corner of his mouth turned up. "Yes, I do know that."

34

"Well, today things just fell into place, and now it's happening, just like I want it to." She launched into a detailed account of her day—leaving out what she could of the visit to the whorehouse—and finally ending with a description of the boarding house she and Graydell had found.

"And when exactly do you plan to move out?" he asked, no inflection in his voice.

"We'll be moving on Thursday," she said. "Graydell is going to get her brother to take us up there. I was hoping I could get your and Mama's blessing on moving out."

"Moving! You're moving out?"

All eyes turned to Mae's younger sister, Ginny, who stood frozen in the door to the kitchen. Ginny squealed and turned in a circle before coming around the table to grab Mae up into an embrace.

"Oh, Mae! That is so exciting! Where are you moving to? Have you got a job? What are you going to do?" She sucked in just enough air to add, "When are you leaving?"

Despite the tension in the room, Mae couldn't help laughing, just for a minute.

Mr. Johnson looked slowly around the room, taking in the expressions of his womenfolk: Ginny so excited she was almost giddy; his wife with a stubborn set to her jaw and a pained expression in her eyes; and Mae, with her shoulders squared back and her chin held high. Mae felt sorry for him. He had three very different women to deal with all at once.

He unfolded himself from his chair, stood, and stretched. She heard his back and shoulders popping. He went to the sink and began to wash his hands, up to his elbows, saying nothing. Reaching for the towel hanging on a nail, he just as methodically dried his hands and arms. Then he replaced the towel and walked out of the room without another word.

Mae opened her mouth but thought better of saying anything else. Five interminable minutes passed before he returned.

"Now, will somebody tell me what's really going on?"

Mama said, "She's got all fired up after a day away from her work here, and she thinks she won't ever have to do this kind of work again. Thinks she's too good for it."

"I would hope you could be happy for me that I won't," Mae spat out. "Maybe I should just go ahead and leave now. I'll pack a bag and go stay with Graydell till Thursday." Ignoring their shocked looks, she stormed out of the room.

* * *

Crying is a weakness. Straighten up. Mae was blowing her nose when there was a knock on her bedroom door.

"Mae? Can I come in?" Daddy asked.

"Sure," she said. She sat up on the bed and tried to clear the tears from her voice.

"Talk to me, Mae," he said, his voice both soft and demanding. He sat on the foot of her bed and skewered her with his gaze.

"I've tried to tell y'all I was planning to move out," she said, looking her daddy square in the face.

He nodded. "I guess I was hoping that was just a childish dream you would grow out of."

"Why does it have to be a childish dream? And why do I have to grow out of it? Didn't you ever have any dreams, Daddy?"

"Well, sure, Mae. I was born right at the turn of the century. Everything was new and exciting. I saw the first automobile in Dixon's Crossing. I couldn't wait to get big enough to reach the controls on one of those things. I hung around old man Wheeler's place every chance I got, and he encouraged me to. I had dreams of living in a big house like theirs, driving a fancy car of my own." Mae heard his voice thicken, and he stopped talking.

His work-roughened hands traced the outline of the green vines twining across her pale pink chenille bedspread. His hand stilled, finally, and he raised his eyes to meet hers.

"But that was a long time ago. I grew up, and I set aside those foolish childhood dreams." He stared at her for a long minute. "I don't want you to go, sweetie. There are hard times coming, even harder than now, and I want all my family to be close by."

Hard times. What do you think we've been living through?

"I'm sorry, Daddy—but I'm going. It may be a big mistake. If I fall flat on my face, I'll take responsibility for that. I have to try. Don't you ever wish you'd tried harder?" She could have bitten her tongue right out of her mouth. Why had she said something so hurtful?

The way he twisted his mouth, she couldn't tell if he was trying not to cry, or not to laugh. She didn't know which would be worse. He wagged his head from side to side like their old red and white bull, then gave a quiet chuckle. She perked up at the sound.

"Then go, Mae. Go and give it all you've got. You're a smart girl, and a hard worker. Maybe you'll do just fine. I sure hope so. Just remember. You'll always have a home to come back to—anytime you want, anytime you need it."

He stood and placed a hand on her shoulder. "Thanks, Daddy," she sniffed, throwing her arms around him.

"Just promise me one thing."

"Anything, if I can," she said, leaning back to scan his face.

"Promise me you won't go off in a huff tonight to the Upton's. Stay here till moving day and see if you can't work things out with your mama."

* * *

Keeping that promise was even harder than Mae had expected. Daddy had informed Mama and Ginny that Mae would be staying until Thursday.

Supper, after all the commotion caused by her announcement, was subdued. Even Ginny, always full of stories and questions, only responded when someone asked her to pass something, and there wasn't much of that. Seemed nobody had much appetite that night.

Mama and Daddy finally pushed back their chairs and moved to the front room to listen to one of their favorite programs, *Deadline Dramas*. Mae and Ginny were able to hear most of the program while they cleaned the kitchen, though Mae was still distracted. It was Ginny's turn to haul water from the well to heat for dishwater, but she didn't even complain tonight. She did, however, do her best to wait for intermission in the program to go out to the porch.

The radio show always amazed them. Three radio actors were given a plot of twenty words that they had to turn into a seven-minute play within just two minutes. Sometimes the story ideas were great, sometimes not so much.

"Those actors are so talented," Mae said to Ginny as she stacked plates. "I know what it was like for us to learn our lines when we did the junior play, and everything was all planned out for us. Even with a complete script, we still had a hard time pulling it off."

"Yeah, I saw the play, remember?" Ginny grinned, pouring a bucket of water into the big pan on the stove. While she waited for it to get to simmering, she wiped off the table and set in place the things that stayed there all the time: the saltshaker, the tin of black pepper, a jar holding toothpicks, Mama's grandma's sugar bowl, a quart jar of sorghum syrup.

Mae used a dipper to transfer hot water from the stove into her wash pan, then carried it to the sink and began scrubbing the dishes—plates and eating utensils first, glasses next, cooking pots last. She layered things expertly, then dipped fresh hot water and scalded the dishes, using as few dips as she could. It was always a test of dexterity and ingenuity to get every dish rinsed without having to heat more water. Ginny wiped the clean dishes dry and maneuvered them into the kitchen's sparse cabinets.

She tried a time or two to ask Mae a question, but Mae shut her down with a look and a whispered, "Later. In your room."

With everything squared away, they left the folks sitting companionably in the front room. Daddy was reading aloud from the Bible now, something from Proverbs, and Mama had her mending basket out. Mae was struck by the sweet family scene as she kissed them goodnight. It hurt a bit when Mama didn't look up at her or wish her a good night, as she usually did. But Daddy warned her with a glance, and she whispered, "Love you, Mama," as she always did.

When she had finally satisfied all Ginny's questions, she hugged her sister goodnight and left the fourteen-year-old to go to her own room. Ginny would probably lose herself in a dogeared movie magazine. Alone at last, she pulled the small red book from her nightstand. Using the tiny key she kept on a chain around her neck, she opened her diary and began to write.

This has been quite a day. Graydell and I got jobs at the Dixie Drive-In in Texarkana and found a place to stay. I'll be leaving home in just a few days to fulfill my dream of building a new life away from Dixon's Crossing.

I had a run-in with Mama when I got home, and it was so bad I was going to leave tonight and go to Graydell's. But Daddy talked me into staying. I'm really glad he did. I was hurting inside, thinking about leaving under a cloud, with Mama so mad at me. I do hope we can at least begin to make up before time for me to leave. I love her, love my whole family. I hope I can make her see that I just want some adventures! And I want to have the chance to make it on my own before I become some man's wife. Is that so wrong?

Ginny doesn't think so. My Lord, you'd have thought I was moving to Dallas, to hear her talk. She's so excited for me. I promised her she can come and spend one of my days off with me, after we get all settled in. I hope I don't live to regret that. My little sister is so boy crazy. I'll have to keep my thumb on her when she comes to visit.

My Lord, I'm getting ahead of myself. But it's only a matter of days now. It really is happening. Look out, Texarkana! Here come the Dixon's Crossing girls!

SEVEN

FRANK CUMMINGS

THE TRIP TO CHURCH on Wednesday night was a somber one. Since it was pretty weather, Ginny and Mae sat on a bench in the bed of the pickup, leaving Mama to sit up front with Daddy. Ginny tried several times to get some sort of conversation started, but Mae gave only perfunctory replies, and after the third time, she gave a snort and quit trying.

When they walked into the building, Mae's eyes sought out Prissy, who was on their usual bench beside Morris. She slid onto the bench next to Prissy, wishing she'd had a chance to tell her of her plans. But now was not the time. She leaned over and whispered in her friend's ear: "I want to talk to you about something after church."

Prissy gave her a questioning look, but she had no time to ask questions, for Brother Williams stood and called the congregation to prayer.

Mae bowed her head along with Prissy, while Morris slipped out of his seat and got on his knees. Mae felt someone jostle her and opened her eyes to see who had caused the commotion. But his shaving cream, something nobody else wore, had already announced him: Frank Cummings. She loved the smell of Barbasol, especially mixed with Frank's

40

own masculine scent. *Girl, you better get your mind on where you are. This is the Lord's House.*

She met his eyes for a second, but quickly lowered her head and closed her eyes once more. *What is he doing here? He hasn't been here since . . . since we broke up the last time.*

Her mind was in a fog, and she heard not another word of the opening prayer. Then the congregation was singing, first "Blessed Redeemer" and then "Just a Little Talk with Jesus," and Mae spent the next hour trying without success to ignore the shoulder lightly touching hers. *I am surely going to hell.*

The congregation stood for the final song and prayer, and Frank turned to her immediately, as if afraid she was going to fly away—though she didn't know how he thought she could, with him in front of her and Prissy behind.

"How's it going, Mae?" Frank asked, his eyes traveling up and down her body. His grin was slow and sexy, and she felt warmth flooding her body. She was determined he wouldn't know the effect he had on her. Not this time.

"Fine, Frank. How have you been?" She stood her ground, not letting Prissy push her any closer to him. Prissy had always liked the two of them together.

"Can't complain. Except for one thing." He leaned a bit closer and spoke softly, so only she could hear. "I'm missing you something awful."

"I'm sure you are," she said, her eyes seeking and finding her mother's. *Wonder what she's thinking.*

"Say, Mae, how about you let me drive you home? I want to talk to you about something."

"After all this time, Frank? What could be important enough to get you out to church?" She couldn't help sounding spiteful, and she hated it, because then he would know she still cared what he thought.

"Come with me and I'll tell you. How about it?" He stared openly at her mouth, and she felt the butterflies begin to stir.

"I'll think about it. Now, if you'll let me by."

He stepped into the center aisle and backed up a bit. She left as quickly as she could, and Prissy was right behind her, hissing in her ear.

"I heard what he said, Mae. Are you going?"

"Butt out, Prissy," she hissed, and the little busybody giggled.

Standing outside with her friends, Mae stewed about what to do. Oliver was scrutinizing her and Frank, his eyes traveling from one to the other. He'd never liked Frank much to begin with, and every time Frank broke up with her, Oliver seemed to detest him just a bit more.

She watched Daddy head toward the truck, head bent toward Brother Williams walking beside him. Mama was still huddled with the other ladies, probably discussing food for the next dinner on the grounds. She finally broke away and came toward the group of young people.

Frank spoke to her familiarly. "Hey, Miz Bessie, how are you this fine evening?" She gave him an indulgent smile.

She wouldn't be so crazy about him if she knew what I know.

"Very well, Frank. Good to see you here."

"Thanks, Miz Bessie. You think we might get up a fishing trip one of these days before the weather gets too hot?"

"We might. I haven't been lately, so I don't know if anything is biting, but we can try."

"That's great. I'll be in touch real soon."

She smiled at him. Mae knew Mama had dated Frank's father once, long ago. *I bet he looks like his daddy. Wonder if Mama ever wishes things were different.* But that was something Mae would not let herself contemplate.

"Miz B., I was asking Mae if she'd like to ride home with me. You think that would be all right?" He actually laid his arm around her mother's shoulder as he asked her this, and her mother actually giggled.

"I think that would be fine," she said, "as long as it's all right with Mae."

Suddenly Mae understood. Her mother was hoping she and Frank would get back together, and then Mae would have more reason to remain at home. *That* wasn't about to happen.

42

Mae felt many eyes on her all of a sudden and, anxious to escape, she said, "Come on, then, Frank. Let's get going." Prissy winked, but Mae ignored her.

Frank took her elbow and steered her toward a Ford coupe. "I borrowed Grandpa's car—I was hoping you'd say yes."

"I didn't have much choice, not without making a scene," she snapped. He chuckled and opened the door for her.

"I'll take what I can get," he grinned, climbing in.

The short ride home was uneventful, Frank keeping his own counsel, and Mae determined not to give him any encouragement. When they pulled into the yard, Frank said, "Listen, Mae. It won't be too long before your folks get here, and I want to ask you something."

Still feeling testy, she snapped, "Whatever it is, the answer is No."

"Don't you want to give me a chance to even ask it?" he purred, one finger trailing up her arm. "God, I've missed you, woman."

How could he get to her like that? Just one little word, "woman," something nobody else ever called her. Yet he always did—"my woman," he called her when they were dating, even back when she was fifteen. Everybody had thought it was so cute.

He took her face in both his hands and brought his lips close to hers, so close she could feel his hot breath.

"Frank . . ."

He touched his lips to hers, softly, knowingly. For he did know her mouth, as no other boy had ever known it. His lips nibbled at hers, and she felt the butterflies again.

"Mae," he breathed, "I've been such a fool. You just drive me so mad at times I can't take it any more, I just have to get away."

She thought back to their last make out session and felt the heat in her face, glad for the darkness . . .

"Mae, sweetie, I had to come and ask you to take me back," he said against her ear. "I've missed you so much it hurts!" His lips nibbled at her ear, slid down the side of her neck, suckled.

She pushed him away and settled her back against the car door. "Now, where have I heard that before?" she drawled. "Oh, yes, the last time you wanted to get back together with me—and the time before that. Why don't I believe you this time? Because I'm sure it's different this time—this time you really mean it."

"You're right, Mae, I've said it before. And I meant it every time, too. But this time it's real. This time I aim to make you believe me."

"And what's so different about this time?" she asked, genuinely interested. He sounded different this time, somehow.

"Because this time . . ." he said, reaching for her hand. "this time, darlin', I'm asking you to marry me."

She jerked upright and yanked her hand out of his grasp.

"What? You've got to be joking!" She started to laugh, but then stopped. Maybe he was serious.

"Do you really think I'd joke about something like that? Have I ever said those words to you before? Ever?"

"Well, no, but—"

"But nothing. I'm ready to settle down with the only woman I've ever really loved. Mae, honey, I want to make a real life with you. My parents never had anything, and then Daddy ran off and left her with all us boys to raise. Couldn't take the responsibility. I'm ready to show you how much you mean to me. I want to marry you. I want to make you happy. I want to love you, to make babies with you." As he talked, he'd been inching across the seat toward her. Now he again took her face in his hands. She left them there for one long, slow, sweet heartbeat. Then, almost reluctantly, she took his hands in hers and shoved them away.

"I can't marry you, Frankie," she said, a catch in her voice and a lump in her throat. She could hardly talk, but she had to try.

"But why not, Mae? You know we could be good together. I know you have those kinds of feelings for me like I do you."

She shook her head. "I believe you believe you love me," she began. When he opened his mouth to dispute her, she laid her fingers across his mouth. "How long before those old urges come back to take you

44

away from me again? Lord, Frank, do you know how much it's hurt me every time you walked away from me and turned to Evangeline?"

"But if you were my wife, I wouldn't want her anymore. I only ever go to her because, well, because a man has certain needs. That's something I don't guess you'd understand, being a woman and all, but . . ."

She laughed bitterly. "Don't understand? Frank, I've wanted you as much as you've ever wanted me!"

"Well, then, why—?"

"Because, dummy, it's different for a woman. You go out and mess around all you want, and men just look at you and think what a stud you are with women. 'Sowing his wild oats,' they say. But just let them find out I was a woman who messed around with you, and you might as well brand the word 'harlot' across my forehead! I'd be ruined."

"I'd better not ever hear anyone say something like that about you."

"Frank, you're missing the point. Now listen to me. It's not just that stuff that makes me say no to you."

"Well then, what, Mae? Are you in love with somebody else? I don't know who that would be, though, because I know there's not a man in Dixon's Crossing that can satisfy you the way I can."

"Do you *hear* yourself? My Lord, you act like sex is the only thing marriage is about, just the chance to have it whenever you want it."

"I didn't mean it like that, but . . ." He put his hand on her thigh and squeezed. "Tell me you don't feel that, Mae. Or this . . ." His hand moved up her thigh.

"Of course, I feel it," she said, pushing his hand away. "I'm flesh and blood, just like you. But I want more out of life than having sex, getting pregnant, and raising a houseful of kids."

"I'd love to have a houseful of kids with you, sweetie." *He just doesn't give up.*

"That is definitely *not* what I want. I want a chance to get out of this little town and do something different. And I will, too. I'm not getting married for years and years—not to you or anybody else."

"That's crazy talk. All girls want a husband of their own, and a family."

"Not this girl. Not now, at least. There's plenty of time for that later. But for now, I'm getting out of Dixon's Crossing as fast as I can. In fact, I have a job lined up in Texarkana, and Graydell and I are moving up there tomorrow."

"You're not serious!"

"I most certainly am! And why shouldn't I be? I'm as smart as nearly any man I know, smarter than lots of them. I aim to make my mark before I settle down. All I could ever be, if I agreed to marry you, would be 'Mrs. Frank Cummings, the little woman', and mother to six or more kids."

"You've lost your mind. I think you let that valedictorian title go to your head, that's what I think."

"Think what you like, it makes no difference to me. But I am getting out of this town. I'm not going to be a farmer's wife."

Frank seemed to jump on this statement as a drowning man might seize a rotten log floating by. "If that's what's stopping you, then we don't have a problem. I'm ready to blow this town, too. My uncle has a job lined up for me in the Oklahoma oil fields, and there are whole trailer camps of couples up there. Us getting married would kill two birds with one stone, so to speak."

He looked so serious that Mae was vaguely tempted—but then she couldn't help it. She laughed. "I can't, Frank. I won't. I've had this dream for far too long, and now it's about to come true. I know, I may fall flat on my face, and I may end up dragging myself back home with my tail between my legs, but I'm going to try. I'm going to go out there and see if I can make it. You know what, Frankie? I think I will."

He stared into her eyes for what seemed an eternity, then he shrugged. "I'm not giving up. You go on to Texarkana, and I'll go to Oklahoma. But one day I'll be back."

"No, you'll go off to Oklahoma and find yourself a good woman who wants the same things you want, and that'll be that." She laughed gently, and finally he grinned sourly at her.

"Maybe so, but don't count on it. You're the one for me, Mae. Now I just have to prove it to you."

"Seems like we both are setting out to prove something, doesn't it?"

"Seems like we'll just have to see who holds out the longest." He winked at her, and she thought of what might have been—but her resolve was strong. She got out and watched him drive away. She shook her head. *Bet you ten to one he's headed straight to Evangeline.*

EIGHT

NEW TOWN, NEW JOBS

"YOU GALS PICKED A nice place," Walt said when he pulled up in front of their new home. Mrs. Swenson stopped her sweeping to watch as the three piled out of the car and started up the front walk, each with an armload.

"Just a minute, young ladies. You do remember the rules about men, don't you?"

"Aw, Mrs. Swenson, he's not a *man*—this is my brother, Walt."

Scowling at Graydell, Walt said, "Pleased to meet you, ma'am. I'd shake, but I'm sort of tied up. This sure is a nice place you've got here." He treated her to his brightest smile.

The landlady looked him up and down. "Well, I guess it will be all right for him to help you while you're moving in. But don't make a habit of it. I have other ladies living here as well, you know, and I have my rules for a reason."

Walt nodded and said, "Lead the way, Grady. Let's get you girls moved into this lovely house."

Mrs. Swenson went back to her sweeping, this time with a smile on her face.

"Way to go, Walt," Mae whispered once they'd reached the top of the stairs. "Jolly good show." She had been working on talking like Mrs. Swenson ever since they had come home from Texarkana, but she knew she still sounded like a River Rat.

"Glad I could help. When I get back home, I'm moving my stuff into Grady's room. It's the biggest bedroom in the house."

"I knew there was an ulterior motive," Graydell said. "Are you sure you packed enough, Mae?" She looked askance at Mae's few boxes.

"I'm just bringing clothes for the next few weeks. I plan to get the rest a bit at a time whenever I go back home on weekends—or whenever Mr. Robinson lets us off."

"So, y'all aren't giving up on Dixon's Crossing totally?" Walt asked, grinning at her. "I thought we'd probably never see you two again."

Mae swatted him on the back of the head as he passed her on his way to the stairs. "Walt Upton, you know better than that. We've just got to spread out wings, that's all."

Thirty minutes later, they were finished unloading and unpacking. Walt had left just as soon as he could, with Mrs. S. keeping a close eye on him as he made numerous trips up the stairs.

In their apartment, the girls surveyed the mess they'd just created. "How did we get so much into that car?" Mae asked, flopping onto the sofa. "Or rather, how did you get so much in it?"

"We did it, Mae! We really did it." Graydell peered into the chifforobe appraisingly. "Not lots of room for dresses," she said. "What do you think?"

Mae looked around. "If it's okay with you, I'd like the bed over in the corner."

"Fine by me. I don't like feeling hemmed in."

"You can have most of the storage, Grady. I didn't bring lots. Let's face it, I don't have lots. A few jeans and some shirts, and a couple of dresses for church. I'll bring more later if we have room."

They set to work to put their things away, and by noon had their respective nooks in some semblance of order. Another half hour, and the sitting room/kitchen/dining area looked as good as it could. *For now. Wait till I get paid.*

"We have a few hours until supper," Mae said. "Want to go explore?"

On their way out, they ran into the other two boarders and stopped to get acquainted. Florene and Julia both worked across the street in the courthouse, secretaries to the County Clerk and Tax Collector, respectively. They all agreed to meet back at "dinner," as Florene called it, to talk more.

"Let's count how many blocks it is to the five and dime," Mae suggested, as they set off on foot to explore their new town. "I wonder where the library is."

"Trust you to want to find a library," Graydell laughed.

The afternoon was perfect for exploring—warm and filled with sunshine, just a few mare's tails scattered across the azure sky. Sparrows ad finches chirped in the oaks and shrubbery of houses they passed, with a mockingbird's sweet—if copycat—tunes loudest of all.

"There's hardly any traffic this afternoon," Mae observed. "We should thank our lucky stars we found such a perfect place to live."

"You're right," Graydell nodded, her ponytail of dark hair bobbing. "Our lucky stars, or our lucky buck." They both laughed.

By this time, they had reached Front Street, which ran parallel to the rail yard. Long lines of train cars waited to wend their way out of town headed for such exotic places as New Orleans, Chicago, San Francisco, New York City. Mae had long dreamed of traveling to those places, but for now she was satisfied just to be in Texarkana.

"Let's go back up to Broad, where there's more going on," Mae said. Broad Street was just one block up from Front Street, but it was an entirely different world from its industrial neighbor. Broad was where all the department stores and five and dimes were located. There were also furniture stores, shoe stores, and various other businesses scattered along the street.

Today they ended up at Wellworth's, the five and dime closest to their new home. In fact, it was only about five blocks away. Wellworth's was a small, locally owned store modeled after the larger Kress's on the Texas side of town. Wellworth's catered to a clientele looking for more basic everyday needs, while Kress's offered dry goods, clothes, and other more upscale items. Wellworth's sold everything from farm tools to embroidery thread. The store also had the best ice cream in town, and that's where the girls were now. Mae had taken only a bite from her chocolate cone when she heard the familiar voice.

"My, my, look what the cat dragged in."

She turned slowly to see Frank, hat shoved back on his head, hands on his lean hips, grinning at her. *I can't get away from him, no matter where I go!* Mae began to wonder if that was a sign of some kind. Maybe it was a mistake to turn him down, after all.

"Have you girls made your move yet?" Frank asked, lazily licking his own cone. He stared over it at Mae as his tongue made circles around the vanilla cone. She glanced away from him, hoping to hide the red she could feel creeping up her neck. *God, why does he get to me that way? And how come he has to know it?*

Graydell answered, after Mae made no move to. "Yeah, we just moved in today. And we'd better get a move on. It's almost time for supper. We don't want to be late on our first day."

"Right, Grady," Mae said, tossing the rest of her uneaten cone into the trash. "C'mon, let's go." She pushed out into the street and strode away, leaving Graydell with her mouth open and Frank grinning broadly.

* * *

Mae squinted as she observed the whiny two-year-old pestering his mother, begging for candy, for a drink of water, to be held in her lap. *My Lord, look at her. She looks about to fall asleep right here on this bus. She hardly seems aware of that little boy, as awful as he's acting. Lord, I'm thankful that's not me!*

51

Graydell got out of her seat and moved forward toward the mother and child.

"Hey, there, sweetie," she cooed to the little boy. "My name's Graydell. What's yours?"

The kid was so startled he stopped tugging on his mother's sleeve long enough to give Graydell a once-over. "Jack," he whispered.

Mae smiled. Graydell had always had a way with the little ones. *But you've got your work cut out for you with this one.*

"We don't have any water on the bus," Graydell said. "But look." She reached into the pocket of her jeans and pulled out a loop of string she always kept nearby. She was notorious for not being able to sit still doing nothing. She sat down on an empty seat across from the boy, feet sticking out into the aisle. The mother watched for a moment and then shrugged as if to say she wasn't worried about Graydell. She turned back to look out the window.

Graydell began her routine of making first crow's feet, then Jacob's ladder. After each one, she tugged on the string and it dissolved into a circle again. The boy's motions stilled, as he watched Graydell's fingers flying. When she held out a complicated pattern and asked him to put his hand inside, he hesitated, then did as she asked. She made a couple more loops above his wrist and then let go with her thumbs. Magically, the loops melted away, leaving the boy's hand free. His eyes grew round, then he laughed and clapped his hands.

"Do it," he said, and Graydell began again. Just as she finished, the bus came to a stop and the woman stirred.

"Come, Jack, we're home," she said. Turning to Graydell, the mother gave her a tired but friendly smile. "Thank you. I just worked all night at the hospital laundry, then picked Jack up from my aunt. I don't know how we're going to make it today when I need sleep so bad, but I sure appreciate you spending these few minutes with him." While she talked, she had gathered her purse and a paper sack and was now herding Jack down the aisle.

"Bye, Miss," the boy said as they stepped off the bus. Mae watched as he stood waving at the departing bus until his mother tugged on his hand, urging him toward a small wood-framed house with a tiny stoop.

Graydell returned to sit next to Mae. "Poor little thing," she sighed. "Living up here with no fields to play in, and not even a front yard, with all this traffic."

"You're a good woman, Graydell Upton," Mae said, nudging her friend. "No way would I have done what you just did. I don't have much patience with kids."

"But you've done great with Miss Hope."

"Yeah, but only because she was easy to deal with. Nothing like that little heathen."

Graydell laughed. "Bet you'd have been fine with her even if she had been like that."

"Don't believe it for a minute," Mae huffed. "Hey, we're nearly there. You ready for today?"

"No," Graydell moaned. "You?"

"I'm worried I'll mix up orders, never mind getting used to dealing with that little change machine."

"Oh, I can handle that fine. It's those skates that have me worried."

"I'll help you, Grady. We've got the whole back lot to practice on."

"I'll need it," she spat. "Here's our stop. Now or never!"

"Now!" Mae laughed, jumping out of her seat. "Let's do it!"

Mae was surprised at how easily Graydell picked up roller skating. Round and round the lot she went, determined to be ready when the first customers arrived. She hated feeling it, but she was also jealous. After all, she'd been skating for years at the skating rink out at the edge of Dixon's Crossing, and Graydell would never even try.

"Look at all the fun you've been missing!" she called to her friend on one pass.

"I know! Just look out now!" Graydell giggled, flinging her arms wide and making smooth motions that reminded Mae of—of all things—a graceful swan.

Mae was, at last, catching on to how to prop a tray on a car's window without spilling its contents all over the driver. She was practicing on Mr. Robinson's old car, and was glad she'd been using empty glasses, or there would have been a real mess to clean up.

She kept at it, though, until she figured she was as good as she could hope to get in one day. Then she skated back to the main building and placed her dirty dishes in the sink.

Mr. Robinson bustled in the back door. "Your friend is doing great out there. And you didn't look so bad yourself, Blondie."

Mae jerked her head around. "Who are you calling Blondie? Me? Well, I've never had anybody call me that in my whole life."

"Can't see why not. Those blond curls, that's all I think of when I see you." Then he was back to business. "Don't forget to write down every single thing the customer wants, Blondie. And remember where the used tickets go?"

She nodded and pointed to a large, six-inch nail that had been hammered through a plank, with the plank nailed to a wall above the prep counter. The nail was safely away from where anybody would walk, but handy enough so you couldn't miss it. It looked to Mae like a simple, yet effective, bookkeeping system.

"Yes, sir. What time do you usually get customers?" She glanced at the clock built into the backsplash of the cook stove. It read 11:05.

A car horn sounded, and Mr. Robinson laughed. "Oh, right about now, I'd say. Go get 'em, Mae!" She grinned and whirled in a circle before skating out the back door. Graydell saluted her as they passed each other. Mae took out her pad and pencil and came to a stop at the first car of the day.

"Hello, sir. How may I help you today?"

The gentleman, in a well-worn but still serviceable brown suit, placed his order after consulting the screen beside the car, and her first day at work was officially underway.

54

There were a few spills and a couple of mistakes on orders before the night closed in on them and customers finally dwindled away. All in all, though, Mae thought Mr. Robinson looked pleased with their work.

"A pretty good day, girls. No customers went away mad--and that's always a good day," he said. "Tell me, what are you going to do with all your earnings?"

"Remember your tips, too," Miss Dora added.

"I almost forgot." Mae dug around in the pocket of the apron she'd been told to use for her bits of change customers left for her. When she counted it up, she was surprised to find a total of a dollar and seventy-five cents. "My Lord, that's amazing! What about you, Grady?"

"A dollar sixty. And this is just a weekday. I bet you have lots more customers on Saturdays, huh, Mr. Robinson?"

"Right you are, Miss Graydell. Now, you two get going. You don't want to miss the last bus back over to Quality Hill."

"No, sir. I sure don't," Mae said. "My legs feel like rubber now. I'd sure hate to have to hike all the way back over there."

"See you tomorrow, girls," Miss Dora smiled as she shooed them out the door. "Sleep the sleep of the exhausted. You'll be feeling all those leg muscles tomorrow." She hugged each of them and closed the door behind them.

Twenty minutes later, they were sitting on Mae's bed with a bottle of rubbing alcohol, taking turns rubbing their aching calves and thighs.

"I was having some second thoughts about this move of ours, Grady." Mae sloshed more alcohol onto her palm. "But looking at that pile of change on the table, I'm pretty sure we did the right thing."

"I'll ask you again in the morning," Graydell said, looking at Mae with her head tilted to one side. She moaned as she rose and stretched. "Good night, buddy."

NINE

TEXARKANA

"HURRY UP, GRADY! TIME'S a wastin'!" Mae said as she finished slipping on her saddle oxfords. "Let's not take this day off for granted."

It was a Friday morning, and since Mr. Robinson had hired a couple more carhops, he had started a rotating schedule for giving the girls days off. Today was Mae and Graydell's. Mr. R. had said he would try to give them at least one day off together, since they both had family so far outside Texarkana. He could be nice when he wanted to.

Mae had heard from Mrs. Swenson that there was a sale downtown at Sears, and since she had a bit of spending money, she thought she'd have a look see. Graydell, always up for a fun time, was applying and reapplying her lipstick at the small mirror over the sink. With a small grunt of satisfaction, she turned to watch Mae across the room.

Mae, usually the first one dressed, was taking an inordinate amount of time getting ready to go, despite pushing Graydell to hurry up. She kept fiddling with the hem of her pants, rolling them up, pulling them back straight down, until Grady had had enough.

"Mae! What is the matter with you this morning? You're acting like a cat in a room full of rocking chairs."

"I don't know. I just feel all jittery, like something is about to happen, but I don't know what. Have you ever felt like that?"

Graydell just looked at her friend with her forehead wrinkled and her full lips puckered.

"Never mind! I guess you haven't." She flipped her pants leg down to its full length, to match the other leg. "Let's go!"

"Great!" Graydell said, linking arms with her. "Watch out Texarkana, the Dixon's Crossing girls are coming!"

By ten thirty, they were on Broad Street ready to window shop, if nothing else. Something seemed different today, though. As they walked along, they kept seeing people standing in small groups, talking excitedly. An almost tangible air of expectation floated around them. Besides that, now Mae's skin was prickling to beat the band. *Thanks for that, Grandpa Johnson!*

Graydell leaned her head close to Mae and said, "What the heck is going on? You'd think somebody died, except that everybody just looks excited and not sad at all."

"You're right. Let's ask somebody."

"No! Mae, you can't just walk up to strangers and butt into their conversation to ask them what they're talking about." Graydell grabbed Mae's arm and propelled her down the street.

"Well then, how are we going to find out, huh?" Mae laughed. "I'm not going to be able to enjoy shopping if I don't know. Pardon me, miss—"

Again, Graydell pulled Mae away from the closest group.

"My God, Graydell! Stop being such an old fuddy-duddy!"

They were standing at the end of the block now, Mae with hands on hips, simmering over Graydell's bashfulness. Then her mouth dropped open, and she started digging in her jeans pocket for a nickel.

"Now what?" Graydell said, but Mae was making a beeline for the newspaper seller she'd spied.

"I don't know, but we're about to find out," she said, nodding toward the paperboy hawking his papers.

"Boy Oh Boy! We Got It! Read all about it!" The scrawny kid might have been ten or eleven, and the stack of papers under his arm looked like it weighed as much as he did.

Handing him a coin, she reached for a copy of the *Texarkana Gazette*. The bold headline didn't really say what "it" was, so Mae began to scan the lead article. Her lips moved as she read, but it took only a few seconds to see this must be what people were talking about.

"You're not gonna believe this, Grady. The government is about to build a huge ammunition plant right outside of Texarkana! That's what's got all these people worked up, it has to be."

Graydell peered over Mae's shoulder. "Wow! It's going to cost how much? I can't even fathom something costing that much."

"Yes, nine million dollars! And this says they'll be hiring lots of people to build the plant and then to run it once it's built. Well, we don't have a chance at getting hired for construction, but I wonder if there might be something we could do after it's built."

"You mean like making ammunition? Not much chance we could do that."

"Oh, I don't know. Daddy's always said I'm a good shot, so if I can shoot it, why can't I help build it?"

"Mae, sometimes things come out of that mouth of yours that just don't make a bit of sense. Come on, let's get to shopping. It's almost time to head to Kress's for a hamburger."

Tucking the paper under her arm, Mae nodded in agreement. "My stomach says not to wait too long."

Crossing into the next block, they stopped to admire the beautiful summer dresses in the window at Madeline's. Then they moved on to Kress's, where Mae picked up a new hand mirror and a matching brush and comb. "My other brush is so old, all the bristles do now is scratch my scalp, and not in a good way," she laughed, depositing her package next to Graydell at the lunch counter. "Now where's that burger we were talking about? My Lord, it smells good in here."

"Yes, and I've been here ten minutes already, waiting for you. I'm about to starve."

"Then let's get you a big juicy burger, Miss Graydell," a voice drawled behind them. Mae felt a shiver going up and down her spine. *What is he doing here? I swear, he's everywhere I go these days. Wonder if he has her with him.* She rotated slowly, hesitant to see. But no. Frank was alone, very alone.

"Mae. How're you doing?" Frank Cummings said, cocking one eyebrow at her. Oh, how she loved those eyebrows. And oh, how Frank knew it. He always knew how to get to her.

* * *

The next little while was stilted. Frank had insisted on buying the girls lunch, and they all moved to a nearby booth. Graydell had slid in and sat like a stone, leaving Mae to sit across from her, and Frank had sat down next to her—a position much too close for Mae's liking. But what was she to do? She resolved to be grownup about the whole thing, but still she placed her purse in the seat between them.

"I see you've heard the news," Frank said, motioning to the newspaper lying beside her bag. "That's really something, isn't it? Building ammunition, how about that? Guess we have an answer to whether we're going to get into this war over in Europe, huh?"

Mae turned squarely toward him. "What do you mean, Frank? There's nothing about that in the paper. We're just going to build ammunition for Great Britain."

Frank laughed. "If you think that, you're not as smart as I've always thought you were."

She bristled at his remark. She couldn't tell if he was kidding or not.

"I don't think the idea of going to war is anything to be kidding about, do you?"

"No, but I wasn't kidding." He shook his head. "It's just a matter of time. I mean, sure, the government wants to get in on building war stuff to help the English, but they're doing it mostly to make money here at home. God knows we need the jobs."

"He's right," Graydell said. "I heard these men talking at the counter while I was waiting for you. They said Mr. Roosevelt has got something up his sleeve, that all the things he's done to get us out of the Depression haven't exactly worked like he'd planned, so he's going to build up a strong military at the same time he'll be selling lots of bombs and stuff to Great Britain." She stopped for breath.

"So, Grady, you've listened to nothing more substantial than gossip like you'd hear at the beauty parlor, and Frank, you've just figured this out all on your own. Y'all are like two little fish swimming in the great big ocean, you know that? You think you understand everything going on there, among all the fishes and what not."

Graydell sat back in her seat and crossed her arms. Frank gave Mae a long, searching look and then he laughed. Whatever reaction she'd expected, that wasn't it. Suddenly she was livid. "Who do you think you are, Frank Cummings? You waltz in here and start spouting off all this . . . this . . ." Here words escaped her.

"Nonsense? Folderol?" He grinned at her.

She pointed her finger and opened her mouth to argue, then dropped her hand. "Exactly."

He was actually laughing at her now, at the whole situation, his shoulders shaking. *How in the world can I find this man so attractive when he's sitting right here making fun of me? Mae Johnson, you better get control of this situation.*

"I'm sorry if you find my opinion so juvenile," she said, drawing farther away from him. "Now, if you'll excuse me, I need to get home." She began nudging Frank, but he wasn't giving in easily. "I said, *excuse me.*" Her voice had risen a notch or two.

"Okay, okay, don't get your—"

"Frank!" she gasped.

Shaking his head again, he stood and held out his hand to help her out of the booth. Looking pointedly at his hand, she slid out on her own and stood facing him.

"Seriously, Mae, and I mean really seriously, I'll bet you we'll be in this war within a year. Maybe sooner."

"I hope you're wrong," Graydell said.

"I do, too, Graydell, I really do."

* * *

"You should have stayed for lunch," Graydell said when she returned to the apartment later that afternoon. "That hamburger was delicious. Mae, just think of it. We can go downtown just about anytime we want, so long as we aren't working. Isn't that terrific?"

"Yeah, terrific."

"What's the matter? You still fretting over your run-in with Frank?"

"I guess so, a little bit. But he got me to thinking—about the war and all. Do you realize that if this country gets into the war, the boys we just finished school with will be lining up to go and fight? And older ones, too, like our brothers, and like Oliver?" There was a catch in her voice as she spoke his name.

"I know, I know. I've tried to put it out of my mind, but it just keeps creeping back in. But surely, after the last war, the government will know better than to get us involved in another war over in Europe."

"You know how that guy Hitler is talking, though—has been for years. He wants to take over the whole world, Grady."

"I know that's how he sounds. But nobody can ever get that much power—can they?"

"I surely hope not." Perking up, Mae grinned wickedly. "At least he likes people who look like me," she said, prancing around the room. "Tall. Blonde. Blue—well, I bet he'd like my green eyes."

"Goofus," Graydell said good-naturedly. "Well, get your tall, blonde self dressed and let's go find a nightclub with some good music!"

TEN

GRAYDELL & GEORGE

"HELLO, DARLIN'," FRANK SAID, leaning down to whisper in Mae's ear. She had sensed it when he walked in the door at the club, and she wasn't surprised he'd headed straight for her table. The familiarity of his greeting was unsettling—but then Frank tended toward the theatrical. He liked to make an entrance, and he loved to make her nervous.

"Mind if I sit down?" She shrugged noncommittally, and he slid into the empty chair next to her. "They make a nice couple, don't you think?" He nodded toward where Graydell was dancing with someone she didn't know.

"Friend of yours?" She felt a tinge of worry. Graydell could fall so easily, and Mae didn't want to see her friend hurt.

"Yeah, George is an okay guy. Graydell seems to be enjoying herself."

"She always does—on the dance floor," Mae agreed. "I don't think I've ever known anybody who loved dancing more than Grady."

"What about you? Why aren't you out there? I remember you liked it pretty well yourself."

She blushed, thinking back to the times they had danced together, when he'd held her close, too close sometimes, and she had his arms around her. *Dammit, why does he still get to me this way?*

"How about it, Mae?" His knee nudged hers under the table. "How about a dance, for old time's sake?"

She so wanted to dance, and she knew how well the two of them fit together. But she also knew how much it hurt when he left. As he always did.

"I don't know, Frankie," she said, but she saw his smile when she used the familiar term with him.

"C'mon, Mae. Just a dance. That's all, just a dance."

She could never resist him if he kept after her long enough, and he knew it. She sighed and stood up—just as "Nobody's Darlin' but Mine" came on. *Wonderful. Our old song.* Why did it have to feel so good to be in his arms again? And why did it have to be this song?

"God, I've missed you, sweet thing," he said, the arm around her waist giving her a squeeze.

She stiffened. "Don't call me that, Frank. You don't have a right to call me that."

He massaged the middle of her back, his hand trailing lazily up and down her spine as he waltzed her around the room. She felt it all over her body.

"I'm sorry, Mae. It's just that when I get so close to you I start feeling things for you like I've never felt for anybody else."

She tilted her head back to gaze into his brown eyes speckled with gold. "Really, Frank? What about Evangeline?"

He stumbled, stepping lightly on her toes. Not like Frank at all. "Sorry," he mumbled.

She stopped dancing and backed up a step. His hands dropped to his side. She stomped off the dance floor, grabbed her purse, and headed for the door. He was right behind her.

"Mae, listen. Stop and listen, just a minute, please." He had her by the arm now, and she couldn't get away without making a scene. Already the people at the table next to theirs were getting an eyeful.

"Alright, just one minute. And then I'm leaving, whatever you say."

"I just wanted to say I'm sorry. I know I'm just a sorry-ass man who doesn't know what's good for him when he finds it. But that's over now. I realize you're the woman for me—you always have been."

"And Evangeline Harper?"

"She's nobody," he scoffed. "Just blowing off a little steam, that's all. There are girls you can have a good time with, and then there are the girls you can be proud to take home to Mama."

"You couldn't have a good time with me? I thought we had fun together."

He ducked his head, refusing to meet her eyes. "Not that kind of fun, sweet thing," he growled. "Understand?"

Oh, she understood alright. It had always been this way between them. When he finally got sick and tired of Mae refusing to sleep with him, he'd go slinking off to that whore. *For that's what she is, and she has been even since before she started charging for it.*

"I'm leaving now." She opened her purse and rummaged inside.

"What are you looking for?" he laughed, seeing the jumble of items inside the bag.

"Bus fare," she snapped.

"Don't be silly. The last bus shut down half an hour ago."

She looked around for a clock. Surely it wasn't that late. But it was. Eleven-thirty by the clock hanging above the jukebox.

"Dang it," she muttered. "I need to find Graydell. Where is she?" She began to scan the room.

"Still dancing with George. Why don't I go round them up, and then we'll see you two girls home safe. How about that?"

Mae weighed her options. Either she'd be beholden to Frank if she let him take them home, or she and Graydell would have to walk about fifteen blocks--and the club wasn't in the best of neighborhoods.

She sighed. Again.

Soon they were on their way, Mae beside Frank, and Graydell and her newest conquest wrapped around each other in the back seat. Pulling up in front of their apartment, Frank said, "I can't get over y'all living right here next to the courthouse. Bet you see all sorts of funny things, huh?"

She ignored the question. "Well, thank you, Frank, for getting us home. Come on, Graydell, we're here."

"Just a minute," she said, and Mae could hear smooching sounds from the darkened back seat.

"Well, I'm going in. Come on soon so Frank can go, you hear?"

"Um-hmm," her friend replied.

She opened the car door and was at the top of the steps before Frank caught up with her. Hearing him behind her, she whirled around. "Don't be following me thinking I'm going to be giving you a goodnight kiss. And don't think we settled anything at all tonight." She drew herself up to her full five-foot-six, so that she was almost looking straight into his eyes.

"Honey, I'm not expecting anything at all from you. But I'll tell you one thing, I sure do miss your kisses. There's no other woman in the world that can kiss like you do when you're serious about it. So that's fine, no kiss tonight. I'm willing to wait. Because I know if you ever really let loose, I won't stand a chance. You'll have me caught up, hook, line, and sinker."

She smiled, despite her earlier resolve. "You better know it, mister. But it won't be you when it happens." She turned back toward the dark car. "Graydell, come on! You don't want Mrs. S. to come out here, do you?"

After a minute the rear door opened and Graydell almost fell out of the car, giggling. George muttered something, and Graydell squealed with laughter. "I am not! You're crazy, Georgie!"

"And you love it," Mae heard him growl. "See you tomorrow night about eleven?"

Graydell had obviously made a date for after work tomorrow. Mae scowled. "Thanks, Frank, for getting my friend involved with one of your pals. I'm sure he's an upstanding young man."

"Hold on there. George really is a nice guy. Sure, he enjoys the ladies. But he'll take good care of Graydell, you watch and see."

Graydell came bounding up the steps, flying past them. "'Night, Frank. C'mon, Mae, we need to go in now."

Mae turned to say good night to Frank and to thank him for the ride home. He stared down at her, then turned to leave. But whirling back toward her, he said, "Aww, the hell with it." Grabbing her by the shoulders, he kissed her soundly, moving his mouth across hers, reminding her of earlier times, hinting at times to come. Before she had a chance to say anything at all, he was striding back to his car, leaving her to stare after him with her mouth still tingling from his kiss.

ELEVEN

THOMAS -- WHAT??

"I NEED TO TELL YOU something, Mae," Daddy said, looking away from the road long enough to be sure she was listening. They were almost home, Mae's first visit home since she'd left. She'd been looking forward to a fun couple of days. But she caught the seriousness of his tone, and a weight settled in her heart. What could make him sound so serious?

"I'm listening," she said, saying a quick, silent prayer.

"It's about your brother, Thomas."

"He's alright, isn't he? Was there an accident?"

"Oh, no, nothing like that. Didn't mean to scare you."

She sat back with a sigh of relief.

"Well then, what is it?"

"Your brother and his wife have got theirselves into a bit of a jam—financially, I mean."

Mae snorted. "Him and just about everybody else. This Depression has nearly got everybody."

"True enough, but some more than others."

"What's going on with Thomas?"

Mae thought she was prepared for anything, but she was still surprised when Daddy explained.

"You know Annette had inherited that piece of land they've been living on from her granddaddy, don't you?"

"Yeah. What of it?"

"You remember Thomas and Annette bought that new Ford last year—on credit?"

Mae didn't like where this seemed to be headed.

"Well, when their taxes came due on the place last year, at the same time their loan to the bank for the farm came due, well, they didn't have enough to pay off the loan *or* pay the taxes."

"You mean because of their car payment?" Mae was flummoxed. How could her brother be that stupid?

"That's about the size of it. Because it's true that if they hadn't been paying on that car, they'd have been able to squeak by."

"Wait a minute." She turned in the seat, not believing what she was hearing. "You mean to tell me they held onto that car and didn't pay their other debts?"

"That's right. The upshot of that was that last week somebody bought their land out from under them."

"Who? How?" Mae sputtered.

"It was a Mister Tilmon from up around Genoa. He's got a government job up at the courthouse, and he knew about the auction sale coming up, so he bought it."

"I saw a bunch of men over on the courthouse steps the other day. I wondered what was going on. Just . . . Just stop a minute. I want to hear all of this before we get home."

Her daddy pulled the truck to the side of the road and killed the motor. "Alright. But that's the long and the short of it. I can't fault this Mr. Tilmon. He did right by Thomas as much as he could. He paid the back taxes on the property, then he paid off the loan they had on last year's crop—"

"That didn't amount to a hill of beans," Mae interjected.

"That didn't amount to a hill of beans," he agreed, giving her a rueful smile. "And then he paid them a right decent amount for the land, on top of all that."

Mae sat stunned. What would Thomas do? Where would they go? *Oh, no, not that.*

"Did he come crawling back to you? He did, didn't he? And of course y'all took them in! What else would you do?" He stared ahead. "Daddy?"

He nodded hesitantly. "Yes, Mae, we took them in. It's not been an easy thing, let me tell you. Your mama—well, let's just say it hasn't been pleasant."

"I bet she blames that Annette, don't she?" Mae slipped back into her childish way of talking, she was that upset.

"I don't want to get into all of that. I just wanted you to know, before you got there, how things stand."

Mae's mind jumped ahead. She knew what was coming next. Still, she was fuming before he even got the rest of the story out.

"Naturally, there's been some changes at the house. Ginny has had the girls move in with her, and T.J. is sleeping on the couch in the living room. And Thomas and Annette—"

"Are in *my* room! Where else is there?" She thought for a moment, calculating, not liking what she knew was coming. "So where am I supposed to sleep?"

"Well, your mama is fixing up a pallet for T.J. in the dining room, and you'll be sleeping on the couch. I'm sorry, Mae! We just didn't know what else to do."

She was silent, and he continued. "You know if you came to us tomorrow and said you needed—or even just wanted—to come back home, we would make a place for you, no matter what."

She did know that. Of course they would. Family always came first, before anything else. Of course they'd taken Thomas and his family in. But still . . .

Her eyes brimmed with tears. She couldn't imagine that her big brother had gotten himself into such a mess.

"And to think, I watched it happening," she said. "I saw all those men on the courthouse steps last week! Can't anything be done about this? I mean, if we could raise the money . . ."

"No, Mae, what's done is done. It's all legal and proper."

"So, what are they going to do? I mean, they don't have any land to farm. What's he going to do to make them a living? He *is* going to make them a living, right?"

"Funny you should mention that. In fact, Thomas has already made some progress in that direction. He went up a couple of days ago and put in an application to work on construction out at the new plants that are coming in. You heard about that, I guess?"

Mae snorted. "I guess I did! It was all over the papers, all anybody's been talking about ever since the announcements. I mean, did me and Graydell pick a good time to move to Texarkana, or what? If we'd waited even another week, we probably couldn't have found a place to stay at all."

Her daddy looked at her out of eyes filled with sadness. "Yeah, I've thought of that. Just another couple of weeks, and I'd probably still have my Mae at home where she belongs."

Mae's laugh was bitter. "And where would you have put Thomas and Annette then? No, there's no more room at the inn."

"Don't blaspheme, Mae," he said.

"I'm sorry, I didn't mean it that way. It just came out. You know me and my mouth."

"Yes, I do," he said, patting her on the shoulder. "But I also know your heart, and I know it's in the right place. So I know you're going to come into that house and be nice to your brother and his family."

"I'll try. But I'm not looking forward to sleeping on the couch. Sure won't be able to sleep in tomorrow," she sighed.

Mr. Johnson smiled and patted her shoulder again. "That's my Mae. Now we better get moving, or your mama's liable to send out a search party for us. Boy, she sure is looking forward to you being home. She's been cooking for two days."

* * *

"Take a walk with me, Mae?" Her brother held out his hand. She was still in shock over the fact that he was back home with his whole brood, but she got up and walked to the door, ignoring his hand.

"Can I go, Daddy?" Tommy asked, jumping up from where he was playing with a toy car on the floor.

"Not this time, sport," Thomas said. "Aunt Mae and I need to have some time together, just us. We won't be gone long."

Mae could see the disappointment in the boy's eyes, in his sagging shoulders. "I'll play hide and seek when we get back, okay, Tommy?" she said. He perked up, turning back to his toys without another glance.

"Tommy sure loves you," Thomas said as they started off down the dirt road in front of the house. "The girls do, too, of course. But that boy thinks you hung the moon."

Mae didn't respond, just leaned down to pluck a sour weed from the ditch, where wild vines grew in abundance, the purple vetch the prettiest. Putting the broken end of the stalk into her mouth, she made a face at the initial bitterness, then set to chewing and sucking the sour juice that gave the stalk its nickname.

"I love them, too, Thomas. I guess those kids are what's making it so hard for me to understand what you've done." *Dang, I hadn't meant to get into this with him. Why can't I keep my big mouth shut?*

"You know there's a Depression going on. Things just happened, and I got in over my head. But I'll get us back on our feet soon and get us back in a place of our own."

"Yes, I know about the Depression. But don't use that as an excuse for your selfishness."

He stopped walking and stood looking across the field of young cotton they were passing. The stalks were only about a foot high. Mae could see that some of the rows had already had a hoe taken to them, the

71

plants evenly spaced about a hoe's width apart, while others still had to be cleared of weeds and given room to grow. She gave a silent thanks that she wouldn't be here this year to do that back-breaking work. She didn't give any thought to who would take her place—she was too focused on the situation with Thomas.

"I can't believe you got yourself in such a situation. My Lord, you didn't have to keep that fancy car you're paying for. I never thought you cared about things like that. Or was it all Annette's idea?"

He jerked his head toward her then, anger sparking from his brown eyes. "Leave Annette out of this, Mae. I'm the one who bought the car, not her. It's my name on the title, and on the loan at the bank. So don't blame her."

"Well, sure, your name's on everything, but that doesn't mean anything. I know women can't go out and buy things on time, can't take out loans. Heck, I can't even open a bank account without Daddy signing for me. The law won't let us women do anything like that. But that doesn't mean she can't be the reason you bought that blamed car in the first place. What I cannot comprehend, though, is that you chose that car over a house for your family, when push came to shove!"

Dammit, *listen*, Mae. For once in your life, just listen, instead of running off at the mouth without having all the facts." He let her go and turned to grab a fence post instead. She opened her mouth, smart remark ready, but then she heard, really heard, what he'd said. Was she jumping the gun? She knew that was one of her many faults. "Okay, I'll listen. Convince me of your need for that car." Seeing a spot of soft grass the cows hadn't reached through the fence and devoured, she plopped down. "I'm waiting."

Thomas said, "Listen without sulking about it, will you?"

She looked away across the field of cows and young calves whiling away the afternoon in the warm sun. *Cows on one side, cotton on the other. I sure don't miss this scenery much.*

When Annette and I got married in '34, we were your age, but I didn't get to graduate like you did. I'd already gone to work full time with

Daddy, you know that. When the Fosters left for California, and their rent house came empty, I went to Mr. J.T. and asked to take it over. He didn't want to let me, cause I was just one worker to take on those acres. But I told him Annette would be joining me in a few months, after we got married—but that we couldn't marry without a place to live. I had to promise him that my *wife* would help me in the fields, to convince him to let me take the place."

"I never knew that, Thomas," she muttered. She shuddered inside, thinking that could have so easily been her fate, too.

"Yeah, well, you were just a kid then. There's probably a lot you don't know, what with the way Mama and Daddy have sheltered you all your life."

"They haven't sheltered me," she protested, spitting out the chewed-up stalk of sour weed. The inside of her cheeks and her tongue felt like she'd been sucking on a sour lemon. Nevertheless, she reached behind her to the fence row, where more of the bitter plants grew in abundance.

"Oh, sure they have, Mae. They made sure you stayed in school, and they've always let you go off and do babysitting and ironing for Mrs. Wheeler, instead of working in the hottest days of the year in the field. When was the last time you picked cotton in the fall?"

She thought of the few times she had actually draped one of those heavy tow sacks across her shoulder, gotten onto her knees, and dug the fluffy cotton out of the bolls that fought anybody trying to take away their beauty. She remembered the tug of the bag, coated on the underside with tar to make it durable, as it got heavier and heavier the longer she picked. She remembered how paltry her bag always looked next to those of Thomas and the black men from the Bend. She could see Daddy struggling to drape the bags on the scales that hung from the frames on the back of his old truck. Her contribution had always been way fewer pounds than most—but it was all she could do. And she hadn't done that in quite a while. Thomas had a point.

"Then when Annette and I married, she went to work right alongside me, and we started trying to turn that house into a home. She'd leave the field several times a day to check on our supper, then beat it back outside and get back to work beside me."

Thomas' eyes took on a faraway look, and Mae imagined he was reliving those early days of "wedded bliss." Then he dropped his gaze, and his shoulders. "And then she got in the family way. Still, she worked inside and outside the house, long as she could. I wouldn't let her pick any cotton that fall, and Tommy was born healthy, so I knew I'd done the right thing. Then pretty soon after, here came Anna, and then Susie. I didn't want my family walking to church! Is that so wrong, Mae?"

His stared hard at her. She thought of the years she'd spent scheming about ways to get out of that life herself. "No, Thomas, it's not. But when things got bad, why did you keep the car instead of letting the bank have it back?"

"It's not that easy these days, that's why. The bank was barely holding on itself. What were they going to do with one more vehicle, when they already had some they couldn't sell? They didn't want it back. They just wanted me to make the payments."

Mae hadn't thought about it like that. *It must have been so hard for Thomas to swallow his pride and ask for help.*

"Thanks to Mama and Daddy, my family has a roof over their head," he said, his voice cracking over the last words. "And thanks to you, too, Mae—if you hadn't moved out when you did, I don't know where we'd be right now. I always thought you were just talking silly when you'd go on about moving to Texarkana. But now, if you hadn't gone and done just that, well, I don't know what might have happened to us."

He came and stood over her, willing her to look up at him. Only when she did so did he sit down beside her. "You can stay mad at me as long as you want, Mae," he said, laying his hand over hers. "But please don't take it out on Annette or the kids."

"I would never—"

"I know. I shouldn't have said that. Sorry."

She covered his hand with her other one. "I'm sorry, too, Tom. I hadn't realized how hard it must have been on you." She gave him a wobbly grin. "Goodness knows, I'm learning all about the responsibilities of adulthood. I'm not there, yet, but I've already learned a lot about being out on my own."

He grasped her hands in his, shaking them a bit, as if trying to rebuild the circulation in limbs fallen asleep—as, Mae supposed, all of her had been ever since Daddy told her about Thomas and his family.

"So, are we good?" he asked.

"We're good," she nodded. "Now let's go play with the kids before the day is all gone."

He stood and pulled her to her feet. "Thank you for being understanding about all this. I promise I'll fix it just as soon as I can."

"I'm sorry, too. Sorry for shooting off my mouth, as usual."

He laughed, the first joyful laugh she'd heard since she got home. It sounded good. But she still hated the thought of sleeping on the couch.

TWELVE

NO, NO, ANNETTE!

"I'M GOING TO TAKE some things back with me," Mae said after supper. "Do we have any big paper bags anywhere?"

"I could get you a flour sack bag," Mama said.

Mae cringed at the thought of toting such a thing on the bus. "That's okay. I think one bag will be all I'll take, anyway." She'd been rummaging in a cabinet and now produced the kind of sack she wanted, a brown paper bag from the general store. "Got it. I'll be back in a few minutes."

"Mae, wait . . ." Annette's voice trailed off as Mae hurried out of the kitchen.

She shoved open the bedroom door and headed to her chest. Opening the top drawer, she frowned. *What is this?* Undies she'd never seen before. *Annette.* She began to riffle through the other drawers. None of her things were there. There seemed to be underwear for Thomas' entire family, though. She wheeled around to look in her chifforobe. Nothing of hers. Nothing. It was only then that her gaze was drawn to the wall behind her bed. All of her pictures were gone, replaced by drawings done by those brats. She stormed back to the kitchen.

76

"What the hell, Annette? Where's my stuff? Did y'all just throw it away? Huh?"

Annette's face was screwed up with anxiety. "I tried to stop you, Mae. I'm sorry you went in there."

"But it was my room." Mae fell into a chair and crossed her arms, glaring at her sister-in-law.

Annette said, "Well, if you'd just give me a minute to explain, I would." The two stared at each other, Mae's green eyes shooting daggers.

"Your mother got me some boxes from the store, and we packed up all your things and put them under the bed. I'm sorry, Mae. I didn't do it to hurt you. We just needed room."

Without a word, Mae left the room and went in search of her belongings.

* * *

By the time supper was finished, Mae had decided she wasn't going to let her first trip home be ruined by her selfish brother and his wife. She wouldn't let a little thing like having her room taken over cause her to have a bad time. Saturday night they had Mama's famous spaghetti and meatballs. "Mama, I know you've tried to show me how, but I still can't match you in the spaghetti department. And biscuits? Forget it." Mama beamed with pleasure. "I've just about made myself sick eating so much."

Annette helped Mae and Ginny clean the kitchen, and they made Mama go into the living room with everybody else to listen to the Grand Ole Opry. The noise coming from the living room didn't sound much like music to Mae, not after what she'd heard live when she and Graydell went out last Saturday night to The Palm Club, where a real live band had played what they called "jazz" music.

* * *

Mama invited Oliver and Prissy to lunch after church, and Mae regaled them with Graydell's and her experiences during their first days at work.

Prissy looked aghast. "I just cannot imagine putting on a pair of roller skates and sashaying up to a car with people I don't know, and being friendly to them and all, and smiling all day long."

Oliver chuckled at Prissy's round eyes.

"You could imagine it if you saw the size of the tips you get if you're nice to people," Mae said. "And Prissy, you're one of the nicest people I know. You'd do great as a carhop."

"Carhop! Is that what they call you? Oh, my goodness." Prissy waved her hand in front of her face. "No, ma'am, not for me. But I'm going to ask Mama and Daddy to go to the Dixie Drive-in next time we go to Texarkana. I can't wait to see you two on roller skates."

Lord, Mae's a pretty thing when she's all lit up like a Christmas tree.

Later, just before time for Mae to go back into Dixon's Crossing to meet the bus, he asked to take her home. "That way you can stay for the service tonight," he said by way of tempting her.

"Oh, Oliver, that would just be wonderful. Would you really do that?"

Assured he meant what he said, Mae then asked, "Would you mind if I took a few things back with me, since I'll have room?"

"Sure, Maisie."

* * *

"These boxes have almost everything I own," Mae said later when they got in the car.

Oliver glanced at her. *Wish I could give you the world, Maisie.*

"All in all, it was a pretty good weekend," Mae remarked, "even if I did lose my room."

"Actually, you didn't lose your room. You already gave it up, remember?"

Mae opened her mouth as if to reply but stopped when she saw the corner of his mouth twitching. "Meanie. You know what I was trying to say." She made a fist and slugged his arm. He grinned to himself.

From the courthouse, Mae directed Oliver around to where their apartment was. He whistled in admiration.

"This sure is a nice looking place," he said. "Now I can picture where you are when I think of you." *Which is always.*

"The room will have to remain faceless. Mrs. Swenson doesn't like menfolk coming around," she laughed.

That makes me feel even better. "But we've got all these boxes . . ."

"We'll just put them on the porch. I'll take them in later. I don't want to give her any reason to throw us out, not with all these new people in town looking for places to stay."

"No, we don't want that," he agreed. Setting a box on the edge of the porch, he said, "That's the last one."

They sat in the swing for a few minutes, and when it came time to say good night, Oliver yearned to hold her hand, to put his arm around her, to sneak a kiss. *Wonder what she'd do. I can't risk it. Don't want to mess up our friendship. But man, those lips are calling to me.*

"What are you thinking about Oliver?" she teased. "You've got this dreamy look on your face. You got a girl or something?"

"No, Maisie. I've got no girl." *But I sure wish I did.*

Driving home, he chastised himself for being so weak, for not telling Mae how he felt about her. It would be a long time before he got to sleep tonight.

THIRTEEN

FOURTH OF JULY

[DIARY ENTRY] JULY 3, 1941

    I'm so excited to be going home for a visit tomorrow. It's just for one day, and I'll have to catch the 5:30 bus to get back tomorrow night. But it will be worth it, since I know the family will be cooking to beat the band! It's funny--I was so excited to get away from that place, and now I'm ready to go back even for just a day. But I do love living here in Texarkana. I know I'm doing the right thing. Especially with these plants coming in—It's so exciting to be in the middle of the action!

    This trip will be special, though. Oliver's birthday is tomorrow, and I got him a card, and I hope to make him a cake. I really miss Oliver, at least as much as I miss my family. He knows I'm coming, and he wrote that he'd be there to meet my bus. That's really nice of him.

    She put the little diary in her small bedside table and left the apartment. At Wellworth's, she spent several minutes reading and dismissing birthday cards. Most didn't fit at all, with their flowers, garden gates, birds, and swings—but when she picked up one with boots and a fishing pole, she saw possibilities. Reading the verse about loyal friendship, she knew this was it.

Besides the card, she picked up a lipstick for Ginny and an embroidered handkerchief for Mama. Then she hopped on a bus and headed up State Line to work. Business was slow that afternoon, and Mae said to Patsy, the carhop working with her, "I feel like everybody in Texarkana but us is already celebrating." Patsy nodded her agreement.

After work, she hurried home to starch and iron her jeans. "Look, Grady. They can stand up on their own," she laughed.

Graydell, who had plans with George at Spring Lake Park, waved Mae goodbye on her way to the bus. Mae still worried about her friend and George, but she knew better than to say anything.

She mentioned nothing about a cake to Oliver when he picked her up at the bus stop the next morning, but she almost ran into the house when he dropped her off. Dashing into the kitchen, she hardly said hello before donning an apron and starting to mix up a pound cake—one of the few recipes she had mastered. She pulled it out of the oven just after ten, just in time to leave for the picnic. She packed the cake into a box and tucked the card she'd bought yesterday inside, too.

"They're having a cake auction to raise funds for new song books. Why don't you put your cake into the auction?" Mama suggested.

"Oh, Mama. I wanted to fix this for Oliver's birthday." *I hope that doesn't sound too selfish.* She held the cardboard box containing her precious cargo all the way to the church, which today served as a community center. Then when everyone had piled out of the truck, she placed it gently on the seat. She'd come back for it later—after the auction.

Mae started squirming when the auction started and she saw all those cakes being bought. She knew hers was as good as any of them, and she briefly wondered how much money she could have raised for the new hymnals if she'd offered her pound cake.

She'd been musing on this when there was a stir of interest in the crowd that made her sit up and take notice. The cake up for sale was Prissy Thibodeaux's famous coconut cake, and the bidding was heating up. Beside her on the quilt, Prissy was looking embarrassed. Mae whispered, "You're going to beat everybody, Prissy."

"Three seventy-five," a voice behind her said. *Oliver*! The bidding climbed higher. "Five fifty!" Oliver said, and everybody gasped. *What is he doing?* A couple more bids, and she heard him say, "Seven dollars! Anybody want to top that?"

Mr. Christensen from the bank, the auctioneer, gave everyone a chance, then yelled, "Sold! To the young man in the straw hat." This drew laughter from the crowd, since no fewer than half a dozen young men were wearing the straw boaters.

Oliver jumped up and went to pay for his prize, then came back and plopped back down. He set the cake gently in the middle of the quilt. "Sure looks good, Prissy," he said. "It even smells good! Why don't I get some plates and we can all share it."

But something unexpected had happened to Mae while the bidding war was going on. First she was surprised—then, though she didn't understand it, she was angry with Oliver for persisting long enough to buy Prissy's cake. It surprised her to feel a hint of jealousy. It wasn't directed toward Prissy, but rather toward Oliver. *Surely he isn't interested in Prissy that way.* Mae felt a lump in her throat, like she was choking. Suddenly she had to get away. She left while Oliver was gathering plates and forks for them. She didn't care. She didn't want any of Prissy's stupid cake. She hurried out to the truck, shoving her cake to the side to sit down.

Under the shade of one of the ancient oaks, she was glad she had a cool place in which to sulk. Yes, she knew that's what she was doing. She was angry Prissy had done something she wasn't willing to do. Angry at herself, angry at Prissy, though she knew that was unreasonable. Most of all, she was angry at Oliver, who had a whole coconut cake now, and who would probably be too full to even try her cake—the cake she had made for him. She crossed her arms and harrumphed.

* * *

Oliver found her sleeping there thirty minutes later. He reached in through the open window and teased at her mouth with a blade of grass. She twisted her lips and rubbed her finger under her nose, but slept on. He

82

grinned and wiggled the grass again, all across her lips. *Sure wish it was my lips brushing yours, Maisie. Oh, well, maybe someday.*

One more tickle and she was wide awake. She jumped when she saw the hand in front of her face, but when she saw it was Oliver, she relaxed. "What do you think you're doing?" she said, her pretty lips drawn into a frown.

Oliver tried to keep his voice natural as he said, "We've been missing you, Maisie. What are you doing out here all by yourself?"

"Nothing. I just felt like getting away from the noise, that's all."

Looking across her, he asked, "Whatcha got in the box?"

"Nothing you'd be interested in, I expect. You're probably full of Prissy's wonderful coconut cake."

"Maisie," he sing-songed, "did you make me a cake? I see you've got one over there, and you didn't have one in the auction, and it *is* my birthday and all . . ."

She stared straight ahead, not replying. He opened the door and leaned in so he could see her face. "What's the matter, Maisie? Did I do something wrong? Are you sick? What is it? Tell me."

She turned toward him in the seat, and he saw tears in the corner of her eyes. *What the devil?*

"Yes, I made you a cake, okay? I hurried to make the bus so I could get home in time to get it made to bring here and surprise you. I even got you a card." She reached under the seat and handed him an envelope. "I wouldn't put my cake in the auction because I wanted to be sure you got it, and I already felt guilty about that. And then you bought Prissy's cake, after bidding it up so I'm sure it sold for more than anybody else's. Didn't it?"

She finally stopped speaking. His heart melted when he looked at her sweet face, and he wanted so bad to take it between his hands and put his lips to hers. *One of these days, Maisie girl, one of these days.* Instead, he reached for her hand. "Come on, Mae, let's go join the others. Then maybe you'd let me drive you home tonight, and I can have some of that cake?"

He was still holding the envelope. "What about your card?"

"I'll open it later, after we get to your house. Okay?"

She dropped it into the box with the cake and took his hand as she climbed out of the truck. He never wanted to let it go.

* * *

The mid-afternoon sun slanted through the one good oak tree that provided a cooling shade for Mae and Oliver, who sat gently swinging. They each held a saucer with a piece of cake and, while Oliver's plate was almost empty, Mae's was barely touched. She couldn't help it—she was still upset over the cake auction. Prissy. *Why did he spend so much money on Prissy's stupid cake? It was probably most of the money he had in the world.*

"Oliver?"

"Hmm?"

"Can I ask you something?"

"Sure, Maisie. Fire away."

But how could she ask him such a thing? *Just blurt it out. That's what you usually do.* When she didn't say anything right away, he stopped the swing and turned to look squarely at her. Feeling his gaze, she turned a bit as well. "Are you and Prissy . . ." Her voice trailed off.

"Are we what?" His eyebrows drew together, and his blue eyes turned icy.

"Well, have you started dating each other?"

He snorted. "Have we what? What gave you that crazy idea?"

"It's not such a crazy idea. You haven't had a girlfriend, and she wasn't seeing anybody last I knew, and you're both surely of age, so I thought—"

"No! My Lord, no." He stood abruptly, making the swing lurch crazily. Mae touched her feet to the ground to stop before she got dizzy. He had his back to her, hands on his lean hips, gazing across the pasture.

"I didn't mean to make you mad. I was curious, that's all."

84

He didn't answer right away. Then he spun toward her again. Running his hand through his hair, he squatted on his heels in front of her. "Is this because I bought that cake?"

She nodded gloomily.

"Mae, you need to get something straight right now. I don't care a whit about Prissy, except as a friend. A friend who's been really lonely since you and Graydell moved off. I just wanted her to know she still has a friend here in Dixon's Crossing. Y'all seem to be having a high old time up in Texarkana, and she really misses you."

Mae felt more guilt creeping over her. "I guess I hadn't even thought of Prissy and her feelings," she said.

"What about me?" He laid his hand on her knee. "Have you thought about mine?"

* * *

His feelings? "What are you talking about?" she asked.

He locked gazes with her. "My feelings. Feelings I've had for you since I was fifteen. Heck, I don't want to go out with anybody, Mae, not until I can go out with you." He took her plate and set it with his, then reached for her hands.

She couldn't believe what she was hearing. Oliver was her friend. They had always been friends. You couldn't go out with a friend--could you? Her mind was in a whirl. *I thought couples had to be like me and Frankie. I fell for him the first time I ever saw him, and he said the same about me. Isn't that the way it's supposed to be?*

"Oliver—"

"You were just a silly kid when I first started paying attention to you. Thirteen. Way too young for me to make a move on you, no matter what some people around here think. I know Brother and Sister Griffin married when she was real young, and it's worked fine for them, but I—"

"Married!" Mae broke in. "Oliver Cranfield, you're talking crazy. I'm not getting married, if that's what you're hinting at. And I'm not marrying you, for sure. You're my best friend."

He scooped the plates out of the swing and dumped them unceremoniously on the ground, flopping down beside her. "That's all for now. Of course, I'm not suggesting we get married right away. But I would like to have a chance to court you before you up and marry somebody else. Especially somebody like that Frank Cummings." He spat out the name as if it were a curse.

When he reached for her hand again, Mae drew back. "Oh, Oliver. Do you mean you've been carrying a torch for me since I was in, what, seventh grade? That's crazy."

He laughed ruefully. "Yeah, I have, Maisie. Didn't you ever wonder why I've never dated anybody?"

"A few times, I guess. I suppose I thought maybe it was this blamed Depression, that you didn't think you could afford a wife."

"That has been in the back of my mind. Maybe it's one reason I haven't asked you out before this. I can't afford a wife, so I guess I thought it would be better if we didn't start dating and, you know . . ."

She knew, alright. Hadn't she fought those urges enough when she was making out with Frank? She might have married him if he'd ever asked, despite her fear of getting stuck in these bottoms. Sometimes she'd wanted him so bad she couldn't think straight.

She shook off those thoughts now, trying to figure out what to say, how to say it.

"Ollie, I just don't have those feelings for you. I can't help it."

"But how do you know? For sure, I mean. We've never kissed, never spent time alone on a real date. Heck, this is the first time I've ever held both your hands at the same time."

She couldn't help it. She giggled.

"Aw, hell, Mae. Now you're laughing at me."

Was she? Or was something else going on? Her mind was in a whirl.

"No, I'm not, really I'm not. It's just nerves. You've gotta admit, you took me by surprise, talking about us this way. I don't know what to think, what to say."

"Say you'll think about it, about us. That's all I ask." He looked at her imploringly. "Please don't say no without promising you'll think about it."

She sighed. "All right, Oliver, I promise I'll think about it." She felt a giggle struggling to escape but managed to squelch it. "I doubt I'll be thinking about much of anything else."

He swept her into a hug, and after a moment's hesitation, she hugged him back. *Just like always. But is it really?*

"You promise me one thing, too," she said against his shoulder.

He drew back. "Anything, Maisie."

"Promise me if I decide I can't go out with you we'll still be best friends."

He nodded, smiling. "Cross my heart."

When he left her at the store waiting for the bus a little later, he took her hand again and said, "Thanks for the cake and the card, Maisie. You have no idea how much they mean to me. I'm going to be praying you'll make the right decision."

"I'll be praying, too," she said.

He leaned forward and kissed her on the top of her head. Long after he'd gone, long after she had made it home and crawled into her bed, she could still feel his lips there.

FOURTEEN

WHIRLWIND

MAE FELT AS IF she'd been sucked up into a whirlwind—one of those hot, dry whorls that blew across the fields and yards during periods of drought, like there had been plenty of lately. The miniature tornadoes would spring up out of nowhere, meander a ways picking up any trash they came across, and carry it off to another part of the yard, making a mess of things.

There was no whirlwind, no cyclone, no tornado. There was only the reality of the two defense plants that were coming to Texarkana.

Mae was fascinated with the goings-on in her new city. While Graydell saved her tips for Evening in Paris perfume and nylons, Mae set aside a bit of change so she could pick up a newspaper now and then. She had even considered buying a regular subscription to the paper. The boy who delivered papers on their street was a natural-born salesman. Little Ben Gregory was a go-getter, alright.

The first time they had talked, he'd been hawking a special edition on a street corner downtown. She'd stopped to buy a paper and had recognized him from her street, where he often delivered papers on horseback.

"Hey, kid, don't you deliver papers over on Laurel?"

"Yes, ma'am. I've seen you a couple of times. Don't you want to get a subscription? It'll save you money in the long run." She'd laughed at his spunk but had resisted his offer. Now he hit her up every time he saw her. Yes, young Ben was going places. She was sure of it.

One day there was a story about the families that had been bought out by the government and were having to move—when there was hardly any place to move to. Another day she read what wages at the ammunition plant were projected to be. It was almost impossible for her to believe that men would soon be earning more than five dollars a day.

The thing that made Mae saddest was the tenant farm families, just like her own, that had been living on the land the government took from owners—owners who at least now had money in their pockets to look for someplace else to live. The tenants were the ones most vulnerable. The land beneath their homes was sold out from under them, and they were given days, or at most weeks, to get out and find a place to go. She read the stories and cried for their plight.

"Listen to this, Graydell," she said one morning while she lounged on her bed. The curtains they had strung throughout the room to give them a sense of privacy were pulled back, all their windows were open, and the morning breeze was pleasant—but Mae didn't even notice. She was too caught up in her paper. "They're bringing in officials from Washington to do something about all the evacuees. Listen to this: 'Seventy-five collapsible houses will be set up on the old Eubanks place near New Boston, and fifty others near Redwater.' What are collapsible houses, anyway? They don't sound very substantial."

"No, I guess not," Graydell said distractedly from her bed, where she was perusing a new Hollywood magazine.

"Graydell, pay attention! This could have been our families if they had decided to build these plants down in Arkansas rather than over in Texas."

"What? Oh, yeah, I guess you're right. But since they didn't, I haven't given it much thought."

"I don't like it. It says here that they're going to 'permanently relocate' those people on land throughout Bowie and Cass Counties in Texas. Well, where are they going to get the money to pay for that land? I mean, all the land belongs to somebody, or are they going to just confiscate their land, too? And where will it stop?"

"Does it say what the houses will be like?"

"No, but it does say sanitation is going to be a problem. And I guess so. It'll take a while to dig that many septic holes and build outhouses for all those houses. This one man they quoted says for sure they won't be moving people to Oklahoma. Seems there's lots of rumors going around about that."

"But the government already gave lots of Oklahoma land to the Indians," Graydell protested. "What about them?"

"Well, it wouldn't be the first time Indians got moved off land they'd been promised by the government."

Um-hmm. I think that's one reason my daddy doesn't have much good to say about the government in Washington. He thinks those people will do just about anything, as long as it benefits them, and that they forget all about us little people once they get there."

"That's true of some, I'm sure, human nature being what it is. But I'll give them the benefit of the doubt, until they show me otherwise." Mae sat up and looked across at her friend. "Just look at this Mr. Wright Patman," she said, gesturing to the paper. "He seems like he's working night and day to try to figure out the best way for our part of the country to get ahead. But still, I don't like the idea of all these tents they're talking about bringing in."

"Tents!"

"Yes, tents. Says they are being brought from a migrant labor camp over close to Dallas. At least I guess the Mexicans can go back home to Mexico. They'll have family there, and maybe houses of their own, too. Since they just spend a few months up here working in the fields."

Graydell rolled off her bed and stood up to stretch. "Well, how about a piece of toast for breakfast?" she said, turning on the stove.

90

Mae took the hint. Graydell had had enough politics for one morning.

* * *

The girls found the nightclubs in town staying open later and later. They didn't go out very often. Serving customers while navigating the parking lot on roller skates was no easy task, and many nights they came straight home and fell into bed.

Graydell had always been outgoing, though, and she could make it only so many nights without urging Mae to go out with her. At first Mae was reticent, but in time she found she had gained a whole new circle of friends, and she became more eager to go out, too.

One afternoon at work, she was surprised in the middle of a yawn to see her brother Thomas pull into a parking space and toot his horn at her. She hurried to his car and leaned in to give him a hug.

"Hey, Thomas. This is a surprise. What are you doing in town today?"

He was grinning from ear to ear. "I got a letter to go out to Red River Arsenal for a construction job. Just got off my first day on the job."

Only now did she realize how dirty his clothes were. "That's great! Let me go put in an order for you. Treat's on me today." She skated off, saying a prayer that Thomas and Annette would get back on their feet soon.

* * *

"My friend Mrs. Goldfield over on Pecan Street says she rented out a tiny room in her boarding house for sixty dollars a month," Mrs. Swenson said at the dinner table one night.

Mae cast a furtive glance at Graydell and the other girls. Nobody said anything, so the landlady continued.

"That doesn't seem quite fair to me," she whined. "Here I've had boarders since way last year and couldn't hardly give my rooms away. Now that I'm all full up, you girls are getting a real bargain, and I'm getting left behind all this new prosperity."

"But we still have the same jobs, Mrs. S.," Mae protested. "It wouldn't be fair, would it, to start charging us all lots more in rent when we're not making more money?"

"I'm just saying, if you all were to leave next week, I could soon be taking in lots more money," she persisted.

"Yeah, but what kind of boarders would you have?" Graydell piped up. "I've been hearing lots about all these men coming into town for construction work. Even the married ones aren't usually bringing their wives. They're here for the money only, and when the plants are built, they'll be gone so fast it'll make your head swim, Mrs. S. Then where would you be?"

Mae gave her friend an appreciative wink. *You tell her, Graydell.*

"I suppose you're right, Graydell. After all, you know how I feel about having men on the premises."

"Yes, ma'am." Graydell grinned into her soup.

FIFTEEN

A NEW JOB OFFER

SEPTEMBER 23, 1941

> *Oh, Lord, I don't know if I'm ready for life in the big city or not! I had a run-in with some women today while I was waiting for the bus, and I have never in my life met up with that kind of woman. To say I was embarrassed would be a great understatement . . .*

Mae paused in her writing. She could feel her cheeks burning as she thought back on the morning's encounter.

"There'll be a hot time in the old town tonight." Mae was alone at the bus stop when she heard the female voices coming her way, singing loudly and with apparent gusto. She turned to look.

A group of several girls, most about her age, was approaching. Their singing continued, but a couple of them skipped on ahead, almost dancing down the sidewalk.

Mae's breath caught in her throat when she recognized Graydell's sister Clara at the edge of the group. Their eyes met, then Clara's lids dropped to the ground.

So that means these girls are . . . prostitutes!

She couldn't believe they were here—right out in public, and in broad daylight. She looked around, wanting a place to hide, but there was

93

nowhere. Besides, she had to catch that next bus if she was going to get to work on time.

As the happy group reached Mae, she glanced down the street to where two older women, about her mother's age, had just spied the group on the corner. They stopped dead still, looked left then right, and hurried across the street in the middle of the block. A car horn blared, but they paid it no mind.

"Same every time," a tall redhead said. "Can't stand to be near us. Bet they're wondering if their husbands have ever been with us." She laughed, and the others joined in—except for Clara.

Mae was of two minds. On the one hand, she knew what her mother would say she should do. She should ignore them and walk away, so nobody passing by would link her with them. But there stood Clara, and Mae felt compelled to speak to her. But what would she say? After all, they didn't have much in common.

But we do have Graydell in common. Graydell loves her sister. And Clara was always nice to me when we were growing up. Maybe she can't help what she's become. What would I have done in her place?

It was decided then.

She strode the few steps it took to get to Clara, then held out her arm. She stood a few inches above Clara usually, but today, like the others, Clara was in heels, so they basically stood eye to eye.

"Hey, Clara, how's it going?" She tentatively touched Clara's shoulder. When Clara didn't pull away, Mae patted her a couple of times, then let her arm fall.

Clara tilted her head to one side and a half-smile touched her lips. "It's good, Mae. Good to see you. It's been a long time."

"Yeah, it has. I guess you knew Graydell and I have an apartment over close to the courthouse."

Clara nodded. "Graydell came to see me one day after y'all got moved in. She told me all about your place."

"Have you each got your own bedroom?" A tall, slim girl with piles of black curls atop her head was looking Mae up and down. "I bet you don't."

Mae gave her a once-over. She wasn't that impressed. "No, as a matter of fact, we share a large room that takes up about half of the upstairs of the house."

"Clara, what's your sister's name again?" the redhead asked, sidling up to them and joining in the conversation as unselfconsciously as anyone Mae had ever met.

"Graydell. Why?" Clara replied.

"Where'd she get a name like that?" another of the girls asked.

Clara said, "My mother had lost a little brother when she was about twelve, and his name was Grady. Daddy named their first kid Walter Junior, then I came along, and he wanted me named Clara. He told Mama she could name her next kid Grady, but she was a girl, too. Mama was determined to use her brother's name, but she wanted everybody to know that baby was a girl, so she tacked the 'ell' onto the end and, I guess, created a new name. I know Graydell hates it, but there's not much she can do about it."

"I didn't know that story," Mae said. I call her 'Grady' for short, and she's never told me anything about your uncle. She may hate me calling her that. She's never complained, though."

Clara reached out to pat Mae's arm. "No, she's fine with it. She told me when you started calling her that, even asked me to as well. I'm so glad she has such a good friend in you, Mae."

Mae felt her cheeks heating. She never could take compliments worth a darn. She always felt like people were just pretending when they said something nice to her.

"Yeah, we get along well. She's a little too crazy for me sometimes, but we have lots of good times together."

"Aren't y'all working over at that drive-in?" the redhead asked. Mae nodded. "How much do they pay you for doing that? Don't you have to wear roller skates and stuff?"

Mae hesitated, not really wanting to discuss her life standing on a street corner, and especially not with these women. But Clara answered for her, saying, "Graydell said she gets thirty cents an hour, plus tips, and those make up to maybe two more dollars a day."

Red hooted. "How in the world are you supposed to have any kind of a life making that little?"

Mae felt bound to defend Mr. Robinson, and maybe herself, too. "We are in the middle of a depression," she said, and there was spit and spunk in her voice. "We make out pretty well, lots better than if I was down on the farm."

Now why had she mentioned the farm? She hadn't meant to have any conversation with these women, and she sure hadn't meant to give anything away about herself. But they just seemed so. . . so normal. So nice.

"Ooh, honey. You ought to come work with us." Red laughed. "Don't you think so, ladies? I mean, she's good looking, in a wholesome kind of way. Men love girls with lots of blond curls, and you've sure got that. You're feisty, but not *too* outspoken. And with those green eyes . . . What do you think, Judy?"

The girl with all the black hair sashayed over and scrutinized Mae so hard she got goosebumps. "I wish you'd quit looking at me like that," Mae muttered.

"Like what, hon? I don't mean nothing by it. But I'm the makeup specialist in our group, and I'm just giving you an expert answer when I say I could turn you into a raving beauty, if you'd let me."

"Thank you, Judy, but I'm perfectly happy the way I am. I mean, I'm sure you could make me look like somebody else altogether, but I'm just going out to the drive-in to work. I want to look nice, because that gets better tips, but I always want to be myself."

"If you went to work with us, you'd have to give up that idea," another girl said. "You'd learn pretty quick that men want a woman who will play roles for them, be whatever he wants them to be. I'm just saying that—"

"What she's saying," Red broke in, "is that you could make as much in a night as you do in a week of serving customers. Maybe two weeks, if you played your cards right."

Mae cut her eyes around at Clara, who stood off to the side, not commenting. She wondered if Clara ever regretted her choice.

"Um, I appreciate the nice things y'all have said about me," Mae began. "But I don't think I'm cut out for that kind of business. I mean, it's fine for you all, but I'm just trying to find my way in life. I'm just gonna need a while to figure out what that is."

The redhead studied her hard for a minute, then smiled. "If you ever change your mind, you come over to our house and ask for Miss Nina. She'll take good care of you. Clara's sister knows where to find us. What's your name, anyway?"

"Mae Johnson. What's yours?"

"They call me Red," she said, and Mae couldn't help it. She laughed out loud.

"What's so funny?" Red asked, squeezing her eyes almost shut to glare at Mae.

"Oh, nothing. I'm sorry. It's just, well, I've been standing here talking to you and calling you 'Red' in my head. I guess you're named right, that's all."

Red tossed her head and laughed. "You're alright, Mae Johnson."

Mae nodded her head a couple of times. "You, too, Red."

In the following lull in conversation, Mae heard, finally, the familiar sound of an approaching bus. "There's my ride," she said, stepping over to the very edge of the curb. "Gotta get to work."

"Bye, Mae," the girls all called out as she boarded the bus. She waved back at them. Turning back to look for a seat, she saw the shocked expressions on the faces of a few of the women passengers. She smiled to herself and found an empty seat.

Now, Mae shook herself out of her reverie, read over what she'd written, and quickly finished her entry. She thought for a minute, then wrote:

There but for the grace of God go I.

* * *

A couple of weeks later, Mae had another surprise.

"Want to buy a paper this morning, Miss Johnson?" Ben Gregory waved a paper at her as she came down the steps early on Tuesday. "I've got a couple of extra copies in my pack."

"Well, I don't know, Mr. Gregory. Anything special going on today?" she laughed. The kid was always hustling.

"Nothing special," he admitted. "Well, except for this little article over on page three. It's about a strike out at Red River Arsenal. Boy, I don't know why they're even trying to bring in a union out at that place. I mean, the contractors are Brown and Root, and everybody knows that Mr. Herman Brown is about as anti-union as a person can get. Why, my daddy says—"

"Here, let me have one of those papers," Mae said, fishing in her pocket for a coin. "Thanks, Ben. You have a good day, you hear?"

"You too, Miss Johnson. Thanks!" The scrawny kid clucked to his horse and was off down the street, tossing an occasional paper and whistling until he was out of earshot.

Mae wasn't sure what had gotten into her this morning, didn't know why in the world she was up so early. But she was sure glad she was. She retraced her steps and entered the boarding house again, slipping into the parlor and turning to page three to read about what was happening out at Red River. The article was just a few short paragraphs, and it was full of generalities. She'd hoped to learn more about the people involved in the strike, but mostly the article quoted Herman Brown, who said he prided himself on paying union wages or better on all his projects, adding that he would never allow a union in any place he had a say so.

I wonder if Thomas got caught up in this. The paper says it was construction workers who were trying to bring in a union. Lord, I hope he stays away from any of that. He sure needs this job. And this Mr. Brown doesn't sound very accommodating.

Mae decided against her planned early morning walk, choosing instead to have breakfast with Mrs. S. and the other boarders. Graydell was still sleeping, after another late night out. Maybe Mrs. S. would have some news about the strike. She went toward the dining room, paper tucked under her arm.

"Hey, Mrs. S., everybody," she said by way of greeting.

"What's got you up so early, Mae? Is Graydell up, too?"

"No, just me. I'd headed out for an early walk when I ran into the Gregory kid, and he sold me a paper."

Mrs. Swenson tittered. "My father used to say of someone he knew that he could sell an igloo to an Eskimo. I wouldn't put it past Ben to have that ability." She shook her head, smiling. "He's quite a young man."

"You got that right, Mrs. S.," Mae laughed. "But he was telling me about a strike out at Red River, among the construction workers. Since that's where my brother works, I wanted to read up on it. But there's nothing much to the article. Do you know anything about it?"

The landlady shook her head. "No, sorry. Let me fix you some breakfast." She hustled off to the kitchen.

Later that afternoon, Mae was surprised to see her brother pull into a vacant spot at the drive-in. She wheeled out to meet him. "What are you doing here? Shouldn't you be at work?"

"Well, normally, yes I would be. But I just finished my turn walking picket, and now I'm headed home for the rest of the day."

"Oh, Thomas, I just heard about it this morning. I was sure hoping you weren't involved in any of that."

"I wish that, too. But there's no way I'm crossing a picket line, not after I paid my ten dollars last week when this union guy hit me up for it. He told a bunch of us that once they brought a union in it would cost twenty-five dollars to join it, but if we joined now, it would only be ten dollars. He also guaranteed we didn't have to worry about striking, cause it's not legal to strike in Texas."

"But then how can they be striking?" Mae asked, perplexed.

"Isn't it obvious? He lied!" Thomas shook his head. "So now I'm waiting to see if I'm going to be a part of the first Brown and Root construction job to be unionized, or if I'm going to be one of the three hundred or so workers that end up getting fired."

"Oh, no! Do you really think it'll come to that?" Mae asked, laying a hand on his arm. "Maybe they'll get it settled soon."

"I'm pretty sure they will," Thomas said with a grimace. "There were guys crossing that picket line all morning to go inside and put in their applications. And the bosses don't care who does the work, just as long as it gets done. Personally, I bet we get our marching papers before the week is out."

"I'll say a prayer for you, Tom." He smiled up at her. "Are you headed home now?" When he nodded, she said, "Wait right here. Let me go fix up a bag of burgers for you to take home to the folks. You can surprise them."

"Thanks, Mae. I know the kids will be thrilled that Aunt Mae thought about them. You're a doll."

"Nah, I'm just your sis, and you look like you could use some cheering up."

"I could at that."

She looked back toward Thomas when she reached the back door. *What a mess! Bet he's right. Bet he's out of a job when this is all over.*

Mae kept up with the news from Red River all week, but it wasn't encouraging. She met Ben outside on Friday morning. He knew by now why she was so interested in the strike, and he shook his head when he saw her sitting on the porch waiting for him.

"It's not good, Miss Johnson. The arbitrator the government sent down snuck onto a train yesterday and left town, and he left word he wasn't coming back. Said there was no use in it. Brown and Root has already hired more people than are out on strike. Somebody from the Chamber of Commerce told Daddy last night they were planning to pay off all the men involved starting today, and then they're letting them go. Just doesn't seem right to me. And I sure hate it for your brother."

"Thanks, Ben. I hate it, too. But I guess we've learned a valuable lesson from this. You never know when you may lose your job over something that seems innocent to you. Lord, I hope I never run up against somebody like that Herman Brown character."

"You and me both. Yep, you and me both. I know one thing. When I'm grown and in business for myself, I do not intend to treat my workers like this Brown feller. No, ma'am. I'm going to be the kind of boss I'd like to work for."

Mae rose stiffly and started back inside. "I bet you will, Ben. I just bet you will."

SIXTEEN

WAR TALK

DECEMBER 5, 1941

> *This has been a sad day for me. It should be a happy one, because today is my birthday. I turned nineteen today. But it's a Friday, and I had to work today, so this is the first time in my life I haven't been at home with my family on my 'special day'. Guess that means I'm all grown up, huh?*

> *I did get a couple of birthday cards, and they were really sweet. I got one from Mama and Daddy. Well, signed from both of them, but I know Daddy. He never signs anything like that. Sometimes he gets Mama a card—but he has never signed any of them! He's so funny that way. And I got one from Prissy and Oliver, too. She took it to church last week and got him to sign it, and they both wrote a little inside, saying how they miss me.*

> *I miss them, too! I know I'm doing the right thing. But I don't think I could stay here if I didn't know I could go back home from time to time. I get to go this weekend, though, and I'm sure looking forward to having a good pecan pie on Sunday—Mama has promised to make one, cause it's my favorite.*

> *I may go out for a while with Graydell after she gets home. When one of the girls didn't show up, she volunteered to work over. I hate*

working Friday <u>nights</u>. The customers get so rowdy. They do tip good, though. <u>Lord, I'm lonesome tonight!</u>

* * *

"What do you hear at the drive-in about these new plants, Mae?" Daddy asked.

They were sitting on the porch on a lazy, unseasonably warm Sunday afternoon, and she was feeling quite content. Most of her favorite people were there—Daddy and Mama, Prissy, and Oliver. They had all just had a piece of her birthday pecan pie. Thomas and Annette had taken the kids on a drive around the country, and the porch was blessedly quiet.

"There's more happening every day," she answered. "Of course, some of it's just talk and nothing else, but the papers are full of it. Ever since we heard about the ammunition plant, and then the big storage depot, people are just excited all the time."

"Did Thomas tell you he got a job at Lone Star?"

"Yeah, on construction. After that awful experience at Red River, I didn't know if he would try again. I'm so glad he did. Maybe they can get a place of their own soon."

"I'm sure they will," Daddy said. "I know they're ready."

No more than I am.

"I'm afraid we may be about to get caught up in this war, after all," Mama said. She almost never spoke up about anything like wars and such, so Mae took notice when she did.

"I hope you're wrong," she said. "People are just starting to get back on their feet after these awful Depression years. And I can't stand to think about all the young guys going off to fight."

"Me, either," Prissy said. "You realize this time it'll be all the boys we just got out of school with who'll be going over to do the fighting? I can't stand the thought."

Mae glanced at Oliver, who was sitting on the porch steps across from her. She couldn't decipher the look in his eyes.

"Prissy, I don't want to hear you talking about that," she said. "It's too nice an afternoon for us to spoil it with this war talk." She dusted her hands together, aiming to change the subject. "So, when are you going to put up a Christmas tree, Mama? Daddy and I usually go out to pick one, but I won't be here."

"That's right. Maybe Ginny can take your place," Mama replied.

"I'm sure she'll be thrilled," Mae thought to herself. But aloud she said, "Good. It's time for her to have some of the fun I've always had."

Daddy had just started talking about a few trees he had his eye on over by the river when they heard a mad car horn blowing, growing louder with each blast. Down the road came Mr. J.T. in his 1939 Dodge, driving faster than Mae had ever seen him. Something was up, that was for sure.

The car swerved into the front yard and stopped, dust swirling madly about them. Oliver and Daddy both stood and stepped off the porch to meet Mr. J.T., who had leapt from his car, his face an ashy shade. *What on earth?*

"Have y'all heard?" he yelled.

"Heard what?" Daddy asked.

"The Japs!" he answered. "The dirty Japs! They've bombed Pearl Harbor!"

Mae jumped up, too stunned to make a sound. She swung around to look at Mama and Prissy. Her friend's just-spoken words came back to Mae. *"All the boys we just got out of school with." And Oliver. Thomas?*

Mr. J.T.'s voice was lower now, and it trembled a bit. "I'm going to all the tenants," he was saying. "I stopped here first, Will. You're my right-hand man, and I'm pleased you'll most likely be like me, not having to send any sons into this war. Thomas should be exempt, with his family and all."

What was the man talking about? The country had been attacked, that's all. Maybe there could be some sort of settlement without going to war. *Sure, Mae, that makes lots of sense. We'll all just sit down at a big table and talk things out.*

Mr. J.T. was back in his car already, heading down the road to the Warren place. For a long minute, Daddy and Oliver stood talking quietly, heads together. Then they turned toward the house, Daddy's hand on Oliver's shoulder, their faces pale.

"Let's get inside and see what we can hear," he said, gesturing for the women to precede him.

Mama hurried to the radio and turned it on, increasing the volume so they all could hear. The KCMC announcer was in the middle of his report, and Mae's stomach filled with lead as he told of how the naval base at Pearl Harbor had been attacked early that morning by waves of Japanese bombers, how observers said it looked like the whole world was on fire.

Mama collapsed into her rocker and put her hand over her eyes, as if by shutting out the light she could shut out the reality of what she was hearing. Daddy stood with his hand on the mantel, head bowed. Oliver remained by the front door, hands shoved deep into his pockets. Mae and Prissy sat together on the couch, clasping hands. So many Sunday afternoons all these people she loved had been in this same room together, talking over the week's events, nothing exciting ever happening. *Lord, what I'd give to turn back the clock, where we could all be 'just visiting' again, with the blamed radio silent.* She feared the radio would never be silent again.

Hearing a sniff, she turned to look into her friend's face. Tears were streaming down her cheeks. Up until then, Mae had been holding her own tears in. But now she cried, too, cried for an innocence she felt slipping away, cried for the almost certain entry into an awful war she was sure would come shortly.

Her eyes locked on Oliver, whose head was bowed. What was he thinking? What was he feeling? As a woman, Mae didn't have to worry about being called up. Oliver did. She couldn't stand the thought of her best friend in the world going off to fight and die in some foreign place.

"I think it would be good for us to have a moment of prayer," Daddy said, motioning to Mama to turn down the sound on the radio.

Prayer? What good will prayer do, now that things have gone this far? God apparently hasn't been listening to prayers lately, because people have been praying for peace and a good economy for almost as long as I can remember.

But she bowed her head just the same, huddling closer to Prissy. If there was no hope of God hearing their prayers, then there would be no hope at all.

* * *

"How can the stars still shine so bright when the whole world is going dark?" Mae was leaning her head on her arm, which was propped against the rolled down window of Oliver's car. The air was still warm, and they had driven out to Spring Lake Park Sunday night to mull over the events of the day.

Her mind in turmoil, Mae struggled to think of something, anything, that would bring her some peace. Listening to the gurgle of the spring in the quiet night, she stared at the sign proclaiming the spring as a stopping place for Hernando de Soto. Local legend had it the explorer had been through the area somewhere around 1540, and de Soto had at first thought he'd found a true Fountain of Youth. He was proved wrong when he died shortly thereafter, something Mae had always found ironic.

Oliver heaved a deep sigh and reached into his shirt pocket to pull out a pack of chewing gum. "Want some Juicy Fruit? That always makes you feel better."

Mae absently held out a languid hand. "Thanks, Ollie—but I don't think anything could make me feel better tonight."

She unwrapped the stick of gum, folded it into thirds, and bit into it, once, not chewing. Her taste buds reacted, flooding her mouth with molten sugary liquid. Mae barely noticed. They chewed in companionable silence for several minutes.

"So, I was thinking . . ."

"You, thinking, Oliver Cranfield?"

They both smiled. It was an old joke between them.

"What would you think about me going ahead and enlisting?"

Mae's head popped up and she swung around to face him. "No!" If he was surprised by her reaction, he didn't show it. "But why would you want to go and do that?"

He shrugged in the moonlit darkness. "It's surely just a matter of time—"

"But still! We don't even know what's going to happen—not for sure."

"Oh, come on, Mae! The Japs bombed us out of the water a few hours ago. You really think Mr. Roosevelt isn't going to declare war when he talks to the country tomorrow?"

"You're probably right," she admitted. "But I don't want you to go!"

"I don't want to go, either. Nobody does. But sometimes we just have to do things we hate thinking about doing. It's part of growing up. But really—do you want Hitler and Tojo taking over the world? We're going to be having kids of our own one of these days. At least I'm planning to." He nudged her shoulder with his fist.

"I guess. Stop trying to change the subject. We're talking about you going into the army, for Pete's sake."

"Not necessarily. There's also the navy."

"The navy!" she spat. "You're not serious."

"And why not? It might be better than being dumped off somewhere over in Europe to fight on the ground. Or don't you remember what your uncle Gerald said he went through back in '18?"

"I remember, all right. I remember him waking us all up night after night when I was little—crying, screaming about his feet burning so bad— the feet that weren't there anymore. No, Oliver, I do not want that for you."

"I don't want to go and fight, Maisie, any more than you want me to, no more than anybody else wants to go. I'm scared out of my skull about it."

"Then don't do it." She grabbed one of his hands with both of hers. "At least not yet. Just wait and see what happens, okay? Just listen to the president tomorrow and see what he's going to do. No need to jump the gun. Is there?"

She was squeezing his hand hard now, as if willing her desire to keep him safe to be enough to make it so.

What's going to happen to my best friend? Mae felt her heart heavy in her chest. *What is tomorrow going to bring? What's going to happen to my world?*

Lost in thought, Mae didn't realize just how long Oliver had been quiet, until he finally broke the silence with two little words: "Aw, hell."

Mae turned away from her perusal of the stars. "Ollie? What's wrong? I mean, I know what's wrong, but what brought that on, just now?"

He slid around in the seat to pin his deadly expression squarely on her. "Mae, we don't know what's going to happen in the future. Heck, we don't even know what's going to happen tomorrow. We don't even know but what the Lord could come back tomorrow, or the next day, and this old world would be gone forever."

Mae felt a queasiness in her stomach—probably because she hadn't eaten any supper. She waited without speaking, sensing Oliver wasn't finished with his thought. Maybe she should have been expecting what came next—but she wasn't.

"With all this uncertainty, I'm going to ask you again what I asked you a couple of months ago. I want you to be my girl."

I should have expected this. I should have made my decision by now.

"Mae, I waited until you turned eighteen, then until you finished school, then while you came off up here to Texarkana and got a job, a place to live. I've tried to wait for you to get all this working world stuff out of your system. But I can't wait any more. I won't. I could be drafted before the week is out."

She tried to stop him. "Hold it right there. I don't want to talk about that."

"Well, too bad. I do. I don't have the luxury of saying I don't want to talk about it. So let me say my piece."

She settled back into the corner of the car seat, waiting.

"I've tried to be patient and not pester you for a decision, but I want you to be my girl. Mae, will you go out with me? I mean, dating, like a real couple?"

Mae sat up straight and stared through the windshield at the dim light playing around the spring, but she didn't speak.

"Mae? Did you hear me? I said—"

"I heard you."

"Well . . . what do you say?"

She laid her hand on his that was clutching the steering wheel so tightly she could feel all his knuckles standing at attention like a row of soldiers.

"Oliver, you know I love you like a brother. That's what we've always been like, brother and sister. Now you're asking me to turn my back on all that for the sake of a few dates."

"Not a few dates, Mae. I mean it. I care about you in a different way than that, and with things so uncertain, I want you to take a chance on us."

"You put your finger on it right there, buddy." He seemed to shrink at her choice of words. "I don't think tonight is the time for us to talk about anything like that—anything that will change our lives in a way where we'll never be able to turn back the clock and get back what we have right here, right now."

"I don't want to lose that, I just want something more, something better." Mae could hear the earnestness in his voice, and also the hurt.

"Ollie, let's face it. You may soon have a job to do for the country. You're probably right. We'll probably be at war this time tomorrow. I'm sorry, but I can't commit to anything tonight. Our world has just flip-flopped on us. I for one am in no position to think about something so earth-shaking as turning our friendship on its head right now as well. I just can't do it."

"So you're saying you won't be my girl?" He loosened his grip on the steering wheel and clasped her hand instead. "Please, Mae, give us a chance."

"I *am* giving us a chance, Oliver. A chance to hold on to the friendship we have while the world spins out of control around us. Can't you understand?"

"No, I don't." He grabbed her by the shoulders and shook her. "I want you, Mae. Worse than I've ever wanted anything."

He tried to pull her toward him, but she pushed against his chest with both hands. "Ollie, stop it! Listen to me! I mean it, listen." But he grabbed her hands and brought one to his lips. If his lips had been on hers, it would have been a bruising kiss, for he put all his pent-up emotions, all his passion, into that one kiss.

Mae was stunned. Partly because Oliver was behaving so out of character for him. Partly because she suddenly felt something deep in her belly that she hadn't felt since . . . Well, since the last time she'd made out with Frankie. *Wow. Where did that come from?*

Just as Mae was on the verge of giving in, Oliver released her hands and turned to start the car.

"Okay, Mae. I'll accept your decision—for now. Just keep in mind I've been waiting for years, and now that I've said my piece, you can be sure I'm going to be repeating it every chance I get." He put the car into gear and backed out of the parking space. "But right now I'm going to take you home."

Mae clasped her hands in her lap all the way back to her apartment, and she sat quite still when Oliver parked the car out front. Without a word, he got out and came around to open her door. Closing it softly behind her, he motioned for her to precede him up the walk. They still hadn't talked at all since the park.

At the door, she turned to say something, anything—but he stopped her by laying a finger against her lips. He sighed deeply, then leaned in. She closed her eyes, wondering what their first kiss would feel like. She sort of hoped it wouldn't feel like she was kissing Thomas. She waited . . . then felt the softest brush of his lips against her cheek, just at the corner of her mouth. By the time she had gotten over her surprise, he was halfway back to his car.

Angry, frustrated tears spurted from her eyes, but Oliver didn't see. She stepped inside and closed the door. Racing up the stairs to her room, she flung open the door to see a startled Graydell look up from her book.

"The hell with men!" Mae declared, stomping across the room and yanking her curtain closed.

"Amen, sister," Graydell muttered, returning to her romance novel. She fell asleep over the book soon after, not having heard the terrible news. She may have been the only person in Texarkana who had a sound sleep that night.

SEVENTEEN

CHRISTMAS GIFTS

MAE STOOD GAZING THROUGH the open curtains at the brightly lit tree. The multi-colored lights were still an amazement to her. When she was a little girl, they hadn't known what a lighted tree was—at least not one of their own. She and Daddy had always brought home a tree of some kind—usually a spindly pine, but once or twice her favorite—a cedar from out in the hills.

Then came electricity, when she was thirteen, and the Christmas tree once decorated solely with cutouts she, Thomas, and little Ginny colored was augmented with two strings of colored lights. It took multiple extension cords to reach from the one wall outlet in the living room to the tree—but it was worth it, Daddy said, to have it in the front window.

Every year Daddy put the tree in a bucket of wet dirt and added the lights. Mama then wrapped the bucket in a piece of red fabric she scrounged up from who knew where. Then all the kids wrapped the tree in strings of popcorn they had spent nights threading, finally adding things they'd made through the years.

Those times were in the past though. This year they had trimmed the tree without her. She'd probably never trim a tree in this house again. Someday she'd have a home of her own, and she and her husband would begin making new traditions. She swallowed the lump in her throat, picked up her bags of presents, and opened the front door.

"Merry Christmas, everybody!" she called, and Thomas' three little ones came running to fling their arms around her. She dropped her bags and went down on her knees to meet them.

"Oh, Aunt Mae, you look so pretty," Anna said, fingering Mae's blonde curls.

"Why, thank you, sweetie. Y'all look real pretty, too."

And they did, in matching green and red plaid dresses with red bows in their hair. It always amazed Mae to realize how much Anna looked like her daddy, and how Susie took after Annette, with her auburn hair and brown eyes.

She stood and looked around the familiar room. Daddy was dozing in his rocker in the corner, but Mama's chair was empty. Sounds of laughter from the kitchen drew her, and she shook off the little ones and headed that way.

"Is this a private party or can anybody join in?" she said from the doorway.

Mama whirled around from the counter, her eyes lighting up. "Oh, Mae. I'm so glad you made it all right. We've missed you." This greeting caught Mae off guard since Mama so seldom showed her emotions.

Annette winked at her from the sink, where she was busy with the supper dishes. "Hey, girl, you got here just in time."

"No, I think I'm a little early," Mae laughed. "Maybe I'll come back in a few minutes."

"Stop that silly talk. Come help me with the jam cake." Mama gestured to the table. "I've got the layers all together, and I'm ready to put the last layer of icing on. Use that imagination of yours to help me decorate it." Mae looked at the bowl of goodies.

"How many layers this year, Mama?"

"Five thin ones with lots of filling," she said proudly.

Mae washed her hands and set to work as soon as Mama finished smoothing on the thickening icing. She'd have to work quickly before it set up. She loved putting the English walnut halves, pecans, and maraschino cherries on, in delicate patterns that would last about ten minutes after everyone took a slice tomorrow after dinner. But a week from now, the family would still be trimming off thinner and thinner slices, making the special cake last as long as possible.

Jam cakes got their name from the fact that their batters and frostings were both so filled with goodies: berry jam, chopped walnuts (both English walnuts, store bought, and black walnuts, from the huge tree at Mrs. Wheeler's place, since she always shared the tangy nuts with all the families on the farm), chopped pecans, raisins, and sometimes other fruits, if they could find and afford them. The layers were dense with these morsels, and the sugary icing was, too, so that a small, thin slice went a long way.

Finished with her creation, she asked, "How's it look?"

"Beautiful, Mae," Annette answered, drying her hands and coming over for a closer look. "Just beautiful. The kids will only get a tiny slice, it's so rich."

"I think that's one of its best points," Mae replied. "That way it lasts longer."

* * *

"You shouldn't have done so much, Mae," Annette whispered, as they all sat around the afternoon of Christmas day, watching the kids play with their presents.

"Well, who am I going to spend all that tip money on, if not my nieces and nephew?" Mae smiled as she watched the girls playing with their new dolls. She'd found one with blonde hair for Susie, and one with dark hair for Anna. Tommy was practicing his "quick-draw" with the buckle-on holster and "ivory-handled" pistols she'd found for him at Kress's. They had been so excited when they opened their gifts that Mae wasn't about to have Annette make her feel guilty.

"I wouldn't take anything for having been here this morning to see their faces when they saw what Santa brought them," Mae whispered back. "Y'all did good, sister." Mae had struggled over them all living back at home, but she was bound and determined to get past her upset. Family was even more important in this day and time.

Ginny has turned into such a teenager. I can't believe the way she gathered up her presents and took them off to her room.

The girl had only come out for the Christmas meal, and now she had disappeared again. She did help with the dinner dishes, but that was expected of all the women.

Mae smiled to herself. *I bet she's busy writing in the diary I gave her. I sure remember when I got my first one. I was sixteen, and I had to buy it with my own money I made babysitting Hope. But I wanted Ginny to have one now. I know I could surely have used one when I was that age. That's when I fell in love with Frank, and I had no place to write down my feelings, to describe our first kiss. Yep, Ginny needs that diary.*

A knock at the door caused the grownups' heads to turn, but the kids played on, unaware. "I'll get it," Mae said, jumping up from the couch. She flung the door open, letting in a blast of winter air. "Oliver!"

"Christmas Gift," he said, ducking his head. She laughed at the country greeting. As the first person to use the phrase, Oliver was supposed to be able to demand a present from her. Lucky for her, she had a new tie already wrapped and ready.

"Come on in before you freeze to death."

"Thanks," he said, handing her a small package.

"Aw, Ollie, you shouldn't have. But thank you. Give me your coat."

He shrubbed out of the well-worn wool jacket and handed it over. While she put it away, he greeted the rest of the family.

Coming back, Mae said, "Come on in the kitchen, Oliver, and I'll feed you a slice of Mama's jam cake."

He winked at Mrs. Johnson. "I was hoping for that invitation. You know Mother makes that fruitcake with all the candied things in it, and I

115

really prefer a good jam cake." He smiled at Mama, and Mae was surprised when her mother actually blushed.

EIGHTEEN

FIRST KISS

"WHEN ARE YOU GOING back to town?" Oliver asked as they ate.

She poured coffee and replaced the pot on the stove. "I have to get back tonight," she replied. "Graydell and I both have to work tomorrow."

"Too bad you don't have a few days off. How are you getting back? Taking the bus?"

"No, Walt said he'd take us. He came and got us yesterday."

Oliver lifted his cup to take a sip, hoping to hide his disappointment. He had hoped to talk Mae into letting him take her home. He'd been talking to himself for the past week, trying to gather enough courage to ask her out again when he got the chance. He'd hoped that would be later today. *Oh, well, there's more than one way to skin a cat.*

"Do you have time to take a ride with me before Walt picks you up?"

"Yeah, he won't be here until five or so. Let me get our coats. If you once get set down in the living room, we'll never get away from here."

He gave thanks for her answer and stood to take his things to the sink. Wouldn't do to get on Mrs. Johnson's bad side by being an ungrateful guest.

After praising the jam cake, he shrugged into his coat and helped Mae into hers. He squeezed her shoulders lightly, hating to let go. She seemed not to notice, and he tried not to be disappointed. He picked up her package from the side table where she'd laid it.

Once outside, he sniffed the air. "I won't be surprised if we get some cold rain sometime tonight," he commented as they headed for the car. He opened the passenger door for her before she had a chance to open it herself as she usually did. Again, she thanked him—and this time, he thought she had felt something. At least he hoped so.

"Where to?" he asked. "I didn't really have any place in mind. I just wanted to spend some time with you."

"I'm so glad you did. I hate I missed the Christmas sermon at church, but I had to work last Saturday to get yesterday off, and then there was just so much to do on Sunday. The drive-in is closed today, of course, but Christmas Eve is just about my favorite part of the holiday, so Mr. Robinson let both me and Graydell off early so Walt could bring us down."

"Well, since he brought you two home, why don't we see if he wants to let me take y'all back?" This might work out, after all.

She hesitated, then said, "If you're sure. But I don't want to put you to any trouble or take you away from your family on Christmas."

He shook his head. "I really want to, Mae. I haven't even seen Graydell to wish her a Merry Christmas. So how about we start at her house?"

She beamed at him, and his heart gave a lurch. *She's so beautiful. And she has such an impish smile.*

"That sounds great to me. You're more fun than Walt."

He grinned back at her and started the car.

They drove the entire river bottoms, waving at the few neighbors they saw outside—mostly a daddy here and there supervising children at play. In a roundabout way they arrived at the church yard, and Oliver pulled in. Reaching into his coat pocket, he said, "Why don't you open your gift, Mae?"

"I didn't know you brought it," she said, accepting the package. It was wrapped in brown paper like they used at the store, but it had a beautiful green ribbon tied into a fancy bow. "Did you do this yourself?" she teased, unknotting the ribbon.

"I most certainly did . . . not," he admitted. "Prissy did it for me. But I picked the ribbon to match your eyes."

Inside was a jewel-toned scarf that slid through her fingers as she admired it. "Oh, it's beautiful! Soft as silk." She folded it into a triangle and draped it over her hair. "What do you think?"

"Yes, Maisie. Beautiful." But he was staring steadily into her eyes. *She's blushing so sweet. And I want so bad to kiss that sweet mouth.*

Before he realized it, he was doing exactly that. He held his breath as his lips moved over hers, surprised and gratified when her lips parted to him. The tip of her tongue tickled his bottom lip and he jumped back in surprise.

Mae's eyes had opened wide, as if realizing what she'd done.

He stared at her mouth hungrily, feeling a sensual grin sliding across his mouth. He wanted her to see how much he wanted her. Then his arms were around her, and his mouth was exploring hers. By the time they parted, he wasn't sure which of them was shaking more.

"Oh, Lord," she said.

"Amen," he replied.

"I think I'd best get back to the house now," she said, settling into the far corner of the seat.

"Whatever you say, Maisie," he grinned, turning the key.

* * *

Back at the boarding house, Oliver helped the girls get their packages onto the front porch and waited as Graydell searched for her key.

"I'd ask you in," Mae said, "but you know our landlady is a real grouch when it comes to guys. You would get inside the parlor, but I guarantee you wouldn't make it up the stairs."

"You don't know how good that makes me feel," he chuckled. "I know you two are in good hands." *I say that, even as I'm thinking about how I'd like to have you in my arms again.*

"Got it." Graydell pushed open the door. "Bye, Oliver. Thanks for the ride." She grabbed her packages and headed for the stairs.

Seizing his chance, Oliver hefted Mae's packages and stepped inside.

"Is that you, Mae?" Mrs. Swenson called from the parlor.

"Yes, ma'am," Mae answered, giving Oliver a crestfallen look. "I'll be back in a minute." She pushed Oliver out the door and closed it behind her. "Is it too cold for us to sit outside?"

"Not a bit," he said, plopping down in the swing. "Come sit with me."

"Thanks for bringing us home. You're such a good friend. I know Graydell appreciates you, too, even if she didn't exactly say so. Something's been eating at her lately, and I don't know what."

"She doesn't bother me. I know how Graydell can be when something's on her mind."

Mae nodded. "Of course you do. We've met so many new people in the last few months, I forget sometimes that I don't have to explain her to everybody."

They swung gently and in silence for a couple of minutes. Oliver finally got up enough nerve to ask her what he'd been wanting to ask all week, whenever he'd thought of this day, which was often.

"So, Maisie, are you ready to go out with me now? I hope what happened earlier will make you say yes."

"I've thought about this a lot, Oliver. I'll agree to go out with you on one condition."

His heart flip-flopped. "Anything," he breathed.

She laughed. "You don't know what I'm gonna ask." He shook his head as if to say it didn't matter, and she went on. "You have to promise me we'll take it slow, and if it starts to feel too weird, we'll go back to being just friends, and no more dating."

He made a crisscross motion over his heart, but he couldn't believe that would happen, not after those kisses. "Promise. But you have to promise me something, too."

"Maybe. What is it?"

"You have to promise you'll give us a real chance. And you'll have to let me know how you're feeling, so I don't go stepping on your toes or anything."

"Promise."

"Seal it with a kiss?" he asked, staring at her lips.

Mae swallowed hard. "Don't think I'm ready for another one just yet."

"Take it easy. I only meant. . ." He leaned forward and planted a kiss on her cheek. "Good night, Maisie. Sweet dreams." He stood and jumped straight off the porch instead of using the steps, then hopped onto the sidewalk, jammed his hands into his pockets, and whistled his way to his car. He didn't look back.

"Well, I never," Mae said, watching him drive away.

* * *

Christmas night 1941

I'm not quite sure how it happened, but I just agreed to start dating Oliver. I know! One of my two best friends in the world. What is happening? The world has gone to war and I'm agreeing to start going out with a guy who's been like a big brother to me for most of my life. But I'll tell you one thing, Diary. I'm going to give this a real chance. Know why? Because when he kissed me this afternoon, my insides went all mushy! Call me crazy, but I think he's beginning to grow on me.

NINETEEN

MISTER J.T.

WINTER THAT YEAR WAS long and hard, and Mae missed the coziness of the fireplace and wood heater at home. January brought an ice storm that kept them all indoors for a solid week, with no way to get to work and no customers if they'd managed it.

April brought the proverbial showers, but Easter weekend turned out to be warm and sunny, so after begging, pleading, and finally bribing the other two carhops to work that Saturday, the girls hopped on the bus and headed home to Dixon's Crossing. It seemed so long since Mae had seen all of her family, and she looked forward to helping color Easter eggs for the kids to find. She had brought a new book for Thomas's kids. *Bambi* was the story of a young deer, and it sounded so interesting that she spent part of her bus ride reading it. She was in tears by the end of the book, and ready to preach to her menfolk about deer hunting. Moreover, she knew she'd have a hard time ever eating venison again.

She also had a hard time concentrating in church on Sunday morning. She kept looking around at the empty spots where boys she knew were missing—already enlisted or drafted, and off to basic training. Thank the Lord Oliver hadn't gone yet, but she knew he could get called up any day. She might not even know it until she came back for a visit. No, surely he'd be able to say goodbye to her before he left. She cast a quick glance at him, up on the first row of benches with the few young men who were left. She hated seeing any of the boys go off to get ready for fighting in this war but dreaded losing Oliver to the army above them all. She just might be falling in love with him. It wasn't fair.

Besides all the missing men, there was the one man right up front who Mae held such hatred for. She had made it through last year's graduation ceremony by keeping her eyes on the outcome: her diploma and her ability to get out of Dixon's Crossing and away from Mr. J.T. She had always disliked the man, but since the year she turned sixteen she had detested him so thoroughly that she now found it difficult to sit through church services while he was there taking part. Today he was serving as song leader, which meant her eyes bored holes in the pages of her hymnal just so she could avoid even accidentally meeting his gaze. As the congregation started into the second song of the morning, Mae couldn't keep her mind from reliving the day that had shaken her world.

It was an early summer afternoon when it happened. The day was beautiful—a perfect day for washing clothes. Mae and Mrs. Wheeler had got an early start, and the sheets had dried by lunchtime. Mae had managed to get each one half-folded by the time she dropped it into the willow basket. Mrs. Wheeler had come along behind her, hanging out the family's personals. She liked to be in charge of those things, and that was fine with Mae. She hated doing Mr. J.T.'s laundry, but money was money—and Mrs. Wheeler seemed to really care a lot for Mae.

"Honey, why don't you take the linens on in and start the ironing. I'm going to sit out front and rest while I watch Hope playing. Day's too beautiful to be inside."

For the boss lady, but not for the hired help. Mae did her best to stifle the resentment. She could be hoeing cotton, and that would be so much worse. She took just a moment to look around before she stepped inside. It really was a gorgeous day. The few white mare's tail clouds were headed east, and they would leave behind just the intense blue sky. To the west, the sky had faded to a blue that reminded her of something . . . *Of course. Oliver's icy blue eyes. And I've never seen anybody with eyes as blue as that eastern sky.*

Lord, what a day you've given us! The blues of the sky, the fresh green of the leaves of the oaks in the front yard where Hope has her swing. I wish we had some nice shade trees like that, and a few of those pecan trees wouldn't hurt, either. She shook herself out of her reverie and opened the screen door, wrestling the basket inside and letting the door slap shut behind her.

Laying the first sheet she came to onto the bed and unfolding it, she began to flick water droplets onto each layer from the sprinkler bottle—a large-sized Coca Cola bottle with a perforated stopper in it. She wanted to put a nice, crisp press onto the sheets.

She loved Mrs. Wheeler's sheets. At her house, every sheet was white, and Mama didn't spare the bleach, determined to keep them white. But the Wheelers had beautiful sheets, several sets for each bed. And percale. They hardly needed ironing. And they were colored. This week, Mr. and Mrs. Wheeler's sheets were a light blue, much like today's western sky. Little Hope's were baby pink, to match just about everything in her bedroom.

"I think I'd rather be chopping cotton than ironing these sheets," she grumbled. But she put her muscle into wrestling with the sheets, glad there were only four to do. Finishing the pink set, she went to Hope's room, where she made quick work of setting the girl's bed to rights. Straightening, she gazed around for a moment, proud of the job she'd done.

"Back to work," she muttered, heading back down the hall. She took her time now, because she knew how Mrs. Wheeler felt about beds being made up well. She reached to the shelf where Mrs. Wheeler kept the small bottle of lavender oil. She was adding a few drops to the sprinkler bottle when she heard him behind her.

"So, this is the reason my bed always smells so sweet."

"Mr. J.T.! I didn't hear you come in." She replaced the stopper and sprinkled a blue sheet, then started ironing again. She hoped he'd be on his way. The way he looked at her sometimes, when no one was around, made her skin crawl.

He didn't leave. "You're turning into quite a young woman," he said, coming to stand so close behind her she could smell his mixture of tobacco and field sweat. He touched his nose to her neckline and drew in a long breath. "My God, girl, you smell as good as my bed," he growled, putting his hands to her waist.

"Please, Mr. J.T.," she said, not knowing quite what she was begging for.

"I saw you on the bridge the other day—you and that Cummings whelp. I saw what he was doing to you—and right out in the open. I saw him put his hands on you—like this." His hands slipped around to cup her breasts. He kneaded the mounds and asked, "Did it feel good, Mae? Did it feel this good?" And he squeezed, hard.

She laid the iron on its stand, even though what she really wanted to do was to slam it against his groping hands. But she knew better. Her family would be off his place with nowhere to go and no work to do. But how to defuse this horrible situation? She gave the heavy wooden ironing board a shove and twisted out and down, away from his filthy hands.

"Stop it!" she cried, backing away across the room. "Leave me alone."

"Just trying to show you how a real man does it, missy." He reached down and began to rub himself, his black eyes boring into hers. "You two have probably been going at it for a while now. Wouldn't you like to find out how a real man pleasures his woman?"

She realized she had backed herself into a corner with no way of escape. Her eyes darted around the room, frantically seeking a way out, but he continued to advance toward her, a sick smile on his face. A moment before he reached her— *Sweet Jesus!* —she heard the front screen door slam and Mrs. Wheeler call, "Mae, come and help me, please! Hope fell asleep in my arms, and I can't carry her much longer."

"Coming!" Mae called, staring up into Mr. J.T.'s mottled face. "Let me by," she hissed.

He grabbed her by one arm and swung her around. "One word of this, and you and your whole family will be in the Poor Farm. Understand?"

She jerked her arm away and ran. Seizing Hope from her mother's arms, she stumbled to the pink and white bedroom and laid the sleeping child on her coverlet. Mrs. Wheeler followed more slowly. "Thank you, Mae. You're a dear. I can't get over how she's grown these past few months. Why, it seems like just yesterday—"

"Mrs. Wheeler, I don't feel so good. Can I go on home?"

Mrs. Wheeler felt her forehead. "What's wrong, child? You don't seem to have a fever."

"Maybe something I had for breakfast. But I need to go. I'm sorry about your sheets."

"Of course. Get some rest. Send someone over if there's anything you need." Mae hugged her and left the room, mumbling her thanks. She couldn't get away from that house fast enough, but then as she drew closer to home, she slowed her pace, letting her breathing return to normal.

What in God's name was he trying to do? Was he trying to scare me into letting him do whatever he wanted? Well, that's not gonna work. I'd much rather tell Mama and Daddy what he did than for him to have that power over me. No, sir, Mr. J.T.

But what am I to do about working there? She flung herself down by the gate post at the lane that would take her back home. Staring across the fields, she saw Daddy bent over the knee-high cotton stalks, rhythmically hoeing weeds. After a bit, she got her breathing under control, and returned to her problem. *I'll just have to have my guard up, always. I can't let him catch me not paying attention again. I can't stop working there. Mama would never let me do that without a good reason. I have a good reason; I just can't tell it.*

Not ever.

What a dirty old man! Mrs. Wheeler must be a saint to put up with him. But she may not even know. I've heard Mama and some of her friends gossiping about one man or another in the community. Apparently married men straying from their vows happens more often than I'd have thought. So much for romance.

Honestly, she hadn't thought about that much at all, not when she was younger. She'd sure the hell be watching out for it now. She rose, swept the dry river dust off her backside, and walked the rest of the way home. Seeing Mama in the garden picking purple hull peas, she maneuvered herself around to the front door so she wouldn't be seen.

In her room, she sat down on the bed and reached for her diary.

What do you think you're doing? What if somebody got their hands on this? I don't mind if they read about Frank kissing me—but this could cause a scandal my family might never recover from. No, I've just got to handle this on my own.

She shoved the little book back into its drawer and lay down on her side, curling into a ball.

The next time she went to work for Mrs. Wheeler, she did a bit of rearranging. She moved the ironing board to the other side of the roomy bedroom where she'd have an escape route if Mr. J.T. ever came in again. She also kept her mind on her business so he couldn't sneak up on her again so easily.

And she never told a soul what happened. Not even Graydell, her best friend in the world.

Mae roused herself from that awful memory to find the congregation singing the closing hymn. *Lot of good it did me to come to church today.*

Dinner on the grounds after church was as good as usual. There was plenty of fried chicken and roast to go around, and canned vegetables. Mr. J.T. had provided the beef for the occasion, and Mae stuck to chicken, fearing beef donated by that man would choke her for sure.

"I've missed having fried chicken on a regular basis," she said to Prissy as they sat on a quilt in their favorite spot under the biggest oak tree's shade.

"Oh? So not everything about living in the city is better than living here?" Prissy's acerbic reply told Mae her friend hadn't quite forgiven her yet for moving to town.

"Well, no, not everything. But Prissy! There's so much to do there. I mean, we can go to the movies almost any time we want to, and dancing at the nightclubs is one of my favorite things to do. You would love it, I know you would."

"Maybe so. But I would not love living around so many people, especially since they'd all be strangers."

"Not everybody is a stranger, Prissy. There's always me." Graydell settled in beside them. "And really, we've met some awfully nice people. You just have to get out there and make friends. Not everybody can be satisfied just knowing the same people forever."

Prissy huffed and turned her face away. Clearly their friend didn't share their views on good living.

"Room for me?" Oliver asked. His plate was so loaded with food Mae wondered where he'd begin eating and how on earth he would put away so much food.

"Always, Ollie," she said, scooting over a bit so he could sit beside her.

Prissy studied the two of them from underneath her thick lashes. *Gosh, I hope Prissy's not planning a wedding shower. That girl's a born matchmaker.*

Mae, tell Oliver and Prissy about your visit to the shoe store the other day." Graydell was smirking around her glass of tea.

Mae felt herself blushing, but when Prissy said, "Yeah, Mae. What did you get?" she knew she couldn't dodge talking about it. She was on the spot.

"Nothing, Prissy." The girl wrinkled her brow, but Mae explained. "Last Tuesday, we heard they'd gotten a new shipment of shoes in down at Watson's. I hurried down there as soon as I got up Wednesday. Things were already pretty well picked over."

"Aw, shucks," Prissy said, wrinkling her nose.

"Then I spotted this pair of bright, cardinal-red high heeled shoes on a stand at the other side of the store. Well, you know me." They all laughed. "I made a bee line for those shoes. Got over there and grabbed one, and it was my size. Looked up to get the other, and this other girl was holding it and looking at the one in my hand.

"Well, I haven't had a new pair of shoes since I turned sixteen, when my feet finally stopped growing—and I really wanted those shoes. But she did, too. So we did the only logical thing. We—"

"Got out in the middle of Broad Street and duked it out!" Graydell chimed in. They all laughed at her.

"Did not. We flipped for them. She won. I was devastated." She shrugged. "But I let her have them without a fight."

"I think that's pretty grown up of you," Prissy said, patting her on the knee. "There was a time when you'd have fought her for them instead."

"Maybe I'm growing up a bit," Mae said, taking a bite of her chicken and hoping this part of the conversation was finished.

TWENTY

GOOD FRIENDS, BAD NEWS, & "RED SHOES"

"THE CLUB IS REALLY jumping tonight," Mae said to Graydell as they stood just inside the door. All the tables were occupied, but most held only a couple of people, as most of the patrons were out on the floor dancing to "Sing, Sing, Sing."

Graydell shimmied her shoulders. "Yeah, and I can't wait to get out there."

Mae scanned the tables, looking for familiar faces. When she spied Morris beckoning to them, she grabbed Graydell's elbow and began weaving their way through the crowd.

"Hey, gals, good to see you!" Morris said, enveloping them both in a brief hug. "The whole gang's here now."

When the song ended, Mae saw this was true. They were joined by Oliver and, surprising to Mae, Prissy.

"Prissy Thibodeaux, what are you doing here?" she said, jumping up to hug her friend. "It's so good to see you out on the town."

Prissy hugged her back. "Mae, I've missed you so much. It is deader than a doornail back home without y'all."

"Well, I'm glad you finally realized that," Mae laughed.

Oliver gave her a hug, too, then included Graydell in his greeting.

"Prissy and I got to talking after church Wednesday night, and we decided to come up here and surprise y'all. We stopped by the Dixie Drive-In first, but the girl who came to our car said you both had the night off. She seemed a bit peeved about that, as a matter of fact."

Mae laughed and winked at Graydell. "Teresa will never figure out how I finagled that. I've got a real friend in Miss Dora, the owner's wife." She punched Oliver in the chest. "Anyway, I'm glad y'all picked this night to come to Texarkana. We don't get many weekend nights off together."

"I'm glad, too," Oliver murmured.

They all settled in for a much-needed reunion, one that appeared to be a one-time-only affair, much to Mae's consternation.

"Yeah, got my orders a week ago," Morris said. "I'm headed overseas in two days. So much for law school." He shrugged his shoulders. "I'll get there someday, though. Just have to take care of this Hirohito fella first."

"Hirohito!" Mae said. "You don't mean to tell me that you. . . that you. . ." She couldn't seem to get the rest of the words out.

"I thought you knew I'd enlisted in the Navy. I don't intend to wait around to be slogging through mud and muck all across Europe when they extend the draft—as they surely will. No sir. I'm going to take this war to the Japs in their own territory. I don't know how long it'll take, or where I'll end up, but I intend to be there when we make them pay for what they did at Pearl Harbor. Maybe I'll even get to see that place someday—pay my respects, you know."

The mood at the table turned somber with Morris's pronouncement. Mae couldn't stand the change. She longed for the days before Pearl Harbor, when Morris was heading to Missouri instead of the Pacific. Suddenly she had to get away from here.

"Hey, Oliver," she said, squaring around and taking his hand. "Dance with me?"

His eyes opened wide and he smiled. "Sure, Mae." They stood and headed to the dance floor, just as the next song came on the jukebox—"I'll Be Seeing You."

Oh, Lord, what a sad song. Guess that'll be Morris' new theme song.

Oliver held out his arms and Mae slid into them, just as she had so many times before. It seemed to be the most natural thing in the world for him to hold her close, and she leaned back in his arms so she could see his face.

"I hate this war." she said. "It's taking all our friends from us. And we don't have any assurance that Morris will ever come back. It's just so—"

"I know, Maisie. Believe me, I know."

Something in his voice caused her to stop dead still. She searched his eyes for something, anything, to give her some kind of reassurance, but it wasn't there.

"Oliver, please don't tell me . . ."

He nodded, and she felt a twitch as he clasped her tighter by the waist. "Keep dancing, Maisie. I haven't told the others."

"Told them what?" But she already knew.

"I got my draft notice a few days ago. And I'm sure I'll pass the physical. I have to report Monday morning back here in Texarkana. I could be leaving in a matter of weeks. I'm basing that on how the other guys have experienced the draft."

She couldn't continue to look into his dear face. *Not Oliver. Morris is bad enough—but not Oliver.*

She laid her cheek against his shoulder and closed her eyes, feeling the stiffness of his shirt and breathing in the familiar scent of starch. He continued moving them slowly around the fringes of the dance floor as the song's lyrics swirled around them, enveloping them in a smoky haze, insulating them from the outside world, and from their friends within—just for a while longer.

I wish this song would never end. I can't go back to that table and listen while Oliver tells everyone he, too, is leaving.

Against the top of her head, Oliver said, "I wanted you to know first, Mae, before anybody else. My folks know, of course, but that's really why Prissy and I came tonight. She was my excuse to see you, to tell you about it."

"Ollie, you are just too sweet. And you're good, and kind, and—"

"Stop, Mae. You're making me sound like a blue tick hound."

That was just the response she needed to get her through this night. She sniffled, then she giggled, and he chuckled, too. So it was that they finished dancing to what must be the saddest song on the radio today, not with tears of sadness, but holding each other up as they laughed. Their friends at the table looked at them as if they were crazy.

"Hey, Oliver has some news, too," Mae said. Now she could make it. With the cover of her tears of laughter, she listened as he shared the news of his draft notice, and nobody thought much about the fact that her tears continued to flow. Nobody except Prissy, who saw through everything.

"Here's my song," Morris proclaimed, when he heard the first strains of "Boogie Woogie Bugle Boy."

"Morris, you've never even held a bugle," Mae laughed, and they all joined in, even Morris.

"Dance with me anyway," he said, coming around the table and grabbing her hand.

Mae jumped up, glad for the diversion. On the floor, though, she got more diversion than she had bargained for. Spinning around the floor with Morris, she caught a glimpse of the girl from the shoe store—and she was wearing the red shoes! She was dancing with a guy Mae had never seen in the club, and when he spun her around, Mae waved to her. A glimmer of recognition, and the girl lifted a hand.

Mae watched their dancing, growing more upset by the second. *He's putting his hands all over her. Wonder if that's her fella. She shouldn't be allowing that behavior, anyway.*

Soon she had her answer. The girl was trying her best to keep smiling, but she was also trying, without much success, to fight off the guy's fast hands. Mae kept an eye on the couple, even managing to maneuver Morris closer to them. She could see now the girl was no longer smiling but was fighting off tears.

"Hold on, Morris," she said. "I've got to take care of something." She strode over to the couple, Morris following close behind, and tapped the girl on the shoulder.

"Hey, honey, are you okay? This guy bothering you?"

She saw gratitude on the girl's face, but before she could answer, the guy said, "Butt out, sister. We're just fine here."

What a bozo. Mae saw red. She drew herself up to her full five foot six and stepped into the guy's face.

"I'll believe that when *she* tells me, Bozo," she said. She hadn't felt this kind of excitement since the day she and this girl had both gone after those red shoes.

Morris jumped in at this point. "Buster, don't be talking to my friend like that."

"You can both take a hike," Bozo said. "C'mon, baby, let's get back to our dance."

"No, I don't want to," the girl said, still trying to pull away from him.

"You heard the lady. Better take your hands off her, right now." Morris sounded more serious than Mae had ever heard him.

As the guy let go of the young woman and drew back a fist, his arm was grasped from behind in mid-swing. Oliver twisted the man's hand behind his back and walked him a few feet away. Mae hadn't even seen him approach. Dancers on all sides gave the group a wide berth.

"You don't want to make a scene, now, do you, mister? Maybe you should move along to another club," Oliver said, through gritted teeth.

"You don't give orders to me," Bozo said.

"No, but I do. And it's time for you to leave," the burly security guard growled into his ear. "Right now. And don't let me see you in here

134

again." He took over from Oliver and escorted Bozo to the door. The lout threw them a hateful glance before the guard shoved him out into the night.

The girl turned to Mae. "Gee, thanks for that. It felt like that guy had six hands. He just caught me off guard."

Mae shook her head. "No thanks needed, huh, guys?" She grinned at her two buddies. "I could have taken the guy, Oliver."

"I have no doubt," he grinned. "But I didn't want to see you get your hair all mussed." Belying his words, he reached out and tousled her hair. But then his hand gently smoothed it back into place.

The girl looked on, wide-eyed, but Mae just laughed.

"Are you here with somebody?" she asked, pretty sure she knew the answer.

"No, and I'm not sure why I'm here at all. I don't usually come to places like this, and I never come alone."

"Aw, that's okay. You're not alone anymore. Besides, I think you and I have something we need to talk about." She arched her eyebrows, looking pointedly at the young woman's bright red shoes.

She caught Mae's glance and grinned. "Maybe we do, at that."

The two guys looked at each other and shrugged.

Mae hooked her arm through the girl's and led her back to their table. "Hey, everybody, I'd like you to meet—Say, what *is* your name, anyway?"

* * *

August 2, 1942

Tonight at the club was exciting in several ways. Some good, some not so much. Oliver and Prissy dropped in to surprise us. Morris told us he'd just enlisted in the Navy and will be leaving next week. While I was dancing with Oliver, he told me he had got his draft notice and is going for his physical next week. Lord, I don't want him to go! On the other hand, I'd almost go with him if I could, if it would hurry this war along. I can't stand thinking about him going overseas! Morris, too, of course.

135

Then we almost had a brawl on the dance floor, and I was glad the guys were there to help.

I was dancing with Morris, and I saw the girl who got the red shoes a while back. This guy she was dancing with was giving her a hard time, so I went over to stop him. But Morris came with me, and then Oliver showed up, too. I still say I could have whipped him, but the guys and the bouncer took care of him.

So I finally got acquainted with Miss Laurie Lindstrom, the girl with the red shoes! She lives here in Texarkana with her parents, but she's wishing she could get her own place. There just aren't many places to be had, so she's feeling sort of stuck. I could really understand that, as bad as I was wanting to get out of Dixon's Crossing! She's got a boyfriend who's already in the service. She said she was lonesome, and she'd got in a fight with her folks because they were trying to fix her up with some doctor here in town, but she's in luv with her boyfriend. Why can't parents just leave us alone? Once we turn eighteen, we can do what we want. I mean, Laurie is nineteen, and she's been working at Red River for several months. She can do as she pleases. Sure, we owe much to our parents. After all, they've raised us. But that's my point—we're already raised now. They need to let us be the grownups we already are.

If our guys are old enough to be drafted and sent overseas to fight another world war, then we girls—excuse me, us women—should be able to go out and work, and play, and live on our own, too

TWENTY-ONE

FIRED!

"I DON'T CARE WHAT Mrs. S. says, she can't just up and raise our rent! We signed a contract." Mae eased her foot out of her roller skate and massaged her aching toes. It was break time, and she was going to take advantage of every stinking minute.

"I know we did, but would that be legally binding if she tried to evict us? I'm just not sure there wasn't some little something in there somewhere that gives her a right to get rid of us," Graydell said. Her skates were already off, and she was sitting on an unopened sack of flour in the corner of the diner's storeroom.

"Let her try. She's only getting greedy because a few of the people in the neighborhood had empty rooms when this craziness started so they can charge whatever they want."

"Yeah, and that's highway robbery," Graydell said. "I can't believe people would do other people that way."

"It's the way of the world, Grady, you know that. Look at how Mr. J.T. always does the families on his farm. Why, he runs the lives of all those people. If you want to work for him, you do things his way or else. Right?"

"Yeah, you're right. I guess I hadn't thought about it exactly that way."

"You would have if you'd been in my place. I can't tell you how many times I watched him shred people's grocery lists, giving them what *he* decided they'd be able to pay for. I griped about that often enough to you, but I guess you can't quite comprehend how bad something like that is unless you see it for yourself."

"I'm sure not," Graydell said. "Hey, let's not talk about all this right now. I have to get back out there now and start all over."

"Sounds good to me. I'm gonna take a cat nap." By this time Mae had both skates off and was reclining in the only chair in the room. "See you in ten." And she shut her eyes and was soon asleep.

* * *

Skates back on, hair again in a ponytail to get it off her sweaty neck, Mae rolled out and back to work. She'd waited on about half a dozen customers in the sticky, sweltering August afternoon when the sound of a horn startled her. She was used to car horns, even heard them in her sleep sometimes, but this one was different. A cross between a trumpet and a train whistle, it was a sound she'd never heard before.

She turned to seek out the source and was surprised to see one of her regular customers, Mr. Draper, grinning at her from the driver's seat of a pink and white Cadillac convertible. The seats were white leather and there was chrome everywhere. *How in the heck did you manage that right now? There are so many rationing things that car should be outlawed.*

"Wow, Mr. Draper! That's a really nice car! It's beautiful!" She couldn't resist touching the back of the seat and running her hand across it.

"Thanks, Mae. I was hoping you'd like it. How about goin' for a little ride with me?"

"Now, Mr. Draper, you know I can't do that. We've talked about this before. We're not supposed to get involved with any of our customers."

"Aw, Mae, you know that rule is just to keep you girls safe. They don't care if you don't."

She had moved around the car to his side and had her order book out and ready. "What can I get for you today?" She gave him her brightest smile, hoping he would get on with his order.

"You can get me you, Blondie," the man grinned. "I want you to take a ride in my new car. No joke, Mae."

"I just got off break, so that would be impossible, even if I wanted to. Which I don't," she added with asperity.

Instead of being deterred, Draper reached out and around Mae, encircling her waist with his arm and pulling her up against the car.

"Mr. Draper, please. I can't do this. I don't *want* this. C'mon, let me go."

He grabbed her wrist and pulled her over the side of the car, almost into his lap, her breast far too close to his leering face. This was too much for Mae. She threw her order book and pencil out behind her and used both hands to push herself away from the grasping man. Once she had her two feet on the ground, she adjusted her shirt. But she couldn't stop there. *This man has to learn his place.* Before she could think twice about it, she reared back and slapped him with all her might.

He froze. She froze.

What have I done? He could have me fired!

Apologize to him.

The hell I will!

Where that internal argument might have ended, and what might have been the outcome, Mae would never find out.

For at the very instant Mae swung at Draper, her boss had opened the back door and come out carrying a sack of garbage. Thus, he witnessed Mae's swing at one of his best customers, even though he completely missed the actions of that customer just prior to the slap.

In a voice that reminded Mae of her old principal, her boss yelled, "Miss Johnson, could I see you a minute?"

Still fuming, Mae took one last look at Draper, his face white with anger except for the large hand-shaped print on the left side of his face. He smirked when he saw her face. "Yeah, Mae, go on and talk to your boss."

Slowly she rolled herself down the almost empty lot.

"Yes, sir?" She would not give him the satisfaction of showing her fear.

He motioned for her to follow him inside.

"Mae, I want you to go out and apologize to Mr. Draper. Right now."

"But, Mr. Robinson, he was getting fresh with me!"

"Now, you probably just misunderstood him. He's a good customer. Go on, apologize."

"I won't. That's just not right, sir! You obviously didn't see what he was doing to me."

"I saw you slap a customer. That's enough for me to see. Right out there in broad daylight? Are you trying to tell me he was trying something in that situation?" He shook his head, as if to say it didn't matter. "Anyway, I need you to go and apologize." After all her hard work for this man, she couldn't believe what she was hearing. Her green eyes blazing, she crossed her arms and stood her ground.

"If you don't apologize, Miss Johnson, I'm going to have to let you go."

"What? You mean you're going to *fire* me?"

Graydell, coming in the back door, heard this, and her eyes grew round.

When Robinson just stared at her, his face the color of the Coca Cola sign that sat atop the building, Mae made a quick decision.

"You can't fire me! I quit!" Standing on one unsteady roller-skated foot, she fumbled with the laces on the other shoe. Jerking it off at last, she flung it aside. Then she repeated the process with the other foot. Grabbing both skates, she marched to the back of the parking lot and raised the lid on the large trash can. She slammed her skates into the bin and turned back to face him.

140

His face was so red she thought he might have a stroke. At the moment she didn't much care. The very idea that he wouldn't listen to her made her livid. When she turned and saw Draper smirking, her anger intensified.

Graydell had been watching with her mouth open. Now she made her move.

She skated out to where Mae stood at the open door, chest heaving. Sitting down on the ground, she worked both her skates off. Then she said, loud enough for the boss to hear, "If Mae goes, I go, too. We're a team. Best friends. You just picked on the wrong girl, sir." With that pronouncement, Graydell stood, skates in hand, and looked to Mae.

Oh, no, Grady, no. Don't do it because of me.

"I quit, too!" Graydell's skates followed Mae's into the trash. "Come on, Mae, let's get our things and get out of here. We're too good for this place."

Mae gulped. *I should have listened to those hookers!*

TWENTY-TWO

OUTSIDERS -- HAH!

AUGUST 15, 1942

I sure fixed things up good today. This customer at work got fresh with me and I hauled off and slapped him. He had it coming, but Robinson saw me and ordered me to apologize to him. The nerve! Wouldn't even listen to my explanation. I felt like I was back in high school all over again. So I quit when he fired me. I saw that in a movie a few months ago and I guess it stuck in my head, cause that's what came out of my mouth—You can't fire me, I quit."

I'm not sorry. Yes, I am. Because, now what do I do? I am not going back to that farm with my tail tucked between my legs. Especially not now, when there is so much going on here in Texarkana. The new ammunition places have brought lots of new, interesting people to town. Wages are going up. But people have come out of the woodwork looking for jobs, too. What's a poor girl to do? I don't want to be a farm wife!!!

And it's not just about me. Graydell quit, too. That was very loyal of her, but I feel so guilty that she's out of a job as well. Besides, now there are two of us who don't have money to pay the rent. Bet Mrs. S. will be tickled pink that we have to move out. Now she can up her prices and take in lots more money—

142

"Lord, Mae, don't you ever do anything but write in that diary?" Graydell said as she blew into the room and flounced onto her bed.

"I needed to write about today. I have no idea what to do now. And, Graydell, I'm so sorry I dragged you into my mess."

"You didn't drag me into anything, honey. I quit of my own accord. I had had just about enough of bossy, spoiled customers, anyway. Robinson was okay as a boss at first, but lately he's got caught up in the whole 'more money' thing, and I'd already had a bad day with him before your situation came up."

"But . . . what do we do now? I am not going back to that farm! Not now, not this way."

"Now? Why, we're going to go out and have a night on the town. Best way I know of to get over an upset. So get up, and get dressed up." She slapped Mae on the leg as she passed on her way to the chifforobe in the corner.

Mae closed her little red book and tucked it under her pillow. "I'm not in the mood to go out," she said, sighing. "I think I'll just stay here and mope around tonight. See if I can come up with any ideas about where to look for a job tomorrow."

"Nope. Not acceptable. We're going to the Jump and Jive, and we're going to find some guys and dance the night away." She shimmied her shoulders and winked at Mae. "Best cure for the blues. Come on. Get up."

"Well, it is Tuesday night, so there shouldn't be a crowd there. Oh, but what do I care? If I have to move back to Dixon's Crossing, I'll never see any of my new friends again anyway."

"Get your butt off that bed, Johnson. You don't sound at all like the girl I knew in school, the girl who was going to make her own way in the world, the girl who refused to be put into a boxy tenant farmer's shack. We'll worry about tomorrow, tomorrow. Tonight we're going to have a high old time." Graydell tossed a bright red dress to Mae—the first clothing purchase Mae had made when she saved enough money. "How about this?"

Mae looked at her friend, now rummaging through clothes for something for herself. "Sure, that's okay. May be the last time I get to wear it for a long time." *It's not exactly church material.*

* * *

An hour later they were walking through the doors at the Jump and Jive. "I'll Never Smile Again" was playing on the jukebox. *Oh, yeah, this is going to be a fun night.* But she squared her shoulders and sashayed into the room as if without a care in the world.

She and Graydell were greeted by Ray, who insisted they join him and some of his friends at a table in the corner. Mae was just as happy to oblige, for, after her somewhat grand entrance, her mood had once again shifted to one of melancholy. She perked up a bit when she saw that one of the people at the table they were being steering toward was Charles Graham, one of the Goodrich supervisors who'd been eating occasional meals at the drive-in.

Charles and Mae had struck up an unlikely friendship on his very first visit to the drive-in, because Mae being Mae, she had determined to make this Yankee see that people in the South were friendly and helpful to a fault. It hadn't started that way.

"Say, where does a fellow go in this town to find a good shoe repair shop?" he had asked her when she brought him his tray of food. "I would know right where to go back in Akron, but I have no idea about Texarkana. Any suggestions?"

Mae had laughed at first, thinking this was one of the corniest lines she'd ever heard in her life. "Mister, where did you learn your pickup line—watching some guy at the movie theater?"

Charles had looked at her askance. "Pardon? I was wondering about where I might go to get these shoes re-soled." He held up a pair of well-worn loafers and turned them so she could see how hard the shoes had been worn down. "Best pair of loafers I ever owned. I'd much rather fix the old than buy new and have to break them in."

"Now, there's a fella after my own heart," Mae had blurted out; then, realizing how she'd sounded, she felt heat on her neck as she reddened.

Charles had laughed out loud at her. Then, as if to ease her embarrassment, he had added, "My wife is great about taking care of things like this for me, but they sent us down here in such a hurry all I had time to do was grab these and throw them in the suitcase. So, do you know of some place I can try?"

Impressed that the man had made a casual reference to his wife, Mae said, "There's a little place just a couple of blocks from here," and had proceeded to give him directions.

A couple of weeks later, he had stopped in again. Grinning at her, he held up the shoes, newly re-soled and shining like Sunday. From that moment on, they had been friends. In spare moments at work, Mae had learned that his wife was back home in Akron, Ohio, that he had been with B.F. Goodrich for seven years, that he was twenty-seven, that they had one little boy but hoped to have at least three, and that he missed his wife terribly. Most important, never once did he hit on her.

Then they had met up here at the J&J. Charles and a few of the other executives from Goodrich had been tasked with getting Lone Star up and running. Unfortunately, the situation when they first arrived wasn't quite what they'd expected. As Mae and Graydell settled in at the table now, he was telling an apparent newcomer about their experience.

"We were sent down here to run this thing," he said, shaking his head, "and there was nothing to run! First time we went out to Lone Star, the day after we arrived, was a sobering experience. I had expected to be here for perhaps two to three months—but now it's been almost a year! Thank goodness we're getting close to going into production."

"Yes, I'm excited to be getting here at just the right time. God knows, I'm ready to get down to business in a calm environment after my last assignment."

"Oh, yeah? Where was that?" Mae asked.

He held out his hand. "We haven't been introduced, Miss . . ." He smiled at her. "I don't enjoy talking to strangers all that much. Name's Yates. Scotty Yates."

She gave his hand her farm girl's grip, noting the uptick in his eyebrow. Good, she'd surprised him. "Mae Johnson."

"You were asking about my last job. I was in Orange, Texas, down on the Gulf Coast. Ever been there?"

"No, but a couple of guys I went to school with have gone down there to do some welding in the shipyards."

"I was there doing liaison work for Goodrich on a job they were looking at doing. It didn't take me long to figure out I wasn't welcome."

"What did you do, rob a bank or something?" Mae grinned at him. "By the way, welcome to the Ark-La-Tex, Scotty."

He threw back his head and laughed. "Nope. Nothing like that. All I had to do was open my damn Yankee mouth. The people there are fed up with outsiders coming in and filling up all their restaurants and movie theaters. Among other things. There was an article in the paper while I was there that said the majority of locals heartily resented us outsiders. Let's just say I wasn't sorry to turn my back on Orange, Texas."

"You won't find that sort of reaction here," Charles said. "There are probably a few folks who would be just as happy if things went back to the way they were, but most of the people I've met are so glad for the influx of industry and cash that they'd put up with us Yanks for the rest of their days."

"That's good to know. How's the personnel situation coming along?"

"Lots of people have applied. But one of the main things Goodrich wants to do is put local people to work as much as possible. This region has been severely impacted by the Depression, and the government has stressed that they want to help the people who live here rather than helping workers from other parts of the country come here to work and send their paychecks back home to people in other states."

"That's admirable of the government, and Goodrich. But tell me, Charles, can the people here do the kind of work we need them to do?" Scotty asked.

"Yes, I believe with the proper training we can develop a decent work force here. This is, after all, work the country desperately needs to have done. I'm sure people here will do their best once we get them hired on."

"Good to hear. I know the education level here leaves something to be desired."

Mae had listened to all of this talk she could take. "Listen, people. I'm getting tired of y'all talking about us as if we're too stupid to work in your big facility and too dumb to realize you're talking about us right in front of us!"

"Calm down, Mae. Scotty here hasn't had a chance to get to know you southerners like I have," Charles said.

"No, sir. You don't get off either! You've been answering his questions, talking right across my face practically. What's wrong with asking *me* whether I can do that work? Why is he asking *you*? You people," she pointed her finger at Scotty, "have a pretty high opinion of yourselves. You come in here and start analyzing us right in our faces and then wonder why the people of Orange didn't like you? Well, I can give you a few reasons. Go on, ask me!"

She gave him no chance to, though. She jerked her arm away when Charles reached for her. "I'm leaving, Graydell. I won't listen to such snobbery, and I won't be treated with such disrespect. You coming, or are you okay with their behavior?"

She stood, and so did Charles. "Mae, please listen. You're right. You're right and I'm sorry. We were rude and inconsiderate. Forgive an ignorant Yankee?"

She was fuming, her chest heaving. She stared at him, her eyes shooting daggers into his, "I'll think about it. But not tonight. Graydell?"

Graydell looked from Mae to the dance floor and back to Mae. "Yeah, let's go. This whole day and night have just been a disaster." She glanced around the table. "Maybe all you Goodrich people aren't as great as I thought you were." She snatched up her purse and linked arms with Mae on the way out the door.

TWENTY-THREE

LONE STAR

"WHO DO THEY THINK they are?" They were back in the apartment and Mae was pacing back and forth in front of Graydell, who was on the couch with her knees drawn up to her chest. "Oh, right. They're *engineers*. God's gift to the South, the poor, backward South. They're here to save us from ourselves. *Can* we do the work. Damn right we can! How do I know? Because we have brains and we know how to use them. That means we can learn to do anything anybody else can learn to do. Besides, we've dealt with more adversity in the last few years than they have in their entire privileged lives!" She whirled around and looked at Graydell, who was now getting ready for bed. "And I know just how to show them what we're made of."

Graydell was in her nightgown and had begun brushing her thick raven hair. Her brush paused in midair. "I've heard that sound in your voice before. It usually means something drastic is about to happen. What are you planning?"

Mae laughed and went to take the brush from Graydell's hand. She began to brush her friend's hair, gazing off into the distance. "Oh, nothing much. But you need to get a good night's sleep, Grady. Tomorrow morning

149

the Dixon's Crossing girls are going to take on the B.F. Goodrich Corporation and the Lone Star Ordnance Plant."

* * *

They waited half an hour for a bus to Lone Star the next morning. The rattletrap old bus, one Texarkana had bought from the 1933 Chicago World's Fair, had a breakdown on the way to the plant, something other passengers told them wasn't uncommon.

The bus dropped them at the front gate, and the other passengers hurried past them after showing their badges. The man at the tiny guard house then turned to the two girls, directing them on up the paved driveway to the administration building. "There's a new one being built, but for now you just go to that house on the right up there." This was a large wooden building that looked to have been a family home before becoming the first building one met when entering Lone Star's property. It shone in the morning sunlight, its recently painted clapboard exterior giving out a friendly feeling.

"Wonder what happened to the people who lived here," Mae remarked. "Whatever, they were probably landowners, from the looks of things, so I'm sure they found another place to live."

"Eventually," Graydell added.

Inside the building, they joined a line of people waiting to see the woman at the front desk. Mae took in the woman's dark navy suit with its long-sleeved white blouse, lace trim erupting from wrists and throat. Red button earrings and a rhinestone flag shoulder pin completed her outfit, and her hair was held in a severe bun at the base of her neck. *Bet she never loses her cool.*

It took about ten minutes to make their way to the front of the line, since each person had to write down their name and address, plus some additional information. Some seemed to take more time than others, as they asked numerous questions which the receptionist couldn't—or wouldn't—answer.

When Mae's turn came, she quickly filled in her information and smiled at the receptionist, moving aside for Graydell, who echoed Mae's response to the section titled, "Type of Position Applying For" by writing in "Production or Office."

"Do you think we'd really have a shot at office work?" Graydell whispered when they'd moved to the edge of the room to wait.

"Probably not, but might as well offer," Mae said with a wink.

When everyone had signed in, "Miss Cool" left the room with her lengthy list. A short while later, a man in a dark gray business suit entered the room. "Listen up, everybody. I'm going to call your names in several different groups and tell you which building to report to next. There will be three groups." He then called ten names and directed this first group to a nearby building. There were fifteen names in the second group, including Mae and Graydell. Mae heaved a sigh of relief that they'd move on together. They left behind a large group of about thirty.

Their next stop was a long building with a large waiting area at the end where they entered. They were called back one at a time to various rooms. Here they were turned every which way but loose, as Mae would later describe it. Finally, they ended up together again, in another waiting room. Only eight of the fifteen made it to this spot, and they smiled shyly at each other, murmuring among themselves while they waited to see what was next.

"Miss Upton, if you'd come with me," someone called. Graydell looked at Mae, who gave her a bright smile of encouragement. One by one, they were called from the room, and Mae was left alone. *Huh. Saving the best for last, I guess.*

Finally, her time came. She prayed she was ready for whatever came next. She'd heard enough talk around the tables at the club to be prepared for her next test. *Dexterity. I remember Charles saying once that if you made it to the dexterity test, all you had to do was take your time— but not too much—and you'd be fine. If you passed, you'd get hired.* She took a deep breath, listened to the instructions, and plowed in.

From there she moved to yet another waiting room—these seemed to be endless in number—where she was happy to see Graydell seated with six others.

"One of us didn't make it, I guess," Graydell mouthed, and Mae hugged her friend.

"Never mind. We did," she whispered. They took seats in the folding chairs and settled in to wait. Again.

After an hour's wait, during which time Mae's stomach betrayed the fact she'd left without breakfast, the group was shepherded down the street to the largest building they'd seen yet. Here they were congratulated and issued a pamphlet filled with rules and regulations. They moved to another room, this one filled with workstations where individuals waited to process them in to working for the government. Nor were they the only ones. The room was filled with people, all kinds of people: men and women, young and old, some looking completely down on their luck, others looking none the worse for wear. Here they got their pictures taken (for badges), were fingerprinted (*like criminals*), and gathered up the myriad pamphlets and slips of paper that told them what Uncle Sam expected of them.

Finished with all that, Mae and Graydell were moved into a smaller group of half a dozen who finally heard their orders for reporting to work. Both girls would begin their government employment in Area B, where they would be doing something extremely important for their country and for their Allies in Europe, whatever that might turn out to be.

Leaving the base that afternoon, Mae gloated, "Let the Goodrich guys put that in their pipes and smoke it."

"Tell 'em, Mae."

"I will. Just as soon as we get home and freshen up. One more night on the town, Grady?"

"Hell, yeah!"

Back at the J&J, they couldn't wait for the Goodrich crew to show up so they could tell their news.

"You don't say!" Charles exclaimed when he heard. "Good for you. I'd been thinking I should see about getting you on. But I'm proud of you for going after it yourselves."

"It was all Mae's idea," Graydell said, patting her friend on the shoulder. "She is so determined not to ever go back—"

"Back home where I'd just be in the way," Mae broke in, giving Graydell a signal to say no more. She didn't want to talk about her old life with these new friends. Not now. Maybe not ever. Not after the run-in she'd had with them last night. She was ready to let go of the past, now that she had a job again, one she'd gotten on her own.

"So, you're going to be in Area B, huh?" Charles broke into her thoughts. "I might see you sometime next week. I'm still moving around a lot at the plant. Just do your best, whatever your jobs are. We're not into production yet, but we will be very soon. Listen and learn, and you'll do just fine."

"Now, come and dance with me, Mae," Scotty said. "You can talk shop later."

She shrugged and went toward the dance floor with him, still unsure how she felt about this newcomer.

TWENTY-FOUR

CALM BEFORE THE STORM

MONDAY MORNING JUST AFTER six, the girls were at the bus stop down the block from their boarding house. The morning was cool, the sun having just risen, but the cloudless sky promised to make it another hot summer day.

"I haven't been up this early since that time a couple of months ago when I stayed out all night with George and we had breakfast before I came home," Graydell mumbled. "That was lots more fun."

"Hush, Graydell. Just be glad we have a job to go to. I for one am extremely happy. I won't be having to go back home to the farm and explain what happened to my job."

"You're right about that, I guess." As the bus stopped in front of them, Graydell said, "Watch out, Lone Star. Here we come."

The days and weeks passed in a flurry of activity as Mae and Graydell struggled to make a place for themselves at Lone Star. One difficulty was that no ammunition-making was yet taking place at the facility.

They were moving crates from one storage area to another one day when Charles caught up with them. "Hey there, girls, listen up!" he called as he strode down the warehouse floor toward them.

They turned to look at him. His eyes were sparkling, and he wore a huge grin.

"What's got you so all-fired excited?" Mae asked.

"Well, Mae, I'll tell you. Area F is ready to go into production. And as of next Monday, you need to start calling me 'Mister Graham'—at least here at Lone Star." He saw the look on her face but plowed ahead. "Hold on, I know we've been on a first-name basis for a while now, but as of next week I'll be one of your bosses, and certain conditions must be met. One of them is—no first names for supervisors."

"I know *that*," she said, then did a double take. "Does that mean—I mean, are we going to be working for you?" She felt a wave of giddiness. Heck, yeah, she'd call him Mr. Graham.

He laughed and gave her a friendly clap on the back. "Yes, you and Graydell—he turned to smile at the brunette—are my first enlistees. I'll need about sixty workers to man F line."

"That's pretty funny, Charles—I mean 'Mister Graham'—you talking about 'manning' the line with two women."

He shrugged. "Just a saying. Didn't mean anything by it. You'll just have to get used to that, too, I guess."

"I guess so." *But I don't have to like it.*

"I'll want to get together with my whole group first thing next week. So be ready Monday morning."

With that, he headed back the way he had come, whistling "Over There."

* * *

Things didn't quite work out as planned. Charles waited until Friday afternoon to give them the news. "Next week is going to be a really big time for us here at Lone Star," he said, as he helped them unload another crate of materials for his office in Area F. "We're all going to be super busy, and you girls are finally going to be split up."

They protested a bit, but they had known the day would come. The place was huge, and the buildings were spread out all over the place. Nobody had given Mae a tour, but in all the weeks they'd worked, she'd managed to observe a good bit of the plant's thousands of acres.

The Gazette had said Lone Star would cover more than 23,000 acres, and she believed it. There were dozens of buildings still going up, plus the dozens already constructed. There were some igloos to temporarily hold ammunition until it could be sent next door to Red River's storage depot, where rumor had it there were hundreds of igloos ready and waiting to take in whatever they at Lone Star could build.

She turned her attention back to Charles, as he laid out their new schedules. Mae was to go to Area P where twenty-millimeter shells would be made, and Graydell was going to Area G to make grenades.

"I guess we can compare notes at home," Mae joked, but Charles shook his head.

"Once you're into production, you can't be discussing anything you're doing out here. Can't be too careful these days."

Chagrined, Mae said, "Sorry, I do know how important that is. It's just that Grady and I have shared things all our lives. It's going to take some getting used to."

He nodded.

"Charles, let me ask you something. Grady and I've been discussing this at home, and we don't quite agree." He set his latest box down and put his hands on his hips, nodding at her to go on. "What do you think about all these Japanese being taken out of their homes and sent to camps where they're under armed guard?"

Graham hung his head and didn't say anything for a minute. Both girls watched him expectantly. Graydell was in favor of rounding them all up, but Mae had been arguing against it.

Finally, he looked at Mae and said, "Well, the government thinks they're a threat, and after Pearl Harbor, I guess we can't be taking any chances."

"That's what I said," Graydell said.

156

"But we're talking about people who are United States citizens," Mae protested. "Lots of them have been here for generations. Do you honestly believe they would spy on their own country? I'm sorry. I just don't believe that."

"I hear what you're saying. And I'm sure it's hard for some of us who don't live on the West Coast to understand how much fear there is out there right now."

"I told Mae she ought to think about what it was like here in the South after the slaves were freed. Lots of whites were scared of the freed slaves. That's why the Klan was founded, after all. Blacks weren't rounded up, but they were kept down by the whites in power."

Graham looked from one to the other of them. "You girls are discussing some very serious subjects. And here I thought all you thought about was where to go dancing tonight."

Mae huffed. "Our whole world is changing, Charles, or haven't you noticed? We graduated just a year ago, and now the boys we were in school with are mostly gone into the service, and we're out here fixing to start making bombs and stuff for them."

"You're right. I guess I'm just seeing a more mature side of you than I've seen before."

"I for one am glad we have these jobs at all. I'll swab out the bathrooms if I have to do that to stay here." She paused. "Well, maybe not that, but most anything else."

"We can do better than that by you gals," Charles said. "Get here Monday morning ready to get to work, and I promise you you'll have some exciting times to tell your grandchildren about someday."

TWENTY-FIVE

PASS THE AMMUNITION

BUSTLING AROUND THE APARTMENT like it was their first day on the job, the girls kept bumping into each other in their haste. At last they were about ready to head out to catch the bus.

"I shouldn't have stayed out so late with George last night," Graydell moaned. "I haven't had but about three hours of sleep."

"It's your own fault, so get your shoes on and let's go."

Two hours and one bus breakdown later, and only an hour later than they were supposed to report to work, the girls finally stepped off the bus and into a whole new level of activity. As the bus pulled away, having disgorged twenty or so disgruntled employees, Mae said, "Goodbye and good riddance! I sure wish we knew somebody with a car."

They walked through the gate, showed their badges, and headed for their buildings and their supervisors. And Mae got her first dressing down due to tardiness.

Great. What a perfect way to start a new position.

"Alright, listen up people. I don't want to say this more than once," the supervisor said, squinting at the motley crew he had in front of him. "My name is John Lineberger. I'll be your supervisor here in this part of Area P. We're going to be building twenty-millimeter shells here. Does

158

anybody know how big twenty millimeters is?" Heads shook, and he sighed. "That's what I figured. Well, you will soon enough. Some of you do already, you just don't know you know."

Mae listened the way her daddy always said was best: "with both ears." Her eyes, though, roamed the room. She guessed the number of people at about thirty, more women than men. Some were about her age, but more were in their thirties and forties. Most of them, from what she could tell, were like her, somewhat nervous. A few looked familiar, and she figured she'd seen them around the plant during the weeks she and Graydell had done all those odd jobs for Charles. "Mister Graham," she corrected herself.

"It's about this big," he held his thumb and forefinger a few inches apart.

Mae grinned. *I think he's talking about a shotgun shell.*

"About like a shotgun shell," he said. Her grin broadened.

This may not be so bad.

"The way the plant is set up, the ammunition won't be 'live' until the very last moment on each line, whether it's grenades, bombs, or shells. That way, barring any accidents, you workers will remain safe. And safety is something the Goodrich administrators know about. So don't worry about something that may never happen. Now, that's not to say you don't need to be careful. You do. Listen closely when you're being given instructions—by me or anybody else—and trust us to have your safety in mind at all times."

She prayed there would be no accidents, but she had grown up on a farm and knew accidents happened. She thought of the day Thomas had taken a fall and broken his arm in a nasty way. They had been playing chase through the field when she darted into the rickety barn behind the house. Always light on her feet, she'd clambered atop the wall that was open at the top, allowing air to circulate through the barn. Then she had sprung down to the ground outside, scooting quickly up next to the exterior wall so Thomas couldn't see her. She heard him scrambling onto the wall behind her, heard him reach the top, watched as he flung himself to the ground, where he landed with a thud and a cracking sound. It had all been good fun until he let out a howl that set the dogs to barking. Yes, she knew all too well how quickly things could go wrong.

She shook herself and brought her mind back to her new supervisor, who seemed to be finishing up. *Hope I didn't miss anything important.*

Lineberger talked on for several more minutes, stressing again the safety issues that had been drilled into them several times already. *The supervisors sometimes act like we're just a bunch of school kids.*

"Now, I know you're all already familiar with the bomb proof, since you've been using one of those facilities scattered around the plant already, depending on where you've been working, to take your breaks and have your meals. Once we get all these lines open, it's going to be imperative for us all to keep to a very rigid schedule for when we use ours."

Mae thought of how hard getting used to all these schedules had already been. *Lord, I'm glad I'm not in charge of making out all these plans.*

"I don't know how many of you are smokers, but if you're one who does, remember what I'm telling you. You can't be smoking anywhere on this entire base except in the bomb proofs. Yes, smoking is strictly prohibited except for those buildings. And do you know why?" He waited.

A woman up front raised a tentative hand.

"Yes, ma'am?"

"Because what we're going to be building is a bunch of different stuff that, all of it, is some kind of explosives?"

"Right you are, Miss—Mrs.?"

"I'm Mrs. Johnie Young, sir." Mrs. Young looked about Mama's age, Mae thought. She couldn't imagine her mother in a group of people like this—going out in public to work, and then speaking up to a supervisor.

She looks like a nice lady. Wouldn't mind working alongside her.

160

"I hope you're all ready to get started, because you have a lot to learn, and perhaps not as much time to do so as you might think."

These people from Ohio sure sound different from us. Mae had gotten so used to talking with Charles she didn't even notice his accent anymore. He was just, well, just Charles. But the jury was still out on this Lineberger fellow.

The better part of that first morning was spent with Lineberger giving them a tour of their building. Mae was amazed at the many steps there were to making one little shell. There would be people in one bay doing just one thing, all day long, before the little would-be shell made its way into the next bay. The whole concept of bays was new to all of them. Each room of the long building was divided from every other room by a concrete wall so thick Mae couldn't even estimate just how thick it was.

"These walls may save your lives someday," Lineberger said. "They're designed so that if there's an accident in one bay—say, a small explosion—the damage will be contained to that one bay, thereby preventing a larger, possibly deadly, blast."

But what about the people in that first bay? Who's to say that first explosion won't be a deadly one? She shivered.

During the afternoon, the workers were sorely tested, as the conveyor belts running from one end of the building to the other were turned on, and the first containers of the various elements of shell-making were sorted out.

Mae was unhappy with her assignment from the start. She and another woman were placed at a table where, at regular intervals, someone would bring them a batch of assembled shells. Assembled, but incomplete. The bottom of the outside of the shell had been crimped, powder had been weighed and inserted, and a cap had been nestled gently onto the top but had not been glued down. This was to be Mae and Hilda's job: gluing the cap to the body of the shell.

While everyone else in their bay could laugh and talk with each other, Mae and Hilda found it took all their concentration to handle the shells safely. With a small, tapered brush, Mae soon learned to apply a bead of glue around the outside rim of the shell, in order to fasten the top on securely.

"Getting the glue on is the easy part," she said to Hilda. "It's getting all the extra off that's almost impossible."

"Almost, but not quite," Hilda said, using one of the many rags that had been provided for that purpose. She held her tongue in the corner of her mouth as she concentrated on wiping off all the excess glue. Hilda's rag had been dipped into a small container of liquid glue remover, what they found out later was exactly what it smelled like: acetone, like they used to remove nail polish.

"Tell me about it. And it's got to be done. I've spent enough years shooting shotgun shells like this to know. If we don't get all this glue off, and there's even a tiny glob left on the outside, it'll jam up the gun and it won't shoot."

"Gee, Mae, so you're a hunter?"

"Yes, I've hunted and fished all my life. Haven't done any of that in a while now, though, not since my friend and I moved to Texarkana."

"You miss living in the country?"

"Nah, Hilda, not a bit. I'm enjoying being a city girl." She punctuated her words by putting the last shell into the container where it would be left to cure.

"Next stop Tokyo," Hilda said.

Please Lord, let out job be good enough for our boys.

* * *

"Miss Johnson, can I see you a minute?" Mae always felt a sense of dread when a supervisor singled her out. She'd only had this one negative experience since coming to Lone Star. *Hey, maybe I'm moving again!* A girl could hope.

She hurried over to him. "Yes, sir?"

"Mae, we're shutting this line's evening shift down for a time, and most people are going to Area B. But I'm sending you to Area E instead.

They need some extra people working on the hundred and fifty-five-millimeter shells, and you've proved to be a very capable worker."

"Thank you, sir. Am I the only one you're sending there?" She sure hoped he'd be sending somebody else.

"No, I'm also sending Mrs. Young. She's not here today, but she'll be going along with you."

Johnie! Thank you, Lord. I won't be by myself!

Their first few days of packing shells went smoothly, and Mae's confidence soared. Then came the day that almost did her in. She had slept late that morning, and she ran out of the house without packing any supper. She was also without funds to eat in the cafeteria, and she was too proud to ask anybody for a loan. It was about nine that night when her body shut down.

"You alright there, Mae?" Johnie asked, seeing the younger woman struggling to reach the top of the large shell she was packing.

Johnie's job was to take the last piece of packing material and hand it up to Mae so she didn't have to do the repetitive climbing up and down motions.

"I'm good, thanks," Mae said, watching the shell she'd just finished riding off down the assembly line that had the large shells held vertically in place. She rotated her shoulders and, unaware she was doing so, put her hands to the small of her back and rubbed.

"Now, you let me know if you need a break. We could change places for a while."

"I might take you up on that, later." She hated the thought of Johnie thinking her weak.

"Suit yourself." Johnie followed the progress of the next shell, picking up the package of filler when the shell reached the right place on the line. It hadn't taken them long to get into a working rhythm.

A couple of shells later, the height finally got to Mae. First she saw black spots in front of her eyes. Next came a dizziness she hadn't felt since she had the flu when she was eleven. Next thing she knew, she was lying on the cool concrete floor with Johnie calling her name. She sounded scared. *Johnie scared? What's going on?* But her eyes refused to open.

Instead, she merely moaned, and asked, "What's wrong? What happened?" Excited voices erupted all around her, intermixed with the humming of the still moving conveyor belt.

"Shut that thing down!" somebody yelled. In just a few seconds, it seemed, the noise stopped.

Mae's eyelids fluttered, then opened wide. She blinked a few times and looked around.

"What happened?" she asked again.

"You passed out," Johnie said. "And no wonder, too. There's none of us that could stand up there, having to reach up to the top of that blasted shell. I've seen them further down the line, and they made height concessions, everywhere but here."

"Well, we can change things here, too," Mr. Ross was saying. "Let's get Mae here up to the hospital and get her checked out. While she's gone, some of you help me mend this situation, okay? Wilson and Hendricks, you two come with me. Everyone else, head on up to the bomb proof and take a fifteen-minute break."

Johnie had helped Mae to her feet and was steadying her. "Come on, Mae. Let's take a little walk."

"No, no," Ross said. "Here's the keys to my jeep. Take it."

Johnie looked at the keys as if they were a snake. "I don't know how to drive!" she protested.

The boss looked at her in consternation. "Are you kidding me?" He glanced around the room. "Who else in here knows how to drive?" Only five hands were raised. He shook his head, flummoxed, and waved his set of keys. "Okay, who wants to drive Mr. Ross's big bad jeep up to the infirmary tonight?" His words sounded gruff, but Mae, who was sitting up now, saw crinkles in the corners of his eyes. "Come on, we gotta get Johnson taken care of and get ourselves back to work."

"I'll take her." The voice was husky, but it was from a female. "Let's get out of here, Mae, before Mr. Ross changes his mind."

Mae looked around to see the woman who matched the voice. It was Ruby, better known as Ruby the Comedian, because she was always cracking jokes and keeping everyone in a good mood. "Dang, I had no idea there were so many sissy women out here who can't—or won't—drive. How about you, Mae?"

"Huh?"

Mae was still pretty much out of it. "Never mind. Let's get you up to see the nurse."

A short while later, Mae had been examined and pronounced fit to work.

Back in their bay, Ruby admitted, "I tried to convince the nurse Mae needed a longer rest, but she's pretty sharp. The nurse, not Mae." Mae faked an angry face. Ruby was alright.

Mae was impressed with the new work situation Mr. Ross had set up for her. From that point on, she had no more issues. At least not until the next move came.

TWENTY-SIX

A LEAVE-TAKING

MAE WAS UP BY seven on Tuesday morning, thankful once again that she was working swing shift, because today Oliver was leaving for basic training. She could hardly stand to think of him leaving, and she sure didn't want to watch him board a train later this morning—but she also couldn't stand the thought of him leaving without her being there to see him off.

She ate an apple, dressed in her best deep green dress, the one Oliver always said matched her eyes so well, put on scarlet lipstick that accentuated her full lips, then blotted most of it off. She brushed her silky hair until every strand shone, then settled her new brown velveteen cloche at a jaunty angle. Surveying herself in the slim mirror set into the chifforobe, she nodded with satisfaction. She would do.

She walked the ten blocks to Union Station, Texarkana's large, modern train depot that straddled the state line on Front Street. She hadn't been there many times, but the place always gave her a thrill. From the street, she entered the Art Deco glass-paned doors and stood looking upward to where there were glimpses of the second floor. She chose the set of stairs to her right and began climbing the marble steps, her heels clicking smartly on the stone. She let her hand trail along the brass handrail until she reached the between-floors landing where the left and right sets of stairs converged.

166

She hurried to the top of the steps. The cavernous lobby was teeming with people, but she spied Oliver and his family right away. She hesitated, trying to decide whether to join them. Making up her mind, she muttered, "The heck with it. I need to say goodbye, too." She plunged ahead. Oliver saw her first, and the way his eyes lit up told her she'd made the right decision. Mrs. Cranfield followed her son's gaze, and when she saw Mae, she just smiled. After a few minutes of stilted small talk, Oliver hefted his duffel bag and said, "Let's get out on the platform. I don't want to miss my call."

Mae was still feeling out of place in the close-knit family group and considered turning around. *But Oliver wants me here, so I'm staying.*

As the air grew heavier, Mr. Cranfield said, "We need to get going, son." He reached out to give Oliver a warm handshake. "Now you follow orders and learn everything you can," he said, stepping back so Oliver's mother could take her turn.

"You take care of yourself, you hear me?"

"Yes, ma'am, I intend to." He smiled gently down at her.

"All right, then. I think we're going to get going now. Do you mind?"

Oliver looked around at Mae. "You staying?" When she nodded, he said, "That's fine, Mama. I won't have to wait by myself. Y'all go ahead."

Mrs. Cranfield reached up to place her hands on his broad shoulders. Oliver bent down and pulled the small woman to him. "Love you, Mama. Take care of Daddy, okay? Don't let him work too hard."

"He always has," she said, her voice muffled against his chest. "What makes you think he would stop now?"

Oliver chuckled. "You're right. Well, 'bye, Mama, Daddy. I'll be back before you know it."

She stepped back from him, her fingers trailing down the sleeves of his jacket.

Mae looked away from this final leave-taking, her eyes filling with tears that she worked hard at blinking away. She smiled at Oliver's parents, and they turned and walked back into the station. Mr. Cranfield's arm was around his wife, and she was leaning heavily on him as they passed from view inside the terminal.

"My Lord, what this war is doing to our country," she observed.

"Yeah, the sooner I get through training and get overseas, the sooner I can get it all shut down."

"I always did like your confidence, Ollie," she laughed, comfortable once again.

He cocked his head and listened to the announcement blaring over the speaker. "That's me. Walk me down to my train, Maisie?" He held out his hand.

She took it, and together they moved toward the stairs that would take him away from her—and that would probably see him return a changed man. She said a silent prayer that wouldn't happen, and then asked what had been on her mind. "Are you going to write to me while you're gone?" She gave him a lopsided smile.

"You bet. And you write to me, too. I'll be gone long enough to get a letter or two." She nodded. "But then I'll be back before you know it. And who knows how long it may be before I get my final orders."

He looked down at his duffel bag, his hand twitching, but then left it there. "Well, bye, Maisie. Be good while I'm gone, okay? Keep building them bombs for us."

"You can count on me."

Checking his ticket against the numbers hanging above the tracks, Oliver gestured. "Lucky me. Here's my train." The air was filled with the sounds of thrumming engines, pigeons cooing in the rafters high above, and the occasional train engine whistle as one pulled out of the station.

Looking around at the busy scene, Mae spotted a familiar figure with a young man. "Hey, there's Laurie!" she said. "Let's go say hi."

Oliver put a hand on her arm to stop her. "Let's don't," he murmured.

But why—?" Then she saw the guy drop his bag and fold Laurie into his arms. She was crying, the tears glistening on her cheeks in the sunlight spilling through the space between trains. As Mae watched, the

168

guy—Derrell, it had to be—lifted her face toward him and said something, then leaned down and kissed her. Mae felt butterflies lift off in her stomach. Laurie's arms encircled Derrell's neck and the two clung together so closely Mae couldn't see an inch of space between them.

"I better get aboard," Oliver said. Suddenly, more than she'd ever wanted anything, she wanted this war to be over and for everything to go back to the way it was.

"Goodbye, Ollie. Godspeed. Be safe—and come back to us soon."

He reached his hand up and stroked her hair, pulling her toward him. His kiss was long and lingering, but when he finally pulled back, he turned businesslike. "Be good, Maisie. See ya around."

Before she could respond at all, he had bounded up the steps of the train and entered a car. She watched him walk to a vacant seat and settle into it. But he didn't look back, not once. She turned and retraced her steps. At the top of the stairs, she scanned the platform for an empty bench. Somehow, she couldn't face going back to the apartment just yet.

She kept thinking about Laurie and her fiancé, about how they'd still been locked in an embrace when she climbed the stairs. She wasn't jealous of Laurie getting those kisses from her fella, but suddenly, she was wishing she'd had more than just the one from Oliver. *It's just this emotional stuff, all these guys leaving. That's all it is. Oliver's special, but it's not like we're engaged or anything.*

That rationale didn't make her heart stop hurting—or keep her eyes from filling with tears. She felt someone sit down beside her and looked up to see Laurie, her eyes red-rimmed from crying.

"I just don't think I can stand this. I should have married that man when I had the chance."

Mae had never been that good at giving sympathy, but she blinked away her tears and did her best. She put her arm around her new friend and patted her shoulder. "There, there . . ." she began.

Laurie went very still. And then she was shaking all over.

"Oh, Mae, you were just what I needed right now. That was the most insincere comforting I think I've ever received in my life!"

Mae jerked her arm back, offended. Laurie just laughed harder. "You should see the look on your face."

"Well, excuse me for trying to help." Laurie just kept laughing, and eventually Mae joined in. "Graydell has always said I'd be useless in a crisis. Guess I'm just too self-centered."

"I love you for trying, anyway. What do you say we go over to the Jefferson so I can drown my sorrows in a giant milkshake?"

Mae nodded. They walked through the terminal, their heels clicking loudly on the black and white tiles. A couple of guys lounging nearby gave them appreciative glances, but neither one noticed. Making their way down the marble stairs, they emerged into brilliant sunshine. Behind them another train whistle blew, as another train began to pull from the station. Both girls pretended not to notice.

* * *

"I was serious about the marriage thing. Derrell kept trying to talk me into it, but I figured he'd spend too much time thinking about me, and maybe he wouldn't be as careful as he otherwise would. I do want him to come back to me in one piece." Laurie swirled the gaily striped paper straw through her chocolate milkshake and took another sip.

They were nestled into one of the small booths in the Jefferson Coffee Shop, a restaurant conveniently located just across the street from the train station. Mae was busy with her own shake, and she could tell Laurie was needing to talk, but she said, "Of course you do. We all do. Oliver and I have just started going together, but I'll bet I'm as worried about him as you are your Derrell. Dang this war, anyway. Y'all should be getting married and raising a family, and Oliver should be finding himself a good woman to settle down with., whether it's me or somebody else. Neither one of them deserves to be shipped off to who knows where to learn to do who knows what." Mae took a long pull on her straw.

"You know, you're really good for me," Laurie said in a soft voice. "I can't believe I've been unburdening myself to you like I have. It usually takes me a while to warm up to people."

"Me, too. Now my best friend, Graydell, she makes friends wherever she goes. I wish I had her self-confidence."

"Graydell. That's an intriguing name."

Mae told Laurie the story behind Graydell's name, and Laurie laughed out loud. "Now, there's a woman who knows her own mind. I admire Graydell's mom."

"Yeah, I guess so. I bet she was surprised, though, when I started calling her daughter Grady as a nickname. So she sort of got what she wanted in the end. Besides, Graydell can work rings around most men. It would also be good if I had her work incentive," Mae confided. "Speaking of my best friend, I'm supposed to meet her at Kress's for lunch—although I don't know how hungry I'll be now that I've had this shake."

"Oh. I won't keep you then. But thanks for taking the time to talk with me, and to try and console me."

Mae laughed at the memory. "Yeah, well, I'll work on my comfort-giving. You never know when I'm going to need it again, what will all these goodbyes being said."

Both girls stood and picked up their purses. Then Laurie reached out her arms. "We're huggers in our family. Would you mind if I give you a hug?"

Mae was sort of caught off guard. People in her family definitely were not huggers, but she nodded and held out her arms. Laurie pulled her close and whispered, "Thanks, Mae Johnson. You've made this terrible day much more bearable."

Mae couldn't help herself. She patted Laurie on the back. "There, there," she said, releasing herself from the hug. Laurie was still laughing when Mae exited the cafe and turned toward Kress's.

Tuesday, August 4, 1942

Well, today was the big day. Oliver left for Louisiana to do his basic training at Camp Claiborne. I'm so tired of seeing our boys go off to war. Morris is gone now, about as far from working on a law degree as it's possible to be. Who knows if he'll ever come back? I'm going to miss Oliver so much. I know we haven't seen as much of each other since Grady and I moved to Texarkana, but I knew he was in Dixon's Crossing, basically just right down the road. Now he's headed to another state. And from there, who knows?

I think it's the uncertainty—the not knowing where he will go, or when—that makes it all seem so bad.

I went to see him off at the Depot. There were so many guys heading out. It feels like Europe and the Pacific are sucking all the men my age out of the country. It's going to be so lonely without Oliver.

While we were waiting, we saw Laurie with her boyfriend, and they were so sad. She and I talked afterward. We don't have that much in common, but I think I could really come to like her. Isn't that funny?

On a different subject. I've been reading through this diary, something I haven't done in more than a year. And I've decided something. I need to grow up. My Lord, the things I used to write about in here. I just sound like such a little girl. Always writing about what we had for supper, and who came to Sunday dinner, and what happened in school that day. I spent so much time writing about things I don't care a fig about remembering, and basically I never wrote about my real feelings, either about people or about important events. I never even acknowledged a single thing about war starting in Europe. At least I did write about Pearl Harbor. It seems war is all there is to write about now.

I just wish I hadn't had to say goodbye to Oliver today. Dear Lord, please keep him safe wherever he goes, and bring him back home to us safe and sound. Amen.

TWENTY-SEVEN

A SUMMER STORM

"HEARD FROM YOUR FELLA yet?" Sue asked Mae on the way back to Area B after five o'clock supper break.

Mae was concentrating on the thunderheads gathering in the west. She had that prickling in her skin that told her a storm was coming. Lord, they could use the rain, but she dreaded the storms that usually threw everyone into the dark. *Wonder how dark it'll be in our building. There's only the one small window.*

"Huh?"

"Where's your head, honey? I asked if you'd heard from that fella of yours." Sue dug two fingers into Mae's ribs.

"Well, he's not quite my fella, even if he wants to be. I wasn't going to have a serious fella for a long time yet, because I want to be on my own without going back to a farm in the bottoms."

"Is that what he does?"

"Well, yes and no. He came from a tenant family like I did, but he finished high school, and he works sometimes in the general store in Dixon's Crossing. But who knows what he'll end up doing after the war? He's just now been sent off for basic training."

"But you'd consider making him a serious beau when he gets back from basic?" Sue persisted.

Mae slowed her pace. "Yeah, I think so. He's been my best friend for years and years, but after we started dating, not long ago, well, I get this feeling when he kisses me, right down here, you know?" She patted her belly.

"Sure that feeling isn't a bit further down?" Sue asked in Mae's ear.

Both women shrieked with laughter, until they had to hold onto each other. But then Mae said, "Maybe so, Sue, maybe so."

They strolled on, walking beside the train tracks, where a long line of empty cars sat like gigantic buzzards, waiting to be loaded with ammunition. It would go over to Red River first, to be stored in the many igloos there. Later the same tracks would send munitions out to the country's coasts to be shipped overseas.

Mae peered into one of the cars as they passed by. She'd heard some wild tales about what all went on inside those cars.

"Hey, Sue, got a question for you."

"Fire away."

"Actually, it's two. Doesn't your husband work somewhere here at Lone Star?"

"Yep. He's a bay leader over in Area P. Jake says it wouldn't be good for us to work together, because I might not do as I was told if he was giving me orders."

"He's probably right," Mae laughed. "Okay, second question. Do you ever look in these boxcars to see if there's anybody in there that you know?"

Sue stopped suddenly. "Only to see if my Jake is in there." Mae's eyes felt like they were going to pop out of her head. Her mouth was a round "O." Sue knitted her brows and frowned up at Mae. The petite little fireball looked ready to spit flames. Then she let out a shriek of laughter. "Got you there, didn't I? I trust my Jake always, and I think he trusts me. But who knows, he may be looking in boxcars just like I am."

They walked on, quiet now. But Mae noticed Sue's head turning toward every open car they passed.

* * *

Mae liked the work here on the detonator line, liked the women she worked with. They were a cohesive unit after being together for the past month, and they were hoping they would all stay together. But with these government Goodrich people, you never knew.

They were all sweating. August in East Texas was always as hot as a wood stove in the middle of winter. Today was worse than usual. The clouds had been gathering all afternoon, huge lumpy clouds that reminded Mae of the piles of feathers they used to amass while picking ducks to cook. Mama always put a number two washtub in the middle of the circle as they worked. Then she'd gather the feathers and tie them into a patterned flour sack, putting them into the smoke house until she had enough to make a new pillow. But these clouds threatened the peace of the afternoon. Indeed, they pretty much promised a storm before nighttime.

With only the one small window at the end of the bay, they were all sweating, jumpsuits clinging to thighs, stiff collars rubbing against throats running with rivulets of pure, salty, sweat. There was a saying among the women of Mae's upbringing. "We don't sweat. We don't even perspire. We *glisten*." Right now, Mae was glistening out of all her pores. Her head, with its phalanx of toothpicks in place and wrapped with the thinnest scarf she owned, was drowning in perspiration.

Lord, I wish we had more than one window. But she was thankful they could open it at all.

Johnie, the most senior person in their women only crew, occupied the workspace where the detonators first came into their bay on the conveyor belt that appeared through a small hole in the wall. Mae was continually amazed at the lengths to which the government was going for safety's sake.

Detonators moved along the belt at a steady but acceptable pace, with everyone having a specific role to play in completing their assembly. Mae worked about ten feet from the end where they were completed, and where Marcell packed each one carefully in a packing crate that held forty-eight. The line could produce hundreds of detonators on each shift. And every one of them was sorely needed overseas.

"Looks like the storm's getting close," Johnie said, glancing behind her at the open window. "Wind's picking up. Lots of stuff flying around out there."

"Getting dark outside, too. At least it'll be through here by the time we get off," Sue said, and several women murmured their assent.

Lightning flashed in the window, followed almost immediately by a deafening clap of thunder.

Mae jumped, as did the women on each side of her.

"That was a close one! Must have been less than a mile away," Frannie, to her right, said. "My grandma always says you can count off the distance by a mile per second between flash and clap."

"I think that one was almost on top of us, then," Mae said, working to complete the detonator in front of her. "Never have liked summer thunderstorms. Always seem to cause some kind of havoc."

"Don't say that, Mae, you'll jinx us!"

"Oh, Frannie, you don't believe in stuff like that, do you?"

"Yes, I do! So hush now."

But it was too late, for at that moment, another giant boom shook their building at the same time a bright flash lit them up from outside.

The lights went out.

Someone screamed.

At the far end of the line Marcell was hard at work packing the detonators into cases. The flash and boom, followed by seeming darkness, brought her to her feet. Unfortunately, she caught the corner of the detonator case on the zipper on her coveralls pocket, and the almost full case crashed to the floor. The next scream was from Marcell herself.

"Oh, shit! Nobody move!" she yelled, but of course almost everybody did. There was a general shuffling to Mae's left as people turned toward the window trying to see what was going on outside.

176

"I *said*, nobody move! There are detonators all over the floor! Do you want to die here?" Marcell sounded close to panic, her voice coming out high and strained.

That got everyone's attention.

"What should we do?" Frannie asked, her voice trembling.

"I for one don't want to die here! Let's get out of here right now."

"I'm with you, sister. Let's go."

"Hold it!" Mae yelled, her voice a command. All shuffling stopped. "Nobody is going anywhere until we get those detonators off the floor."

"And how do you propose we do that in the dark?" Ruth, the woman to her left, asked.

Mae thought for a moment. "Here's what we're gonna do. We're going to gather up those suckers." Explaining as she moved, Mae removed her boots and put them on the conveyor belt, which had stopped when the lights went out. Then she eased into a squatting position and used both hands to sweep the area around her. She found three detonators and eased them onto the conveyor belt, too. "Y'all just stay calm. There's really a good bit of light coming through the window, now that my eyes have gotten used to no lights overhead."

"She's right," Johnie said. "It's pretty bright down here. And I don't see any detonators."

"Don't take anything for granted," Mae cautioned.

"Okay, ready for me next?" Frannie asked. She repeated the sweeping procedure Mae had used, and in a few minutes her four detonators had joined Mae's.

Then it was the turn of the two women to Frannie's right. They found a total of eight.

"I'll go next," Ruth volunteered.

She found only one detonator. All the way down the line to Johnie, women slowly cleared the floor. They found no more.

Marcell asked, "Who's close to the telephone?"

"I am," came a reply from a steady sounding Johnie. All were listening intently, and there was an air of partial relief when they heard Johnie explaining the situation on the phone.

The workers were discussing the likelihood that they had found them all when the door burst open and a flashlight beam swept around the room.

"Y'all okay in here?" their supervisor, Mr. Wilson, asked in a shaky voice.

"Of course we are," Mae spoke up, and others said yes at the same time.

Wilson shone his light toward her, striking her full in her bright green eyes. "Hey there, Blondie." Somehow the nickname had followed her from the drive-in. The light swept her up and down, pausing at her socked feet. Sweeping the floor with the light, he saw that everyone was in their socks. "What the—?"

"It's okay, Mr. Wilson. I just knocked over a case of detonators in the dark, and we've been gathering them up." Marcell explained Mae's plan. He shone his light up and down the conveyor belt, where little groups of detonators lay side by side but not touching.

"What the—?" he began again. "Why in the hell were you doing that? And in the dark?"

"Everybody wanted to get out of here," Frannie started to explain, "but we were scared to move with all those detonators scattered around, so."

The bay leader looked at her quizzically for a moment, then started to laugh. Once he started, he couldn't seem to stop. The women looked from him to each other and back at him. When his laughter let up, he shook his head and said, "Ladies, those detonators aren't harmful at all until they've been added to whatever ammo they're for, and that doesn't even take place on this base. You were never in danger at all."

They all looked at each other, and to a woman, their faces began to take on extra color, some reddening terrifically. Mae's was one of those.

178

She looked around the room at her fellow workers, then sighed. "Oh, my gosh! I am so sorry, y'all. I can't believe I was so stupid."

"Who're you calling stupid, Mae? We were all thinking the same thing, and we all ended up in our sock feet and on the floor," Sue said, stepping up next to Mae and slipping an arm around her waist. "At least now we know if we do have an emergency, we'll be alright, cause we've got Mae Johnson in our bay."

She blushed redder than ever. Wilson said, "Y'all come on down to the bomb proof and get yourselves back together. Have a little extra break on Uncle Sam, okay? Maybe we'll get power back soon."

The crew didn't wait to take advantage of his offer, slipping on their boots and streaming past him into the rain-soaked lot.

"Thank God," Frannie muttered. "I could sure use a smoke right about now."

TWENTY-EIGHT

A NEW KIND OF POWDER

"I'M SURE NOT THRILLED about having to move again," Mae grumbled as she and Johnie headed for Area E, where tracer pellets were made. "But I'm really glad a friend is going with me." She linked arms with the older woman. "Know what, Johnie? You treat me more like a daughter than my own mother does."

"Oh, Mae, don't be like that. Wait till you have children of your own. Until then, why don't you try to go a little easier on her. I know she loves you. She just may not be very open with her feelings." She tugged on the arm holding hers tightly.

They bent their heads into the lashing wind and rain from the sudden cloudburst that had caught them unawares.

"Change the subject?" Johnie said, leaping across a puddle of water that had appeared almost instantly when the rain began while they were in Administration getting their new assignments sorted out. The puddle hadn't been there when they went over.

"Nah, go ahead. Don't like talking about family stuff anyway." *And don't need another mother telling me I'm not giving the first one a real chance.*

"Somebody was telling me an interesting story about these pellets we're making. They say before the war, the machinery was being used in a factory that was making aspirin tablets."

"You don't say! Boy, this war is sure bringing lots of changes. It's strange. Before the war, nobody around here had much money. Now pretty much everybody who wants to work has a job, and a good one, but there's not that much to buy, what with rationing, and the changes in what factories are producing."

Johnie nodded and pulled open the door to their new building. Soon they found their bay leader and learned their new assignments. Johnie was sent into the next bay, while Mae was told to take a seat at the long table that took up much of the workspace. She looked curiously at the other women at the table, about ten in all. In front of each of them was a set of scales and empty containers that looked too small to be of much use. She soon found out how wrong she was.

By quitting time, her back and neck muscles had her entire body jerking. She had spent all day and night, except for her dinner break, for which she had no appetite, bent over those small scales. She used a spoon to dip into the igniter powder and tilt it ever so slowly onto one side of the scale to try to make it match the weight lying on the other side of the scale. At one point, she'd been so frustrated she slammed her fist onto the table, startling the other women and causing all their scales to swing crazily.

"Oh, hell, y'all! I didn't mean for that to happen. I'm just having a hard time with this." Mae was usually able to adapt quickly, and her struggle left her irritated.

She'd also been distressed to learn they all had to remove their coveralls before they headed to the bomb proof for fear of some spark igniting their clothing. Then they had to hurry back to get into the jumpsuits for the rest of the night's work.

Now she curled into the corner of her bus seat, closed her eyes, and tried to ignore the frequent lurches and stops along the road to Texarkana. Graydell tried to start conversation a couple of times, but Mae just moaned and shook her head.

She was dragging when they got off the bus. Graydell said, "Something's really wrong with you." It wasn't a question. Still Mae wasn't talking. "Let's get you home and into bed," she said, patting Mae's shoulder.

Once in their room, Mae pried her work boots off and fell onto her bed, moaning softly.

"What can I do for you, hon? Are you sick? Is it your stomach?"

"My back," Mae mumbled into her pillow. "And my neck. And my shoulders."

"Damn, girl, what'd they do to you out there?"

"Made me weigh powder, a little at a time. And it had to be perfect. Grady, I don't think I'm going back. It's too hard. And I hurt too much."

Graydell's mouth fell open. "What are you talking about? That's nonsense. Nothing can be that bad. If you quit this job, you probably won't get another one. I heard rumors about the plants putting out orders not to hire people who quit one of them."

"I don't care. I can't do it."

Graydell stood looking down at her friend. "After all the times you swore to get out of Dixon's Crossing, no way you're quitting. Let me think . . ." She rummaged in the cabinet and came out with a rubber hot water bottle. Putting the kettle on, she said, "Hold on, Mae. We're gonna fix you up." While the water heated, she found the bottle of liniment and went to sit beside her friend. "Here, get your shirt off. Come on. No, don't go to sleep on me. Turn over. That's my girl." She helped the fumble-fingered Mae undo her buttons and had her lie down on her stomach. With a soft cloth, she began to rub the liniment into Mae's aching muscles.

Mae jerked when the cold liquid first hit her skin, but soon Graydell's manipulations of her muscles had her groaning with something close to pleasure. When the kettle began to sing, Graydell filled the hot water bottle. Wrapping it in a towel, she laid it gently between Mae's shoulder blades and pulled the quilt up to help hold the heat in. Only when

Mae relaxed into sleep did she remove her own shoes and get ready for bed.

Mae slept till noon. When she woke, she rolled over and sat up. "Oh, man, I feel better. Are you there, Grady? You need to go into nursing, girl."

Graydell peeked around the curtain and grinned. "Does that mean you're not quitting your job today?"

"What are you talking about?"

"You said last night you couldn't do this new job they gave you and you were quitting."

"That's crazy talk. If I quit this job, I won't get another, and I'll be on my way back to Dixon's Crossing in a heartbeat."

"Glad to hear it. Now get up and get downstairs before Mrs. Swenson puts the food away."

By the time they broke for dinner that night, Mae was threatening to quit again. But it was under her breath.

TWENTY-NINE

SMOKIN' IN THE GIRLS' ROOM

"I DON'T CARE WHAT they say. I just don't think there's any danger of an explosion just from a cigarette! My gosh, I grew up in the country, and we always smoked when we took target practice with our guns. And that's ammunition!"

Mae glanced up from eating. They might not have a very big stove in their little apartment, but it was plenty big to cook vegetable soup and bake cornbread. She was able to relish her dinner again, now that she had transferred away from the powder weighing and back to shell building. She didn't know many people here yet, but thank goodness Johnie was here, too. Fate seemed to keep throwing the two of them together, and Mae was glad.

She looked toward Jewel now, the one who'd spoken. Jewel was a feisty young woman who worked on the main line of their bay, while Mae and her crew worked at a nearby table. She looked to be about Mae's age, but the two hadn't spent any time getting acquainted. Mostly they were coming to know the people nearest to them.

"I don't know . . ." Johnie said. She had become pretty much the mother hen to all of them. "Mr. Roberts seemed pretty serious about it yesterday. I'd hate to see any of you get reprimanded for that. I hope y'all try to do what the rules say."

"Aw, Johnie, what are they going to do to us? Fire us? They need us all to keep the line running smoothly," Jewel said.

Johnie arched her brows but said nothing else.

Mae was just glad she didn't smoke, so she could spend her little bit of free time eating and napping.

Later that afternoon, Mae noticed Jewel looking over her shoulder before heading toward the bathroom in the far corner of their bay. *She's sure acting weird.* Then another woman went to the bathroom, too. Funny. They didn't usually go to the bathroom more than one at a time. She shrugged her shoulders and put her mind back on her work.

Minutes later, Nelda whispered into her ear, "Do you smell smoke?"

"I hadn't noticed—but now that you mention it . . ." Mae scanned the room, seeking the source of the smell. Then she saw it—bluish-gray smoke drifting lazily out of the vent above the door to the ladies' bathroom. "Oh, no," she muttered. "Those girls are just asking for it."

Sure enough, only a minute or so later, Mr. Roberts opened the door and came bustling in from outside. "How's everybody doing?" he asked, flashing a smile from one worker to another.

He stopped dead still halfway down the room, sniffing the air. Then his eyes went to the vent, and Mae saw his neck redden, then his face. He stomped over to the bathroom door, crossed his arms, and waited. The only sound in the room was the conveyor belt motor.

After a couple of minutes that seemed more like an hour, the door opened and Jewel and the other girl emerged, stopping short when they saw their supervisor.

"Hold up," he said, as they tried to sidle by him. "You gals have been smoking in there." It wasn't a question.

"No, sir," Jewel protested. "Just using the facilities."

"Facilities my foot," he snorted. "You see that vent up there? Your smoke was just rolling out here to beat the band." He was gesturing wildly with both hands. "I'm going to tell you one time, and one time only. And everybody in here had better listen up, too. The next time I catch somebody smoking in there, I'm coming in there, and there are going to be strong consequences!"

He wheeled about and slammed out of the room.

"He's sure got his drawers in a wad," Jewel remarked, sashaying back to her workstation.

Mae saw shocked glances from several of the women. She wasn't shocked, not really. If those girls were willing to disobey a direct order so soon after being reminded of it, well, who knows what else they might disobey? *I'm not so sure I want to work in the same place with them. They may end up getting us all in trouble. Or even killed. But I need this job.*

* * *

Several days went by without incident, and Mae almost forgot about the smoking issue. Work on the line had picked up substantially after Lone Star received a huge new order from Uncle Sam. The war news wasn't good, and it was obvious the military was beginning to pour more and more munitions into both Europe and the Pacific.

Occasionally, there was a bit of overtime for some of them, volunteers only so far, and Mae had not yet stayed over. She was thinking about whether to volunteer and trying to decide which day of the week would be easiest, when she smelled the smoke. "Oh, no! Not again," she muttered under her breath. She glanced around. Sure enough, Jewel wasn't at her post. And there were two more empty spots on the line.

As if by design, or like it was meant to be, Mr. Roberts walked into the room from over in the next bay, which he also supervised.

"Well, I'll be damned," he muttered. He hitched up his pants, change jingling, and, shaking his head the whole time, strode down the room to the bathroom door. He gazed for a moment up at the smoke curling out of the vent, then jerked the door open and barged in. *A rooster in the proverbial hen house.*

Screams erupted immediately, but they were soon cut off. Mae could hear his voice but, try as she might, she couldn't make out the words. When the door opened, the supervisor came out first, followed by three red-faced women. Roberts went back out the way he had come in, saying not a word.

As the women took their places, Jewel said, "My gosh, I never thought he would come in there with us! He's a man. He's got no business in the women's bathroom!"

"And y'all have got no business *smoking* in there," someone said.

"What did he say to y'all?" someone else asked.

"Not much. Just said to get back to work and we'll talk about this later," a somewhat chastened Jewel said.

They continued to work but still murmured among themselves about what might happen, but none of them were prepared for his response.

About half an hour after the set-to, the conveyor belt died. At least that's how Mae would describe it later. It had never stopped before, not right in the middle of a shift. They all sat looking at each other.

"I'll go see what's up," Johnie said, opening the door into the next bay.

"That won't be necessary," Roberts said, meeting her and motioning her back into the room. "Everybody outside. Gather up over by the flagpole."

Quietly they began to file out of the room. Once outside, Mae saw the group from the bay next to theirs already huddled together on the far side of the flagpole. With one accord, Mae's group gathered on the near side, facing the others.

Mae looked up into an azure blue, cloudless sky at the three flags fluttering in the lazy breeze. The largest of the three poles held the American flag. On an adjacent pole were the Texas flag and the white "E" flag Mae was so proud of. Each quarter when the government gave out the "E" for Excellence flags to Lone Star as one of the institutions around the country that was exceeding expectations—in production, in purchase of war bonds, or both—plant officials stopped work on a few lines so

187

everyone working there could come outside and watch the new "E" flag being raised. Workers and management alike were justifiably proud of those white flags. *Bet we won't be invited to the next flag-raising.*

Roberts appeared next to them and maneuvered to where he could see both groups of women. They were all women, as were several more groups around the plant. At least, that's what Mae had read in the paper.

"I know it's not the first shift of the day," the supervisor began. "But considering what I'm about to talk about, I think it would be fitting for us to say the Pledge of Allegiance together. Right now."

He looks about as serious as the undertaker at a funeral.

He laid his hand over his heart and they all, to a woman, covered their own. He began, "I pledge allegiance to the flag . . ." and a chorus of female voices joined in.

Tears came to Mae's eyes, as they so often did when saying the Pledge. And as on all those other times, a vision of her classmates off on some foreign battlefield, wounded, maybe dying, came into her mind. At the end of the pledge, she whispered, "Amen."

Roberts cleared his throat amid a generalized rustling among the workers. Mae cut her eyes around at Jewel, wondering what the girl was thinking right now about the situation she had put all of them into.

"I'm sorry to have to call you all together to talk about something that should never have become an issue. Sorrier than you know." He looked around at all of them, then continued. "A situation has arisen over in bay ten, but I've called bay nine out to hear me also, since I'm your supervisor there as well. Despite my demands and threats, which I've made as your supervisor based on the plant's regulations, some women in bay ten have willfully disobeyed the rules by continuing to smoke in the ladies' bathroom."

About twenty heads turned and twenty pairs of eyes from Mae's group glared at Jewel and her friends huddled together at the edge of the group. They turned back to hear what else their supervisor had to say.

"Therefore, as I warned the offenders a week or so ago, there are now going to be severe consequences for their actions. As of this moment, the ladies' bathroom in bay ten is locked and will remain so for the foreseeable future. Workers in ten will have to wait until they have a chance to go to the bomb proof to be able to use the restroom."

A gasp came from the bay ten group, but he seemed not to hear, or at least to care. "Now, you women in bay nine, I haven't had any trouble out of any of you. Your bathroom will remain open unless I find out you've been doing the same thing."

He put his hands on his hips and looked toward bay ten. "Any questions?" He was greeted by silence. "Good. Now everybody get back to work. We've got some time to make up."

It was a chastened group that returned to work in bay ten that afternoon. Mae could hear sniffles coming from Jewel's end of the room, but she had no sympathy for the twit of a girl. *Wait till I give her a piece of my mind.*

* * *

At supper several women made a beeline for the bathroom facilities in the bomb proof rather than starting to eat. Mae got out her sack and started in on her peanut butter and jelly sandwich. Not her favorite food, but it would sustain her, and that's all that mattered.

She had been in a foul mood ever since the gathering that afternoon, and it didn't help when Jewel and one of her friends sat down at her table. It was only made tolerable when Johnie sat down as well.

"How's it going, Mae? We never get to talk much now that we're so far apart on the line. Not quite like when we were working as a team on those 155-millimeter shells, huh?" Johnie asked.

"It's very different, alright," Mae agreed, and took another bite of her sandwich. Seemed the peanut butter was gumming up her mouth today. She must not have put as much jelly as usual. She took a few swallows of water.

"What was it like working on shells?" Jewel asked. "I've only worked on this line, and I've wondered what it's like in other places."

"Well, for one thing, everybody on that line followed the rules and did as they were told," Mae said, laying her sandwich down to stare across at Jewel.

"Don't get all high and mighty with *me*," Jewel said. "I wasn't the only one who was smoking."

"I don't believe you," Mae sneered. "You may not have been the only one, but you were the first, and you kept it up, and had others following you, thinking y'all were being so smart. Then you get Roberts' wrath on all of us. They should have just fired the lot of you and left everybody else alone!"

"Take it easy, Mae," Johnie said quietly, laying a hand on Mae's arm. "We all have to work together, no matter who was in the right and who was wrong."

"How can you take it like that, Johnie? You, who have never done anything wrong since you've been working here. And I know you've had opportunities—times when what they've told you to do made no sense, but you did it anyway."

"I just try to mind my own business and do the best job I can."

"It doesn't seem right at all. Little Jewel over there acts like nothing at all has happened. And all this is her fault."

"Don't talk about me like I'm not here!" the brunette hissed, heat rising in her cheeks. "You're not my boss."

"You'd better thank your lucky stars I'm not," Mae retorted. "You make me sick, you and your friends and your cigarettes. I wish you'd choke on one, one of these days. Oh, and the ashes, too."

"And I hope you choke on that sandwich," Jewel replied.

Mae was on her feet in an instant, fists knotting and muscles in her forearms flexing. Her green eyes flashed as she shoved the bench back out of her way. Jewel stood, too. The two stared at each other, eyes glaring.

Sit down, Mae," Johnie urged in her soft voice. "I care about you too much to lose you. You're a good worker, a good person. Back down from this now, before things get out of hand."

190

Mae looked down at the older woman. "You want me to just *take* that kind of talk, that attitude, and do nothing?" She was incredulous. Growing up in the country, she'd learned to stand up for herself and what she saw as right, and she wasn't about to stop now.

"That's exactly what I want," Johnie said. "Mae, you need to be the bigger person here."

"Bigger person? What does that make me, chopped liver?" Jewel spat out. "You talk to her like she's somebody special and I'm just a nobody."

Johnie was tugging on Mae's arm, and finally Mae sat back down on the bench, feet facing away from the table, back turned to Jewel.

"Well, you see, Miss Jewel, I haven't known you near as long as I've known Mae here. I've worked close with her in several places before they transferred us over here. I know what she's made of. I can't say the same about you. So, yes, I'm more concerned about keeping her from doing something to put her employment in jeopardy. And you know, I have a feeling it's only a matter of time before you get yourself tossed out. I just don't want to see Mae go with you." Johnie's voice had remained quiet, her composure sure.

Mae looked at her in wonder. *I've never seen Johnie really rattled, but no occasion has really presented itself before today. I'm amazed at her patience and her concern for me.*

She leaned over and gave her older friend a hug. "I hope I'm half as wise as you are when I'm—" She reddened, realizing what she'd been about to say.

"When you're what? Old like me?" Johnie let out a rolling laugh and kept it up until tears were streaming down her cheeks. She fanned her face with a paper napkin and wiped her eyes. "Oh, Lordie, I hope you are, too, dear Mae." She turned to look at Jewel. "I hope you, too, learn something from this today, Jewel. I really do."

Virgie walked up then and laid her hand on Mae's shoulder. "I'm with Johnie. I see what a good worker you are, sitting there across from me day after day, always keeping up, usually doing more of the work than I do.

191

You need to stay right here. Our boys overseas need every one of us who have their best interests at heart. We have hard work ahead of us, and you need to be here."

Mae ducked her head, then met the other woman's eyes. "Thanks, Virgie. I was just thinking about them this afternoon at the flagpole, about all the men going into battle day after day, month after month, and the medics who are trying to patch them back together when they're injured. I bet they would be ashamed of me right now." She turned to look at Jewel, who had also resumed her seat.

"Jewel, I apologize for saying those things to you. I may still feel that way, but I've got no business saying it, especially not in front of all these people." *Well, it may be a half-hearted apology, but it's better than nothing. I just can't say something that's not true—for better or for worse.*

Jewel said, "Sorry. I've learned my lesson about smoking. I'm sorry it's caused trouble for everybody else." She glanced around the room, and here and there someone glared at her—but just as often, someone smiled.

"Okay, ladies. Now that that's out of our systems, it's work time!" Johnie said, and they all began to pack away their lunch things. "Last one back to the line is a rotten egg!"

Mae sprang from her seat and raced for the door. She hadn't been part of a good footrace for ages.

THIRTY

A QUANDARY

MAE SNATCHED THE LETTER from the hall table and rushed upstairs. Plopping onto her bed, she took out her pocketknife and slit open the envelope. Removing the letter, she thought, "Gosh, I've been missing Oliver more than I ever thought I would."

August 2, 1942

Dear Mae,

I'm sitting down to write to you while I have a few minutes. That's about all we have in basic training. I'm down here in Louisiana, not that far south of Shreveport, at Camp Claiborne. It seems to be a pretty nice town, what I've seen of it. At least the local people are nice to us whenever we go into town on leave.

On the way down, our train stopped in Shreveport to meet up with another troop train, and we got off for a couple of hours. The USO people there were super to us. They had sandwiches, coffee, and donuts for us, and the food was sure delicious.

It's a lonely life down here, despite the fact that I'm in the middle of hundreds of other guys. You know I don't find it easy to talk to people I don't know. Of course, I'm getting to know people pretty quick since we're thrown into situations were we have to depend on each other. But I don't want to waste your time writing about that.

Mae, I want to talk to you about this war we're in. You know how I feel about killing someone. I'm just not sure I can do it. We grew up being taught murder is a sin. Of course, we were also taught about faith in God, sometimes through Bible wars. I remember especially Joshua and the battle for Jericho, where he had to march round the walls of the town seven times and blow his trumpet. After six times, nothing had happened, and I'm sure, like many men, he was discouraged. Many men would have stopped before then, but Joshua pressed on, and as soon as he made that seventh trip around and blew his horn, <u>the walls fell down!</u> We learned about faith and trust, but we also learned about fighting and dying. learned about warfare and fighting over territory. Now we're fighting for our freedom, and the freedom of others, and that to me seems even more important. Now I know I need to reset my mind and be ready to do whatever is necessary. I'll just have to trust God to get me through this.

Mae looked up from her reading. She couldn't imagine being in Oliver's shoes and having to wrestle with such a decision. Her heart hurt for him.

Now I'm down to the part of this letter I've been putting off. Not because I don't want to say it, but because I want to say it the right way—meaning in a way to get your attention.

Well, he sure had her attention now.

Mae Johnson, I have loved you for years. I don't mean the kind of love a guy has for a friend. I love you like a man should love a woman. You're the woman I want to spend the rest of my life with, starting right now.

I love you for your loving spirit, your fire and determination (even though that's what took you off to Texarkana and made me afraid I'd lose you to some no-account city boy before I ever had a chance to win you for myself), your smarts, your compassion, and of course your wonderful free spirit. Our children would be a perfect mix of you and me. I love you, Mae. I want to marry you. Now, today. Since that's not possible, I want to marry you the day I get home from basic. I know that won't be possible, either, but then I want it to be the quickest wedding ever.

I plan to keep on asking you until you say yes, sweetheart. However long that takes, that's how long I'll be asking.

All my love,

O.D.

She stared at the letter, reading that last part over again. *O.D. Just his initials, Oliver David. Wonder why he didn't sign it Oliver. And I wonder what he's going to decide about fighting.* She couldn't imagine being in Oliver's shoes and having to wrestle with such a decision. Her heart hurt for him.

Still in a sort of shock, she kept rereading the letter. Maybe she'd imagined it. No, there it was, all of it. Oliver loved her, wanted to marry her, wanted to have *children* with her, for Pete's sake. *What in the world happened to him on that trip to Louisiana?* She folded the letter and slipped it back into its envelope. She would have to give some deep thought on how to answer this surprising letter.

* * *

The letter left her preoccupied in the following days. At home, she was quiet, no longer the bouncy girl Graydell was used to. At work, she found herself thinking of Oliver and trying to imagine him sitting down to write those things to her. He had never, ever voiced anything of the sort to her. She had to admit, she'd felt something the few times they'd kissed, especially when he was getting on that train.

She was thinking of The Letter, as she now called it, as she exited the bathroom next to the bomb proof one night. Rounding the corner, she collided with someone coming out of the colored bathroom attached to hers.

"Oh, sorry," she said automatically. When she looked into the face of the young black woman she'd barreled into, she did a double take. She knew this girl.

"Keesha? It is you, isn't it?"

The girl looked her up and down, her brows knitted together. A light dawned in her eyes. "Miss Mae? It's been a long time. Yes, it's me, LaKeesha."

"LaKeesha, right. Hey, how've you been, girl? It's been a while."

"I'm fine. It has been a long time. What, maybe two, three years?"

"About that. I haven't worked the fields since I turned sixteen."

"Well, I haven't worked the fields since these plants came in," Lakeesha grinned.

"That's wonderful," Mae laughed. "Always glad to see anybody get away from that kind of work, especially my friends. So, where are you working here? I'm over in Area G, making grenades."

"I work all over the place," was all Keesha said.

"Gee, what do you do?" Mae didn't know of any job that had people "working all over the place."

Keesha looked at the ground and mumbled, "I clean the bathrooms."

Mae swallowed her first response. She knew blacks were relegated to custodial and kitchen work, and it had never really bothered her before. But—Keesha! The two of them had played side by side when they were too young to hoe and pick cotton in Daddy's fields. By the time they were eight or so, Keesha had had to take her own sack and get to the back-breaking work. Over the years, Mae saw her only occasionally in the fields, or if she brought her daddy a lunch. They would make eye contact and smile at each other. If it hadn't been for those times, Mae doubted she'd have recognized the black girl today.

"I've gotta get back to work," she said, backing away. "But dang, Keesha, it's good to see you!" She beamed at the young woman.

"It's good to see you again, too, Miss Mae."

She was halfway back to her line before she realized Keesha had called her "Miss Mae." She felt herself flushing at the significance of that. "Gotta do something about that next time."

* * *

196

The meeting with Keesha and The Letter from Oliver had Mae's head spinning like the Tilt-a-Whirl at the Four States Fair, and sleep felt very far away on that Sunday night. She tried to stay in bed, hoping sleep would come, but eventually admitted it wasn't going to work. She tiptoed to the French doors, hoping to open them quietly, but a creak caused Graydell to sit up in bed.

"Mae, you okay?"

"Shh, Grady, go back to sleep. Sorry, but I've got some things to think about."

Graydell padded across the floor barefooted. "Then come on, girlfriend, let's get outside in the fresh air and get these issues settled, whatever they are." She pushed Mae ahead of her and steered them to two rockers that faced each other. The night was sultry, with a lazy breeze bathing their skin in a heat so dry it seemed to Mae even worse than no breeze at all. Heat lightning flashed far away to the south, but it promised no relief.

"I didn't mean to worry you, Grady," she said now. "You should just go in and get back to sleep."

Grady snorted. "Fat chance of that. We're always there for each other and that's not about to change now. You've been moping around for days, so spill it."

With a grin, and a silent thanks for this woman who was such a dear friend, despite her ways that Mae sometimes found impossible to understand, she did just that. Once she started talking, the words poured out. Graydell sat back and listened without interruption.

When Mae said, "And that's about the gist of it," Graydell shook her head.

"Oh, hon, no wonder you've been acting strange." She paused, then asked, "And how do you feel about what Oliver wrote? Do you have those feelings for him?"

Mae heaved out a sigh that could have been heard on the courthouse steps. "I don't know," she wailed, rocking back and forth. "I mean, I never thought I did, but then a few times, before he left, I had these stirrings in my belly that I'd only ever had before with—"

"Frank!" Graydell spat out. "Girl, you've got to get over that man. He's nothing but bad news for you, and you know it."

"Yes, I know it," Mae snapped. She stopped rocking. "Oh, I'm sorry Grady. I'm not mad at you. It's true what you say. But I didn't say I was pining after him, did I? I'm just saying, I never felt like I did with him, not until—"

"Until what? Did Oliver try something with you?"

"No! Gosh, no. He'd never do anything like that, not without me giving him some kind of invitation."

Graydell's posture relaxed. "That's what I thought. After all, we've all hung out together for years. I was sure I knew him that well."

"Exactly. That's what has me so confused. How could I suddenly start having this kind of feelings for him, after we've spent so much time together and all? When I read that letter, I couldn't believe he's been in love with me all this time and never said anything. Why would he be like that? How could he not say anything?"

"Well," Grady retorted, "Maybe because you've been wearing your heart on your sleeve for Frank Cummings since you were about fourteen."

"Have I always been that transparent?" Mae was truly surprised.

"Maybe not to other people, but to me and Oliver, yes. How many times did y'all break up and get back together? Oliver couldn't help but see you were miserable while Frank wasn't around, and you were all giddy when y'all made up."

Mae continued to rock and think. She knew she'd always felt the way Graydell was describing, but she hadn't known how much it had showed.

"You're right, Grady, as usual. I see that now. Do you think I might really be over him this time? I mean, I wouldn't want to turn to another man if I thought I was just missing Frankie."

She thought of all her favorite memories with Frank, during the good times. Fishing trips where he fished and she read romantic poetry and daydreamed of them having a life together; sitting in the yard swing with him, sneaking kisses nobody could see, tracing his eyebrows with her fingers until he would suddenly whip his head around and grab her finger with his lips and wrap his tongue around it, sending chills right down to her core. Riding home with him from church on his horse, her arms clasped tightly around his waist, her cheek pressed against his shoulder. Those memories and so many more, like the way he always talked about her to other people, calling her his "woman," when she was still a skinny fourteen-year-old. Lord, the man had had a hold on her ever since she first laid eyes on him. Had she finally broken that hold?

"So, what are you going to do about Oliver?" Graydell broke into her thoughts. "It's not fair for you to keep him dangling if you're still involved with Frank."

"I'm *not* involved with Frank." Mae protested. "We haven't been together for more than a year now."

"You know what I mean. You may not be *with* him, but if you've still got those feelings, can it be okay to start something up with Oliver?"

"I hear what you're saying. But the thing is, I think there just might be something to these feelings I've been having about Oliver. How will I ever know, if I don't give him a chance? But would it be right to start exploring things with him when he's about to go off to war? You know that lots of couples are jumping into marriage before the guy leaves for overseas. I'm scared, because Oliver wants to go that far before he leaves, and I don't know if I'll be strong enough to say no to him, even if I'm not ready for that. For marriage. Does that make sense?"

"Honey, I think you already know what you want to do. So just do it. *After* you sleep on it. Let's go to bed, and you should try to wipe that letter and this entire conversation out of your mind. Get a good night's sleep, and let your conscience guide you in the morning. Oh, man, I sound like an advice columnist." They both laughed. "Then write the letter you know is the right one."

Mae stood and yawned a stretching yawn. "Right. You're right, Grady." She grabbed her friend's hand and pulled her to her feet, giving her a quick hug. "I am so lucky to have you as my best friend."

"That goes both ways, dearie."

When Mae got back in bed, the moon was so bright she could make out all the shapes in the room, so she turned toward the wall and squeezed her eyes shut. Sleep came, but not a peaceful one, since the faces of Oliver and Frank floated through all her dreams, like horses on a carousel.

* * *

August 11, 1942

Dear Oliver,

I got your sweet letter a few days ago, and I've been thinking about what you wrote ever since. First of all, I want to remind you that I don't plan to marry for several more years. I want, no, I need, to be on my own, independent, long enough to grow up, really grow up. Besides that, we've only had a few dates, and I don't think that would be a good start to being married. My first thought was, What happened to that man on that train to Camp Claiborne? But my next thought was, Do I have any of those feelings for him? Honestly, I'll admit, there have been times when I've felt something different when we were together. And honey, your kisses did set me on fire. But what does that really mean?

So here is my answer. No, of course I won't marry you when you get home. You may have been in love with me for years, but these emotions I have are too new, too raw, for me to act on them rashly. That wouldn't be fair to either of us.

But if you're willing to take this slow and to give me time to explore my feelings, I'm more than willing to go out with you, and only you.

What I won't do is jump into something so precious just because "there's a war on." Too many couples are doing that, and most of them don't have any idea of what love really is and should be. There just seems to be this sense of urgency, this need to belong to somebody, almost

200

anybody, and <u>right now</u>. This war may go on for years, and it'll probably get worse before it gets better. I don't think I could stand to send the man I loved off to fight and maybe die. I know that old saying, "Absence makes the heart grow fonder," and all that—but I doubt it would be the case with us. You've only been gone a few weeks, for Pete's sake.

I do love you, as a dear friend, one of my best friends in the whole world. As I've told you, I want to be sure that we don't endanger that friendship by trying to turn it into something more. Now, if that happens in a natural way, that's fine and dandy. Just don't come home from Louisiana expecting me to jump into your arms, because that won't happen. I'll be there to meet your train, if I'm not working. You can ask me out on a date whenever you want to, and I promise I'll say yes to that, and we can see how things develop.

But whatever happens, we cannot allow anything to destroy, or even weaken, our real, true friendship--because friends like you come along only a few times in a lifetime. <u>And I won't lose you that way!</u>

Hurry home—

Mae

She read over what she'd written, folded the pages, and slipped them into an envelope. Rummaging in a drawer, she found a purple three cent stamp. She gazed at the eagle's spread wings that made a beautiful "V." She loved the "V for Victory" campaign, even if it had started with Winston Churchill, the British Prime Minister. She always laughed at the newsreels when they showed Churchill getting out of a car, clamping his cigar between his teeth, and giving the Victory sign.

Victory soon. And bring Oliver back home soon, so we can get this settled.

THIRTY-ONE

A MYSTERY ILLNESS

WORK KEPT MAE DISTRACTED from thinking too hard about Oliver and their situation. Being transferred several times made her always the "new kid," always learning new production techniques, new rules. She wondered if she would ever begin to feel at home in her job.

A day came that caused her to feel like, finally, her position at Lone Star might be solidifying. Charles caught up with her in the bomb proof at supper. "Miss Johnson, could I speak with you for a minute?"

"Sure, Mr. Graham," she said, trying hard to keep a straight face. That became impossible when she heard his news.

"I'm going back home to Akron to get my wife and little boy. I've found us a house over in Beverly Addition, and I wrangled some time off. Man, I'm excited! It's been way too long."

"That's wonderful Ch—Mr. Graham."

"And when I get back, I plan to get you and Graydell moved to Area F. It's taken a while, but I've finally managed it. I've taken over swing shift, and there's room for a few more people there."

"That's great. Although, I don't know about Graydell. She's just changed to days, so she may not want to move again. If she doesn't, do you think . . ." She paused, afraid of sounding presumptuous.

202

"What is it, Mae?" They had walked outside where no one was around, so they were falling back into their old familiarity. "C'mon, spit it out." He grinned down at her.

"Well, I was wondering, if Graydell doesn't want to leave days . . . There's this woman I've been working with pretty much ever since I got here. I was thinking, maybe she could move with me instead of Graydell?"

He cocked his head and gave her a stern look. "Nothing has happened between you and Graydell, has it?"

Nothing except I don't approve of her boyfriend. "No, of course not," she answered. She just got tired of swing shift and I didn't, that's all. Tell me about your new place. Gosh, I feel like I already know Evonne, you've talked so much about her."

He laughed. "And I've talked a lot about you to Evie. I can't wait for the two of you to meet."

I hope she's as nice as Charles. She may not want to get acquainted with a southern girl, a hick from the river bottoms.

"Earth to Mae," he said. "Give me this woman's name, and I'll see what I can do."

Mae went back in and gathered her supper things, then headed out ahead of the crowd to stop off in the four-square public bathrooms. As the stepped into the building, her nose was assaulted by an awful smell, one she hadn't encountered except in the outhouse back home. "Oh, no, there's a stopped-up commode again," she muttered.

The sight she saw almost made her ill, but not because of all the sludge. There was Keesha, her childhood friend, pants legs rolled up halfway to her knees, her braids coiled atop her head, bent over the first commode, scrubbing for all she was worth. A dirty plunger lay beside her, and water, mixed with urine and excrement, covered the concrete floor.

"Bathroom's closed," Keesha said, looking over her shoulder. "Oh, it's you, Miss Mae. I'm sorry, but you'll have to go someplace else. I still got to clean up this mess."

"No problem," Mae said, backing out of the room. Outside, she leaned her back against the warm brick wall of the toilet facilities. *My*

Lord, to see someone I know having to do that kind of work. I'd have died off if someone had seen me having to do that! Tears sprang to her eyes, hearing again the way Keesha still called her "Miss Mae." She hated it, hated the way it made her feel, as if she were complicit in keeping blacks "in their place." She'd argued with her daddy for years over his use of the word "Nigger" that he used sometimes when he talked about the workers he hired from Nigger Bend, the black community a few miles down the highway.

"That's what they call theirselves," he always responded. But Mae knew instinctively he was wrong. She'd learned enough from Keesha to know blacks used the hateful word toward other blacks they saw as lazy or mean. They never called their family or their friends such a nasty word. "Colored" was bad enough, especially when the only job her "colored" friend could get here on this government job was cleaning bathrooms. She made it to the bushes nearby just in time, losing her lunch along with losing her sense of right and wrong.

* * *

Sure enough, Graydell stayed on days. The friends had always traveled to the plant together by bus or in a carpool, but now they hardly saw each other. Mae's trips to and from the plant were different, too, since the driver she'd ridden to work with also moved to days. That meant Graydell still had a ride, while Mae was back to riding one of the rickety, smelly buses. She didn't even mind *that*, she liked swing shift so much.

She had a few friends who also rode the bus, and sometimes they'd all stop at one of the restaurants that stayed open for the night workers; more often than not they were more than ready to get home to their beds.

Mae wasn't happy with Graydell and George together, though she knew it was mostly because he was Frank's friend. Only once did Mae try to caution her friend to watch out for George, and she quickly learned to leave the topic alone.

"Just because you don't get along with Frank, that's no reason to assume any friend of his can't be trusted. I like George, Mae, I *really* like him. So butt out!"

204

And Mae did.

Most nights when she got home about midnight, Graydell was still out—somewhere. Sometimes she made it in before Mae fell asleep, more often she didn't.

One night the two happened to cross paths. In the light of the half moon, Mae was surprised to see Graydell and George on the porch when she came dragging up the steps. Graydell was on George's lap, her skirt was hiked up, and Mae was embarrassed to see his hand inside the front of her unbuttoned blouse.

Mae looked away, opened the door, and went inside. She leaned against the closed door for a minute. *Oh, Grady, what are you doing?* She crawled upstairs to bed. Before she got her boots off, Graydell came into the room and plopped down on the sofa.

"I guess you think I'm just like my sister, huh?" she said. Her back was ramrod straight.

"What? Why do you say that? I never entertained such a thought."

"I know you saw what we were doing, and I know you think good girls don't do such things."

"Hey, Grady. Hold on. I can't say anything about that. Frank and I had some pretty heavy petting sessions sometimes, and we were just kids."

Graydell slid around on the sofa so she could face Mae. "Are you serious? You don't think bad of me?"

"Hell, no, I don't think bad of you. I worry about you, that's all. I mean, how well do you really know George? I know you don't like me saying this, but you did meet him through Frank. I just don't quite trust him. And I love you like a sister, always have. I don't want to see you get hurt."

"I won't get hurt. I'm a big girl now. So stop worrying about me. I'll be fine, okay?" She came to stand next to Mae's bed. Mae stood and hugged her.

"Okay, if you say so. But remember—if you ever need me, or need to talk, I'm here. I'll always be here for you, Grady."

"Thanks, buddy. And I'll be here for you. Always. Now, let's get some sleep."

* * *

Between work and pondering what her feelings for Oliver really were, Mae had little time to worry about Graydell's love life. She wished with all her might Oliver would hurry and get through with basic training so he could get home and they could get things settled. The waiting made her all antsy.

One Saturday afternoon, she mailed a letter to him and then spent a few hours shopping up and down Broad Street. After a lonely lunch at Kress's, she was shocked to meet Frank coming down the stairs when she got home.

"Frank! What are you doing here?"

"Hello, Mae. Just helping out a friend. How are you?"

She didn't answer him. "What friend? And what were you doing upstairs? You know how our landlady feels about men on the premises."

"Hell, yeah, I know about her hang-ups. Well, I checked to see if she was here before we came in."

He tried to push past her on the stairs, but she stood firm in his path. She didn't even feel the usual stomach butterflies when he moved very close to her.

"Exactly who is 'we'?" It had to be one of three people, and if he'd ever met the other women who lived here, she wasn't aware of it.

She put a hand on his arm and squeezed. There was nothing romantic in her gesture, and Frank stared at her hand and refused to meet her eyes.

"Fine. If you must know, I was doing a favor for Graydell. But she didn't want anyone to know, so don't say you saw me, okay?"

Mae's stomach seemed suddenly to be full of rocks, and she felt a tingling set in from her neck all the way down to her toes. She cringed inside. She'd had a feeling like this only a few times in her life, and every time, something awful happened soon afterward. She pushed past Frank and hurried up the stairs.

She found Graydell behind her curtain, covers drawn up. She couldn't tell if her friend was sleeping, so she tiptoed to the bed.

"Grady?" she whispered. "You okay?"

There was no movement, no sound. Mae stood watching the measured breathing, but she didn't have the will to force herself on Graydell. If her friend didn't want to talk to her, there was nothing she could do about it. She tossed her packages on her bed, eased out of her shoes, and lay back with a sigh. Before she knew it, she was fast asleep.

She woke in darkness, the only light the almost full moon that shone through the French doors. *What time is it?* Her stomach told her she had slept through supper time. She reached for the lamp but then remembered Graydell. *Wonder if she's still here. I hope she's okay.*

She sat up on the side of the bed and stretched, feeling her muscles begin to respond. *Think I'll straighten our beds so we can sleep easier tonight—if it is still night. Clock says 9:30, so it must be.* When she finished her bed, she crossed to Graydell's and turned back the bedspread to straighten the sheets. Then she saw it.

There was a drying puddle of blood on Graydell's sheet. "Guess she's on her period," Mae thought aloud. "She must be having a rough time this month." Mae set about remaking her friend's bed. She found the one extra sheet Graydell had and, after putting an old towel on the mattress to soak up the blood, smoothed on the fresh sheet. Then she took the stained sheet to their small sink and began scrubbing out the blood. She was still at it when the door opened and Graydell walked in.

"What the hell are you doing?" she asked, slamming the door. Mae turned from the sink to face a stormy-eyed Graydell, her back against the door and her arms crossed. Mae had never seen such fury in her friend's eyes, black as night and emitting sparks.

Mae ignored her. "Hey, Grady. How're you feeling? I woke up and you were gone, so I was going to make your bed. I guess you're having a rough time this month, huh? It's a good thing it's the weekend. I'm glad you have tomorrow to rest up."

Graydell stared at her a moment looking puzzled. "Oh, um, yeah, I guess so," she said. "But you don't have to do that, Mae."

"Yes, I do," Mae said, turning back to her scrubbing and rinsing. "What are best friends for, if not to help each other out when it counts?"

Graydell crossed the room and put her hands on Mae's shoulders. "Thanks, Mae. You're a girl's best friend. No, that's not right." She shook Mae's shoulders gently. "You're *my* best friend."

"And you're mine. Now get back in bed and cover up. You don't need a chill on top of having bad cramps."

"You're righter than you know," Graydell said. Gently she settled down onto the bed and slipped out of her house shoes. Sighing, she lay down and started to pull the sheet up.

Mae came over and reached to cover her with the quilt. "Can I get you anything? Have you taken aspirin?" She was surprised to see tears glistening on Graydell's cheeks. Grady, who never cried.

"I'll be fine," her friend replied. "I just need some more sleep. And yes, I took aspirin when I first woke up."

"Well, okay, then. I'll let you get back to sleep. I'll probably go down to the parlor and read for a while until I get sleepy again. I really went out like a light when I got home this afternoon and found you asleep." She was careful not to mention seeing Frank inside the house. "I guess I was extra tired, too."

She bent down to brush a stray curl out of Graydell's eyes, and her fingers brushed her forehead.

"Graydell, you're burning up! I thought you said you already took aspirin."

"I did." Graydell pushed Mae's hand away. "Just leave me alone, Mae. Go on down and do your reading. I'll be better in the morning."

But she wasn't better. In fact, to Mae she seemed worse. Mae tried to get her to eat some scrambled eggs she'd brought upstairs, but Graydell just shoved the plate away and turned over. Mae patted the back of her head, then slipped her hand onto Graydell's forehead.

"Your forehead is hotter than it was last night! We need to do something for it. That's probably why you can't eat."

Suddenly Graydell began to shake so hard her bed shook. Mae was beside herself. "I don't know what to do for you, Grady," she whined. "Do you need to go to the hospital?"

"No!" Grady said between gritted teeth. "Just leave me alone. Please. I'll be alright soon."

The shaking finally passed, and Graydell drifted off to sleep. Mae curled up at the foot of the bed. When Graydell woke about noon, she seemed better. Mae touched her forehead and was relieved to feel it covered with sweat and much cooler.

"Do you think you could eat something now?"

She managed to get most of a piece of toast down her friend, but Graydell insisted Mae go about her usual business and leave her to her bed.

Mae fretted through that day and night, feeling helpless. She couldn't help being concerned, for Graydell had always had an easy time with her monthly periods. For the past few months, she had kept up her frenetic pace, going from work to play and right back to work again, and Mae had not once caught her lying in bed due to any kind of illness at all.

Wonder if she and George broke up. Maybe that's why Frank brought her home. She knew better than to bring up the subject. Grady was obviously having the worst period of her life, and it was no time to ask if she had just lost her boyfriend. That topic could wait for another day.

Graydell spent most of Sunday in bed, only getting up to go down the hall to the bathroom and to get occasional glasses of water. Finally, about eight that night, Mae coaxed her into sipping some of the vegetable soup she'd cooked for work the coming week. She wouldn't, however, eat any cornbread.

Mae was up and down throughout the night to check on Graydell, whose fever went through cycles of spiking sky high and returning to almost normal. Mae fixed cool cloths for the feverish times, when Graydell reluctantly allowed her forehead to be bathed, and she took the aspirins whenever Mae held them out to her.

They didn't discuss anything of consequence during that long weekend. Graydell was too ill to be forthcoming, and Mae feared making her friend angry enough to refuse her help altogether.

In the early hours of Monday morning, she fell into an exhausted sleep herself, and when she opened her eyes at seven that morning sunlight was shining on the hardwood floor. She sat up abruptly, swinging her legs to the floor and looking across to Graydell's bed.

I hope I haven't slept through a crisis.

"Morning, Mae," Graydell's weak voice came from the depth of her bed covers.

Mae padded across the room to sit at the foot of her friend's bed. "Oh, Grady, are you feeling better this morning? I've been so worried."

"A little, I think. How about you? Have you been getting any sleep at all?"

"Oh, sure, plenty," Mae lied, trying but failing to stifle a wide yawn.

"Why don't you go back to sleep, and I'll wake you in time for you to eat something and get ready for work."

"That sounds great. If you're sure you're okay—"

"I'll be fine. I'm going to take a bath. I'm staying home today, maybe tomorrow, too. I just need a little more time to get over this."

Mae nodded and returned to her bed, where she turned her back to the room and stared at the wall. Suddenly she wasn't sleepy at all. She had just had the most horrible thought. She couldn't go on without knowing whether she was right, but she had no idea how to broach the subject with Graydell. If she was right, it might bring disaster to their friendship. Despite her unease, Mae finally slept, but fitfully.

THIRTY-TWO

UNIMAGINABLE

WHEN MAE GOT HOME Tuesday night, Graydell had fixed some toast and scrambled eggs for them. While they ate, she informed Mae she felt well enough to get back to work.

"That's great, Grady!" Mae enthused. "Your friends have asked about you every day when I'm coming and they're going, and I know they're anxious for you to come back."

"Not as anxious as I am," Graydell said. "I've had about enough of that tiny bed over there. You know I've never been one to take to my bed—"

"Like Prissy? Bless her heart." They laughed.

"Yes, I do love the girl, but you would think nobody in the world had ever experienced the world just like Prissy has. If I were her mother, I'd probably strangle her," Graydell said.

Mae took her empty plate to the sink and came to sit back down, but she kept her gaze on the tablecloth. *How do I begin this conversation? It's always been so easy to talk to Graydell about anything and everything. Lord, please give me the right words.*

"Graydell, can we talk about something?"

"Tonight? It's almost one in the morning. Can't it wait till later?"

Mae looked up at her friend. Graydell was still pale, and she would have to get up early. She wavered, and the moment was lost.

"Sure, Grady, that'll be fine."

"Thanks. I'm so tired, despite what I just said about being sick of lying around. It's been so boring here by myself, and I look forward to work, but my body says it's time to get some more sleep. Go figure." She shrugged, taking her plate to the sink, too. Then she surprised Mae by washing out the used utensils before going to bed.

"I could do those," Mae protested.

"Nope, get ready for bed. Maybe I'll see you at the plant. Say, how's that soup holding out? I could eat some for lunch tomorrow, if there's plenty."

Mae opened their tiny Frigidaire and checked the soup. "Yep, there's lots left. I ended up not taking any today. Help yourself. There's cornbread, too."

"Thanks, Mae. Now, get to bed. I'll try not to wake you in the morning."

"Bet you won't. 'Night, Grady. Love you."

"Love you, too, my friend. Sleep tight."

* * *

There was no opportunity for the friends to have a serious discussion until the weekend. Mae had planned to go home for the weekend, but she needed to clear the air with Graydell more than she needed to see her folks. So on Wednesday afternoon she mailed a brief letter to her mother, saying she might need to work that weekend, and so was postponing her visit.

It's been so busy out at the plant for the past couple of weeks. I feel like my time is coming up soon, so I probably won't make a trip home until after I work a shift of overtime. Give everybody my love—even that stinker of a kid sister.

She actually did stay over on Thursday night. She worked four hours extra, getting home about an hour before daylight. She collapsed onto her bed without doing more than taking off her boots. She didn't hear Graydell at all when she left a couple of hours later.

When Saturday arrived, both girls slept in, rising in time to make some tuna salad. Over lunch, they discussed their plans for the rest of the weekend. When Graydell didn't say anything about George, Mae felt she had to know what was going on.

"You don't have plans with George tonight? I haven't seen him around lately."

Graydell's expression darkened, as if all the light in her world had gone out that very second.

"No, no plans. There won't be any plans with him in the future, either."

"Really? Oh, Grady, I'm so sorry. You seemed pretty serious about him, the best I could tell."

"I thought I was. I thought I *loved* him. But after I found out what he was really like—I could never care that much about a man like him."

"What do you mean by what he was really like? What did he do?"

"I don't want to talk about it," Graydell whispered. "It's no use."

Mae took a deep breath and plunged in.

"Graydell, I've spent the past week worried sick about you, and I'm so happy to see you finally looking like your old self—mostly. But watching over you, cleaning up after you—"

"You didn't have to do it. I could have taken care of myself."

"Sure you could, sweetie." Mae sat back in her chair.

"I don't want to talk about it, I said. Why can't you leave it alone?" Tears welled in Graydell's dark and brooding eyes and spilled down her cheeks when she finally blinked. "Why can't you leave *me* alone?"

"Because I care about you. You're my best friend, and I've felt like a nurse instead of a friend this week. Nurses take care of you, but friends take care of you *and* share your problems."

The tears continued to stream down Graydell's cheeks. "Don't make me talk about it, Mae. I'm already so ashamed, and I don't want you looking down on me."

"Why would I do that? Haven't we always said we could forgive each other anything?"

"It's not you I need forgiveness from," Graydell said, wiping her eyes with a dish towel.

"Then who? George?"

"No! Not him." But she would say no more.

Mae said, so softly she wasn't sure Graydell would hear her but in a voice she could barely make work, "Were you sick because of your monthly, or . . ." She could not make herself say the words. It was Graydell's turn now. Would she open up or not?

"No," her friend answered back, speaking as softly as Mae. Both women spoke in low voices, as if the walls had ears. Sometimes it seemed as if Mrs. Swenson did. "It wasn't my period. It was . . . It was a baby." She burst into tears again.

Mae's worst fears had just been confirmed.

"Oh, honey, I'm so sorry. Does George know you lost the baby?"

Graydell was shaking her head wildly, her black curls flying. "No, you don't understand! It wasn't like that."

Mae was confused. "What do you mean? And what did Frank have to do with it?" Graydell lifted her eyes to meet Mae's. "Yes, you don't know this, but I met Frank on the stairs last Saturday, when you were so sick. He told me to go easy on you, that you weren't feeling well."

Graydell gave a bitter laugh, "Well, that was sure the truth. And at least he stood by me—which is more than I can say for George."

"Stood by you? So George does know about the baby, that you lost it?"

"He knows there was a baby. He didn't want anything to do with it—or with me." She spat out the next words. "He even said maybe the baby wasn't his, that maybe I was just trying to trap him, that I wanted to get married before he went off to war so I could collect his pay."

The flood of words hit Mae like a slap in the face. She'd never liked George, but she couldn't imagine any man saying such things to someone he was supposed to care for.

She jumped up and ran around the table to put her arm around Graydell. "Sweetie, I can't fathom a man who could behave that way! Why, goodness knows, you spent just about every waking hour with him. You wouldn't have had time or opportunity to fool around on him even if you were that kind of girl. He is just one sorry S.O.B.!"

Graydell stopped crying and looked up at Mae. She gave a hiccup, trying not to get strangled on the air she had sucked in. "I've never in my life heard you talk about somebody that way."

"Well, he is. I just spoke the truth."

"Yes, he really is a sorry S.O.B., and I'm a dummy for not recognizing that until it was too late."

"Don't beat yourself up over that. There are plenty of girls who put their faith in the wrong man." Realizing her last words may have hurt Graydell more, she added, "I mean, it would be nice if we could always know the men we fall in love with for years beforehand. But then I guess the world would get to where it would be a pretty boring place."

Graydell blew her nose into the dish towel, then dropped it onto the floor. "I guess you're right. But I could use a bit of boring right now. I'd sure like to turn back the clock to about three months ago, to see if I could make a better choice when I got together with George."

"Well, you've learned a valuable lesson at least."

"That I have. I guess our mothers were right, and everyone else, telling us we should 'save' ourselves for marriage. The debt you pay if you don't is almost unbearable."

"I'm sorry, Grady. I'm so sorry you lost the baby."

"Oh, I didn't *lose* the baby, Mae. I got *rid* of it."

Graydell spoke quietly but with a fierceness that took Mae aback as much as her actual words had.

"You *what*? Are you saying you—that you had a—an—"

"Abortion. God, I never thought I'd say that word in relation to myself."

215

Mae moved back toward her chair in a daze. She couldn't be hearing this. Her best friend could not have just said she had an abortion. She couldn't have said she "got rid of it." Not Graydell.

"See, Mae? That's why I didn't want to ever tell you! I can't stand the idea of you looking at me like—like you are right now. And when everybody else knows, everybody will be looking at me the same way as you."

For once in her life, Mae was at a total loss for words. She couldn't wrap her mind around the words she'd heard coming from Graydell's mouth. She stood and left the table, retreating to the balcony, where she curled into a ball in one of the rockers. Graydell didn't follow her. When she went inside later, her friend was gone.

THIRTY-THREE

SATURDAY IN THE PARK

A WEEK PASSED WITHOUT the two friends setting eyes on each other. When Mae got home at night, Graydell's curtain was drawn tightly around her bed. When she woke sometime mid-morning, Graydell had already been at work for hours.

She must feel as tense as I do. We have got to work this out. But it seems bad to ruin two weekends in a row over this.

That was Mae on Wednesday, when she realized that, again, she'd slept through Graydell getting dressed and leaving for work. At work herself, she was distracted, frustrated, and careless, causing her bay leader to comment, "Now, ladies, let's not have everyone start acting like Blondie here, or we're all liable to get blown to smithereens!"

Johnie tried to talk to her on their dinner break, but Mae just shook her head, tossed her half-eaten sandwich in the trash, and headed back to the line early for a change. She could feel Johnie's eyes on her from time to time, but the older woman didn't try anymore to get her to open up.

By Friday night, she had determined she would be up before Graydell on Saturday, and she set her clock for seven. But she tossed and turned for hours, and when the insistent clang of the alarm finally reached her, she groggily fumbled to push the button in, cussing a bit when it eluded her. She emerged from the sheets about eleven, and when she pulled her curtain, Graydell was already gone.

I'll be damned if I stay in this apartment all day brooding. Think I'll catch the bus and head out to Spring Lake Park. The park was the closest thing in Texarkana to the woods back in Dixon's Crossing. If she'd been home and had fallen out with Graydell, that's exactly where she'd be. She dressed in jeans and a plaid shirt, turning up the cuffs on both, and slipped into saddle oxfords. Tying Oliver's scarf around her ponytail, she set out.

Oh, Ollie, how I wish you were here. For half an hour she'd been sitting on a bench staring at the water, brooding over the confrontation with Graydell, oblivious of the kids playing chase around her. Lovers strolled by hand in hand, stopping occasionally for an embrace, but she hardly noticed. *I'm sure you'd be able to fix things. But you're not here, are you? And it's not even like I could write to you for advice about this. Graydell would never forgive me if I shared her secret. She may never forgive me anyway for walking away from her the other night. But the outcome of this is all up to me. Lord, I know you won't hold this against her. So how can I? Please help me find a way to make things right between us again. She's my best friend—next to Oliver.*

She stood and physically shook off the malaise that had held her captive for the last few days. Physical activity, that's what she needed. She set off on the trail that circled the small lake. The early autumn air had a hint of crispness to it. Billowy clouds were reflected in the clear spring water of the lake. Taking in deep breaths, she finally began to feel more like herself. Reaching the far shore, she broke into a whistling rendition of "Little Brown Jug," one of her favorite Glenn Miller tunes. Lost in the effort to capture the correct notes, she was unaware she was being watched from the very bench she'd recently vacated, until she'd made it almost all the way back around the lake.

"Say, if it isn't the Whistling Woman from Dixon's Crossing!" She broke off in embarrassment, glancing around to see where he was. Frank was sitting on *her* bench, Graydell beside him. *What the hell?*

She made her way slowly to the two people in the world she'd most wanted to see, if for very different reasons. She looked imploringly at Graydell. "Hey, how are you, Grady? We've been missing each other all week."

Graydell shrugged. "Figured that's the way you'd prefer it." The brunette didn't look at her but stared across the lake, with its rippling waves glistening in the sunshine. The dark scowl on her face told Mae she was still hurting.

"What brought you two out here today?" she asked, looking directly at Frank.

"Oh, we didn't come together," he said. "Guess everybody decided it was a good day to spend in the outdoors."

"I was just leaving," Graydell said, standing and picking up her purse.

"But you just got here," Mae protested. "Can't you stay a while?" She could see her friend wavering. Graydell looked down at Frank, who took the hint. *For once in his ever-loving life.*

"Well, you ladies carry on. I need to see a man about a horse." He stood and tipped his hat to first one then the other. "See you soon, maybe." He whistled "Little Brown Jug" all the way to his car. *Wonder where he got that car. And where he got the money for it. Probably bootlegging.*

"Want to sit awhile?" Mae asked, sitting down in Frank's spot. Graydell looked as if she were almost afraid to sit down. "C'mon, Grady, please?" Graydell finally eased back down onto the bench, perched as if ready to take flight at a moment's notice, like the sparrows that had alighted in the nearby rose bush.

Graydell was watching the little birds intently, and Mae chanced a comment. "They remind me of the house sparrows that are always trying to build mud houses under the eaves back home. Mama knocks their houses down as soon as she sees them going to work, and they just move up higher at the end of the house where she can't reach."

Graydell smiled. "Yeah, my mother, too. I don't mind them, myself."

"Me either. There are probably lots of ways we have that are different from our mothers." She took a deep breath and plunged ahead. "Grady, I'm so sorry for the way I bolted out of the room the other night. It was stupid, and—"

"No, that's alright. I don't blame you. I wouldn't want to be in the same room with someone like me, either. Not after—"

"Not after almost *dying*?" Mae broke in. "Grady, I could have lost you! Every time I think back on how sick you were, I could kick myself for not making you go to a doctor."

"You couldn't have made me, even if it killed me. There's no way I could face anybody else after what I'd done."

"Hey, you're human, like all the rest of us. You know, because I've told you before, how I used to carry on with Frank. He has no idea how many times I came close to going all the way with him."

"But you didn't. That's the difference between us."

"Yeah, but I was so young then. I was just too scared of what my folks would do if something like that happened and they found out. I really wanted to."

"I thought George loved me, Mae. I really thought he did. He said so, over and over, and he talked about us having a life together. And dumb me, I believed him." She took a handkerchief from her purse and wiped her eyes, then blew her nose.

Mae reached for her instinctively and drew her close. Graydell put her face into Mae's shoulder and let her tears fall unheeded. Her shoulders shook as she cried, and Mae felt tears welling in her own eyes. "We've always said we could forgive each other anything," she said, her voice husky, "but can you forgive me for walking away from you when you needed me?"

Graydell drew back. "Forgive *you*? What about you forgiving *me*?"

"We both know I'm not supposed to be passing judgment against you or anybody else. We learned that even before we started school. And how many instances are there in the Bible of God, and then Jesus, forgiving people who'd done much worse things? No, Grady, I'm the one needing forgiveness, for not supporting you when you were so down."

"You can still be friends with me, after what I've done?"

"If you can still be friends with me," Mae said, her grin wobbly. "I don't just want to be friends. I want us to go back to being best friends."

"Best buds? You got it," Graydell said. The two hugged again, tighter this time.

"Honk! Honk!" came from the lake as a huge white gander waded ashore and headed toward them, letting them know they were in his territory. Graydell's squeal gave him pause, and Mae's flapping arms finally brought him to a stop a few feet away. He shook from head to splayed feet, smoothed his ruffled feathers, and padded away without a backward glance.

"That's what we should do," Mae said, standing and giving her body a very deliberate shake. "Shake off everything that's happened in the last few months, and just start over."

"Deal," Graydell said, imitating Mae. The two laughed and hugged again, then headed off to the bus stop arm in arm.

THIRTY-FOUR

HELLO, DARLIN'

"LOOK WHO'S BACK IN action!" Scotty Yates said as Mae walked up to her favorite table at the Jump and Jive. "You've been gone too long. How about a dance to celebrate?" He held out his hand, beckoning to her.

Laughing, she dropped her purse on the empty chair, smiled at Charles and Evonne, and gave Scotty her hand. Evonne winked. "I've only missed a couple of weeks. Don't make such a big deal over it."

"Two weeks without our Mae is like two months without other girls," he said, as he twirled her around in one of his fancy jitterbug moves.

Her eyes scanned the dimly lit room as they danced their way around the floor.

"Have you found a girl yet, Scotty?"

"Nope, still looking. Why? You available?"

"Me? Oh, no," she laughed. "I was thinking about a friend of mine."

"Miss Graydell?" he asked, as he spun her around at the end of the song. "I've asked her out a few times, but I think she's too hung up on that Snow guy."

She picked up her purse and slid into the chair, looking at him across the table. "You should try again, if you're still interested. You might be surprised by her response." She gave him a wink.

His eyebrows rose. "Really?"

She nodded, then turned to say hello to the others. She had done her part. Anything else would be up to Scotty.

* * *

Mae hated the seat she'd inherited tonight. She usually arrived early, but she'd been so caught up in the drama with Graydell that she hadn't felt like going out at all. But then Graydell went to a movie with a couple of women she worked with. The two had made their peace, but it was proving difficult to get back the easy closeness they'd shared before. Suddenly Mae couldn't stand the thought of being in the apartment alone.

She tried, really tried. She turned on the radio and tuned in to The Opry, something that used to bring her pleasure. She got out the linseed oil—but the furniture was so sparse it didn't take long to polish it all to a shine. She picked up the paperback she'd started during Graydell's worst nights, when she'd wanted to stay awake. But the book reminded her of what Graydell had done, and she threw it against the wall. *The only option is to get out of this apartment.*

So here she sat, her back to the room at large. Everyone else at her table was out on the floor, so she scooted her chair around so she could watch them. Her mind drifted to the last time she'd seen Oliver. It had been eleven whole weeks, and she found herself missing him more than ever.

"Hello, darlin'," the familiar voice whispered into her ear. She had been waiting for this chance. She spun in her chair to see that Frank had sat down in the seat next to her. She stared into his gorgeous brown eyes, and he winked, the bastard, his mouth slipping into his old, familiar one-sided, full-lipped smile.

She said nothing, simply stared at him, and finally his smile began to fade. She hoped he could feel the chill in her eyes, the contempt she felt for him.

"We're not talking tonight, sweet thing?"

That did it.

"Don't you *ever* call me that again," she spat out, her green eyes flashing.

"Aw, you know you love it," he said, laying a hand on her knee.

She knocked it away. "Don't, Frank. Just . . . don't."

"You're serious, aren't you?" She continued to stare, willing all the disgust she felt to show in her eyes.

"What's wrong with you, Mae? You're not acting like you at all."

"That's because I'm trying to figure out where to start in giving you a piece of my mind."

"For what? Oh, Graydell."

"Yes, Graydell. She was too sick to talk for *days*! Her fever shot sky high, but she wouldn't even *talk* about seeing a doctor. I couldn't understand why she fought me about it for so long. But when I finally figured it out, and she admitted it to me—"

Frank jumped up and grabbed her hand. "We don't need to be airing this in here." He looked around the room at the crowd of people. Come on."

She fought him for a minute, but when she looked around, she saw Scotty eying the two of them. His face looked like a thundercloud, so she gave him a reassuring smile as they headed for the door. He shrugged and turned his attention back to his dance partner.

Outside the club, Frank took off across the parking lot, but Mae stood where she was, still in the light of the Jump & Jive's neon sign. He stopped when he realized she wasn't following him. He turned to see her standing with feet apart, arms crossed in her visualization of a warrior's stance. *Or maybe Tarzan.*

"You need to understand, Mae," he said, walking back toward her.

How can he look sexy to me, when I'm so disgusted by him?

"Graydell came to me, not the other way around."

"Why would she come to you, instead of to her friends? That makes no sense."

224

"Maybe she thought y'all would look down on her." Mae opened her mouth, but then closed it again. Maybe he had a point.

"I didn't intend it. It started when I walked in on her and George having a fight over at our place."

"What!"

"Well, not a *fight* fight. But George was drinking—it looked like he'd been going at it for a while—and Graydell was crying. I felt so sorry for her, cause ol' George was acting like she was just nothing but a piece of trash. And he was always carrying her around on a platter. I couldn't figure out what had changed."

"I never have liked that man," Mae said. "I tried to warn her away from him."

"He's a pretty good guy—but he was sure acting different that night. He drained his beer and said, 'I'm out of here. Maybe *you* can talk some sense into her.' Then he just left. I thought Graydell had been crying before, but she really started squalling then. And she started spilling her guts. She couldn't seem to stop, and . . . I don't know how much she told you—"

"Enough," Mae spat. "She told me she got pregnant but George didn't want anything to do with her or the baby. Then she said you helped her get an abortion. But Frank, how could you?"

"Hey, wait a minute. I didn't ask to get involved. I just sort of fell into it. I'd had some experience with this guy—"

"You mean you've taken girls to him before?" Mae was stunned. *I thought I knew this man.*

"Well, yeah," he admitted. "But only a couple of them were girls I was involved with. The rest—"

But she didn't let him finish. "Are you telling me you've helped girls who were pregnant with *your baby* to get abortions?"

He stared back at her, wordless but unbowed.

"Don't you have anything to say for yourself?"

"Why should I? You're not going to accept anything I have to say." He spat on the ground, so near Mae instinctively moved her shoe.

"You know there's no excuse you could give me that would be acceptable."

"It would be to anybody who had even an inkling of how the real world operates."

"Oh, I know how it operates, at least your world. I know men like you and George do your best to take what you want, when you want it, no matter the cost. If y'all had any decency, then he would never have walked out on Graydell and she wouldn't have felt like she had no choice but to get that abortion."

"Don't be blaming me. I was just trying to help out a friend."

"I do blame you! Graydell wasn't thinking straight, and she could have *died*. Did you think of that?"

"Nobody's ever had a bad time before, nobody I ever took to him."

"Oh, so that made it okay to for you to take my best friend to this *quack*? She had chills and fever for *days*. And she bled. My God, Frank, she lost so much blood." Her voice quivered.

"Aw, I hate to hear that. But she's okay, isn't she? She looked okay Saturday."

"I guess so, but she's been through a lot. I don't know if she'll ever be okay about getting rid of that baby. I know I wouldn't." A couple came out of the club, laughing as they swept by Mae and Frank. She waited until they had reached their car to continue. "You men are all the same. You're always after us girls to have sex, but then you're never around when something happens."

"And you girls are all the same. You put out just enough to get us guys all hot and bothered, then you just quit putting out and leave us to our own devices."

"We do no such thing! Think it's easy on us? We have feelings, too."

"That's another thing I admire about Graydell. She at least went after what she wanted. So she got caught, and George didn't back her up. That's one reason I helped her."

226

"Lord, keep me from any kind of help like that, from you or anybody else!"

"You won't have to worry about that, sweet thing. You never had a hard time calling a halt, and you'd always seem so cool and collected—after."

She didn't even know she was going to slap him. But she reared back and struck him across the face as hard as her farm girl's arm could. The slap whipped his head hard to the right. They stared at each other without speaking.

Frank closed his eyes for a moment and sighed. When he opened them again, there were tears glistening in Mae's eyes.

"Aw, hell, Mae," he growled, grabbing her by the shoulders and pulling her tight against him. She stood stiffly in his arms, but he ground his lips against hers. She could taste alcohol on his tongue as he thrust it into her mouth, along with a strong hint of the Camel cigarettes he favored. The familiarity captured her for a moment, and she relaxed her lips to allow him entrance. The kiss went on and on, and she began to feel dizzy from the lack of enough air, but he only gave her a second to grab a breath before he descended on her again.

His hands roved over her back before dipping a bit lower. Keeping one at her waist, holding her close, he slid the other hand around and cupped her breast. "Oh, Mae, sweetie, I've missed this so much," he said, squeezing gently and using his thumb to tease at her nipple.

For just one small moment, Mae was right back where she had been with Frank so many times. He always awoke feelings in her she knew she shouldn't give in to, no matter how much she wanted to. She'd never wanted to end up in the same situation as Graydell. And now there was Oliver. What she had with him was the real thing. *What would he say if he could see me right now? Why am I even allowing this at all?*

She clasped his hand and shoved it away from her breast. "No, Frank, don't. You know you have an effect on me, but you don't really know me anymore. No, stop," she said as he reached for her again. She was finding it difficult to speak—her lips and tongue were numb from his wild kisses.

"Here we go again," he began. "Just like old times. You tease and then you back off."

"Shut up. If you keep talking like that, I'm going to have to slap you again," she managed to say. "I didn't start this, and I certainly wasn't 'teasing' you. I was trying to tell you how wrong you are in your thinking. Can't you see what I'm talking about? *You* kissed *me*. Even if I ended up kissing you back, that doesn't mean I want to have sex with you."

"But you do want to, don't you?" he whispered.

"No! Haven't you been listening? I said you don't know me anymore. And it's true. I've changed. I've grown, and I'm growing up. And I'm in love with someone, really in love."

He took a step back from her. She could sense as much as see him clenching and unclenching his fists. "Who is he? Some army guy in a fancy uniform, I guess? Where did you meet him? What do you know about him?" He leaned in toward her, his face only inches from hers. "Does he kiss as good as I do?"

She couldn't help smiling. "It's not somebody I just met. It's Oliver. Oliver Cranfield."

"Cranfield! You've known him all your life. You never dated each other. You're just having a relapse from us breaking up. That has to be it."

"Oh, get over yourself, Frank! Not every girl is always going to fall at your feet. I'm certainly not. Yes, it's true we've known each other forever, and I do know just about everything about him. I love him, I really do." She couldn't resist saying, "And yes, Frank, he kisses at least as good as you, maybe better."

He ground out a curse. "Fine, Mae. I guess we've said about everything that needs to be said. I hope *Oliver* makes you a very happy woman." He spat on the ground again, spun on his heel, and stalked away into the darkness.

I'm sure he will. And now you can go on back to Evangeline.

228

THIRTY-FIVE

FRANK – AGAIN!

MAE YANKED OPEN THE front door. She was late and she was exasperated. She was supposed to meet Prissy at Kress's in twenty minutes, and her hair had given her fits today, of all days. Finally, disgusted, she had gathered it all into a high ponytail and said the heck with it. It had felt funny bobbing down the stairs, making her feel like a little girl again.

She sniffed. *Camels*. She looked around to see Frank sitting in the porch swing, lazily blowing smoke rings.

"What the heck are you doing here? I don't have time to deal with you this morning."

"That's a fine way to greet an old friend," he purred, coming close to her.

"You're not a friend of mine, not anymore," she said, locking the door behind her and taking two paces toward the steps. "You have no business being here."

"Oh, yes, we have business," he said, his tone serious for once. "I need to talk to you."

"Well, I don't want to talk to you." She hated remembering their recent confrontation.

"Please, Mae. We need to talk . . . or at least I do."

"I don't have time to listen," she said. "I'm meeting Prissy in twenty minutes, and it's a fifteen-minute walk to Kress's."

"Then let me take you. I'll get you there fast, so we'll have time for that talk."

"No, Frank, I don't want—"

"Mae," he said, his voice velvet. "Just a few minutes. I want to apologize for what happened a while back."

She was taken aback. This was a first.

"Really?" She felt herself hesitate.

"Really. Come on, my car's just up the block."

She hesitated, but finally said, "Well, okay, I guess. But don't make me late! I promised Prissy."

"Then we'd better hurry."

Once in the car, Frank turned to face Mae. She searched his face, looking for the Frank she knew so well, the one who always had a wisecrack, but all she saw was a serious expression, one she'd only seen a few times, mostly when they were making out.

"I want to say how sorry I am about what Graydell went through. I'm sorry I ever introduced her to George Snow. He's always been a good friend of mine, but after the way he treated her, and the way he reacted when he found out she was pregnant, well, I told him how I felt about the whole deal, and I told him to get lost."

"Wow, Frank, that's . . . that's surprising, for sure. But I'm glad to know you can realize the wrongness of the whole thing."

"I know. I did what I felt was best at the time. Graydell came and told me what she wanted. I tried to talk her out of it, but you know what she's like when her mind is made up."

"I do know," Mae agreed. "We had a long talk about it. I realized how much she was determined not to put her mother through what Clara did."

"I thought that was part of it. She was just so desperate for help."

"And, of course, you knew just where to take her." She let the malice creep into her voice. She wasn't about to make this easy on him.

"Well, I thought I did. I mean, I've taken a few girls there before, but it was a different doctor when we got there. I didn't know he was such a quack, Mae, honest I didn't. The other doctor always did a good job, and the girls were fine after."

"Who had you taken there before? I mean the ones pregnant with your baby." *Let's see how honest he's willing to be.*

"Oh, come on. I can't tell you that. Rather, I won't. They were good girls, just got in a fix and needed help, and I supplied it."

Maybe he did have an ounce of honor. "But you have gotten girls pregnant."

"Once was a long time ago. I was fifteen. In fact, it was just before we moved back to Dixon's Crossing and I met you. Daddy helped me get her to this place where I took Graydell. Then I took another girl that I got in trouble, before you and I ever dated. She told some of her friends, so when they got in trouble I helped them, too. That's all, Mae, I swear."

Mae zeroed in on what he had said first. "Your *daddy* took you?" She was flabbergasted. What kind of father was Mr. Cummings?

"You've never met Daddy, have you? He thinks he's God's gift to women. That's probably why Mama left him in the first place. He ran around on her their whole lives. He'd come home and they'd make up, and Mama would end up pregnant again. Then Daddy would go out looking for someplace else to get his satisfaction, up till time for Mama to have the baby. He always got back home in time for that."

"My gosh, Frankie, what a horrible way to live. You never told me any of that."

"Yeah, well, it's not something that's easy to talk about. I always wanted you to think well of me, and I didn't think you would if you knew."

"You thought I'd think bad of you because of what your daddy was like?"

"I was embarrassed, I guess, more than anything else. I mean, look Mae, look at your family. They're good people, and they care about each other a lot, anybody can see that. I bet your daddy never looked at another woman in his life after he hooked up with your mama."

Mae grinned to herself. The very idea of her parents "hooking up" with each other . . . She and Mama had had one conversation about that subject, and she still couldn't believe Mama had talked about it with her.

She could still see her mother sitting in the rocking chair, while Mae sat on the top step, and they had their "talk" about the birds and the bees. Mama had cautioned Mae about going with boys, and what the boys would want from her. Then she had shocked Mae by talking about her and Daddy's courtship, in detail.

"Your daddy even begged me to, you know, to sleep with him, after we'd been going together for quite a while. I'd been expecting him to ask me to marry him, but then he came out with *that* instead. Well, you can bet I sent him packing that night, and I didn't know if I'd ever go out with him again.

"But he came around the next day and asked me to go walking with him, and I did. He cried and said how sorry he was to have asked me that, that he knew I was a good girl, and he would never ask me that again. Leastwise not until we were married."

"Was that how he proposed to you?" Mae asked. Her mother laughed.

"No, but it wasn't much more romantic than that. Your Aunt Blanche was going with your Uncle Eugene at the time, and Eugene and your daddy cooked up a scheme to ask us both at the same time. That's how we came to have a double wedding."

That had been about all her mother had ever said along the lines of sex. Mae knew what it was all about, of course, had for years. And she had sure felt those urges plenty of times when she'd been dating Frank.

"Are you listening to me, Mae? I said, I want to go out with you again. I want you to give me another chance."

"What? Frank, we've been through this plenty of times for us to know it's not meant to be."

"That's where you're wrong, sweet thing. I think we *are* meant to be together. Know why? Because you are a good girl, and you'll make me a better man. I've always felt like that about you. Now I want to really make a go of it with you. I want us to get married and—"

"Whoa! Frank, have you lost your ever-loving mind? We haven't even dated in forever. I just got out of Dixon's Crossing. I've got some living to do before I get married. And when I do get married, it's not going to be to somebody I'm not sure about. And you can't blame me for not being sure about *you*, not when every time we got to a certain point you broke up with me and took up with Evangeline again. And—"

"Okay, Mae. I get it. You're right, I haven't ever been fair to you. But surely you know I don't care anything about Evangeline. She's been a good friend to me, but she has way too many friends, if you know what I mean."

"If you mean you and half the boys in the county have had sex with her, then, yes, I know what you mean."

His eyes widened. "I can't believe you just said that."

"I'm all grown up now, Frank. Hadn't you noticed?" She was getting just a bit tired of dealing with him. But he surprised her again.

"Yeah, I've noticed." He laid a hand on her thigh. "I've noticed plenty. That's one reason I'm asking you to marry me. I want to get you in my arms, in my life, in my bed, before I lose you to somebody like Cranfield, for God's sake, just by saying nothing. Doing nothing."

His hand inched up her thigh, until she laid her hand over his and held him where he was.

He slid closer to her and put his other hand at the back of her head. "I'm crazy about you, Mae. I guess I have been ever since I first laid eyes on you in ninth grade. If I hadn't messed around and quit school, I bet we'd still be together."

His hand massaging the back of her neck felt so good—that always had been the way he could get to her. *And he knows it. But not this time.* This time Oliver's sweet face slipped in between them.

"Stop, Frank. No, just stop it." She took a deep breath and lifted his hand from her leg. "I'm willing to accept your apology about what happened with Graydell, but that doesn't mean I want there to be anything between the two of us. I don't."

He intertwined his fingers with hers and raised her hand to his lips. "But I love you. Doesn't that mean anything?"

She broke free from him and waved both her hands in the air between them. "No! That is not what I want, Frank. I told you, I'm seeing Oliver. He's the man for me. Either you can start driving right now and take me down to Kress's, or I can get out and walk." She reached for the door handle.

He held up his own hands in protest and slid back under the steering wheel. "Okay, if that's what you really want. You don't have to walk, I'll take you."

She kept her hand on the door handle until he started the car and pulled into the street. She was doing the right thing, she knew it. Frank did not fit into her plans for making her own future here in Texarkana, or into her future with Oliver, if that was meant to be. That's all there was to it.

Five minutes later, he pulled into a space right in front of the store. "Thank you for the ride, Frank. And thank you for explaining a bit more about that deal with Graydell. I have to run now."

"Anytime, sweet thing, any time." He winked at her, but made no move toward her, and she opened the door and got out.

She stepped up onto the sidewalk, her cheeks ablaze. She would be glad when he no longer had any effect on her at all. Turning toward the store entrance, she saw Prissy standing just inside fingering a swag of lace fabric, watching her through the window. Prissy frowned and nodded, as if to say, "I knew you couldn't stay away from him."

Great. Now I have to deal with Prissy, too.

THIRTY-SIX

AND A RED CONVERTIBLE

"LOOK, GRAYDELL, THERE'S LAURIE," Mae nodded toward the door where a group of women had just come in.

"Who?" Graydell looked. "Do we know any of them?"

"You know, Laurie. The girl who got the red shoes I wanted," Mae laughed.

"Oh, yeah. Didn't you say you talked to her a while back?"

"Yeah, the day Oliver left for his basic training. She was seeing her fella off to go overseas. She works at Red River."

Mae caught Laurie's attention and waved. After the women were settled at a table nearby, she called, "Laurie, pull your chair over. I want you to meet my best friend."

Laurie did, and after introductions were made, she asked, "Graydell, do you work out at New Boston with the rest of us?"

"You bet. I'm working on Area G right now, the grenade line. What do you do over at Red River?"

"She drives a jeep all over the place and flirts with every good-looking guy she sees."

Laurie's mouth flew open. "Mae! That's not true, and you know it."

Mae giggled and patted Laurie's shoulder. "Of course, it's not. I was teasing." She grabbed Laurie's left hand and thrust it up for Graydell to see. "See here, Grady. Laurie's got this real handsome fella that wants to marry her when the war's over."

Graydell's eyes grew round. "Wow, that's a beautiful ring, Laurie."

Laurie blushed. "Thanks. Guess I better get back to my friends."

"Hey, let's pull our tables together," Mae suggested.

Then it was time for more introductions, after which they all got down to what they had come here for—the dancing. The girls were undeterred by the scarcity of male partners—the few men there were in great demand—and simply took to the dance floor in groups of three or four, practicing the moves of a new dance one of the women had learned while visiting a cousin in Little Rock. By the time they all felt comfortable with the steps, they were out of breath and needing a break.

Two of Laurie's friends had found male dance partners, and Laurie sat back down next to Mae and Graydell.

"Have you got moved out on your own yet?" Mae asked.

"No, and it doesn't look like I'll ever be able to." Laurie propped her chin in her hand and pouted. "I know I have a nice home to live in. I just can't help being a bit jealous of all of you women who have your own places."

"Graydell, Laurie was off at college when the plants came in, and by the time she moved back to Texarkana to go to work here . . . Well, you know what the housing situation has been like ever since."

"Boy, do I. We were lucky to have moved up here right before all hell broke loose."

"We have lots of room, even without separate bedrooms. But me and Graydell don't mind. After all, we stayed over at each other's houses half the time when we were growing up, anyway."

"Yeah, we do have lots of room," Graydell added. "Mrs. Swenson, our landlady, actually had the apartment set up for three girls. We have three beds to deal with, but we do have curtains strung up so we can have a little privacy when we want it."

236

"That's right," Mae agreed, looking thoughtful. "We do have lots of room."

Her mind was racing. *What if Laurie moved in with us? We could split the rent three ways instead of two, and Laurie could get out of her parents' house.* She was hardly able to pay attention to the conversation, busy as she was trying to find a way where she could get Graydell away for a confab.

Finally, a guy asked Laurie to dance. She demurred at first, but Graydell piped up, "Go on, Laurie. This is Roy. He's a friend of mine, and he's an OK guy. Now, Roy, this young lady has already met the love of her life, and she's just waiting for this blamed war to end to marry him. So treat her right, you hear?"

Roy grinned and winked at Laurie. "All I want is a dance, miss. No strings attached." He held up both hands in a sign of surrender.

Laurie laughed. "Well, in that case . . ." She stood. "I'd love to."

With Laurie out on the dance floor, Mae started in on Graydell to have her move in with them.

"But I don't really know her," she protested. "What if we don't get along?"

"You will," Mae said with assurance. "You're both great gals. What could go wrong?"

As usual, Graydell was no match for a determined Mae, and by the time Laurie returned from her dance, it had been settled. It was only left for them to let Laurie know.

* * *

Mrs. Swenson had been much harder to sell on the idea than Laurie had been. "I've never met this young woman," the landlady protested. "What if she's not a nice girl?" Graydell turned beet red at the question, but Mrs. S. seemed not to notice.

"She is a nice girl," Mae said.

"You girls already have that big apartment at the end of the house."

Suddenly Mae had an inspiration. "That's right, Mrs. S.! And we appreciate it. How would it be if Laurie is willing to pay the same as what

Graydell and I have each been paying? That would get you a good bit more income. And you know how we are about meals. We eat out and take our lunches most of the time."

She could see the wheels turning in their sweet little landlady's head. "Does this girl have a steady job? Can I depend on her being able to pay her way?"

"She does. She works in Administration at Red River. And her parents live right here in town. They're real nice people." Mae decided not to mention exactly what Laurie did at Red River, or the fact she'd never met the Lindstroms.

The landlady picked up her spoon and pointed it at Mae. "Well, alright, I guess that would be agreeable. But if she ever gives me any trouble, it's going to be on your head, Missy." She bent over her bowl of oatmeal.

Mae and Graydell exchanged pleased glances. Mae couldn't wait to telephone Laurie to give her the longed-for reprieve.

Before they'd finished breakfast, Mae heard the plop of mail dropping through the slot in the front door. That was one of the many things she liked about living in Texarkana. The mail came early, and you didn't even have to walk out to the road to get it.

"I'll get the mail," she said, jumping up from the table. When she returned, she handed Mrs. S. a couple of envelopes but clutched one tightly.

"From Oliver?" Graydell asked, smirking at her.

Mae nodded.

"You go on upstairs and read it, and I'll help Mrs. S. with the dishes."

"Graydell, that's sweet of you," Mrs. S. said, as Mae whirled around and left the room. "Yes, really sweet." She patted Graydell's shoulder. "You're a good friend to give her some time alone."

Plopping onto her bed, Mae took out her pocketknife and slit open the envelope. Removing the letter, she began to read. Gosh, she had been missing Oliver.

August 31, 1942

Dear Mae,

My, how I'm missing you.

She grinned, but her eyes were misting.

They're keeping us really busy here. We went on a twenty-mile hike last week. I nearly wore the soles off of my boots. But the army doesn't care. There's always another pair of boots. And talk about keeping those things shined! Our drill instructor had better be able to see himself in them when it comes time for inspection. Which can be any time at all, day or night. I've learned how to make a bed that would make my mama proud, too. In fact, there's no end to the things I'm learning. I'm going to come back to Dixon's Crossing a changed man.

"Not too changed, I hope. I like you just the way you are," she said. Funny how her feelings for that man were changing. How could they have been such good friends for so long without her realizing what he really meant to her? *Because of Frank. You've spent way too long letting him twist you around his little finger.* She returned to Oliver's letter.

A bunch of us have been going over to the USO Club whenever we get some release time. That's not often, but we go when we can. It's right here on base, so it's not like we're free to go out and get drunk, so of course some of the guys are always complaining about that. But for me, the USO place is just fine. There are always girls to dance with. And plenty of chaperones, too, to make sure there's no hanky-panky. Not that I'd be involved in any of that. I'm missing my Maisie too much. All I want is to get through these next few weeks and get back home to you. Of course, I don't know how long I'll get to stay at home. It's up to Uncle Sam as to what happens next after I'm through with basic.

And it's up to you, sweetheart, to make me a truly happy man by saying you'll marry me after I get back. I told you. I love you, and I'm going to ask you to marry me every chance I get, until the day you finally say yes.

Mae gazed out the window at nothing, thinking about the words she'd just read. *He sure is determined. But I'm determined, too. I'm not going back to that farm except to visit.*

She went back to reading.

I know what you're thinking right now. You're probably saying to yourself you're not about to up and marry somebody from the river bottoms, somebody who'll take you right back to the place you just got away from.

She laughed out loud at his perception. He really did know her better than anybody. *And he still loves me.* A tingly feeling began in her stomach and radiated outward. This was new, something she'd never experienced before. Not even with . . . No, this was something new entirely.

As she turned to the next page, something fell from between the sheets of paper. She picked up the small object. A picture of Oliver, with writing on the back. Gosh, he looked so handsome in his uniform. And serious. She could almost feel his stern gaze coming straight off the picture to skewer her. She flipped it over and read: "To the girl I love with all my heart. I'll be home soon, and then I'll ask you again to make me a happy man by marrying me. Love, O.D."

She marveled he had managed to put so many sweet words on that one little photo. "I need to go down to Woolworth's and get a frame. I'll do that as soon as I finish his letter."

So I'm going to make you a promise. I will not ask you to move back to the bottoms until after this war is over and I'm once again a free man. For now, we can look for a little place somewhere there in Texarkana until I get my orders. And while I'm gone, you can stay wherever you want—with your friends or in our place. Although, I'd rather you moved back in with them so you wouldn't be lonesome.

Duty calls. I love you, Maisie!

O.D.

Mae felt a tear slide down her cheek. She was surprised at how very good Oliver's plans for them sounded to her. He was actually making plans around her, not giving her any ultimatums about what her life would be like married to him. But she had promised herself not to marry too soon. Well what, really, *was* too soon, in the midst of this world they were in?

She was staring out the window, her eyes unfocused, when Graydell came in. "I'll be glad when Laurie gets moved in," she said. "If you're going to be mooning after good old Oliver all the time, at least I'll have somebody to talk to."

Mae's blush said it all.

Later that afternoon, Laurie arrived with more bags and cases than the two girls had had between them when they made their move. Going out to help her bring things in, they stopped to gawk at the car by the curb.

"What's the matter?" she asked, noticing their stares. "Haven't you ever seen a convertible before?"

"One or two," Mae said slowly. "But not one this—"

"What?" Laurie laughed. "This red?"

"Now that you mention it. Yeah, this red."

"Father bought it for me when I turned eighteen last year. Of course, it wasn't new, but it had been well cared for. I went off to Texas State College for Women in Denton, close to Dallas, but we came back home when the war started and my brother got drafted."

"We?" Graydell asked.

"Me and Myrtle, the car, silly," Laurie giggled.

"You named your *car*?" Mae asked.

"Doesn't everybody?" Laurie said, reaching into Myrtle's trunk for another box. "Let's get these all inside, and I'll take y'all for a spin."

THIRTY-SEVEN

WHERE'S LONNIE?

"AND THEN SHE DROVE circles around the big post office about ten times, us all laughing like crazy." Mae was regaling a small crowd with her descriptions of Laurie's car during their supper break on Monday night. There were almost a hundred people in the bomb proof, but hardly anyone else was paying attention, so Mae was putting on quite a show.

"Has anybody seen Lonnie Jackson tonight?" The questioner, wearing an anxious frown, had stuck his head inside the door without coming inside.

Mae looked around at a bunch of puzzled faces. Apparently nobody had. "Thanks anyway," the man said, darting out.

"I've never heard of Lonnie Jackson," somebody said. There was a murmur of agreement.

"I know someone by that name. We grew up in the same place," Mae said. Abandoning her audience, she hurried outside the bomb proof. She spied the man striding briskly toward the road leading to Area P.

Whistling, she yelled, "Hey, mister!" He turned to look at her.

"Have you seen Lonnie?" He headed back toward her.

"No, but I wondered if he was the guy I grew up with in Dixon's Crossing."

The man thought for a minute. "I'm not sure, but I remember him talking about growing up in the country, somewhere on a cotton farm, I think."

"That's probably the same guy. Why are you looking for him?"

"Here's the thing," he said. "He works in another bay from me, and he's been riding to work with me and some other guys. He rode out with us today, but he didn't show up for supper. I've been asking around, and nobody seems to have seen him since about four this afternoon."

"That's strange. Wonder where he got off to. You think maybe he got sick and went on home?"

"I don't think he would have left without telling some of us."

"You're probably right. Well, I hope you find him." She started back toward the bomb proof. "Hey, would you mind letting me know if he shows up? I work in bay ten in Area F."

"Sure will, if I get the chance. What's your name? I'll tell him you were worried about him."

"Mae Johnson. I appreciate it. Hope he's okay."

They parted ways and Mae headed back toward her work spot. Thinking about the last time she'd seen Lonnie, one day in Mr. J.T.'s store when she was so mad at him for cutting the supply lists—again—she hadn't stopped to talk with the young man. She was happy to see somebody else from down in the river bottoms getting one of these good Lone Star jobs. Caught up in a crowd leaving the bomb proof, Mae felt somebody grab her by her elbow. She whirled around and found herself swept along by Johnie, the sweetest woman at this plant, she had long since decided.

"What's your hurry?" Johnie laughed, forcing Mae to slow down. "It's not like that man of yours is going to be waiting at the door for you when we get there."

"Don't I wish!" Looking past Johnie, Mae spied Keesha at the far edge of the crowd, hands in her pockets, head down. "Hey, I see a friend of mine. Meet you back at the shack." Johnie released her elbow, and Mae started weaving through the throng. "Keesha! Wait up!" The girl jerked her head up and looked around. Then she ducked her head and sped up, almost in a run, moving quicker there on the edge of the workers than Mae could from her place at its center. "Keesha! LaKeesha!" she called again, but the girl never looked back.

"Did you get to talk with your friend?" Johnie asked her a few minutes later when she arrived at their building.

"No, I didn't. And it was the funniest thing. I'm sure she saw me. Looked right through me. Then she took off like a bat out of he—heck."

"That's strange. Are you sure she saw you?"

"Yes, I'm sure. We've met up a couple of times lately, and she's always been friendly. I don't know . . ."

"What makes you think she might have wanted to avoid you?"

"It's how we know each other, I guess you'd say. Her family sometimes hires out to Daddy when it's time to pick cotton, and Keesha and I used to play together. She's from down in the Bend, you see."

"Ah, yes."

The Bend was the nice way of describing the black community where Keesha lived. The place usually had that awful word in front of Bend, but Mae refused to call it that.

"She was real friendly the first time I saw her out here," Mae said. "And the second time, well, I came up on her cleaning up a mess in one of the women's bathrooms."

Johnie nodded, her lips pressed into a straight line, her brow furrowed. "I'm afraid your friend Keesha is probably embarrassed."

"Embarrassed. But why? It's honest work."

"Honest, maybe. Equal to your job? No. She'll never be able to hold a job like yours, work alongside you like I do. Because she's colored."

"And that's just wrong!" Mae sputtered.

"I agree, but we're in the minority around here, in case you hadn't noticed. Most of the people we work with would have a cow if the supers brought in coloreds to work next to them. And I think those Goodrich people know it. Somebody high up has to have let them know they can

244

keep the status quo around here. Because I think a big lot of them would just walk out if they had to work in the same place as coloreds, with the colored people making the same pay as them."

"I'm afraid you're right, Johnie." Mae sat down at her workstation and waited for the next grenade to come her way. "But it just isn't right, not at all," she muttered.

Next to her, Gracie said, "Pardon?" But Mae just shook her head. No need to get a big controversy stirred up.

For the rest of the night, Mae's mind wandered between Keesha and Lonnie. She knew she was helpless to do anything about either one. Her carpool discussed what might have happened to Lonnie on the way home that night. It seemed there had been an all-out search conducted, but he'd been nowhere to be found.

On her way to her line the next afternoon, Mae spied a familiar figure ahead of her. "Lonnie!" she called, and he turned. Seeing it was her, he stopped and waited for her to catch up. She grabbed him by both arms. "Where have you been, Lonnie Jackson? You had everybody worried last night."

He gave her a sheepish grin. "I'm sorry, Mae. I feel so stupid. It was my own fault."

"What was? Where were you?"

"I could make a long story of it, and someday I probably will, but right now I'm just gonna confess. I got locked in one of the igloos."

Mae's jaw dropped. "What igloos? How'd you go and do something like that?"

"It was easy," he said, still grinning. "I was with a bunch of guys, and we were taking a truckload of crates of the fifty-five-millimeter shells over to Red River to the igloos for storage. Well, I had worked over the night before, and there were plenty of guys to unload those crates, so I just . . ."

"You what?" she asked.

"I kind of eased off toward the back, found a pile of rags back there in the dark, and decided to take a little nap."

"Oh, Lonnie, you didn't. Don't tell me they left you."

"Okay, I won't tell you," he said, his grin getting wider. "I guess I was more tired than I'd thought. I went so sound asleep I never heard anybody say anything about leaving. It's my own fault I got left all night."

"All night!" Mae was horrified. She'd long had a healthy fear of the dark. "I can't imagine what that must have been like."

"Do you have any idea how dark it is in one of those places when the door is sealed up?"

She could imagine, sort of. She'd grown up sleeping in complete darkness, after all. But seldom was it what she would call "pitch black," because the moon and stars could be very bright when no other lights were around. She had also lain there many nights with the rain pattering on the roof. Nothing was darker than the darkness of a midnight rainstorm after the thunder and lightning has passed. But an igloo. She shivered to think of it.

"The worst part of it all," Lonnie went on, "was being found by the guard at Red River this morning, then getting brought back over here and having to confess to one of the Goodrich bigwigs that I'd been slacking off on my job. I really let lots of people down—much less all the people who were out looking for me. I feel like such a fool."

"Oh, Lonnie, it could have happened to anybody. Don't be so hard on yourself. Wait till I tell you what's been happening on my line. It'll probably make you feel better."

She launched into a description of the events in her bay over the past couple of weeks, culminating with the women's toilet being shut down. It still galled Mae to think of Jewel and her selfishness. When she finished, he stood there, shaking his head.

"See, Lonnie? People all over the plant are having to learn how to keep to those rules and regulations. And what is the moral to your story?"

"Don't go anywhere by yourself, and don't be trying to get out of doing your work."

THIRTY-EIGHT

OLIVER'S HOME!

A KNOCKING ON THE door woke the girls Saturday morning. "Mae? There's a man downstairs to see you," Mrs. Swenson called. "Are you awake?"

"I am now. Be down in a few minutes," she called. Bustling into some decent clothes, she grumbled, "I'm not in the mood to fight with Frank today." Graydell and Laurie gave each other looks and headed back to bed.

Five minutes later Mae burst back into the room. "Grady! Laurie! Get up. Help me get fixed up. Oliver's here."

Dressing and fixing her hair in record time, Mae was back downstairs. Oliver was in the parlor, and he rose when she came in. "Lord, Maisie, you look gorgeous." She couldn't stop blushing. "You didn't need to get dressed up for me, though. I told you before you looked beautiful."

"With my hair a mess? I'm sure—"

"That's what I liked. I've been sitting here imagining we were married and I was seeing you first thing in the morning." He laughed. "You're so cute when you blush. I never knew that, because we've always been just pals. I love it. Let's me know you're thinking about me in a different way." He reached for her hand and pulled her down onto the sofa.

"Now that your landlady isn't around, how about a proper welcome?" he whispered, staring hungrily at her newly lipsticked mouth.

She put a hand to the side of his face, letting her thumb trace his square chin. "Oh, Ollie, it's so good to see you." She leaned forward and his arms came around her. She gave in to his kiss, wondering at the strength of his embrace. Soon they were both trembling.

"I have to go back Sunday afternoon, then I have four weeks left. What do you say we make the most of this weekend? Go for a ride with me?"

She laughed. "How, on the bus?"

"Oh, ye of little faith. I caught the bus earlier and went home to get my old car."

"You didn't! Without me?"

"Had to get the folks' welcome out of the way. Now the rest of my time is all yours."

"They're okay with that?"

"They have to be. That's the way it's going to be."

"What are we waiting for?" She jumped up and held out her hand.

Their day together was perfect. They bought hamburgers downtown and took them out to the park, where they walked and talked for hours. They had supper at the Hotel Grim Coffee Shop and strolled down the street to the Strand Theater, where they sat in the last row. Mae felt his arm tighten around her shoulder when the newsreels came on, and she felt tears sliding down her cheeks. She couldn't imagine Oliver in such places. Beside her, Oliver squirmed.

When the musical came on, she nestled her head into his shoulder, and he touched his forehead to hers. "Let's get out of here," he whispered. She nodded.

In front of the apartment, they clung together in his car. "God, Mae, I love you more than I ever thought possible." He kissed her hungrily, his mouth moving over hers. His hand inched from her waist upward, and she gasped when he cupped her breast.

"Ollie—" she said against his mouth, placing her hand over his.

"I'm sorry, baby." He made as if to move his hand, but she held it there, guiding his fingers to her nipple. "Oh, Mae," he groaned. "I want you so much."

She left him to his own devices and opened her mouth, and her heart, to him.

He nuzzled at her neckline, and she worked to undo the buttons on her dress. But he pulled back to look into her eyes. "Marry me, Mae," he growled. "I need you so much."

It was the word "need" that gave her pause. That's what she'd worried about, that maybe Oliver was another of those guys not wanting to go off to war without a woman of their own at home.

"Ollie," she said again, sitting up and straightening her clothes. "We can't do this. Not like this. I'm sorry. I can't."

"Then marry me, sweetheart! I love you, and I know you love me. What's stopping you?"

She reached for his hand, and she wavered, thinking of where it had so recently been. "I'm not ready for marriage, Ollie. I'm sorry, but I can't. Not now. I'm going inside. Come see me tomorrow before you leave?"

He sighed. "Sure, Maisie. I'll be here in the morning." She kissed him once more, a kiss filled with love, and promise, and resignation. Then she left him there.

Early the next morning, Mae padded out to the balcony in her pajamas and flopped onto a rocker to think about yesterday. *I'm so confused. I thought I knew what I wanted. Now I'm not so sure.*

"Morning, Mister," she heard little Ben Gregory call out just before the thunk of a tossed paper hit the Stevenson's porch next door. "Who're you talking to this early, Ben?" she muttered. Puzzled, she leaned over the balcony. "Oliver! What am I going to do with that man?"

She sighed, then called down to him. He looked up at her and smiled. "I'll be down in a jiffy," she said, and he nodded.

She took special pains to freshen up and find just the right outfit. A lacy white blouse with cap sleeves, a full skirt in spring green, and a white leather belt to cinch her trim waist. White flats. Chunky green beads at her throat, pearl drop earrings. Everything green and white. She smiled at herself in the mirror and picked up her purse.

"Look at our Mae," Graydell sang out. "Where are you off to so early?"

"Oliver's downstairs. Looks like he slept in his car all night. Gotta go." And she was out the door.

Sunday was as magical as the day before. They drove to the country and surprised their folks at church, and Mama insisted on feeding them afterward. Then Oliver had another surprise for her.

"I'm going to teach you to drive," he announced, stopping the car in the middle of the road. "Trade places with me."

"What? No! I can't do that," she protested.

"Sure you can. I want to leave my car with you until I get back. So you have to learn." He opened the door, got out, and grabbed her hand to pull her under the wheel. "Come on, it's easy."

She looked at him in consternation but settled herself under the steering wheel. "See, here's the brake—his hand guided her left foot—and the clutch, and here's the gas pedal—he moved her right foot into place, caressing her leg as he did so, and sending shivers over her. Then he ran around the car and got into the passenger seat. "Now, here's how to work the gears."

He then led her through the main aspects of shifting gears, letting her practice without the motor running. She didn't mention to him that her daddy had already showed her the mechanics of driving, though she'd never driven. Finally, Oliver pronounced her ready to start the engine.

"Already?" Can't I practice some more?" she moaned.

"You can practice while you drive. Now start the car." He looked down his long nose at her. "Not scared, are you?"

He reminded her of all the times he'd dared her before, and she'd never failed to take the challenge. She wasn't about to let this be the first time. She reached for the starter.

"I did it! I did it!" Mae cried a few minutes later as they flew down the road, dust rolling up behind them.

"You're doing fine, Maisie," Oliver laughed, his army-cropped hair barely moving in the wind.

Their windows were down, and the breeze made her feel shot full of electricity. Who knew driving could be so exciting? They drove every road around Dixon's Crossing, with Oliver helping her practice her arm turn signals. She knew these already, just had to remember to use them. "Up for right, straight out for left, and down for stop. I got this."

"Ready to drive back to Texarkana?" he grinned.

"No! You take over!" But he shook his head. "If you're going to drive while I'm gone, I have to know you can handle traffic."

Her stomach knotted, but she squared her shoulders. "Okay, then," she sang out. "Here we go." She put the car back into gear and after a bit of a lurching, stuttering start, they were off.

Mae did insist that she park the car behind Laurie's and that they walk to the station. She wasn't ready to be alone behind the wheel. Not yet.

Oliver hefted his bag and they set off, taking every minute they had.

"You going to miss me, Maisie?" he asked, swinging her around to catch her in an embrace. "You going to think of me every night? Think of what our wedding night will be like?" He pulled her even tighter against him.

Mae threw her arms around his neck. "Oh, Ollie, I don't want you to go! I feel like we're just finding each other, and we need more time. At least I do," she finished.

He released her and they walked on hand in hand. "I'm going back to camp and I'm going to pray harder than I've ever prayed for anything," he said. "You do the same, okay? God will send us the right answer."

She looked at the building looming in front of them. The sounds of trains anxious to be on their way came to them on the street. Trains whistled in the distance, some arriving, some leaving. People hustled by them into the station.

"How can anyone be so anxious to send someone they love away?" she said, not expecting an answer, and receiving none.

On the platform a few minutes later, Mae finally felt what Laurie must have felt that day she sent Derrell away. Oliver scooped her into his arms and whispered, "When this is over, I'm never going to let you go again. Never, you hear?" His lips crushed hers, and their tears mingled as they said goodbye.

* * *

Thinking of Oliver kept Mae preoccupied over the next few days. At home, she was quiet, no longer the bouncy girl Graydell and Laurie were used to. At work, she found herself thinking of Oliver's letters, and of the things he'd said to her while they were together. She couldn't be sure she was ready. She couldn't be sure Oliver wasn't behaving like lots of other soldiers, the guys who wanted something—someone—to cling to while they fought. That wasn't what marriage was supposed to be about. It should involve two people getting to know each other, spending time together, having common ideals and common plans for their futures. Yes, they needed to be attracted to each other sexually. She wasn't one of those women who thought sex was only for making babies. She firmly intended to enjoy her husband "that way" when the time came.

She was pondering all these things a few nights after Oliver had gone back to Louisiana, having read his latest letter. Again, he had proposed. She couldn't sleep for thinking about it. Finally, she got up and padded quietly to the French doors. She tried to open them quietly, but that little creak was still there. Graydell stirred.

"Mae? You okay?"

"Shh, Grady, go back to sleep. Sorry, but I have some things to think about."

Graydell slipped her feet into house shoes and padded over to where Mae still stood in the door. Laurie raised her head, but her roommates waved to her to go back to sleep. "Come on, girlfriend, let's get out to the conference room and get these issues settled, whatever they are," she whispered. She pushed Mae ahead of her and shut the door. She steered them to their favorite rockers. The night was warm, with a gentle breeze, but Mae tucked her bare feet under her, feeling chilly, though not from the weather. Moonlight streamed onto their corner of the balcony, and she could see Graydell's furrowed brow.

They hashed out Mae's problem for the next hour, with Mae vacillating between thinking she was ready for marriage to Oliver and wondering if she'd lost her mind. In the end, Graydell wasn't much help.

"I think you already know what you want to do, so just do it. *After* you sleep on it. Wipe that letter and this whole conversation out of your head and get a good night's sleep. Then write the letter you know is the right one."

"Graydell, is that the only advice you ever give, to go get a good night's sleep?"

Graydell shrugged. "Worked last time."

Mae had intended to write to Oliver the next day, but she slept too late, after her middle of the night talk with Graydell. *Guess it won't hurt to wait one more day.*

THIRTY-NINE

FINAL ANSWER

"DID Y'ALL HEAR ABOUT Joshua?" Sue asked. Several women were busy changing into their coveralls. Mae scooted past Rosemary to get to the mirror and grabbed a handful of toothpicks to go to work on her hair.

"Joshua who?" Rosemary asked.

"You remember, Joshua Combs, the tall, blond, good-looking guy we met last year from Dixon's Crossing."

Mae had been thinking about Oliver and her situation, but now she jerked her head around to look at Sue. "What about him?" He had gone off to join the Navy right after Pearl Harbor and she hadn't heard from him since.

"His folks got the news last week. He got killed somewhere in the Pacific."

Mae felt the tears spring to her eyes. "How? I mean, where?"

"Nobody knows. They just got a telegram, and it said he had been buried there. Maybe even at sea. Wouldn't that just be awful?" Sue said, shuddering.

"That's all they know?"

Sensing something in Mae's voice, she looked up from lacing her boots. "Oh, honey, I forgot you were from Dixon's Crossing. I guess you probably knew him, huh?"

"Yes, I did," she said, her voice thick with tears. "In fact, I went to church with him. He was a few years older than me, but yes, I knew him. Lord, I hate to hear that. He's from a real nice family."

The conversation turned to other matters, but Mae was oblivious. All she could think about was Oliver and the fact that he would be going overseas one day soon. *Too soon.* She couldn't stand to think about it. *Oh, Lord, what am I going to do about Oliver? I don't want to lose him! I care too much about him.*

Drying her tears, she moved out to her bay and set to work. She nodded hello to Charles but didn't speak. As the afternoon wore on, her thoughts whirled around Joshua and Oliver. Mechanically, she packed the grenades as they got to her. One after another . . . She cocked her head and stared at the pin in the grenade she was holding. Something wasn't right. She nestled it into the box reserved for defective grenades and continued packing. A few grenades later, she noticed another one, this time with the pin only partially screwed in. *This thing won't detonate. Nothing is connected. That's no good for our boys.* She set this one aside as well.

Charles had been watching her without her noticing. Now he came to stand over her. "What's the reason you set aside those two grenades?"

Mae jumped. "Oh, you startled me," she said, fanning herself. She then told him about her concern that one of the grenades would explode if it got jostled in transport, and how she thought the other one wouldn't explode at all.

He examined the grenades in question. "You've got a good eye there, Mae. Think I'll make you my roving inspector. Mrs. Harper is going out on maternity leave next week. You can take over then."

On another day, Mae would have been beside herself with giddiness at this promotion. Today, though, she simply thanked Charles and went back to work. He shook his head, watched her for a moment, then left the bay.

Mae looked around at the other people, each one doing a specific job, over and over and over. Just as she was packing grenade after grenade. What monotonous work. Yes, she was about to get to do something different. But in reality, all she would be doing next week would be walking from one end of the line to the other, observing her co-workers. Routine, never-changing work.

She thought suddenly of days on the farm, working in the cotton fields. Hoeing from spring into summer, then waiting for the tight green bolls to swell and finally burst, giving up their fluffy fibers to the fingers clutching at them. Day after day, until the field had been stripped, the sacks of gathered cotton had been weighed, and wagon loads of the sweet-smelling stuff had gone off to the mill.

Other chores then occupied everyone for the rest of the year until spring, when it was time to start the cycle all over again. So often there was little to no cash to show for their efforts. But one thing you could say about life there. You wouldn't starve. Not with the fishing and hunting and canning. Even in a bad cotton year, she had never gone hungry.

Would it be so bad living back in Dixon's Crossing? Things are going to be different after the war. I can see those changes coming, even now. People around here have money, for one thing. I won't be surprised if most of Mr. J.T.'s tenants leave his place and go out on their own. Maybe Oliver and I could do that—

What am I saying? I sound as if things are already settled between us, as if getting married is inevitable. Is that what I really want?

"Well, what if it is? It's not like this job will be here for me when the war is over. This place will be shut down and padlocked overnight, and we'll all be out of work. What then, my girl?"

So you're thinking of getting married just so you'll have somebody to take care of you?

"What? No! Just thinking, that's all. Thinking that no matter where I go, where I live, I'll always end up doing some kind of monotonous job. Why not do it with someone I love?"

Love. So you're saying you love Oliver Cranfield?

"I guess I am."

Mae smiled to herself, thinking about the letter she was for sure going to write to that man tonight.

* * *

September 4, 1942

Dear Oliver,

I got your sweet letter, and I've been thinking about what you wrote ever since then. First of all, I want to remind you that I didn't plan to marry for several more years. My decision has not been made in haste. But I might as well get to the point. My answer is yes. I know now how much I love you. I've always loved you, but not in this way. Not in the way that makes my insides go all watery thinking about seeing you again, kissing you again. You know, I don't think it would seem so bad to live on a little farm—as long as it's with you. Like Ruth in the Bible, I'm ready to say—

Whither thou goest, I will go, and where thou lodgest, I will lodge.

Thy people shall be my people, and thy God my God;

Where thou diest, I will die, and there will I be buried."

Yes, Ollie, in answer to your question that I'm sure you're asking about now—Yes, I'm certain. Now, hurry home!

All my love,

Mae

She read over the letter. Satisfied, she put it in an envelope. Tomorrow couldn't come soon enough. She was too keyed up to sleep. Padding out to the balcony, she rocked for hours, until the warmth and soothing early fall sounds of night lulled her into a peaceful sleep. "I wonder how long I'll have to wait to hear from Ollie," was her last coherent thought. She woke to thunder rumbling and wind-blown rain hitting her in the face. As the stood and stretched, she muttered, "Lord, I hope this isn't a sign."

FORTY

FINAL QUESTION

HOW LONG WOULD IT take for Mae's letter to get to Camp Claiborne and for Oliver to get a letter back to her? She figured she'd hear from him by Saturday, or Monday at the latest. She hovered around the mail slot every morning, always there to scoop up the miscellany and sort through it. But no letter came. A week passed, then two. She dressed for work without saying more than a dozen words to Graydell and Laurie. At work, she was mopey and subdued. She checked grenades along the line, plucking one now and then and taking them to the recycle bin.

Charles said, "Mae, I don't get it. I thought the new job would suit you."

"It does," she replied, but her bad mood didn't lift.

By the end of the second week with no letter, Mae was fit to be tied. The girls walked on eggshells around her in the apartment, never knowing what might set her off. Moody and mopey, Mae stomped down the stairs on Saturday morning to wait for the mail. But again there was no letter.

That settles it. I missed my chance. He's most likely given up on me. I just waited too dang long, and he's decided I'm not worth it.

Slump-shouldered, she dragged herself back upstairs, where she lay down on her bed and curled up into a little ball.

"Want to go shopping?" Graydell asked, probably expecting the answer she got.

"No, Grady, you go on," Mae sighed. "Have a good time."

She was still in the same position when Graydell returned a couple of hours later.

"Okay, that's enough, Mae. Come on, get up."

Mae flopped over and sat up. "What time is it? Hell, what day is it?"

"It's still Saturday, about four. You've got to get off that bed, you hear me? Get dressed, and let's go find some food. Mrs. S. was frying chicken when I came in."

"I'm not hungry."

"I don't care. You're going to eat whether you like it or not."

"Why hasn't he written me, Grady? You know him almost as well as I do. It's not like him not to answer. Especially after a letter like I wrote him."

"He's probably tied up with finishing his basic training. Who knows, they may have moved him from Louisiana to some other state. He may be out on maneuvers. He may not have even had a chance to read your letter yet."

Mae perked up. "You really think so? Yeah, you're probably right." She got up and stretched. "What did you say there was for supper?"

The rest of the weekend passed quietly enough. Laurie had gone straight to her parents' house after work on Friday, and they didn't see her until late Sunday evening.

"I can't believe how much I enjoyed being home," she said, getting ready for bed. "I was in such a hurry to get out of there, and now I enjoy going back every chance I get."

"'Absence makes the heart grow fonder' isn't just for guys and gals, I guess," Graydell said. "I guess it's for families, too. I know I enjoy going back to Dixon's Crossing now."

"Me, too," Mae said from her bed. She was sitting cross-legged with all of Oliver's letters splayed out before her. She was reading and re-reading them, trying to imagine what would happen when he came home. Her dreams that night were of the two of them strolling through the woods back home, holding hands, stopping now and then for a lingering kiss.

* * *

Mae was putting on her saddle oxfords on Wednesday when she heard a commotion outside their door. Footsteps, loud and insistent, were headed upstairs.

"What in the world? It sounds like a herd of elephants out there!"

Graydell peeked around her curtain. "What's going on?"

Mae shrugged, but finished tying her shoes before standing. She was only halfway to the door when a pounding began.

"Eula Mae Johnson, are you in there?"

Her heart actually skipped a beat. She felt it.

"It's Oliver!" she exclaimed, giving Graydell a quick, excited glance.

"Well, let the man in," Graydell laughed.

She flung open the door but shrank back from what she saw there. It was Oliver, all right, but she'd never seen him look like this before. He was grinning from ear to ear, his hair was mussed where, it seemed, he had just jerked off his cap. His hands held the cap, along with a giant bouquet of flowers.

Directly behind him Mae spied Mrs. Swenson. The overwrought landlady was using all of her varied vocabulary to try to get Oliver's attention. The man was nothing if not determined, however, and he kept ignoring Mrs. S., which was contributing to Mae's sense of the surreal.

"You people know my rules," she was saying. "No men on the second floor!"

Mae couldn't help it. She giggled.

* * *

Oliver continued to ignore the landlady, drinking in the sight of Mae, his Mae, the Mae who had said she would marry him. He was about to find out if that could really be true. But suddenly he wasn't so sure he wanted to hear her up close and personal answer—especially in front of an audience. It would be bad enough with just Graydell here, he thought, and he'd known her all his life. But this little worrisome woman behind him. Well, he didn't even know her, except through Mae's laughable imitations of her.

Backing his ears, he thrust the flowers into Mae's unprepared arms and she almost dropped them. He didn't care. He stared into her gorgeous green eyes for a long moment when time seemed to stand still. At last, satisfied with what he saw there, he asked, "Did you mean it? Or were you just trying to pacify a lonely soldier?"

Finally, she whispered, "Yes, and no."

Yes and no? What does that mean?

Only when she responded did he realize he'd spoken out loud. She was giving him a goofy grin, a look like he hadn't seen on her face for probably at least five years.

"It means, my dearest Oliver, that yes, I will marry you. And no, I was not just trying to pacify you."

Everyone was silent now, even Mrs. S., who had placed her hand on her heart and was leaning against the wall for support. Graydell was still looking out from behind her curtain. "Just imagine it," she whispered. "My two best friends in the world—together."

Oliver let out a whoop and grabbed Mae up to swing her around and around. "Oliver, put me down! You're making me dizzy," she protested.

He lowered her gently, slowly, until her feet were once again on solid ground, and continued to gaze into her eyes.

"Those incredible eyes," he said, rocking her gently from side to side. "I want to wake up looking into those eyes until the end of time."

"Oooo-kaay!" he heard Graydell say. "That's about all the mushiness I can stand." Mae looked around, but Graydell's curtain was now drawn as far across her space as she could get it.

Oliver heard a sniffle from the landlady. "That's the most romantic thing I've heard since my Albert proposed to me in the middle of the shirtwaist factory floor."

When he deciphered what she'd said, Oliver threw back his head and chortled. "So, this proposal I've been working on for three days, or really three years, is still only second best?" He beamed at her. "Gotta do something about that." Digging into a pants pocket, he took out a tiny cardboard box covered in a layer of gilt that sparkled as he turned it around. Dropping to a knee, he uttered words as old as time itself. "I love you with all my heart, Mae Johnson. Will you do me the honor of becoming my wife?"

Mae cleared her throat, and still her reply came out a bit strangled. "I love you, too. Yes, Oliver, yes, I'll marry you."

"It's about time!" Graydell squealed, running across the room to embrace them both, her desire for privacy seemingly forgotten.

Oliver wrapped his arms around Mae and danced her back into the room. He didn't even look behind him before he kicked the door shut, leaving the startled landlady staring at the closed door, her mouth ajar. "Well, Al, if you think I'm going to send that man away, you've got another think coming." Chuckling to herself, she turned around and started down the stairs. Back in the parlor, she gazed at Albert's picture she kept in a place of honor on the piano he had loved so much. "Did you hear that, Al? There's going to be a wedding."

* * *

After a quick trip to Dixon's Crossing for Oliver to ask her daddy for his permission, which he didn't have to do, but that made her love him even more, the next two days were a flurry of activity the likes of which Mae had never known. Not even when her brother married Annette after a months' long engagement had everybody been in such a tizzy. Everyone but Oliver, that is. The man was infuriating in his quiet, contented self-satisfaction.

"You act like all of this is nothing special," she pouted on Thursday, as they left the courthouse with their paperwork complete and their marriage license in hand.

"Oh, no, sweetheart. All my insides are like water spilling into the boat when I forget to put the plug in. And I do feel like I'm drowning—drowning in happiness." He pulled her to him and gave her a long, lingering kiss, right there on the courthouse lawn, with people on all sides.

He looked around. "What's the matter? Haven't you ever seen a man in love before?"

Mae was blushing beet red by this time, at least she thought so. In fact, she continued to get even redder, and the scattered folks around started clapping, with a few wolf whistles thrown in for good measure.

Oliver folded his long, skinny frame into a curtsy, taking her with him. When they straightened, she whispered through a wide smile, "Can we get out of here now?"

Bending to give her one more kiss, "For good measure," he whispered.

He swept her into his arms, and she let out a surprised shriek. Then he marched across the courthouse lawn, on across the street, straight up the boarding house steps. "If you would do the honors?" he said, dipping her so she could reach the doorknob.

Once inside, he set her on her feet, giving her a final, searing kiss. "Until tomorrow night," he growled into her ear. She felt herself heating up from the inside out.

"You're crazy, Cranfield," she chided him gently.

"Crazy in love, Johnson. Now, I'm off to round up a JP. You go on and do what you ladies always do before a wedding, whatever that is."

With that, he was gone. *The room seems so much bigger without him in it. I pray that feeling lasts forever. Please God, don't ever let us lose this magical feeling for each other.*

In her heart, though, Mae felt a foreboding she couldn't explain, but one which she was determined to ignore.

FORTY-ONE

THE BIG DAY

IT WAS FRIDAY JUST before noon when Graydell finally lost it. "I can't decide how to wear my hair. Should I pin it up or leave it down? Gosh, I've never been a maid of honor before," Graydell wailed. "I don't even know what I'm supposed to do."

"I hate to think what you're gonna be like when *you* get married." Mae smiled at her best friend. "You're supposed to calm down and keep me calm," she said, glancing up from her ironing. She had decided on a pale blue skirt and weskit she hadn't worn in ages, and the suit was sorely in need of pressing. "Do you think my straw pumps will look okay? I've had them for years, but I don't wear them often. I thought they might be good enough."

"You could go barefoot and Oliver wouldn't notice." Graydell stared into the mirror a moment more, then let her hair fall, shrugged, and began rummaging in the chifforobe. "Now, where are those shoes? Oh, here they are." She eyed the pumps. "Yep. These will do just fine." She held them next to the skirt Mae was putting finishing touches to. "Don't you agree?"

"Yes. Now, I need to decide about jewelry."

Graydell set the shoes down and opened a drawer. "You need something borrowed. Here, wear these." She held out a pair of clip earrings shaped like flowers and made up of seed pearls.

"Oh, Grady, they're gorgeous! Where did you get them?"

"They belonged to my Grandma Jones. I'm planning to wear them when I get married."

"Oh, I shouldn't use them before you do."

"Don't be silly. Who knows when I'll find a man to put up with me?"

"I'm so lucky to have you for a best friend." Mae donned the earrings, hugged Graydell, and went to stand before the mirror.

"I'm the lucky one," Graydell said, with a catch in her voice.

Their eyes met in the mirror. "We're both lucky," they both said at the same time, and they laughed together.

A knock on the door caused Mae to jump. "I hope that's not Oliver. I'm not supposed to see him yet."

"Don't worry. Get behind your curtain and I'll get rid of him."

But a moment later, Mae heard Graydell's relieved voice. "Mrs. Johnson. Ginny. Y'all come on in."

"Where's my little girl?"

"Mama, I'm not your little girl anymore," she protested, emerging from behind her curtain.

"I'm just joshing," Mama said. "This is all so exciting. I couldn't sleep after you and Oliver came down Wednesday night so he could ask for our blessing."

"Me, either," Ginny said. "I've been trying to decide what to wear ever since y'all left."

"You look cute in anything, Squirt," Mae laughed. "And you look great in that yellow dress. Just don't show me up." She shook Ginny by the shoulders.

Ginny gave her sister a lingering glance. "Dang, Mae, with the glow you're wearing there's no chance of that happening."

Mama unpinned her hat and sat down on the sofa, laying it beside her. "You're really sure about this?" she asked, skewering Mae with green eyes that matched her daughter's.

"Yes, ma'am, I'm sure," Mae said, sitting beside her and meeting her gaze again. "As sure as I've ever been about anything."

Graydell glanced from one to the other. "C'mon, Ginny. Let's see if Mrs. Swenson needs some help with the arrangements."

"But I . . ." Ginny began. Graydell grabbed her by the arm and propelled her out the door.

"I'm glad they left us for a few minutes."

"Me, too. Graydell's been about to drive me crazy with all her fussing."

"I hope you won't think I'm fussing, too," Mama said, reaching for Mae's hands. "But I wanted to be sure. You're my oldest girl, and I don't want you to make a mistake." Mae squeezed her hands. "So, I'm just going to ask you . . ." Her voice trailed off.

"What is it, Mama?"

"Well. It was just over a year ago that you moved out, and you said then you didn't plan to marry for several years. As far as I knew, you and Oliver were just friends. I can't help wondering what's changed your mind all of a sudden. Eula Mae, have you got yourself in trouble? Is that's what's behind this wedding?"

"Mama! How can you ask me something like that?" Mae jumped up and began pacing the room. "I guess I should have expected that from you. You never have given me the benefit of the doubt about anything."

"That's not true," Mama protested. "I'm proud of the young woman you've become. But these things just have a way of happening when men and women think they're in love with each other."

Mae was fuming. "I don't *think* I'm in love with Oliver, Mama. I know I am. And I know he loves me." Mae turned to gaze out the French doors at the quiet courthouse. Everything appeared normal, though her head was spinning right now.

"You haven't answered my question."

Mae whirled to face her mother, red blotches suffusing her fair skin. "Okay. I'll answer your damn question, since I see you're not going to let it go. Hell, no!" Mama gasped, but Mae kept on. "No, I'm not 'in trouble'. I'm not pregnant. There is no way I possibly could be. Oh, don't look at me that way. I'm sure you wanted to ask that, too. Yes. Mama. I'm still a virgin. I've never been with a man—not Oliver, not Frank, not *anybody*."

Mae was fuming. How could her mother ask her such a thing—and on her wedding day? She was already a bundle of nerves trying to get everything together without being questioned about stuff like this.

"I'm sorry you're upset," her mother said. "But I had to ask. Your daddy and I—"

"Daddy! Y'all have discussed this? Discussed whether Oliver and I—whether we have had *sex*?"

"Oh, my gosh!" Ginny screeched from the door she'd just flung open. "Well, have you?"

Mae threw up her hands. "Oh, my Lord." She crossed to her curtain and jerked it closed behind her, effectively slamming a door in their faces. "Would everybody just go away and give me some peace and quiet!"

There were a few whispers and some rustling, then Mae heard the door shut, and all was quiet. She took a few deep breaths, determined not to let the conversation ruin her entire wedding day. Calmed at last, she rose and returned to her ironing. She had just started on the weskit when she heard the door open.

"Mae?" Mama said, tapping on the door. "Honey, I'm sorry. Can I come in?"

Mae shrugged. "Sure, come on in." She kept her back turned, concentrating on the blouse with its complicated peplum. She could feel her mother's eyes on her but refused to turn.

"Here, let me." Mama laid a hand on Mae's arm. Mae was shocked into setting the iron down and moving aside. Her mother had never offered to help her like this before. "I really am sorry I said anything. I know you're a good girl. And I know Oliver is a fine young man. We—I—should have trusted y'all to be getting married for the right reasons. You've never given me any reason to question your virtue."

Somehow, the word virtue broke into Mae's angry defenses. After all, she hadn't acted very virtuous sometimes with Frank, and her thoughts and actions sure hadn't been virtuous toward Oliver lately. She felt a giggle trying to break out, and finally she let it go.

Mrs. Johnson looked up from her ironing. "Well, I never," she muttered.

"Mae only giggled more. "Oh, Mama, you must have—at least a few times."

Her mother set down the iron. "Eula Mae! I can't believe you just said that." Her cheeks were flaming, and seeing her discomfort only caused Mae to laugh harder. She laughed until tears were streaming down her face, laughed until suddenly she was sobbing, the tears continuing to fall.

"Oh, Mae, honey, come here." Mrs. Johnson led Mae to the sofa and pulled her down to cradle her in her arms. She crooned as she rocked back and forth. "Come on, Mae. Stop crying. You'll have your face all blotchy. We don't want Oliver changing his mind when he sees his bride, do we?"

Mae sniffled and blew her nose on the handkerchief her mother held out. "That's better. That's my baby." Mae looked at her mother as if she were a stranger. Who *was* this woman who was being so nice to her?

Mama was digging into her purse. "It's a good thing I brought extras," she said, pulling out another handkerchief. "This was my mother's," she said. "I was hoping you would carry it for your something old."

Mae fingered the delicate lace edging of the hanky. "It's beautiful, Mama."

"Your grandmother did that lace tatting herself. She used to tuck this one into her belt when she started to church. She never used it, always carried a plainer one for that."

"I'll do the same. Thank you, Mama."

268

"Can we come in now?" Graydell said from the doorway. "I need to get dressed." She and Ginny came in. "What am I saying? The *bride* needs to get dressed. And there's menfolks downstairs who are beginning to look restless."

* * *

"Ready to do this?" Graydell asked. She was adjusting the ruffles of the peplum at Mae's back. "There's still time to back out if you've changed your mind."

"After we've got ourselves all gussied up?" Mae grinned. "Not on your life. I'm going to marry that man today."

"Everybody's ready," Laurie said, peeking in. "Mrs. Swenson's playing a prelude until Graydell gets downstairs. She'll change to the Wedding March and then you can come down. Got it, Mae?"

"Got it. I still can't believe she's letting us get married in her house."

"Letting you? From what I heard, she insisted. And wait until you see."

They all laughed as Laurie said, "Group hug."

"She's really a softy at heart," Graydell said. "She said her Albert would never forgive her if she let you two get married at the courthouse."

"Let's get this show on the road. Go on, Laurie, I'm ready. I'll see ya after I'm a married lady."

Laurie gazed at her dreamily. "I can't wait till Derrell gets back home and we can tie the knot, too. Good luck, Mae." She gave her friend a quick hug and hurried out.

"Let's see. . . You've got something old?" Graydell asked.

"Grandma's hanky." Mae waved it.

"Something new?"

Mae touched her throat. "Necklace from Oliver."

"Borrowed—my earrings. Blue—your suit. Good. Oh! A penny in your shoe." She plucked a coin from the side table and said, "Lift your

269

heel." Slipping the penny into the pumps, she smiled in satisfaction. "Guess that's it, then."

"That's it, Grady," she smiled, hugging her best friend. "See you downstairs."

Laurie waved to Graydell at the top of the stairs, and she started down. Mae waited until the music changed again and followed. *Lord, please don't let me trip on my way down.* She tucked the handkerchief into the nosegay of yellow chrysanthemums from Mrs. Swenson's garden, said a quick prayer of thanksgiving for Oliver, and took the first step into her new life.

Mae's father smiled as he took her hand at the bottom of the stairs. "You look beautiful, Mae. You remind me of your mother on our wedding day." She felt her throat tighten at his words, and she kissed him on the cheek. Then she lifted her eyes to where Oliver stood in front of the dormant hearth. Instead of a fire, there was a huge basket of flowers sitting in the empty fireplace, but she gave them only a passing glance. Oliver's blue eyes darkened when he saw her, and Mae felt that stirring deep inside.

Yes, this is the right thing. This man is the right one for me, the only man.

Daddy walked with her to where Oliver, his brother Ray, Graydell, and the Justice of the Peace stood. Ray had just received his orders to leave for Europe, and he and Oliver looked so handsome in their uniforms. "But my guy's better looking," Mae thought, unable to keep the smile from her face.

The ceremony lasted less than ten minutes. Mae had sneezed once during the recital of her vows—*blamed flowers*—but Oliver's recitation was strong and sure.

The dining room held more flowers in several vases. *She must have rounded up every vase on the street.* Mae was amazed at what Mrs. S. and the girls had accomplished in such a short time. The thing that brought tears to her eyes, though, was the square, three-tiered white wedding cake adorned with flowers, and with a tiny ceramic bride and groom perched on top.

"Where—how—where did this beautiful cake come from?"

"It's from Mom and me," Laurie said. "We didn't know what to get you for a wedding present, so we decided on this. Mom did the baking and I decorated."

Mae hugged her friend tightly. "It's perfect. But now, who's going to make yours when Derrell comes home? You know I could never create something like this."

There was general laughter. "I don't care if I even have a cake," Laurie said, "as long as there's a wedding."

As she and Oliver moved to cut the cake and everyone gathered around to watch, her eyes lifted to where Johnie stood in the back of the room. When their eyes met, Johnie smiled broadly and gave her a nod of approval.

FORTY-TWO

AT LAST

"MOTHER SAID OURS WAS the most beautiful wedding she'd ever been to," Oliver said, loosening his tie as he stood gazing at his new bride. His icy blue eyes pierced her straight to her heart, and she smiled, nose buried in her bouquet.

The cake had been cut and served, and the guests had all departed. Graydell had gone with Laurie to the Lindstrom's for the night, leaving the apartment blessedly empty for the newlyweds.

"It was beautiful," Mae agreed, running water into a quart jar for her nosegay. "The flowers, the music, the cake—everything."

"The bride," Oliver said, putting his hands on her shoulders and nuzzling at her neck. She felt that new feeling again. "I'm sure glad the landlady agreed I could come upstairs," he growled.

The early autumn sun had almost reached the horizon, lending a warm glow to the apartment. Mae stepped away from him and busied herself with straightening the room. "Gosh, we left this place in a mess," she said, putting the iron in the cupboard and folding the ironing board, which she slid beneath Graydell's bed. "Want me to make some coffee?"

"No, thanks, I just want you." A shiver went over her at not only his words, but the deep rumble of his voice. He motioned for her to join him on the sofa. "The apartment's fine. Leave it for now." He took her face in his hands and covered her mouth with his.

That first kiss seemed to go on forever, as their mouths began to really get to know each other. His hands moved from her face to the back of her head, where his fingers tangled in her curls. His lips trailed across her face and descended to her neck, where his pearl pendant necklace nestled, as if it had already found its home.

"I hope you like your present," he said against her skin.

"I love it. And I love you for giving it to me. And I love my ring. I can't believe you found time to get it engraved." She held her hand out and gazed at the gold band with its small twinkling diamond set between two even smaller emeralds.

"The green is for your eyes," he whispered.

"But you didn't need to get it engraved," she insisted.

"Why, pray tell, not?" he said sitting back with his eyebrows knitted together.

"Because, my darling, I'm never taking it off." She leaned in and kissed him again.

"How about we get out of these clothes?" Oliver said. "I had Ginny bring my duffel up earlier."

"Ginny! Well, I just hope she hasn't pulled any pranks with your stuff."

"I think I got my bluff in on her. But we'll see. Now, where did she put it?"

"It's on Laurie's bed."

"That was swell of the girls to go over to Laurie's folks' for the night."

"Yes, it was. I don't know where we'd have gone otherwise." She stood and walked over to Laurie's corner. "This is what we do when we want privacy. "She gestured with the curtain. "So, I'll close my curtain and change."

He put his hands on her waist and pulled her tight against him, and she swallowed hard as she realized how aroused he already was. "Don't take too long." He slid his hands up to cup her breasts. "I'll be waiting." She shivered, and he chuckled.

She pulled her curtain and slipped out of her shoes, sliding them under the bed. It felt so good to get them off. She laid the lucky penny on her nightstand. Next, she removed her suit, which she hung carefully in the chifforobe. She looked at herself in the mirror. *Well, you're a married woman now. No, not yet.* She wouldn't feel married until she and Oliver came to know each other in the Biblical sense.

She turned toward her bed, where a gift-wrapped box lay. Her gift from Graydell. "Don't you dare open it until after the wedding, after we're all gone." She slid the baby blue satin ribbon off and peeled back the paper. When she lifted the lid, she gasped.

"Everything alright in there?" Oliver asked.

"I'm fine. Don't come in yet."

She heard him laugh, but she was busy lifting out the white silk gown. It felt so cool under her fingers. She held it up against her and looked in the mirror again. She couldn't believe such a thing was hers. Nightgowns had always been practical things at home, made by Mama out of the soft cotton flour sacks. Mae had picked her least worn one to wear tonight. But now, she had this beautiful gown to wear. For Oliver. *Thank you, Grady.*

Hurriedly, she removed her slip, bra, and stockings. Standing in just her panties, she felt suddenly shy. Should she take them off, too? *Not yet.* Letting the gown fall over her head, she marveled at how it clung to her body. The straps were satin, and a satin bow was tied between her breasts. She ran her hands over them, smoothing the lovely fabric. Running her hands through her hair, she thought back to how Oliver had held her a few minutes ago. She looked at her breasts in surprise. *Apparently he's not the only one already aroused.*

She pulled her curtain back far enough to see Oliver. He was wearing pajama bottoms that hung low on his slim hips. She felt his smoldering gaze on her, his eyes traveling from her face to her bare feet and back again. She did the same to him, taking note of the dark hair scattered across his chest. More hairs, a dark line, ran down his stomach to disappear into his pants. She tore her gaze from his hips, and they smiled at each other. She wondered if he was as nervous as she was.

He took the few steps to meet her and touched her lightly on the shoulder, letting his hand train down her arm. "God, you're so beautiful. Come to bed, Maisie." He reached to turn back the covers. He sat on the side of the bed and pulled her onto his lap. "I don't know what I've done to deserve you. I love you so very much."

She laid a hand on his cheek and kissed him, softly at first, but as his arms tightened around her, her embarrassment disappeared. *There's no need to stop this time.*

She tilted her head so their foreheads met. "I love you, too, Ollie." The words still felt new coming off her tongue. "I'll love you forever." And in that moment, she knew with a certainty it was true.

He swung his legs onto the bed and laid her down beside him. "Nervous?" He smiled down at her.

"Not when you look at me like that. I know it'll be okay."

He grinned. "I hope it's better than okay, sweetheart. I promise to take my time. The first time."

First time? Eek.

She nodded, and his mouth closed over hers. She couldn't believe she was lying here with only the silk between them. Propping on his elbow, he gazed at her as the last rays of the sun gilded her hair before slipping out of sight. His hand roamed over her body, found her hipbone and kneaded it, sending chills of anticipation over her.

When his hand moved to her breast, he sucked in his breath. Sliding the satin strap down her arm, he exposed her nipple. When he dipped his head and licked lazily, the pink bud stood at attention. He laughed, then growled, and took it into his mouth. Mae arched her back, begging for more. She sighed and gave herself up to the exquisite sensations flooding her body and her mind.

* * *

She woke early on Saturday, after only a couple of hours of exhausted sleep. She was on her side, with Oliver spooned up against her in the tiny bed that was much too small for the two of them. His hand was cupped around her breast. She smiled a wicked smile, remembering all the things they had done last night—and this morning. When the moment came, there had been a fierce pain, one so sharp she cried out. When Oliver had hesitated, she had dug her nails into his back. "Don't stop!" she'd begged, and he had plunged ahead, taking them both to places Mae had only dreamed about before.

Her heart was so full that she felt tears welling up. As gently as she could, she wiped them away, hoping to let him sleep. "Good morning, Mrs. Cranfield." Oliver nuzzled her neck as his hand tightened on her breast. "Wish I could wake up like this every morning for the rest of my life." Mae heard the low timbre of his voice, deeper than she'd ever heard him before, and felt him move behind her. *I do that to him. Glory be.*

She twisted in the bed to look at him. His dark brown hair, always so well groomed, was all askew this morning. Dark stubble covered his cheeks.

"I love you, Mr. Cranfield. I wish we could wake up in a bigger bed for the rest of our lives."

"Nooo," he growled. "This one suits me. I like being this close to you." Moving his body over hers, he added, "Think it fits us just right."

A loud growl from her stomach made Mae pull the sheet over her head. "Oh, that is so embarrassing."

"Is my bride hungry?"

"Well, I didn't eat much yesterday, with so much going on."

"Oh, you're hungry for real food?" He laughed and pulled the sheet down. "Don't hide from me, lady. Don't ever hide from me."

"But it was embarrassing," she insisted.

"Only because our situation is so new. We've been friends forever. I couldn't count the times we've heard each other's stomachs, how many times I've belched in front of you, and you just laughed at me. You'll just have to learn how not to be embarrassed."

"It's different now. I'm different. It will never again be like it used to be."

He looked at her in consternation, his brow furrowed. "Why, Maisie? Why won't it be the same?"

"Because," she said, sliding out of bed and reaching for her robe hanging from the bedpost. "Because, my dear Ollie, now it's going to be so much better." She kissed his forehead. "I'll be back in a flash, depending on what you want for breakfast."

"Know what I'd really like?" His eyes turned a smoky blue.

She sighed in mock exasperation. "Well, I think I can guess, but we need real food."

He sat back against the headboard. "I was talking about real food, ma'am."

"Oh. Well, in that case, tell me what you want."

"I want some more of that wedding cake." She laughed and shook her head. "Men," she said.

"Not men. Man. One man. Your man!" he called after her, but she was already out the door.

FORTY-THREE

TOO GOOD AT SAYING GOODBYE

THE HONEYMOON LASTED TWO days and two wonder-filled nights. Graydell and Laurie came by the day after the wedding to have Sunday dinner with them. Mrs. S. had outdone herself in the kitchen. Over a meal of roast chicken and vegetables, field peas, and her famous rolls, which Mae was too drowsy to enjoy fully, they had discussed every aspect of the wedding. Graydell had them all in stitches with her mimicry of the attendees, and of Mae's sneezes during her vows.

Laurie and Mrs. Swenson came out with trays loaded with more slices of cake, and while they ate, she and Graydell exchanged glances.

"Think we're going back to my parents' tonight," Laurie said. "We started playing gin rummy with them last night, and we realized we haven't had much fun like that lately."

"Are you sure?" Oliver asked. "I can find us a motel somewhere if y'all want to come back to the apartment."

"No need for that," Graydell chimed in. "Mr. Lindstrom is a hoot. And he does not like to lose in a card game. It's the most fun I've had in ages."

"Well, if you're sure," Mae said. "I just feel bad, like I've kicked you two out."

278

"Don't be silly. I'm having a great time," Graydell said. "We'll run up and grab a few things, and we'll see you after work tomorrow." She paused. "Or are you going in tomorrow?"

Mae looked at Oliver and raised her eyebrows. "I'm not sure. We haven't planned that far ahead. I don't really know how long Oliver is going to be here."

"Actually, I was trying to find the right time to tell you."

"Tell me what?" There was a definite catch in her voice.

"I got into the Medic program. I have to report to a school in Illinois as soon as I can get there." He reached for Mae's hand. "I have to leave first thing tomorrow morning."

His words cast a pall over the room. Mrs. Swenson quietly loaded plates onto the tray and excused herself to the kitchen. Mae's roommates slipped out, leaving the newlyweds alone.

"When exactly were you going to tell me?" She couldn't even bring herself to look at him.

"I don't know, honey. I wanted to. I just couldn't find the right time. I knew you'd be disappointed."

But Mae just sat there, silent. Suddenly, she bounced in her chair. "Oh! I just now heard what you said. You got into the Medic training. Ollie, that's wonderful!" She beamed at a very surprised Oliver.

"You're not mad I have to go right away?"

"Well, I don't want you to go now, of course. But, Oliver! Don't you see what this means? It means you won't have to fight. You can spend your time helping the wounded rather than carrying a gun."

"At least in theory. I'm not so sure there's that much separation between the two positions. I don't want you to get your hopes too high."

"Oh, but I am. Now, I want to go to a movie."

"Now?" he asked, looking perplexed.

"Yep. Right now. I want to go sit in a dark movie theater and make out with my husband in the last row."

"I'm gonna pretend I didn't hear that," Graydell said, breezing in with a bag on her shoulder.

Laurie waggled her fingers as they left.

Mae pasted a bright smile on her face. She would not let Oliver see her disappointment. Not tonight.

* * *

His leave-taking on Monday was another matter altogether. Mae hated herself for it, but she couldn't stop the tears when she stood by Oliver's car with him. They'd stayed in the apartment all of Sunday, making love and making far-reaching plans for their lives after the war.

"I know it's silly, trying to say now what our lives will be like after this is all over. The world is already a different place, and I don't think things are likely to go back to the way they used to be," Oliver was saying as he polished his boots. "But I have so many dreams for us, Mae."

"I know. I do, too. What's so bad about making plans? Nobody says we'll have to stick to them. But at least we can talk about the future. And then I can dream about it after you're gone."

He dropped the brush, wiped his hands on a rag, and crawled across the floor to where she was lying on the floor on a patchwork quilt. "Want to make another memory before I go?"

She grinned and pulled him to her. She was wearing one of his army shirts with it buttoned once. She wore nothing else, and Oliver slipped his hands inside. She broke away from him and, rising to her knees, pushed him back so that he lay stretched out before her. "Take your pants off, baby," she crooned, and he lost no time in obeying her. She leaned down to kiss him, and before he knew what she intended, she had straddled him. Instinctively he groped her hips, and she whispered in his ear, "Let's make a memory that will last until you're back in my arms forever. How about it, soldier?"

His body gave her all the answer she could have wanted.

With his car packed, she couldn't face the thought of him leaving. Not when they had just made such a commitment to each other. Thoughts of the past two days whirled in her mind, and she wanted more. It wasn't right for him to have to go away again so soon.

"It doesn't matter if I'm here or a thousand miles away, darling Mae. You're going to be right here," he said, patting his heart, "and I'm going to be right there." He placed his fingers over her heart, letting one of them slide over her nipple.

"Oliver!" she said, covering his hand with hers. "We're out in public." But she didn't remove his hand.

"Yes, and we're legally married. I just wanted to say goodbye to the little guy."

"You're crazy, you know that?"

"Yep. Crazy in love, that's me."

"Write me as soon as you get there?"

"You know I will. You be careful out at that plant, okay? Watch those grenades. And make sure all the guys know you're a married woman now."

"I don't want you to go, Oliver," she cried, clinging to him. *Damn. I wasn't going to do that. Come on, Mae. Straighten up.*

He held her by her shoulders. "Look at me, Maisie." He stared into her eyes, wet with tears, and reached to wipe them away with his thumbs. "Your eyes are sparkling like emeralds, so much brighter than the ones in your ring. Someday I will put a ring on your finger like you deserve. Someday." He leaned down and covered her mouth with his, as if trying to get as close to her as possible. "Love you," he choked out as he backed away and got into the car.

She stood staring after him, long after the car had turned the corner and was out of sight. A soft rain began to fall, mixing with the tears running down her face. Mae felt as if the whole world, and maybe even the angels, were crying with her.

FORTY-FOUR

RIDING THE RAILS

THE FIRST THING MAE saw when she opened Oliver's letter was four ten-dollar bills. "What the . . .?" She fingered the money but set it aside to see why Oliver was sending her money. She made more than his army pay. She'd told him already she didn't need anything. Maybe he wanted her to save it for after the war. She'd find out soon enough.

October 20, 1942

My Sweet Mae,

Lord am I missing you! But that's about to change. I have great news, the best news possible. The base here is overcrowded, and there's not enough housing for all the recruits. So they decided some of the men could live off base in private housing. They held a drawing, sort of like for the draft, and put all the names of men who said they'd like to live elsewhere. You probably wouldn't be surprised to learn that was the majority of us. But you might be surprised to learn yours truly was one of the lucky ones to have his name drawn. Yes, your loving husband has an okay from his government to rent a place in town, and Uncle Sam will even pay for it. So I marched over there (actually I drove) and gave the place a once over, and I found a little house. For us. I want you to come to me, Maisie.

"He says 'I want you to come to me'. Lord, that man can turn my insides to mush with just —how many? —eight little words."

The house is very small. But it does have a full-sized bed, and that's all we need. There's a kitchenette, too, in case we decide to have a bite to eat. So, what do you say? Pack a bag, buy a ticket, and get here as quick as you can. I put down a deposit, and I'm sure hoping you're missing me as much as I'm missing you.

All My Love,

O.D.

Mae scanned the letter again. She couldn't believe it. She was going to Illinois. She let out a squeal and started calling, "Graydell! Laurie! Y'all get up. You can sleep later. I've got news! The best news!" They were both sleeping in this Saturday morning, but she didn't care. She had to share her news with them, and right now. Laurie came awake immediately, as usual. Graydell was harder to rouse, since she hadn't been in bed that long, after a late date night with Scotty.

"What's such good news? Laurie said, yawning. "Is the war over?"

Me stopped her dancing momentarily. "Boy, Laurie, you really know how to pop the balloon, don't you?"

Graydell padded in to plop down on the sofa next to Laurie. They both looked at Mae expectantly. She flashed the wad of bills at them. "Know what this is for?"

"You robbed a bank?" Graydell grumbled. "If so, it doesn't look like you made off with much loot."

"Oh, no, I haven't done anything illegal. I just got a letter from my man."

"He robbed a bank?" Graydell persisted.

Laurie laughed and nudged her. "Why don't we stop guessing so Mae can tell us her news? Then we can both get back to sleep."

"Bet you won't," Mae teased. They both gave her dark looks, so she said, "Oh, all right. The base is overcrowded where Oliver is, and they're letting some of the men take rooms or houses in town. And Oliver is one of the lucky ones. And I'm going to Illinois!" She danced around the sofa as she shared this information, and when she stopped in front of them, they both just stared.

"Well? Isn't anybody going to congratulate me?" she asked when they continued to sit with their mouths open. "Grady? Laurie? Isn't this the most wonderful news?" But she was beginning to get the feeling they didn't quite share her excitement.

Laurie recovered first. She jumped up and hugged Mae. "That is wonderful, sweetie. So he's sent you money so you can go up there to be with him?"

"Yes, and oh, I have so much to do. I have plans to make." But she hung back, waiting to hear from her best friend.

"Oh, hell, Mae. Of course, I'm thrilled for you, and for you and Oliver," Graydell said. She stood and embraced her. "It's so wonderful for you. But I'm going to miss you! And what about your job? Are you just going to up and leave Lone Star?"

Mae was incredulous at the question. "Why, of course I am. Oliver is my husband. My place is with him. I can't go overseas with him when he finally does ship out. But if Uncle Sam is happy with him staying here a few more months, and he's making it possible for me to be with him, well, sure I'm going."

"Of course you are." Graydell smiled, finally and truly awake.

* * *

The trip to Illinois would have been unbearable if Oliver hadn't been waiting at the end of it. She had packed light, just one small case. He wouldn't care if she wore the same clothes every other day. *Or not at all.* Mae had never traveled anywhere by train before, had barely been out of Arkansas, and she was both scared and excited at the beginning of her trip on Wednesday. She only had to change trains in Memphis and St. Louis, but in St. Louis she ran into trouble. So many troops were embarking there that she was booted off and had to wait for a later train, and that put her behind. She fretted and fumed, until she remembered she could send a wire ahead to Oliver. Then she sat down in the station to wait, bundling her jacket into a pillow so she could sleep on the bench. The first available train pulled in on Friday morning, and Mae dragged herself and her case on board. Her new ticket led her to the third passenger car and she hurriedly found an empty row. Stashing her case in the rack, she fell into a seat. With the aisles full of people, she quickly moved to the window seat. Sighing, she shrugged out of her jacket and prepared to use it once more for a pillow.

"Do you mind?" She looked around to see a woman of about thirty gesturing to the empty seat. She was taller than Mae by a couple of inches, and her reddish-brown hair was piled atop her head. She looked a bit like Betty Grable. Mae shook her head, smiled, and then gazed back out the window again. She hoped her seatmate wouldn't be a big talker. Mae, herself, was too exhausted to make small talk.

"And then he said, 'Well, then get yourself up here, sugar,'" Thelma said, with a laugh at the end of the lengthy story she'd just told. "So here I am, on my way to the big city of Chicago. Where are you headed?"

"The same place, sort of," Mae said tiredly. "Oliver's picking me up there and we'll drive from there to his base at a place called Rockford."

"Yeah, Rockford's a really busy place these days. Isn't it exciting, following our men around the country?"

"I guess so," Mae replied. "It'll be exciting when I see mine, I know that. We've only been married a few weeks, and we only had a couple of days for our honeymoon."

"Oh, you poor thing!"

"It's alright. There are plenty of other women in the same boat as me," Mae smiled.

"Yes, but still. Harry and I've been married seven years now, and I still miss him like crazy. Why, you two just got started. Two whole days, huh?" She shook her head and patted Mae's arm. "Rest up, honey. That man's gonna eat you alive," she whispered.

Mae took her at her word and nestled her head against her jacket, gazing into the darkness at nothing. Exhaustion soon overcame her.

Early Sunday morning, Mae woke to the sound of the conductor announcing their arrival in Chicago's Union Station. Her body ached, her head hurt and she knew she smelled to high heaven. *What a way to meet Oliver. . . if he's even here. Lord, please let him be here!*

"Come on, sugar, let's move," Thelma said, stepping into the aisle and reaching for their cases. "This one yours? Good, let's go."

Mae stumbled off the train behind her new acquaintance. Once inside the station, Thelma and Mae hurried to the arrival lounge. "There's my man!" Thelma exclaimed, waving to a handsome officer of about thirty-five. He rushed to meet her, swinging her into the air and then enveloping her in a bear hug.

Mae was standing a bit forlornly, watching the couple's happy reunion, when she heard, "Mae! Over here!" By the time she'd turned around, he was there. And she was in his arms, and his mouth was crushing hers. And she was laughing and crying at the same time. And the awfulness of the last few days melted away, and her world was right again.

"Newlyweds," she heard Thelma say, laughing. "God love 'em."

* * *

Once in Rockford, they had breakfast at a diner Oliver had found close to the base, and Mae got him caught up on the news from home. Afterward, he drove her around the base and some of the little town, showing her shopping areas and the downtown, which was about the same size as Texarkana's Broad Street. Seeing Mae nodding next to him, he smiled at his exhausted bride and turned toward their new temporary home.

"Wake up, Maisie," he said, nudging her gently. He felt like picking her up and carrying her inside. Poor girl looked beat.

"Hmm? Oh, I'm sorry, Ollie. I can't believe I fell asleep on you." She sat up and looked around. Seeing the small structure with its tiny front yard, she asked, "Is this ours?"

He hoped she'd be happy with it. He'd fixed it up as much as he'd had a chance to, but it needed a woman's touch. He hopped out of the car and came to open her door. She stood looking at the house for a long minute, then he saw a smile begin to play at the corners of her mouth. He grabbed her case and held her hand as they walked to the door.

"Want me to carry you over the threshold?" he asked. She nodded. He opened the door, scooped her into his arms, and strode inside. He didn't put her down until he'd shown her the entire place, such as it was.

"It's like a grown-up's doll house," she laughed, and he could hear her old spunk returning. She ran her hand over the pale yellow coverlet on the bed. "Pretty."

He could hear the hesitation in her voice. This war was causing people to accept a lot of things they hadn't before, but he'd be damned if he laid his Maisie in used bed covers.

"Honey, I bought these at Sears. They're brand new. Of course, you can buy whatever you'd like, but I had to get it ready for you." He saw the relief in her eyes. Turning back the covers, he plumped the pillow and said, "Why don't you lie down and rest up from the trip?"

"Are you coming to bed, too?" God, how he wanted to. He'd been dreaming of their two days and nights together ever since he left.

"Not right now," he said. "Get some rest. We'll have plenty of time for—"

"For getting reacquainted," she smiled. She turned her back and began to remove her suit. When her skirt fell to the floor and her jacket followed, he gazed at her slim figure.

"Mae, are you eating enough? You look thinner to me." He laid his hands on her shoulders and let them slide down her arms. *Yes, definitely thinner. We'll see about that.*

She slid between the sheets without answering. He watched until he was sure she was asleep, then he stripped to his skivvies and eased into the bed from the other side. *Time enough, old man. Time enough.*

FORTY-FIVE

ADJUSTMENTS

THE FIRST WEEK WAS a magical reunion. Mae learned her way around town, bought groceries, and began to learn how to be a housewife. Oliver brought home a small table radio, and she marveled at the number of stations they picked up. She listened to news reports from the war zones, always while he was in class. During supper, he liked to share with her the things he was studying, and she was so proud of all he was learning. Late at night, they fell asleep in each other's arms, fully sated with lovemaking.

During the second week, boredom began to haunt her days. There was just so little to do in the way of housekeeping. Oliver left for the base before she woke, and she ate breakfast and lunch alone, never very hungry. She found a small book shop in her wanderings and picked up a couple of paperbacks, but she'd never been a voracious reader like Graydell, and . . .

Wonder what Graydell and Laurie are doing these days. Wonder if they miss me. I doubt it. She dressed and walked a few blocks to her new favorite five and dime to buy writing materials. Back home, she wrote to the girls, to her folks, to Prissy. *Prissy would hate it up here.*

Fall had hit here already, and the wind blew every day. Her only pleasure came from the little time she had with Oliver. And he seemed to be busier and more preoccupied every day. He toted home bags of books

288

and notebooks and apologized to her when he studied until almost bedtime every night.

"I guess this isn't what you had in mind when you came up here," he said one night as he sat at the kitchen table, books spread out around him. "I admit, I didn't know we were going to be quite this busy."

Mae finished wiping down the stove and came to put her arms around him. "Hey, don't you worry about me. Spending an hour or two with you is better than going to bed alone every night at home."

He reached around and drew her onto his lap, kissing her deeply, lingeringly. "Aw, hell," he growled. "Forget the books. Let's go to bed." She jumped up from his lap.

"I thought you'd never ask, baby!"

They made love frantically at first, hungry for each other as if afraid it would be their last time. When Oliver fell into an exhausted sleep, Mae lay awake letting her eyes roam over every inch of his body. *One of these days, he's going to be gone, and these memories will be all I have— for the duration. However long that is.*

When she couldn't stand it any longer, she leaned over and began to let her tongue and her hands explore this man she loved so much. She felt his hands massaging her head and looked up from her ministrations. "My God, Maisie. You're incredible." She felt incredible at the moment, and she slid her leg across his so that she was lying half atop him.

She whispered in his ear, "Show me things, Ollie. I want to do things for you—with you."

"Honey, you're the only woman I've ever been with. I'm not like lots of guys. I don't know everything about this."

"Then we'll learn together," she purred, positioning herself above him. By morning, they knew much more than they'd known before.

In the third week, Mae came to a decision. She needed a job. She was bored and feeling useless, as if the only thing she was good for was cooking and sex. Their love life was wonderful. There just wasn't enough of it.

"I'm going to look for a job tomorrow," she announced one night at supper.

Oliver put down his fork and stared down his long nose at her. "What for?"

"For something to do. Ollie, I get so lonesome here all day, waiting for you to come home. I need to be doing something, anything."

"You're my wife. Isn't that enough of a job?" She heard the dangerous deepening of his voice.

"Well, sure it is, honey. When you're here, it's great. But you're not here much."

"You knew that before you came."

"Knowing and experiencing are two different things," she said. "I've been working so long it seems wrong *not* to be, now. I won't take a position that will keep me from being here to fix your dinner and spend evenings with you. Just something part time, to pass the time, you know?" Surely he'd understand.

"I don't want my wife working. I can provide for you without that." She saw that stubborn tilt of his chin.

"Oliver! I've been working for two years now. I was working when you married me."

"That was different. That was war work. There's none of that here. I'm serious, Mae. You need to forget about that silly idea. I don't want you working, and that's that."

She sat stunned. This was a side of Oliver she'd never seen, not in all the years they'd been friends. "You're just being pig-headed," she spat out. "I refuse to sit here and stagnate while you go off and play doctor. It's ridiculous." She was sorry as soon as the words were out of her mouth— but then he doubled down on his ultimatum.

"I refuse to have you going out looking for work! And that's that. We'll hear no more about it." He took his plate to the sink and retreated to the living room with a textbook.

Mae sat and fumed. *No man is going to tell me what to do. Especially when what he's saying doesn't make sense. What happened to*

290

the man I married? She ran water in the sink and tossed the dishes in. By the time she got to the pots and pans, she was so mad she was sloshing water all over the floor. She didn't care. It wasn't *her* house. She strode into the tiny bedroom. *Maybe I need to get back to my 'war work'. Yes, that's what I'll do.* She got out her suitcase and started packing. Half an hour later, she walked into the living room and said, "I've decided to go back home. You don't need me here. And what I want doesn't seem to matter. So tomorrow morning, I'm taking the bus into Chicago and I'm going back to Texarkana." Before he could reply, she whirled and left the room. When he came to bed hours later, she pretended sleep, and he let her be.

* * *

Oliver stood looking at his sleeping bride in the predawn light pouring through the window. His heart hurt to think of how upset she had been. But in his heart, he knew he was right. He stepped into the kitchen and read over the note he'd written. He'd tried to placate her without giving in, and he prayed she'd come to her senses. He placed the note on the kitchen table and closed the door softly behind him.

Mid-morning, he was back. He ran to the front door and hurried inside. The silence that greeted him was deafening. He knew she was gone, but he called her name anyway. Checking the kitchen table, he saw his note torn neatly into two pieces.

Damn that woman! I can't believe she really left me.

He checked the closet. Her clothes and her case were gone. The bed was made, the house spotless. But it was so empty without her. His heart ached for hurting her.

Maybe I can catch her. He prayed all the way to Union Station. Inside, he scanned the waiting rooms. He checked the big board of arrivals and departures, finding only one train going in Mae's direction today, leaving at noon. The big clock showed 11:30. *Thank God. I have a chance.* He continued his search, finally going out to the platform. Frantically, he looked for a head of blond curls. Then he saw her. She was sitting on a bench, alone, twisting a handkerchief in her fingers.

"Oh, sweetheart," he muttered, walking up to stand in front of her. "I've been such a fool. Just a damn fool." He knelt before her, looking up into her red-rimmed eyes. "Forgive me?"

She burst into tears and flew into his arms. "I'm scared, Ollie. I'm scared we'll keep hurting each other."

"Come with me, Mae. Please, I love you, baby. Please . . ."

She gazed into his eyes, her emerald ones still swimming in tears. "Can I look for a job?" *Stubborn wench.*

"No, honey. I'm sorry. You can't." She drew back from him, but he hurried on. "I came back home to tell you my news. I'm being sent to California for some special training. That's what I came to tell you. I have to take you back to Arkansas, and then I'm on another train."

She blinked once, twice, and burst into tears again. He held her and crooned to her, no idea what he was saying. Gradually her tears subsided, and she blew her nose.

"So, I don't have to get on that train to go back to Texarkana?"

""No, baby. We're going to drive. You and I are finally going to see some of the country like we've always talked about. We'll make it a real honeymoon, okay?"

She nodded. "I love you, Ollie."

"Oh, God, I love you too, Maisie."

He picked up her case and held out his hand. "Let's go pack up and hit the road, honey. It'll be an adventure."

"I like adventures," she said, sniffling. They walked out of the station hand in hand.

292

FORTY-SIX

SOLDIER BOY

MAE WAS FEELING MIFFED. No, she was just put out. Or maybe both would describe her. It was Saturday night, and she was all alone in the apartment. Laurie was out to dinner with her parents, and Graydell was out on the town with her latest boyfriend. *I hope she learned her lesson with that terrible experience with George. And Lord, I pray Scotty will be a good man for her.*

Oliver was off in California learning more about being a medic. She was proud of him, yes. But, Lord, she missed him. Especially on nights like these, when they would have all the privacy they needed here in this apartment that seemed large enough to house an entire company of enlisted men. *Ha! What a time Mrs. S. would have with that, trying to house an entire company of guys. She'd probably go across the street and round up some policemen to roust them all out. On the other hand, she could probably handle the job herself.* But the point was, the apartment was large, and tonight it felt especially empty.

She knew she was lucky to still have a place in this apartment, lucky to have her job. The plants were so desperate for workers that Charles had welcomed her back to the grenade line, where Johnie and the others seemed genuinely glad to see her. If it weren't for the war, she wouldn't have been able to pick up right where she'd left off. Then again, if it weren't for the war, she wouldn't be living here at all. She'd be somewhere with Oliver, doing who knew what, but doing it together.

She was lonely. She wanted her husband. And she wanted him *now*.

She decided to wash her hair.

Setting out shampoo, towel, and pitcher next to the kitchen sink, she stripped down to her underwear and wrapped her robe tightly around her. No need to be getting her clothes wet. She always made a mess washing her hair. She picked up the paperback Graydell had insisted she read, turning to read the blurb on the back. *Great. Another cheesy romance.* She had found it next to impossible to become interested in any love story other than her own ever since Oliver put that ring on her finger. She held up her hand and kissed the little ring. Sitting on the bed, she began to brush through her hair, fantasizing about being with Oliver again.

There was the tread of heavy footsteps on the stairs. They sounded male. Mrs. S. wasn't in, or she'd have surely already sent whoever it was packing. The steps stopped right outside her door.

"Who's there?" she asked. "You don't have any business here, so please just go away."

After a few seconds, she heard a deep baritone voice reply, "I was sort of hoping for a warmer welcome from my sweet bride."

Oliver!

She threw open the door and jumped into his arms, wrapping her legs around his waist. No easy feat, as he was carrying both flowers and chocolates. His love offerings fell to the floor at their feet as he lustily caught the leaping Mae. She flung her arms around his neck and covered the side of his face with kisses. He bussed her lips once, heartily. Laughing, he stood her on her feet.

"Who were you expecting, anyway?" he laughed, running his hands underneath her robe and not finding much in the way of resisting fabric.

She swatted him on the shoulder, giggling. "Not expecting anybody—but you can come on in, soldier."

He bent to pick up his dismissed gifts and followed her into the room.

"How did you get here? I mean, when did you get here? I mean, oh, honey, it's so wonderful to see you! I don't care how you got here, where you're going next. I'm just so grateful you're here."

"Me, too, Maisie. Now come here and give me a proper welcome." He flounced back onto her little bed and held out his arms.

She gave a Cheshire cat grin and took a step toward him, then another, as she loosened the belt of her robe and let it slip from her shoulders. "Sadly, my husband has been away, and I had wondered if he was ever coming back."

Oliver crooked a finger at her. "Well, he's here now, and he really needs his woman."

"That so?"

"Damn straight."

"Well then, here I am." She climbed onto the bed, straddling him with her knees. He reached out with both hands and stroked her thighs.

* * *

Much later, they were spooning on the little bed, Oliver's back against the wall, an arm and a leg thrown over Mae.

"Honey, how long can you stay?" She tried to keep her voice casual, but even in just those few words she was sure he would hear the catch in her voice. *Drat. I was trying so hard. I don't want him to go away thinking I'm going to be a crybaby about this—even if I am, later.*

"I'll have to leave tomorrow night. I've got a ticket on the ten 'clock train headed toward New York. We ship out on Wednesday, so I should get there in time with no problem."

Mae sat upright suddenly, causing the sheet to slip toward her waist. Oliver's eyes darkened a bit as he looked at the curve of her breast.

"So soon? That is not fair," she spat. "Those generals must not love their wives very much or they'd have more concern for yours."

"Oh, darlin', I think it's Hitler's generals who don't have loving wives. It's their schedule we're working on these days, sad to say." As he spoke, he reached out and tweaked the nipple that was staring at him so saucily. It instantly sprang to attention.

Mae sucked in a breath and leaned in toward him. "All right. It's a good thing you have a loyal wife who doesn't go out at night," she said, staring deeply into his eyes. He took the gift she was offering and squeezed her breast. He pulled her toward him and took the rosy nipple into his mouth, nipping gently, then a bit harder, moaning from deep within himself. She squirmed and moaned softly in answer.

He detached his mouth and asked, "Want to go out for a bite to eat—after?"

"Yes," she said. "After."

* * *

Oliver sat back in the booth and sighed with satisfaction. He pushed his empty plate aside and slipped an arm around Mae. She giggled when he nuzzled her neck. He knew she was especially ticklish there, and he enjoyed hearing her giggle. "I love your laugh, Maisie," he said against her neck. "I wish I could bottle up that laugh and take it with me. I'll never forget it, but it would sure be nice to take out a small bottle, uncap it, and have your musical giggling take all my cares away, as I know it would."

"I'll miss your arms around me in the night, more than anything else," Mae said. She turned toward him and searched his eyes, wanting to memorize every facet of his personality showing there.

He winked at her, and her heart contracted about two sizes before growing close to bursting. "I got you something to remember me by," he said, his deep voice going even deeper.

"You didn't have to do that. I'm always going to remember everything about you, sweetie."

"That may be, but here it is, anyway." He reached into his uniform pocket and took out a small, rectangular box. Taking his arm off her shoulder, he moved to open it. Inside was a pin a bit shorter than her little finger, shaped like a capital "V." Embedded within the pin's outline was a series of rhinestones.

"Now, I know what you're thinking, Mrs. Cranfield. You're thinking I went out and bought you the biggest set of diamonds you've ever seen and had them set in this little dinky pin instead of having them made into a nice, serious wedding ring for you."

She giggled.

"Really, it's just a silver pin with some pasty rhinestones—but it's a very important little pin. Know why?" She shook her head. "Because, Maisie, I want you to wear it until I get back home to you. Several of the guys have bought these for their wives and girlfriends, and I really liked the idea. The "V" stands for "Victory." You know, victory in Europe and in the Pacific both."

Mae's voice was husky when she said, "Oh, Ollie. I'll wear it every single change I get to, you know that, but—"

"But nothing. I know you can't wear it to work. But I want you to wear it when you go out places." She started to shake her head, but he continued. "Yes, you're going to go out places, honey. You're young, you're working your butt off out at that plant, you have friends who will be going out, and you," he poked his finger into her chest, then tapped it on her nose, then waggled it in front of her face, "you, too, are going to go out and have a good time."

"But what if I don't want to?" she protested.

"Doesn't matter. I refuse to be sitting in a field hospital somewhere over in Europe thinking about you back here moping around your room while everyone else is out having a good time. Now, do you want me to be preoccupied, worrying about you, where I'm liable to stick my head out of some foxhole and get the blamed thing blowed off, or are you going to keep me happy in my little hellhole?"

297

She placed both hands on his cheeks and leaned in to kiss him, a long, searing kiss that had an older couple seated across the room from them looking at each other with a secret smile, as if to say, "We could show them a thing or two."

"You are the sweetest husband a girl ever had. You're not really gonna be in a foxhole, are you?" That thought made her queasy.

"Nah, just a little exaggeration," he assured her.

"I'm proud to wear your pin. And, okay, I will go out sometimes. Just don't ask me to go every night, or even every week. I can't keep up with those girls anymore. I've turned into an old homebody. All I want to do is read, sleep, and rest—and think about you."

"I guess that's as good as I can ask for. What man wouldn't want to have a woman like you keeping the home fires going for him?"

They sat quietly for a couple of minutes, relaxing into the music playing on the jukebox. At least they were relaxed until "I'll Be Seeing You" came on the jukebox.

"Speaking of home fires . . ." Oliver began.

Mae had already grabbed her handbag. "Let's go," she laughed, pushing him out of the booth.

* * *

Sunday morning came too soon, and Mae was surprised to realize neither Laurie nor Graydell had come in at all last night. When she went down to get a glass of milk from the kitchen, however, she noticed some unusual shapes in the parlor and backed up for a better look. There, sprawled out on the matching divans, were her two roommates, arms flung out in all directions, one snoring gently and the other on her stomach with a cushion over her head.

Lord, I do love those girls. Thank you for giving them to me. Swooping into the room, she swatted Laurie on her rear and flopped onto the couch with Graydell.

298

"You gals are the best ever. But you shouldn't have. We were expecting you to come on in."

Laurie struggled to her knees and sat up, yawning. "Well, Mae, dear, you may have been expecting us—but we certainly weren't expecting *you*. Or should I say, *you two*?"

"Nope," Graydell piped up. "Two's company, and three may be a crowd, but four is definitely above my pay grade. Or something like that."

"Well, we'll be out of your hair in a jiff," Mae said. "My sweetie is taking me to church this morning."

"Need to do some confessing, do you?" Laurie said with a leer.

"Heck, no. Everything I did last night was with the full consent of my lawfully wedded husband. I'm going to church today to *give thanks*."

On her way to the kitchen, she stuck her head back around the corner to add, "And to say a special prayer of protection, too."

FORTY-SEVEN

KISSES & PROMISES

"YOU THINK YOU'LL BE alright up there in New York City by yourself?" Mae teased Oliver as they walked up the steps at Union Station. "I mean, there's no telling how many young, beautiful girls will be there to meet your train."

"Doesn't matter. I've got the one I want." He watched her going ahead of him up the stairs. When she got to just the right angle, he swatted her bottom, and she let out a shriek that echoed in the stairwell.

"Oliver Cranfield, you stop that," she said, staring down at him over her shoulder.

"Better hurry up, or I might just take a bite," he laughed, snapping his teeth together.

Mae hurried to the top of the stairs and turned to wait for him, her face a nice rosy red. He grinned at her discomfort. It was sure turning out to be fun being married.

"Aw, come on, Maisie. I'm sure people hanging out around the terminal here have seen worse things than that." He grabbed her around the waist and maneuvered her away from the steps and onto a bench, where he set out to show her how much she was going to miss him. *Lord knows, I'm going to miss her.*

"I don't know when I'll have a chance to write to you," he said, turning serious. "Several days on the train, and then who knows what, when we finally get there. I'm sure they'll be bringing guys in from all over the country. I hear they're packing those ships as full as they can before they sail for Europe."

"Yeah, I heard that, too. I know it's not going to be anything like mailing letters here in the States. But I know they have a special way of sending letters from overseas."

"You're talking about V-mail?"

She nodded. "Laurie says they take a picture of a page and then send the negative somewhere, where they print a miniature page that she can barely read. Lord, I hope Derrell makes it back. He's somewhere in the Pacific, that's all she knows. And things are so bad over there."

"I have to admit, I'm glad I've already been told I'm going someplace in the European theater. I know what people told us about the hell they went through in trenches during the First War. But hopefully the commanders learned something from that experience. Maybe things will be different this time."

"I'll pray for good winter weather. And that's enough of that talk. Tell me again how much you're going to miss me while you're gone." She reached up and removed his cap, settling it atop her curls. "Gotta run my hands through this head of hair one more time." When her fingers reached the back of his head, she pulled him toward her and parted her lips.

Accepting her invitation, he met her with a lazily thrusting tongue, hell bent on memorizing the taste and the feel of her. This was going to have to be enough for months, probably even years. He couldn't think of not seeing her for years. He wouldn't. Life would be difficult enough if he just thought of their separation as being months long.

When she whimpered against him, he decided maybe he should think about ending the kiss. When he did so and pulled back to look at her, her eyes were glassy with want. He was sure his looked the same.

"Oh, Maisie, I wish things were different. I wish we could be getting on this train together and riding off into the sunset on an extended honeymoon."

"I know. Just imagine, we could buy tickets for a sleeping car and ride across the whole country and back again. We could have our meals delivered to our car, and we could make love watching all kinds of landscapes go by the window. We wouldn't have to worry about onlookers until the train started slowing down."

"Then we could pull the shades," he said, "and just keep on loving each other."

"You hold that thought until this war is over," she said huskily. "I'll be ready to go as soon as you're free."

"Free. That's what this war is all about now, isn't it? We're really fighting for our freedom. The Japs and the Krauts can't make it if they don't win this war. And we can't allow them to win."

"Ollie, promise me something?"

"If I can. What?"

"Promise me you won't go and volunteer to get closer to the fighting than you have to."

He opened his mouth to protest, but she laid her fingers over his lips. *God, I love the feel of her so much.*

"Hear me out. I know you, remember? Seems I've known you forever. I've watched you tend to hurt animals on the farm. It didn't matter what their problem was, you always jumped into the middle of things and tried to make it all better. I love you for that, but please. Just don't be so quick to jump in over there."

He had been nibbling on her fingertips while she talked, but now he released them and said, "I can't make that promise, Mae." He sat back against the arm of the bench and gave her a penetrating look. "And would you really want me to? You know what I'll be doing when I get to where the fighting is. I'll be doing my dead level best to save lives. Our soldiers' lives, honey. Think about what a responsibility that will be. I won't promise

302

not to jump into a jeep and take off to look for the wounded. I doubt they'll be coming to us on their own."

They both jumped when a loudspeaker near their heads came to life. "That's me," Oliver said. "Come on, baby." He folded her into his arms. "Always remember how much I love you, and that I'll be thinking of you all the time. Don't let it worry you if you don't hear from me for a while. I promise I'll write when I can, and you promise to do the same."

"I promise. I love you, too. More than I ever thought I could love anybody."

"Do me a favor, Maisie?"

She smiled. "Anything."

He reached into a pocket and pulled out his pen knife. "Let me have a lock of those golden curls?"

Without hesitation, she pulled a long strand from the underside of her hair and tilted her head while he cut. Gently, slowly, he sawed until the tress sprang free. Like a love offering, she held it out to him. "Wish I had a ribbon to tie it for you," she said, smiling.

He took it from her and kissed it, then kissed her. "It's fine. I have the perfect place for it." Taking out his wallet, he slipped the little curl in front of her picture. "That'll do for now. Guess we'd better go."

They rose and joined the knot of people moving out onto the platform and down the steps. There seemed to be soldiers everywhere, most of them accompanied by girlfriends or wives, many with their whole families there. His parents had decided to say their goodbyes this morning. Every time he or his brother left, it seemed to take a little more out of his mother.

When he found his train, he set his bag down and hugged her tightly. He could feel her heart beating against his chest. He laid his lips on top of her head and said, "I love you, Maisie. I'll see you in my dreams until you're back in my arms."

"I'll write to you all the time. I'll miss you every minute of every day." Her arms were around his waist, holding on for dear life.

"Bye, Maisie. Love you."

"Bye, Ollie, and Godspeed. Love you."

* * *

She didn't know if he'd heard, because he had bounded up the steps and, as always, found a seat without looking back.

She turned and walked slowly back the way she'd come. As she had the last time he left, she waited for the train to start moving, only then pushing through the crowd of people to cross the broad, open platform and watch the train carrying her man away. A brisk autumn wind whipped dust up into her eyes, and her tears came faster. This time the train was moving in the opposite direction, headed for New York City. Again, she watched until the blinking light on the caboose disappeared around a curve.

We're getting altogether too good at saying goodbye. Please, God, let this be the last time.

As she had pretty much expected, Mae didn't receive a letter from Oliver for several weeks. When that day came, she was, as always, waiting for the postman. When the V-mail envelope dropped onto the carpet, she snatched it up to see who it belonged to. This time—praise God, this time—she didn't have to leave it on the hall table for Laurie. She raced up the stairs and settled on her bed. Gently, lovingly, she slid her knife under the flap and slid the small, folded pages out to try to figure out where to start. Finally, she found the "Dearest Mae." She kissed the words and began to read.

December 4, 1942
Dearest Mae,
It's late, but I wanted to write to let you know we got here safely. That's kinda silly, too, isn't it? It's not like you're going to be getting this letter right now. It'll be weeks before it gets to you. I guess it's really that I just want to feel like I'm making contact with you, you know? Cause it's like I'm losing touch with you—I can feel myself slipping away. And this thing is just getting started for us, so I can't let that happen. I guess writing to

you is my way of putting my arms around you and holding you close to my heart. That's where you are, you know, no matter what I just said about slipping away. I will not let this war do that to us! I promise.

She felt a lump in her throat at his words, so scary for her, sitting here alone on the bed where they'd made love the first time, and other times, too, each one inscribed in her heart. She wiped tears from her face and continued to read.

I can't tell you where we are, of course. If I try, they'll just come along and scratch it out. But I guess I can probably say it's cold. Ha ha. Wonder what it's like back home right now. Wish I was there to cuddle up with you and keep you warm, you know what I mean. Take that, Mr. Censor. Are you blushing yet? Him, Mae, not you. I know you--you're giggling and waving your hand in front of your face. With just a blush of redness on those rosy cheeks. You know, I was just getting used to being in your bed and boom!! They took me away from you. But I'll be back, I promise I have that final night of ours together to help me hold on until this war is over and I'm home for good.

I do feel blessed of God, though, to be going to a place where I can do some good. There's so much killing and dying on the battlefield—I can see the results of that already, from the men in hospital here.

I miss you, my beautiful, spunky bride. You take care of yourself—for me.

Your loving husband,

O.D.

P.S. Happy Birthday!

Oliver David. Maybe someday they'd have a son they could name after him. Someday, when this horrible time was over. She read the letter three times through, then took the box of his letters from under her bed. Kissing the envelope, she placed it inside. There was already a blue ribbon waiting for the time when she could bundle his letters from overseas together, much as she'd done with his earlier letters from around the country.

She sat back to think about what he'd said and what he hadn't said. There was nothing there to tell her where he was, nothing at all. It was cold everywhere in Europe right now. She knew he'd made it to Europe, knew he was probably in a staging area. So, he wasn't where the fighting was, not yet. He was most likely in England, or maybe Scotland. Probably not Ireland. Yes, most likely England. But where? She went to look at the world map she had tacked onto the wall just after he left. She was going to put a thumbtack somewhere on England's west coast. She could always move it later, if she ever found out where he'd landed.

Let's see, Manchester looks like a likely place. Or maybe Glasgow? Manchester for now.

She checked the time. She'd have time to make a diary entry before she left for work.

January 5, 1943

I finally heard from Oliver! Praise the Lord, he's made it to Europe safely. I think he's somewhere in England, though of course I don't know for sure. It was my first V-mail letter. They're not so easy to read, but I managed. Heck, I'd use a magnifying glass if I had to. I can't wait to tell the girls and Mrs. S. Our landlady has been almost as anxious as I've been for this letter.

I'm making it okay at work. There are plenty of other women in the same boat I'm in. If this keeps up, there won't be any men at Lone Star at all! Right now, most of the men there are forty or older, some much older. Not that I care. There's only one man for me. I'm going to pray for a mild winter. Not so much for us, but for Oliver, wherever he is. Our men don't need to be fighting the cold as well as fighting the enemy.

I'm going down to lunch now. On my way to work, I'll mail the letters I've written to Oliver already. Oh, Lord, I'm so thankful for the mail. At least I know he was okay four weeks ago!

EPILOGUE

MAE BOLTED OUT OF bed and made a run for the bathroom. She made it just in time. *Wow, this flu bug is a strange one. I feel worse early in the day and better as the day goes on. Very strange.* She wet a washcloth and wiped her face, taking it with her back to the apartment.

Graydell was running water into the kettle and didn't look around right away. When she'd set it on to heat, she leveled her gaze on Mae.

"What?" Mae said. "Well, I'm sorry I'm sick. I'm trying to stay away from you so maybe you and Laurie won't catch it, too. That's all I can do."

"Oh, I'm not worried about catching it. I don't think you should worry yourself about that, either."

"What do you mean by that? And why are you looking at me that way?"

Graydell came to sit on the sofa and patted the seat beside her. "Come here, Mae. Sit down. No, don't worry about the germs." She was almost laughing now.

"What the hell? This is not funny!" Mae sat down anyway, far away from her friend.

"Mind if I ask you a couple of questions?" When Mae shrugged, she began. "You're feeling worst when you first wake up, right?" Mae nodded. "And you've been extra moody?"

"Well, I'm missing my husband. That's enough to make anybody moody."

"I know, hon. But . . . Well, have you not stopped to think that maybe . . .?" She hesitated on the next words.

"Maybe what? Spit it out, Graydell." But suddenly, seemingly as soon as Graydell had started this line of questioning, she knew.

"Oh! Oh, my God. I'm going to have a baby. Grady, I'm going to have Oliver's baby!"

"Yes, my dear," Graydell drawled. "I believe you are."

"I have to tell him. I have to write and tell him." She jumped up and ran to collect her writing things. "Oh, he's going to be so excited. What am I talking about? *I'm* so excited." She came back to grab Graydell's hands. "Oh, Grady, isn't it wonderful?"

But Graydell didn't seem so excited, Mae realized. "Oh, sweetie, I'm sorry. I didn't think. This can't be easy for you, not after what you went through."

Graydell shook her head. "No, Mae, it's okay. It's not bothering me that way. But—do you think you should be writing and telling Oliver about this just yet?"

"What do you mean? Why not?" But then she realized why herself. She wasn't far along at all, probably not more than a couple of months. She knew enough about women's matters to know she was in the most dangerous time, except for the seventh month, which according to old wives' tales was the scariest month for a woman's pregnancy.

"You're right, Grady. I need to wait. I could write Oliver today and lose the baby before my letter even gets to him. Okay, I'll wait. Guess I should wait to tell my folks, too. And Mrs. S. If she notices, I'll tell her, but if not, I'll wait. But Laurie. I have to tell Laurie."

"Yeah, she'll probably kill both of us if she finds out on her own," Graydell laughed. "You probably won't see her until Saturday."

"Yes, Saturday. I'll take y'all out to dinner to celebrate." Mae turned off the stove. "Tea?" she asked, beaming.

The weeks dragged by until Mae had missed her third period. Then she went to see the doctor so he could tell her what she already knew. When he finished his very embarrassing examination, he washed his hands and said, "Congratulations, Mrs. Cranfield. You're very much pregnant. I'll send my nurse in to go over some things with you, nutrition and diet, taking care of your changing body, things like that. Oh, and things that might be a sign of trouble."

Trouble?

"Did you see anything that would make you think there might be a problem?" Mae asked, frowning.

"Not at all. In fact, I expect you to have a perfectly normal pregnancy and birth experience."

"So, when can I write to give my husband the good news? He's overseas."

"As soon as you'd like. Your pregnancy is completely normal. Now, excuse me. I have a few more pregnant ladies to attend to."

Mae managed to sit through the nurse's detailed instructions, but as soon as she was dismissed, she headed across to the drug store with her prescription for vitamins. While there, she perused the greeting cards, finally selecting one with plenty of room for her to write Oliver with their news.

But she couldn't stand to wait until she got home to write him. She ordered a soda and sat down in one of the booths, pulling out her pen and taking a sip of the cherry coke.

January 25, 1943
Dear Oliver,
I have the most wonderful news. . .

ACKNOWLEDGMENTS

This book actually began thirty years ago, when I chose the topic for my dissertation at the University of North Texas in Denton, Texas. I entered the doctoral program in 1991, with the goal of getting my degree in much less than the average of seven years, and I reached that goal in August 1995, four years later. Along the way, I met some wonderful people who helped me on my way. From professors such as Randolph B. (Mike) Campbell, Donald Chipman, Donald Pickens, and James W. (Jim) Lee, I learned to trust my instincts and to stand up for what I believed in. From my fellow students (Beverly Rowe, Linda Hudson, Lisa Thompson, Mark Barloon, and others), I learned the joys and fears of going through graduate school together. One of our profs, Gus Seligman, introduced us to his class by saying, "I must warn you that graduate school is at best an adversarial relationship, and not a place to form lifelong friendships." We looked around at each other, shrugged, and met after class for dinner, as usual. The last letter I received from Linda Hudson was earlier this year, two weeks before she passed away. Lifelong friendships, indeed.

The topic I zeroed in on for my research was "Defense Industries in Northeast Texas, 1941-1965: The Social and Economic Impact on Bowie County." As part of my research, I interviewed people throughout Bowie County, Texas and Miller County, Arkansas who had worked at the local defense plants during World War II. Those interviews introduced me to some fascinating people and allowed me to get much better acquainted with others I'd known all my life—including my own father, Noah Brown; Ildea Cutchall, with whom I attended church; and Geralene Young, Miss Red River 1943. Every interviewee left me feeling both humble and grateful.

Occasionally, while asking questions and taping interviews, I would hear someone make a statement that gave me chill bumps, and I would think to myself, "That needs to go in a book someday." But with my degree fresh in hand, I was too busy getting settled in my chosen career—teaching History and Geography at Texarkana College. Many years later, some of those statements have found a home in Leaving Dixon's Crossing and the books to follow.

I would like to thank a few special people for their help. Understand, this is far from a comprehensive list of those I am indebted to. It's never possible to remember everyone who had a hand in helping us along as we write.

I suppose I should begin with Professor Ronald Marcello, who was the Director of UNT's Oral History Program during my years on campus, and for many years before and after. If it weren't for the classes I had with him, my interviews wouldn't have been half as interesting or complete as they were. I'd also like to thank all those professors who pushed me to make my own decisions rather than only taking their advice. Their support helped me to grow as a person, and I tried to follow their examples in my own classroom.

Thanks to Jamie Simmons, Archivist at the Texarkana Museum Systems' Museum of Regional History, who helped me locate photos from which I chose the one that graces the cover of this book. My friend Laura Lis Scott, designer extraordinaire, took that photo and ran with it to give my cover a truly unique look. I'd also like to thank my old friend, Dr. Beverly Rowe, for her fantastic pictorial histories of Texarkana. I referred to her books often as my characters navigated the 1940s streets of Texarkana. Beyond that, Beverly and I shared our studies at UNT, two trips to Scotland, the same faculty hall at TC, and many, many talks, trips, and secrets.

I own a huge debt of gratitude to my husband, which I hope comes through in the fact that both this book and my first book (2015) are dedicated to him. Bill passed in October 2019, shortly before Covid-19 hit, and the two things together upended my life for a time. Because of his going, I made the decision last fall to move from the country home we had shared for twenty years. With the help of my son and grandsons, I packed up a POD and my car and moved to Mississippi to live with my daughter. I am thankful to her for having made me feel so welcome and for helping me begin a new life here on the Mississippi Coast.

A NOTE TO MY READERS

Now I really must get busy finishing books two and three of this series. Tentative titles are *Under Familiar Stars* and *Secrets and Scars*.

Under Familiar Stars will see Mae still having adventures and experiencing terrible events in Texarkana and at Lone Star during 1943-44. At the same time, Oliver will be facing trials of his own as he struggles to remain true to himself, and to Mae, in the European theater of war.

And in *Secrets and Scars*, the terrible war years will finally come to an end. But what will life be like back in Texarkana? If Oliver makes it back home, you can bet he'll be a changed man. What about Mae? She will have had to come to terms with events in her life she had never expected. Will she be too changed for Oliver? Will they be able to find their way back to each other? Or will he come home at all?

Stay tuned for the rest of their story and for that of the Texarkana area. Book two should be out by the end of 2021, and book three should follow in the Spring of 2022.

If you enjoyed *Leaving Dixon's Crossing,* I would greatly appreciate it if you'd leave even a brief review on your favorite storefront or reading group. For example, Goodreads, Amazon, Barnes and Noble, etc. We authors really do live for our readers' comments and support.

Please go to my website: http://www.janetbrantleywrites.com

Have a look around. It is there and in my newsletter that you'll be able to keep up with my writing and what's going on in my life. Sign up for my newsletter while you're on site, so you'll be aware when I decide to do a giveaway or announce my next venture. I hope you'll be there with me! And contact me at: janetbrantleywriter@gmail.com

Made in the USA
Columbia, SC
02 October 2021

46129045R00195